*To those who revel in literature, languages, and dangerous love.*

# MILO

E.L. LEWIS

# CHAPTER 1

## TROUBLE COMES KNOCKING

A LONE TEAR ROLLS DOWN MY CHEEK, THE FIRST ONE I've shed since she left this world. Three weeks. I haven't cried in three weeks. I didn't have time to cry. I couldn't. If I cried, I feared I'd never stop, that I'd live in a perpetual state of agony. Of grief. Of sadness.

*Stop crying. Stop.*

I should've let myself feel this loss earlier. Not now. Not when I have five minutes left on my break. Not when the bank manager already commented on my smudged make-up. Not when I have to face customers for the next two hours before we close. Just two more hours and I can go home to an empty house. Two hours until I can climb into bed and stay there until my next shift. Two hours. You can do this, Kiara.

Two *fucking* hours.

With glossy eyes, I scroll through my camera roll, my heart aching as my grandmother's smiling face looks up at me with her signature red lips.

You were all I had left, nana, why'd you have to leave me too? Are you with Mom and Dad right now? Are they happy? How about Grandpa? Is he up there? Did they let him in? He was kind of a dick, but I think he made the cut...right?

Tears spill onto my screen, seeping into the crevices. Damn it. Flipping my phone around, I wipe it against my thigh and take a deep stabilizing breath as the backroom door creaks open.

*Already?*

"Kiara!" Bethany, the fifty-year-old bank manager barks, her shrill voice echoing through the sterile empty room. "Your break is over. I need you up at the front." She narrows her judgmental eyes at my chest, her thin lips pursed. "And button up your blouse. This is a bank, not a brothel. What would your grandmother say if she saw you walking around looking like that?"

She'd probably tell me to unbutton my blouse even further; grandma wasn't a prude, at least not at home. But to the small town of Hawthorne, Nana was a saint and a recluse, barely leaving the house, except for church. She was wary of the outside world, she never even let me go to school. *I'll teach you everything you need to know, dear,* she'd say to me.

And she did.

With a tight-lipped smile, I fasten the top button of my standardized white blouse. "Better?" I stand up and slip my phone back into my purse.

"Much." Bethany's uppity arrogance radiates off her stumpy body. "I know this is only your first day, but you've had a week of training. If you read our employee manual like you *said* you did, you'd be well versed in our dress code." She takes a purposeful step toward me. "I gave you this job because your grandmother was a dear friend. Don't make me regret it."

I fight the urge to roll my eyes. "And I'm so thankful for this opportunity, Bethany," I say, my tone sweet, grateful, despite the fact I want to smack this priss over the head with a rotary telephone. "You've gone above and beyond to help me, so thank you."

Bethany tosses me a smug smile. "I am a very kind and generous woman. It's in my nature to help those in need."

"Yes, you're *very* kind." People who are kind and generous seldom refer to themselves as such, but I'm not interested in starting a confrontation. "I'll get back to work now."

"Go on now." She shoos me out of the room. Once she closes the door, I immediately unbutton my shirt. Fuck you, *Beth*. If she gave me a uniform in the correct size, we wouldn't have this problem.

As I walk past Evie, my only other coworker, to my computer situated on the far counter of the bank, the streetlights flicker on, casting shadows of the trees lining the block.

I groan, resting my elbow on the ashy wooden counter, my gaze flicking up to the clock hanging next to the sign that reads Hawthorne United Trust.

God, it's only 6 p.m. but darkness has enveloped the sky, no hues of color, no evidence of a sunset, just grey dim clouds. It's miserable. Completely dreary. No one's going to come in. Not today.

Why didn't I bring my phone out here? I could've finished watching *Les Enfants Du Paradis*. I wanted to finish it with Nana. But now I'll have to watch it alone. I'll have to watch everything alone.

The next fifteen minutes pass in silence. Evie doesn't talk to me, her attention focused on the game of solitaire she's playing on her computer. I'd play too but it's not fun when you always win. Computers are intelligent but they have flaws. Like humans.

A howling suction of wind draws my attention to the front doors. A man in a beige trench coat enters the bank, followed by two shorter, fatter men in his tow.

Great. People.

I straighten out my shoulders as I follow his contemplative cold gaze that jumps between me and Evie.

*Not me. Not me. Not me.*

His decisive amber eyes land on mine and he strides toward me, the sharp edge of his stubbled jaw tensed, a barely noticeable sheen of sweat gracing his olive complexion.

I clear my throat, a lack of oxygen in my lungs as he stops in front of me. My pulse quickens. Crap, he's gorgeous. The two dodgy men stand close behind him, watching him with a hawk-like gaze. Bodyguards?

"Welcome to Hawthorne United, my name is Kiara." I swallow away a ball of nervousness in the back of my throat as he scans my face intently, his gaze dim, almost scared. "Identification and account number please."

"Of course," he says in a thick Italian accent. He reaches into his pocket slowly, carefully, and pulls out a black leather wallet. He slides a driver's license and bank card across the counter, his tattooed knuckles bruised, dry, speckled with...blood? What the— "Here it is, my identification."

I blink, grabbing his ID and angling it against my keyboard. I frown as I type his name into the system. "Alexander *Smith?*" I raise an inquisitive brow. "Not a lot of Smiths from Northern Italy."

"I beg your pardon?" Mr. Smith asks, his voice hoarse.

"Northern Italy? That's where you're from, right?"

He doesn't look pleased or impressed. "What is it that makes you think I'm from Northern Italy?"

"Your accent." I pull up his file. "I take it you're from Milan? Turin? Genoa?"

"I do not believe that is any of your business." He taps his fingers impatiently against the counter, a sudden air of urgency bouncing between our bodies.

"Apologies," I say quietly. Maybe that was rude. Hopefully, he doesn't file a complaint. I need this job. "So... how can I help you today, Mr. Smith?"

He cranes his neck toward the burly men hovering behind him, his teeth clenched. "I would like to access my safety deposit box."

"Oh, okay." I bite my lip. He should've gone to Evie. "I can go get my manager for you. It's my first day, I'm not really sure how to—"

"*No.*" His deep voice startles me as he fishes a brass key out of his pocket. "I would prefer to keep my business here as discreet as possible. That is what this establishment offers, is it not? Discretion?"

"Yes, but—" I pause. "I haven't accessed the vaults before, so I don't—"

"It is quite simple," he says in a low hum, methodically rolling the key slowly between his long fingers. His dark eyes flicker across my face. "You take this key—" He holds it up. "Insert it into a lock—" He points it at me, licking his lips. "And *twist.*"

"Oh." Is all that escapes my lips, my breathing shallow.

"So easy—" He pauses as his icy gaze pierces mine. "Unless you are an *imbecile*, that is."

Wow. I scoff inwardly, ignoring the fact that my cheeks are burning up. Who is this man? So fucking condescending.

"Fine." I snatch the key from his cocky fingers, angry at myself for finding him so alluring. "Follow me."

I round the corner, waving for Mr. Smith to follow me down the white hallway that leads to the secure vaults, two sets of heavy footsteps echoing behind us.

I pause. "Only authorized personnel can enter the vault, your...*associates* must wait out here."

Mr. Smith stiffens. "They go where I go," he states in an assertive tone, almost challenging me to refuse him. "I grant them permission."

"Fine," I sigh, clicking my tongue. "But they have to wait outside the vault in the hall. That's the best I can do. I don't want to be fired on my first day."

Mr. Smith glances over to his two *friends* who toss him a begrudging nod. Maybe they're *his* bosses. "That will do." He motions down the hallway. "If we can hurry this along, time is of the essence."

"Big Thursday night plans?" I ask, leading him to the secure section of the bank.

"Yes," he says distantly. "Big plans."

Alrighty then. Not a talker I see. We stop in front of a vaulted metal door, and I scan my security badge before entering my employee code. The door releases pressurized air before opening.

"After you," he says and I step inside, scanning the sterile surrounding. Hundreds of stacked silver mailbox-like slots sit in the middle of the room. "It is number 406."

"406?" I search for the correct section, acutely aware of the whispers coming from the two men lingering outside the vault door that's propped open. They're speaking...Russian?

"*This is going better than we thought,*" one of the men snickers in a language I learned last year. I narrow in on the correct box and unclip my set of keys, opening the first slot and removing a rectangular box. *"He is an idiot like his brother."*

*"Igor will be pleased,"* the other man replies. *"And to think we almost used a real bomb."*

My head snaps up to Mr. Smith's tensed expression. Bomb?! Did he say bomb?! I mentally flip through the employee handbook. Was there a section on this?!

"Sir?" I whisper cautiously, gripping his brass key in my hand. A sense of fear spreads through my body. Oh my God. "Are you here under...*duress?"*

"What?" he seethes. "Why would you ask such a *ridiculous* question?"

My all-too-curious gaze drags down the length of his body until I reach his hard chest, the barely noticeable outline of various shapes poking through the large tan trench coat. Holy fuck. My heart hammers.

"Is that a bomb?" My voice is barely a whisper, my palms clamming up, throat dry.

Mr. Smith's entire person darkens. "Just open the fucking box," he spits. "Now."

"What is taking so long?" one of the men calls out. "We are in rush."

Oh God... They're not his friends. Or associates. Or employees. They're—

"The box," he breathes, a hint of desperation in his voice.

"Mhmm..." I grip the key between my fingers and slide it into the safety deposit box, uncertain of what to do. What the hell do I do? Do I tell him? I should tell him. Or maybe not...

"It's not real," I blurt out as the lock clicks open and I peer up at Mr. Smith with a wince. Fuck. Maybe I shouldn't have said anything.

*"What?"* His lip twitches. He leans his body toward me, his face an inch from mine. He's so close I could count the faded freckles on his nose *"What* did you say?"

"The bomb—" I swallow, my gaze darting over his wide shoulders. They're staring at us. "It's not real."

"How do you know?" he asks in a low hum, expertly controlling his body language. *"Tell me."*

"I—I understand Russian." I force a smile in case his apparent *kidnappers* are sensing that something is wrong. "They said it's not real."

A devilish gleam of relief flashes in his eyes. "You are confident that is what they said?" I press my lips thinly. Why am I telling him this?! "Answer my question."

"Mhmm," I hum my response, unable to lie, unable to look away from his full lips. What am I doing?! I should just let them leave and call the fucking police. Idiot.

He glares at me, clearly not satisfied with my reply. "Yes or no, *Kiara?"*

My name rolls off his smooth tongue like a damn sedative. "Yes," I breathe. "I'm confident."

Double idiot.

"I see." Fear dissipates from his frigid features, his shoulders relaxing, like he's reenergized, *reborn.* He nods toward the box, a ghost of a smile on his scheming face. "Open it."

I hesitate. Why is he—

"I said *open the box."*

"Okay," I whimper, my knees weak as I lift the metal lid.

Before I have time to react, Mr. Smith reaches inside the container and pulls out a black pistol with a cylindrical attachment on the barrel. A knowing smirk sprawls across his menacing face.

"Grazie, *Kiara."*

*What the fuck?!*

He whips his entire body around, his arm extended, firm, as he states in an unwavering tone, *"Per mio fratello."*

And without hesitation, he fires two soundless shots: both Russian men collapsing on the ground like dominoes, blood gushing from the holes in their foreheads.

"Oh my God!" I cover my mouth, frozen, unable to move as thick crimson blood flows over their open eyes and onto the marble floor.

He killed them. They're—they're dead.

Mr. Smith points the gun at the security camera in the corner of the room and fires another shot. He grabs a USB stick out of the deposit box before he coils his murderous fingers around my forearm and tugs me toward the door.

"Exit. Now." He pushes me out of the vault, stepping over the lifeless bodies. He leads me down the hallway toward the emergency exits, the barrel of his pistol pointed against my back.

Oh, I fucked up. I fucked up bad.

# Chapter 2

## Flashes of Color

I like to think that I've lived a hundred lives.

I've been a young waitress in France with the goal of bringing joy to people's lives. I've been an heiress chased by a reporter through the vibrant streets of Rome. I've been a cancer-stricken father struggling to raise his children while dealing with an alcoholic spouse.

But now I don't think watching foreign films, for days on end, counts as living.

The reality of my life can be summed up in one word: mundane.

I've done nothing. I've *seen* nothing. Not in real life. Not in the flesh.

Not really.

They say your life is supposed to flash before your eyes when you die. I see nothing.

A blank canvas that has yet to be painted. A starless night. A black vortex.

A void.

"Are you going to kill me?" I whisper as Mr. Smith guides me down the scarcely lit sidewalk.

The sharp November air prickles at my skin and sends a shiver down my spine. A couple passes us on the street, neither of them paying attention to me, neither of them noticing the terror on my face. So oblivious. So fucking useless.

Do I scream? Do I yell for help?

The bank had cameras. He didn't care. He'll shoot me. On the spot. And then he'd shoot whoever would try to help me. I know he would. I don't know *how* I know that. But I do.

"Keep walking." He presses the pistol harder into my back as he pulls out his cellphone and types a message; the brief clicking of the keyboard indicates that it's a short text. I would think you would need more than three words to explain this situation to someone.

"Who are you?" I ask with a shaky breath, my eyes dry, surprisingly tearless. Mr. Smith ignores me. "Just let me go. I won't say anything, I promise."

"You are walking too fast. You need to relax and slow down. We don't need to draw unwanted attention."

Is he being serious right now? *We?* That's exactly what *I* want to do. Bring on the attention. *All* the attention. If I had a horn, I'd blow it.

Or...

Or maybe I wouldn't.

Everyone knows about fight or flight, a person's instinctive response to stress or trauma. But there's also freeze. And fawn.

I think I'm freezing.

But I refuse to fawn.

"It's kind of hard to relax when you have a gun pointed at your L2 vertebrae," I murmur as we turn into a dark alley.

I've seen enough movies to know that an alley means death.

"Turn around."

I close my eyes, turning toward him, my breathing ragged, uneven.

This is so fucking stupid. I did this asshole a favor. I helped him! And now he's going to kill me? In an alley? Not even a glamorous death.

How upsetting. How infuriating. How *unfair*.

Opening my eyes, I find myself teetering away from fear and edging closer to frustration, *anger*.

"I saved your goddamn life!" I clench my fists and stare into the barrel of his gun. "Is this how you repay kindness? By killing innocent women?"

"Unfortunately, you are incorrect, Kiara," he says, a melancholy smile on his face. "As you so astutely pointed out, this bomb is not real, thus I was never in any real danger."

I glare at him. "A technicality."

Mr. Smith lets out a low chuckle. "A grave one." He takes a step closer to me, adjusting his grip on the gun. "It is a shame though—" His pitch-black eyes skim my face. "To rid the world of such beauty."

"If that's the case, you can always let me go." I ignore the rising of my traitorous chest. "Preserve the beauty...so to speak."

"I do not make messes, I cannot clean up," he says, almost apologetically. "And you are, regretfully, a mess."

"I—"

My response is interrupted by his cellphone ringing. He's not seriously going to answer his phone, is he?

"*Pronto*," he says, lowering the gun as he props the phone against his ear.

Oh. He's answering. Not like he's in the middle of attempted murder or anything. He begins pacing, turning away from me. I look around. Of course, nowhere to run. I guess I'll just stand here and wait for my untimely demise.

What an anticlimactic end to my anticlimactic life.

Several seconds pass by, Mr. Smith's back still turned to me. His attention focused on whoever he's barking orders to on the phone. My gaze snaps to the pistol, hanging so precariously off his index finger. He really is quite cocky, isn't he?

Maybe I could—

Manifesting the energy of a prima ballerina, I gracefully glide toward Mr. Smith, ensuring that my feet make no noise, that I don't breathe, that silence surrounds us. When I'm mere inches away, I suck in a sharp breath and latch onto the gun. His head whips toward me as I snatch the pistol from his fingers, but he's too late.

Holy crap, this thing is heavy. Using both hands, I extend my arms and point the gun at Mr. Smith, a sense of murky pride spreading through my body.

I flex my muscles so that my arms don't shake. "Let me go."

I'm in charge now. I have the power.

Mr. Smith sighs. "*I will see you in five minutes, Marchello,*" he says in Italian. "*I need to solve a little problem first.*" He hangs up, tilting his head to the side as he stalks toward me. What is he doing? Is he crazy? "Kiara put down the Beretta. It doesn't suit you."

I re-grip the pistol. "Seeing as I'm the one with the gun, *I'll* be making the demands." I take a step back as he continues walking toward me. "How do you plan on solving this *little problem* without the upper hand?"

"Hmm." He takes three large strides in my direction,

forcing me to retreat back further. My back hits the brick wall. "You know Italian?"

"I know a lot of things," I whisper as his chest meets the tip of the pistol.

Oh God, he's a lunatic. Does he think I won't shoot?! I will. I fucking will.

"Is that so?" Mr. Smith chuckles, clicking his tongue. "Do you know what a *safety* is?"

*What?*

In the millisecond it takes for my gaze to lower down to the weapon, he's already snatching the pistol out of my hands. He snakes his fingers around my neck, knocking my head back into the wall, his grip restricting airflow, making me choke.

"Such a silly girl." His calloused thumb grazes along my quivering bottom lip, his sweet breath blowing into my mouth. "You never take your eyes off your target."

"I don't want to die." His fingers loosen around my throat but he doesn't let go. "Please."

"You will either die by my hand." He caresses my jawline, his body flush against mine. The jagged blocks of the fake bomb press into my chest. "Or by the Russians." He pauses, his charcoal eyes meeting mine. "It is better *this* way, *bella*. At least I will not torture you first."

"Please..." I fight back tears, defeat washing over me like a tidal wave. My hand grips his, attempting to drag it down. "*Per favore. Ti prego. Non farò niente.*"

"It does not bring me joy to end such a young and beautiful life." He sighs as he drops his hand and takes a solemn breath. "But begging will not help, even if it's in Italian."

I clench my teeth together. This is it. There's nothing else I can do. I'm out of options. Maybe I'm ready. Yes. I'm ready.

I'm ready.

"Just do i—"

Police sirens blare in the distance and my head snaps toward the wonderful sound.

Oh my God. Yes.

Mr. Smith reaches for his cellphone, a frown marring his brows as he reads a message.

"*Cazzo!*" He runs a frustrated hand through his dark thick hair. "It would seem that destiny has other plans for you, *Kiara*." He grabs my arm, leading me out of the alley and toward a parked black SUV with tinted windows. The door swings open, revealing two older men in the front seats, both dark-haired and frightening. "Get inside the car."

"No!" I attempt to jerk away from him, the sirens getting louder by the second. They're almost here.

"Get in the *fucking* car." He pushes me inside and hops in, slamming the door shut. "Do not scream or I will cut your tongue out before I kill you."

Waiting for death is exhausting.

"How very Russian of you," I sneer, eliciting a grin from Mr. Smith. *Psycho.* "I thought you don't torture people."

"I adjust *very* quickly." He turns his attention to the man in the passenger's seat as the driver pulls out onto the street. "*Did you clean up, Marchello?*" Mr. Smith asks in Italian.

"*Yes, the manager will erase the tapes and our men will discard the bodies,*" he replies, briefly glancing at me. "*I am sorry this happened, Milo. We should've known what they were doing. I'm so sorry. If you want to kill me, I will accept that fate.*"

Milo? What the fuck...

"I do not wish to spill more blood tonight." Mr. Whoever-the-fuck-he-is removes the trench coat, exposing the bomb wrapped around his chest. *"We will deal with the Russians later. I would like to take this off now."*

*"It looks so real."* Marchello examines the various crossed red and blue wires. *"How did you know—"*

"He didn't," I snap. They're talking like I'm not even here! "I told him." I face Mr. Smith, whose eyes are glinting with subtle amusement. "And *who* are you exactly?"

"How did you know?" Marchello asks me warily as I keep my attention on my annoyingly handsome captor. I have serious issues if I'm fantasizing about a man who's going to kill me. This can't be healthy. "How did you know that it was fake?"

I sigh, trying to read Mr. Smith's blank expression as he unclips the explosive vest off his body. I really hope it *is* fake. "I speak Russian," I murmur, wincing as Mr. Smith detaches the last wire and flings the vest to the floor. Oh, thank God. Still alive.

For now.

"You do?" Marchello purses his impressed lips. "And Italian as well?"

"And French and Spanish and German and Arabic," I mutter absentmindedly. Mr. Smith's groomed brow quirks up as I list off the languages I've learned over the years. "Plus, a little Korean. Not a lot though."

"Who are you?" Marchello asks.

*Me?*

"You first." I cross my arms, my gaze dancing between the two Italians. "Who are you, Mr. Smith? I think I deserve to know the name of the man who will eventually put a bullet in my brain, don't you think? It's not like the dead can talk. Might as well concede to this tiny request."

Leaning back into his seat, he studies me intently like he's plotting something. My death, no doubt. With a quick glance at his associate, he reveals in a smooth tone, "Emilio Di Vaio." He pauses, conjuring up a coy smirk. "But those close to me, call me Milo."

I blanch, his last name ringing in my head.

"D—Di Vaio?" I stammer. "As in..."

He smiles, evidently proud of his mafia ties. "Yes, as in *Santi Oscuri.*"

I nod slowly, realization dawning on me. "And the Russians at the bank...they were...?"

"Bratva," Milo confirms casually with a shrug. "A particular faction of the brotherhood that is causing quite a headache as you might have noticed."

"Uh-huh." So, he wasn't lying when he said the Russians would kill me. They would probably dismember me if they found out I foiled one of their grand plans. "Well thanks for telling me. At least I'll die with all the facts."

Milo glides his fingertips along his lips, cocking his head to the side. "Perhaps there is an alternative solution." His amber eyes soften, just a bit. "Instead of death, I am now willing to offer you protection."

"What?" I frown at his sudden change in plans. Marchello looks equally confused but he doesn't question his apparent boss. "Why would you do that?"

"It would be highly beneficial to have someone under my employ with your particular skill set," he explains. "It is not every day one meets a polyglot."

I blink. "So, you want to use me as your own personal Google translator?"

He smirks. "I want to use you for a lot of things, Kiara, but yes, translating is one of them."

# Chapter 3

## Fickle Like Promises

*I want to use you for a lot of things, Kiara.*

*Things*: objects or acts that one need not, cannot, or does not wish to give a specific name to. In Milo's case, I'm certain it's the latter. But given his gritty suggestive tone, dilated pupils, and the slight twitching of his upper lip, I can fill in the blanks quite easily, *too* easily. Subtlety is not this man's strong suit, evidently, neither is timing.

Not ten minutes ago, he had a pistol pointed at my head, ready to shoot without a second thought and now, he wants *things*? The nerve of this man.

I am offended. Thoroughly, wholeheartedly, undeniably *offended*. Or at least I want to be.

I *should* be.

I refuse to be as capricious as a criminal, yet I can't help but find my curiosity piqued by the tempting glimmer of pleasurable promise in his garnet eyes.

*Mmm.*

What *kind* of things...?

I blink. Dear God. *No.*

Yanking my disloyal eyes away from his enticing face, I

inwardly cringe at my fickle reserve. I will not succumb to his dangerous charms.

I won't.

"So, in exchange for my...*skills*, you'll keep me safe?" I ask, refusing to acknowledge his earlier statement. I can analyze his intentions later. There are far more important *things* at hand right now, like my life. If the only options are to work for him or die, I don't have much of a choice.

Although, working for the Italian mafia *does* pose its own set of problems. *Santi Oscuri* are notorious for their constant...*turnovers* in staffing, at least according to the various European newspapers my Nana hoarded over the years.

No one lasts long working for a criminal organization. But I suppose *eventual* death is better than *imminent* death. Everyone dies, it's a given, I just always thought it'd be decades before I was reunited with my whole family. At this moment, I'm not sure which half I'd meet.

"I will ensure that no harm comes to you," he states with unfaltering confidence. "As long as you are with me, I can guarantee that you will be safe."

"I would prefer if you didn't lie to me, Mr. Di Vaio," I say, skeptical of his overly assured pledge. "There are no guarantees in life."

"A pessimist, I see." He lets out an amused hum. "You are far too young to be so cynical, Kiara."

I scoff. "And you're far too optimistic for a man who just had a bomb strapped to his chest, fake or not. If you can't guarantee your own safety, I doubt you can guarantee mine."

His jaw clenches. I've hit a nerve. "You would prefer to die than take my offer then?"

"Of course not." I frown, taken aback by his confusion.

"All I'm saying is that you shouldn't make promises you can't keep. I will happily accept your protection, but I don't anticipate a long and prosperous life. You can promise me that you'll try your best but I'm not an idiot. I know how this ends."

"You *are* a cynic." He licks his lips. "We will fix that."

"I'm a realist, Mr. Di Vaio," I explain, unbothered by my outlook. "There's a difference."

He smirks, shifting his body toward me. "You may call me Milo." His rapidly changing demeanor is giving me a headache.

"You said only those that are close to you call you Milo. We just met."

His large, battered hand finds its way to my thigh, his fingers coiling around it slowly, applying minimal pressure. He leans into my ear and whispers, "It seems as though we are *very* close right now."

I control my breathing, ignoring the fragrant oaky musk of his cologne. Gently placing my hand on top of his, I push it away. "We both know you weren't talking about proximity, *Milo.*"

"I enjoy the way you say my name." His lips curl up into a satisfied grin. "It is like you are scared of me. I will not bite you, Kiara." He pauses. "Not yet."

My eyes harden, irritated that he can read me so well already. "If you want something to *bite*, perhaps you can get a *chew toy.*"

Milo expels a low laugh, his gaze flickering to Marchello who's pretending not to listen. "*She is funny, no?*"

"*Yes,*" Marchello agrees in Italian, like the puppet he is. "*Very funny.*"

I roll my eyes.

"*Allora*," Milo holds out his hand, inviting me to seal my fate, "do you accept my offer, Kiara?"

I gaze heavenward, shaking my head, incredulity bouncing between neurons. I can't believe I'm doing this. He killed two men in front of me today and now I'm supposed to work for him? Yes, they were bad men, horrible probably, but does that make it okay? Is a life less important if it's corrupt?

If I were a good person, I'd hold steady in my principles; I'd choose death over selling my soul to the devil. But evidently, I'm not a good person. I choose life. Even if that life kills me; perhaps not physically, but morally, which might be even more terrifying.

With a heavy sigh, I extend my arm forward, his hand encircling mine slowly, a ghost of a smile on his face.

"I accept." The heat from his palm radiates through my body like he's filling me with the flames of hell.

"Excellent." He smiles, knowing that he's marked me, that he's chained me to a new life, that my very existence rests in his hands. "We will go over further details at my estate."

"And where is your estate?" I rub my hands together, trying to scrub away the invisible filth. "Manchester?"

"In *Genova*." He types out a message on his cellphone. "We are going to the airport right now."

I blink. "Right now? We're going there *right now*? B-But I don't have anything with me! I don't have my wallet, phone, laptop, Kindle, *clothes*." I pause, panic setting in. Oh shit. "My locket. I need my Nana's locket; I can't leave without it." I tap the driver on the shoulder. "Excuse me, you need to turn around—"

"Please relax," Milo sighs, as he types out another text.

"My men have already collected your belongings from the bank—"

"But I need to go home!" I insist, my voice rising. "I need to get—"

He peers up at me from his phone, eyes dark and stern. "*Shh.*" I begrudgingly snap my mouth shut. "I already have people going to your home to retrieve your requested items. Where is your passport located?"

"In the nightstand by my bed." I attempt to keep my tone even, relaxed. "My locket is there too. It's a silver sphere." I pause, frowning. "Wait, how do you know where I live?"

"Your wallet."

"You went through my *wallet*?" I cross my arms. "Such an invasion of privacy."

Milo expels a soft laugh. "Get used to it, Kiara. There will be eyes on you all the time now."

Dread washes over me. What did I do? Why did this happen? Why did I accept that banking job? Why didn't I take a later break? Why did he have to choose my till? Why did I tell him about the bomb?

Why?!

"Perhaps you would like a sedative," Milo suggests. "It will take the edge off. You have had an eventful day."

"I'm fine," I breathe, my hands shaking. "I'm fine."

"You are not." He nods toward Marchello who passes him a black tin. He slides open the container and picks up a rectangular pill and snaps it in half, holding out a piece. "Take it."

"No, I'm not going to take random drugs from someone I *just* met. Are you crazy? I'm fine."

Milo lets out a sigh, his eyes fluttering shut for a brief moment. "It's Xanax and it will help you sleep. We have a two-hour drive to the airport and then a two-hour flight to *Genova*. You should rest, Kiara." He puts the pill in my hand. "It is pure, I promise."

I purse my lips, eyeing the benzo warily, my heart thumping with anxiety. "I'm surprised you're not *forcing* me to take it."

"I do not force women to do anything." He shrugs. "I have no need."

"Well, that's comforting." I hesitate for a second before popping the Xanax into my mouth, the sharp edge of the pill scratching my throat. He's right, I need to relax. "How long does it take to work?"

"It will be quick. Just close your eyes and enjoy."

And I do.

With the stress of recent events and the potency of the sedative, I drift off to sleep effortlessly.

At first, everything is serene.

Calm.

Quiet.

Light.

But not for long. It never lasts long.

It's dark now, too dark, thunderous growls echoing all around me; screeching screams, piercing howls of demonic forces surrounding me. The air is thick, heavy, painful to breathe. My feet are bare, my heels digging into shards of obsidian glass, penetrating my skin, cutting through veins, sending spikes of agony through my core.

No, where am I? Help! Help!

Mounds of wasted earth rise all around me like it's breathing, gasping for air. And then I feel it, the magma oozing through the cracking molten rocks behind me, gushing down my body, burning it. I can't run. I can't— My head snaps down to the ashen ground, a decaying hand emerging from the volcanic debris, and another one, and another one, and another one.

*Kiara.*

Their heads burst out, twisting, turning, inhuman, possessed. They look familiar. So fucking familiar. *Ubiytsa,* they rasp in unison, their yellow eyes locked on mine as they drag their rotting corpses toward me. *No, I'm not. I'm not a murderer. I'm not.* I want to scream but no sounds come out. My legs can't move. I'm stuck. Frozen. Paralyzed with fear.

*Kiara.*

A hand coils around my ankle and yanks me down, my head slamming against the ground, jagged rocks scratching my back as more hands feast upon my limbs. No. No!

*Kiara! Wake up!*

I gasp, my body jolting upright. Rays of sunshine beam into the room, my forehead drenched in sweat, my breathing ragged, heavy.

It was a dream.

"Kiara, are you alright?"

Gripping my chest, my eyes flutter open slowly, cautiously. I crane my neck, my blurry vision starting to focus on the man hovering above me.

Oh, it wasn't a dream.

"Where am I?" I whisper, my throat dry, sore.

"*Genova,*" Milo explains in a gentle tone. "In your room."

We're here? Already? I look around, barely able to register the regal decor, the lavish furniture, the dark aesthetic of my surrounding.

"My room?" I wipe the moisture off my forehead.

"Yes, your room..." He narrows his eyes, observing my every movement. "You were screaming, Kiara."

At least someone heard.

"I had a nightmare." I prop myself against the headboard. "How did I get here? Why didn't you wake me up earlier?"

"I tried but you were unresponsive. Perhaps I gave you too much. I will adjust accordingly," he says, almost apologetically. He pauses before adding, "It is Friday morning."

I blink. "What?"

"You slept for eighteen hours. I was almost worried you were in a coma."

"Well, you're the one who drugged me." A cough escapes my lungs. "Your fault."

"Perhaps..." He scratches his gruff dark stubble. "You should take a shower now. All the belongings you requested are in the closet, plus some new clothing." His unreadable gaze sweeps across my body. "I had to guess your size, but I believe that everything should fit."

"You bought me clothes?" I ask with an unintentional scowl. "I could've done that myself."

"Not me personally," he smirks. "One of my assistants went shopping. Do not worry, she has great taste. Her name is Luisa, she is here to help you with anything you need."

"My own lady-in-waiting," I sigh. "How exciting."

He ignores my sarcasm and gestures to the bathroom. "Go shower, Kiara. We have many things to discuss."

"I'm sure we do."

With a nod, Milo exits my room and I lazily slide out of the king-sized bed, banishing the flashes of my dream from my mind. It wasn't real. They're not real. Listlessly, I saunter toward the marble slabbed bathroom, slipping my clothes off with every step until my feet reach the heated tiles of the glass-encased shower.

Hot water spurts down my face, flowing down my breasts, my waist, washing away the emotional dirt that has rendered me lifeless. Scanning the various products stacked against the built-in shelves, I lather my hair and body in lavender-scented suds, the fragrance relaxing, soothing.

Just as I'm rinsing out my hair, a steady flashing of red light draws my attention to the corner of the bathroom.

Is that...?

Is that a fucking camera?

# CHAPTER 4

## EYES OF THE CASTLE

WITH A WHITE COTTON TOWEL WRAPPED AROUND MY body, I cross my arms, staring up at the security camera in the corner of the bathroom, fuming, utterly dismayed.

*This motherfucker.*

Thank *God* the toilet is situated behind a separate door otherwise, I would erupt with humiliation knowing that someone was watching me...*go*. Milo did say that I should get used to having no privacy but this?

This is unacceptable, improper, *intolerable.*

*Go take a shower, Kiara.* Well, now I can see why he was pushing it so hard. What a sick, twisted pervert. I refuse to be a channel that he and his goons can turn on whenever they're feeling frisky and need a little peep show. I've already degraded myself by agreeing to work with the goddamn mafia and I would like to preserve the smidgen of dignity I have left. I wonder how many other cameras are hidden in my room. Does he think I won't mind? That I won't protest? That I won't *do* something about it?

How naive.

Grinding my teeth, I storm out of the bathroom, scanning the bedroom for a blunt object. As luck would have it, Mr. Di Vaio seems to be a sculpture aficionado, so my options are vast. I hope he's not attached to any of them.

On second thought, I hope he *is*.

Perhaps the marble lion licking his paw? I run my fingers along its smooth white surface, lifting it up. Pure marble. No. Too heavy. I continue looking. Maybe the archangel Gabriel? I shake my head. No, that would be sacrilegious. Nana would be disappointed. My eyes dart to a bronze Hercules with the weight of the earth on his shoulder. Hmm. This seems like it could be *quite* aerodynamic.

Snatching the metal statue off the sleek black dresser, I traipse back inside the bathroom, hoping that my hand-eye coordination will not fail me. Maybe the season of baseball my parents signed me up for when I was ten has been ingrained into my muscle memory.

Here's hoping.

Pursing my lips, I line my feet up with the ogling camera, my fingers coiled around the spherical earth of the statue. Taking a steady step backward, I wind up my arm and fling the bronze Hercules toward the camera, quickly jumping back in case it ricochets. I smile triumphantly as the lens of the camera shatters upon impact, the red light dimming as the statue falls to the ground.

I smirk at my handy work. That's better. *Now* I can get ready in peace.

Milo might be a voyeur but *so far,* he's not a liar. The outfits Luisa picked out for me are phenomenal, everything designer and nothing under a grand. I've always wanted to own couture, to feel glamorous with expensive fabric draped over my body. Perhaps this is the silver lining. I might no longer have a soul but at least I have Chanel. It could be worse.

Removing an off-the-shoulder chiffon blouse and a black pencil skirt from the velvet hangers, I lay the items on the bed before perching on the upholstered gold stool in front of the rococo vanity table. I barely recognize the woman looking back at me. I'm in Italy, a country I've always wanted to visit, yet I don't feel the joy that's supposed to come with checking an item off one's bucket list.

I adjust the flap on the towel hugging my body as I scan the tubes and containers of make-up in the drawers, shocked to find that the BB cream matches my skin tone. Maybe Luisa color matched me while I was in my Xanax coma.

Nana always told me to find happiness in the little things whenever I was feeling miserable, drained, *empty*. When your entire world collapses and you lose the most important people in your life, the little things become your life source. The chirping of a bird. The smell of Earl Grey. The warmth of sunshine on your face.

Today, it's make-up.

As I'm about to apply a gorgeous shade of taupe shadow to my lids, Milo and three of his henchmen come bursting inside the room, weapons drawn, ready for battle.

God, they're so dramatic.

"Alright, alright, I'll use the *gold* eyeshadow," I joke to myself, letting out a soft laugh. Milo stops in front of me, his expression stern, serious. Unbothered by his tense reserve, I continue to do my make-up. "Is there a problem?"

"Is everything alright?" He thoroughly scans the bedroom, hovering behind me, pistol gripped tight. "We received an alert that a security camera had been tampered with."

Oh, that's why they're here. *Oops.*

"Yeah, I threw Hercules at it." I close one eye and sweep the shimmering dust across my lids. "Was I not supposed to do that?"

"You *what?*" he seethes, facing the mirror so that I'm looking at his reflection. I take in his unbuttoned white dress shirt, a tuft of chest hair peeking through the collar, two gold chains around his neck.

"I... *disabled* it." I give him a sweet smile. "I hope you don't mind."

"Those cameras are connected to sensors on the windows, *idiota.*" He waves his associates away before snapping his gaze back to mine. He holsters his gun and runs a frustrated hand through his hair. "They are there for your *protection.*"

"Right, the windows, sure," I scoff, craning my neck toward him, my body following as I stand up. "They're pointed directly at the shower. I'm not an *idiot*, Milo."

"Do not flatter yourself, Kiara." His jaw twitches with irritation as he sweeps his lecherous gaze across my spilling breasts. "If I wanted to see you naked, I would. And it *most certainly* would not be through a *screen.*"

I bite my lip, tilting my head to the side.

*So fucking arrogant.*

"Is that what you want, *Mister* Di Vaio?" I toss him a coy pout and cross my arms, inadvertently pushing up my breasts to create more cleavage for him to leer at. "To see me naked?"

He sucks in a sharp breath, dragging two fingers across his lips. "Do not tempt me, Kiara." He flicks his strained gaze up to my defiant eyes. "You are not the only person who struggles with *controlling their impulses.*"

I swallow, cursing myself for taking us down this road.

I'll simply feign ignorance since he already thinks I'm an *idiota*.

"A bit trigger happy, are we?" I take a step away from the man that's causing my core to ache. "I imagine that's an undesirable trait for a man such as yourself."

He blows air out of his nose, stifling a smile. "Not the impulses I was talking about," he smirks, stalking toward me. "But you knew that."

I clear my throat, refusing to be rattled by this devilish man. "I don't want any cameras in the bathroom. That is non-negotiable."

"I find it endearing that you believe you can negotiate with me, *gattina*." He lifts his hand up to my face and drags his thumb slowly along my jaw, outlining my face like he's painting a masterpiece. "Need I remind you who works for whom?"

"*Kitten?*" I scoff, fighting the urge to lean into his touch as I swat his hand away. Mind over matter. Always. "I am not a child and don't wish to be addressed like one, thank you very much."

He grins, scratching his chin. "I would argue that destroying thousands of euros worth of security equipment is very child-like, no?"

I glance at the brown leather watch strapped around his wrist and note the brand. Patek Philippe. Of course. "Well, *I* would argue that a man who can afford a one hundred-thousand-dollar watch can afford a little camera, *no?*"

His gaze briefly glances to the luxury Swiss watch, his lips twisting up in amusement. "What can I say? I have expensive taste. But that does not mean your actions go without punishment."

I blink. "Punishment? What are you going to do? Send me to time-out?"

A frown mars his eyebrows. "I am not sure what this *time-out* means but I doubt it is the punishment *I* had in mind." His voice turns smoky, taunting, full of deviant insinuation. "This will be your only warning, Kiara. I would recommend that you refrain from destroying any more of my property in the future... unless you're curious, of course."

I bite my lip, pushing the minute itch of curiosity out of my mind. "You're giving me a warning? How very diplomatic of you."

"I do not give warnings often. You will soon learn how *undiplomatic* I can be."

For the first time since I've been catapulted into this world, I find myself scared by the words rolling off Milo's tongue. There's a promise in his tone, an undeniable truth that sends a shiver down my spine.

"Understood." The reality of who this man is sets in. This isn't a good man. A kind man. A man who will forgive. This is a man who kills. Who slaughters. Who has no remorse.

"Kiara..." He cups my chin, tilting my head up. His expression softens. "I do not mean to frighten you."

I clench my teeth. "I'm not *scared*."

"But you are." His faintly cruel eyes burrow into mine. "You need to understand that there are consequences to every action but as long as you listen to me, I will not hurt you, neither will anyone else."

"And if I *don't* listen to you?"

"Let us hope it does not come to that," he states with an edge before reaching into this pocket. He pulls out my grandmother's locket. "Your necklace."

I take a deep breath. He sure as hell knows how to segue topics. "Thank you," I mutter as he dangles it above my palm.

"Would you like me to put it on for you? It is very beautiful."

"No." I shake my head, a melancholy smile on my face. "I can't wear it, I'm allergic to silver."

"Oh," he hums with a slight frown. "How unfortunate."

"Yeah," I sigh, placing the locket on the vanity table. "It's just a keepsake now."

"I see," he says lightly, heading toward the door. "*Allora*, you should finish getting dressed, Kiara. Luisa will be here momentarily to escort you to my office. I will see you soon." He pauses, cocking his head to the side as I sit back down on the stool. "I have *many* questions for you."

I narrow my eyes. "Questions?"

"Yes, I am very curious as to why my private investigator could barely find any information on one Kiara Payne." He lifts an inquisitive brow. "Who are you?"

I blink. "You did a background check on me?"

"Of course." He lets out a melodic chuckle. "I had to make sure I wasn't going to be working with a *criminal*."

I grin in spite of myself.

"Hilarious. Do *I* get to see *your* background check?"

"Now *that* is hilarious."

# CHAPTER 5

## BETWEEN THE LINES

"*MI SCUSI*, KIARA?" A GENTLE KNOCK ON THE DOOR draws my attention away from the oval mirror. *Good timing.* I put down the blush brush and turn my head. "It is Luisa, may I come in?"

"Yes, come in." I stand up and adjust the black chiffon blouse, making sure it's even on both shoulders.

There's no lock on the door, she could've barged in but instead, she knocked. Interesting. How polite. A rarity, I'm thinking.

I give Luisa a careful once-over as she enters my room, not at all surprised by her striking beauty; a petite figure, long thick Caramel hair, doe-like brown eyes, slender nose.

Objectively speaking, she's gorgeous, more so than me. I've always envied short women, there's a certain dainty quality to them that I think I'm missing.

Luisa smiles as she approaches me. She scans my outfit with pride. "Do you like the clothes I bought for you?" she asks. "I think it suits you very well, no?"

"Yes." I run hands down the curves of my hips, my

fingers gliding along the satin texture of the mini pencil skirt. "They're very nice, thank you."

"It's my pleasure." She passes me a cellphone. "Milo told me to give this to you. There are some numbers programmed into the phone, mine, his, a few others you might need. I can go over them later."

"I already have a phone." I take the cell from her hand and twist it in between my fingers. "Why do I need another one?"

"I'm not sure, I was just told to bring it to you." Luisa lifts her shoulders into an unbothered shrug. I suck in a sharp breath. Ask no questions. Of course. "Are you ready to go? Dr. Giardini is expecting you."

I blink. "Doctor? I thought I was meeting with Milo?"

"*After* the doctor. Milo has requested a comprehensive physical. It is standard for all his...*employees*."

I expel an airy scoff. What a caring employer. "I have no choice but to go, correct?"

Luisa's lips curve up into an apologetic smile. "It will be quick; he is a good doctor."

I'm *sure* he is. I doubt the mafia would hire incompetent physicians.

"Fine." I place the phone on the vanity table next to my grandmother's necklace before following Luisa out of the door and down the dim hallways of Milo's grand estate.

This villa is nothing like I've seen before; distressed faded white walls with grey bricks shining through, blood-red carpeting, gold detailing on every picture frame hanging on the walls, refurbished sconces from the nineteenth century. It's like an ancient castle that got a modern facelift, a twenty-first-century homage to The Palazzo Medici. It's mesmerizing, like I'm walking through the halls of history.

"How long have you worked for Milo?" I ask as we make

our way down the stairs, my hand sweeping along the ornate railings. Luisa's high heels echo through the vast emptiness of the house. "Are you his assistant?"

"Assistant? Me?" Luisa lets out a soft laugh as if the idea is simply preposterous. "No, I manage the estate for Milo. My father, Marchello, is Milo's...*assistant*. We grew up together. My father has been the advisor to the Di Vaio family since his youth. He previously worked for Milo's father and brother before they—" She pauses, rounding a corner. "This way."

"Oh," I hum with a nod, trying to make out the similarities in features between Luisa and Marchello. I make a mental note to ask Milo about his family. I doubt Luisa will elaborate any further if I ask. "And do you enjoy managing the estate?"

"Of course." Her tone is laced with prestige and power. "It's my home."

"Right."

Now it's mine too. For the time being.

Once we get down to the floor that the infirmary is situated on, Luisa stops us in front of a glossy black door. "Milo's office is right upstairs, I can come back to show you or—"

"I think I'll find it." I give her a tight-lipped smile. A moment of freedom seems like something I should savor. "Thank you, Luisa."

"Text me if you ever need anything," she says sweetly. "I'm here to make this *transition* as easy for you as possible."

"Thanks."

Luisa knocks on the door for me as if I'm incapable of doing it myself. "Kiara Payne is here," she states before waving goodbye.

The door swings open, revealing an elderly man in his

sixties; salt and pepper hair, crow's feet on the edges of his aged eyes, a stethoscope draped over his lab coat.

"Miss Payne, please, come in," he says in a hoarse tone, ushering me inside. "Please sit." He holds out his hand "I'm Dr. Aldo Giardini, a pleasure to meet you."

"Kiara Payne." I shake his hand as I perch myself on the medical examination table. This better be a verbal exam, I'm not getting undressed.

"This will not take long." He retrieves a clipboard from the far console table and slips on a pair of thick-lensed glasses. "Your medical history was difficult to attain so please bear with me as we go through the questions."

I stifle an incredulous laugh. Difficult to attain? It should be impossible. I'm starting to suspect that doctor/patient confidentiality is nonexistent if you have wealth and power.

For the next ten minutes, Dr. Giardini goes through his extensive list of questions, asking me about vaccines, family history, any surgeries I've had, my blood type. He's professional, respectful, *clinical* during the entire conversation.

That is until he asks me, "Are you a virgin?"

My jaw drops. "Excuse me?"

He peers up at me from the clipboard, unflinching as he asks again, "Are you a virgin, Miss Payne?"

I cross my arms defensively. "Is that a standard medical question?"

"Yes."

I purse my lips, unconvinced. "Did Milo ask you to ask me if I'm a virgin?"

"No."

I click my tongue, shaking my head. "Are you lying to me?"

"No. I am not."

"Mhmm." I narrow my eyes. "Would you *tell me* if you *were* lying?"

"No," he states, a ghost of a smile on his face. "I would not."

For fuck sakes.

"No, Dr. Giardini," I sigh. "You can tell *Milo* that I am *not* a virgin." I tilt my head. "Will he be pleased or disappointed?"

The doctor doesn't answer as he scribbles down a note. "When was your last sexual encounter?"

I clench my jaw. He's unbelievable. This can't be protocol.

"Five minutes ago." I keep my expression neutral. "I fucked one of Milo's guards before I came here." I lean in closer to the Doc whose eyes are bugging out of his sunken face. "He had a *huge* cock, I *loved it.*"

He clears his throat. "I take it you are joking."

"I don't know? *Am I?*" I give him an innocent shrug. "Maybe Milo should check the security footage."

Either I've rendered the doctor speechless or he's having a *petit mal* seizure. I wonder if there are cameras here. Or a microphone.

"Are you on birth control?" he continues after a few seconds of silence.

"No, I'm not," I say, getting tired of this inquisition. He lifts up an inquisitive brow, I elaborate, rolling my eyes, "I use *condoms.*"

"Only condoms?" He purses his lips. "Nothing else?"

"Yes, Dr. Giardini, only condoms," I sigh, hopping off the table. I'm sensing this is the end of the line of his *intrusive* questioning. "My previous gynecologist told me I only have a 4.4 percent chance of getting pregnant, those aren't great odds so *no,* I'm *not* on birth control."

"Very well." He averts his prying gaze as he flips through the pages of my past. "Alright, we are finish—"

I exit the medical office before he can finish his sentence, my blood thrumming with irritation as I march up the stairs toward Milo's quarters. Again, he must think I'm an idiot. If he was curious about my sexual past, he could've just asked. He doesn't strike me as a timid man, but I suppose he doesn't want to show his hand this early in our...*arrangement*.

Not wanting another confrontation, I take a leveling breath before knocking on his door. "Mr. Di Vaio?"

"It is open," he calls out and I turn the handle, peeking my head into his lavish office. My mouth hangs open as I scan the grandiose interior. So much fucking velvet. Milo's eyes follow me as I enter the room, trailing up and down my body as he purses his cunning lips. "I think I prefer the towel."

I roll my eyes, gliding toward the rows upon rows of tattered books sprawled along the far wall. "I'm sure you do." I tilt my head to read the names of the titles. "Do you enjoy reading?"

"When time permits." The smoky timbre of his voice buzzes through my bones as he joins me by his extravagant collection of European literature. "Do you?"

"Mhmm." I pull an old copy of *The Divine Comedy* off the shelf and handle the bindings and pages with a delicate touch, amazed that I'm holding such an iconic piece of art in my hands. I flip to the first page, my eyes widening. "Oh my God, this is a *first edition*."

"Most of them are first editions," he says casually, like they're not worth millions. "Would you like to read it?"

I flicker my perplexed gaze toward the frustratingly handsome man in front of me. "I would, thank you," I say hesitantly, unsure of what to make of his sudden *kind* countenance.

"Of course." He gives me a stoic nod, gesturing toward his desk. "Please sit, Kiara."

Oh, time for more intrusive questions.

Milo pulls a folder out of a drawer once we're both seated, flipping it open. "So, tell me, Kiara..." He scans the documents. "Why was my investigator barely able to find any information on you? You have no social media accounts, no educational history, no employment. Nothing. Who are you? The truth."

Carefully placing *The Divine Comedy* on his desk, I recline in my seat, crossing my legs. His eyes dart to the exposed creamy flesh of my thigh. I inwardly smirk. Shameless.

"It's not that interesting," I say, looking over this shoulder toward the oil painting of two Italian men, both possessing a strong resemblance to Milo. "Who are those people?"

Milo's lip twitches. "Where were you born? Tell me."

I sigh. Clearly, we're not moving past this. "I was born in Virginia, in the States. When I was thirteen, my parents passed away, so I moved to Hawthorne to live with my grandparents."

"My condolences," Milo says. "May I ask how they died?"

I close my eyes, memories of that day still so painfully vivid.

*"Daddy, drive faster!" I whine, squeezing my bladder tight. "I have to pee!"*

*"We're almost home, sweetheart," Dad says, smiling at me through the rearview mirror. "Ten minutes."*

*"Honey! Watch out!" Mom screams as rays of winter sun reflect off the black ice on the highway. "Slow down!"*

"Shit!" Dad turns the wheel, our bodies flinging side-to-side as the car skids, slides, screeches.

"Kiara, hold on to something!" Mom orders and I do. I grip the handlebar as our car spins out of control, nearing the edge of the highway. My temples pulse from the speed, the fear, my heart racing as my dad tries to reclaim control of the car.

But he can't.

"Mom!" I shriek as our bodies lift up into the air for a brief second like the first drop of a rollercoaster. The car veers off the highway, through the railings, and plummets into the tree scattered ravine, the impact bashing my head against the window.

And then nothing.

Buzzing. Dull buzzing. The odor of leaking gasoline. The smoky smell of fire. Muffled voices. Tapping. Clawing. Shattering. My back scraping against shards of glass.

"Can you hear me?"

I groan, my eyes fluttering open. I'm in a stranger's arms. I don't know you. Who are you?

"Back up, Connor! It's going to blow."

"Fuck!"

And I'm carried away.

Only me.

I clear my throat, sucking a sharp breath. "A car accident. I was the only survivor."

# CHAPTER 6

## LIES IN THE EYES

MILO'S GAZE IS UNWAVERING AS HE STARES AT ME WITH understanding, compassion, *sympathy*. For a brief moment, he looks almost human.

Innocent.

It's unnerving, uncomfortable, uneasy.

And I don't need it.

I don't *need* his sympathy. I don't need to relive the past. Talk about it. Dwell on it. Think about how things could have gone differently. There's no point.

None.

Nothing will bring them back. Nothing will bring anyone back.

"I—"

"So anyway," I cut him off, moving past this undesirable topic, "I moved in with my grandparents who decided to homeschool me."

"Homeschooling?" Milo asks, evidently picking up on my tense body language and not prying further into my parents.

"Yes." I stand up, a dull burst of anxiety preventing me

from sitting still. I turn away from Milo, scanning the various Leonardo Di Vinci prints hung on his dark grey walls. "They *tried* to enroll me in a normal high school. It didn't work out."

"Why?"

I shrug, not bothering to look at him. "PTSD or something." I take in the detailed anatomy of the renaissance painter's work. "I was planning on going to university but then my grandfather passed away and I couldn't leave Nana all alone. We had some family money, so I didn't have to work."

At this point, I don't care that I'm telling him everything. I'm going to die anyway. There's no point in lying, in hiding the truth.

"You did not attend university?" he asks. I crane my neck toward him; he's lost.

"Does the University of Wikipedia count?" I tilt my head. "If not, then no."

Milo frowns. "If you never received formal training, how is it that you can speak seven languages?" He pauses, reclining in his leather chair. He links his fingers across his torso. "Or were you lying?"

"Would you like to quiz me?" I let out a genuine laugh, amused that he thinks I'd lie given the circumstances. "I'm not lying but I also can't give you a concrete answer." I pace in front of his desk, gliding my fingers along the back of the gritty chair. "My grandmother, she was a—" I pause, biting my lip. "A worldly woman, eccentric at best, and when my grandfather died, she spiraled a little, if you will. She didn't want to leave the house; she didn't want to do anything."

I dart my gaze to Milo who nods, indicating that he's following.

"I think she felt bad for keeping me in Hawthorne so

every few months, she'd go through these obsessive phases where she'd choose a country and our lives would revolve around it," I explain, attempting to find the right words.

"It started with Spain. We'd watch Spanish movies, TV shows, eat Spanish food, read Spanish books, with translations, obviously. But somehow, I started to pick up the language. At first, I thought it was because I took some Spanish in grade school but then the same thing happened with French, Italian, Russian, you get the picture."

Milo blinks. "You are telling me that you became fluent in seven languages by watching *films?*"

"More or less," I say, circling his desk. I pause in front of the arched checkered window that overlooks a grand courtyard, a pool in the center. "Once I noticed how easily I was picking up words, phrases, I studied the languages more thoroughly, and after six/seven months, I became fluent. According to the internet, I'm a hyperpolyglot—" I turn my head toward Milo who's spun around to face me. "Supposedly, I possess a particular neurology that makes me skilled at language accumulation."

"That is—" Milo licks his lips, processing my explanation. He lets out a breath. "You're remarkable."

"No, I'm just lucky." I shrug, turning away from him, watching trees sway in the wind on the fringe of the cobblestoned courtyard. Several men dressed in suits walk around the perimeter. "I just happen to be born with this ability. I didn't work for it. It was given to me."

His chair squeaks as he stands up and stalks up behind me. "There is no need to be modest, Kiara—" My breath hitches as he sweeps strands of hair off my shoulder. He arches over, whispering in my ear, "You are remarkable."

I suck in a shaky breath, twisting my body to face him, his chest an inch away from mine.

"Is a cat remarkable for always landing on its feet?" I fight the urge to reach out and touch the sculpted ridges of his chest as my back presses up against the jagged window-panes. "Or is it just a cat?"

"Well —" Milo smirks, resting his palm above my head. He leans closer to me, caging me with his hellish body. "I have always found pussies to be *quite* remarkable."

I force a scoff, my breathing ragged. "Charming," I murmur, denying Milo the satisfaction of seeing me squirm. *Bastard.*

"You're blushing." His gaze dances across my burning face. He's clearly pleased with himself. I don't dignify his annoying observation with a response. He segues when he's certain I have nothing to add to his lewd remark, "But truly, Kiara, it is worrisome that you cannot see what a gift you have been given."

"It's only a gift *now* because it's what's saved me from being executed by *you*." I weave under his arm, escaping his burrowing intense gaze. "*But* I suppose it *has* served a greater purpose."

Hanging his head, Milo expels a low chuckle before slowly turning around. He leans against the window, crossing his arms. "Some optimism." His top lip quirks up. "Finally."

I roll my eyes.

"So now that I've answered all your questions," I take one more stride backward so that there's optimal space between us, "I think it's time you answered some of mine."

"You may ask me whatever you'd like." He pushes himself off the window and perches on the corner of his desk. "But I will tell you only what you need to know."

"I figured as much." I nibble on my bottom lip, surveying his neutral features, attempting to recall everything I've studied about micro expressions. "What is it that you and your *family* do?"

For half a second, his eyebrows perk up, his lips clipping up into a smile. Amusement. I'm fairly certain.

"I own a chain of hotels and casinos across Europe," he answers flatly. "I'm a businessman."

This is going to be tricky.

"Most regular businessmen don't get kidnapped by the Russian mob. Might want to consider changing professions." I pause. "Why *did* they kidnap you? Hmm?"

He shakes his head. "Not relevant."

Hmm... Let's turn it up. I've always wanted to put my self-education to the test.

"What do you *really* do?" I take a step forward, my gaze bouncing between his lips, eyebrows, and nose. The trifecta of human emotions. "Gunrunning?" Nothing. "Extortion?" No. "Drugs?"

The right corner of his lip tightens and rises. Contempt? Interesting. Not the reaction I was expecting. I was anticipating pride.

"Drugs? How unoriginal," I muse, striding closer to Milo who's narrowing his eyes at me, body tense. "Do you *make* the drugs, *traffic* them, or *sell* them?"

His lip twitches, one eye briefly squinting. Traffic.

I think.

I tilt my head, continuing on my rampage. "And the hotels and casinos are what? A front for money laundering?"

His jaw clenches. "I did not say that."

"You didn't have to," I smile, blessing Paul Ekman and his research. "You can't conceal a biopsychosocial reaction." I pause, cocking my head to the side. "The amygdala— it really *is* the *snitch* of one's brain."

"What?" he asks through his teeth. "What are you talking about?"

"Not relevant," I repeat his words. This angers him like I knew it would.

"What makes you so confident that you are correct in your...*assessment*?" He takes a purposeful stride toward me. "Tell me."

I shrug. "A party trick."

"Kiara..." His eyes darken. "Do not play games with me."

"If I were playing a game, Mr. Di Vaio. I believe this would be *checkmate*."

He stares at me warily, uncertain of how to react. He can either move past this, sticking with his story, or acknowledge that I'm correct.

"I am a businessman, Kiara," he says, unfaltering in his lie. "That is all you need to know."

So predictable already.

"So, what is it that you want *me* to do for *you*, Mr. Di Vaio? You speak Italian so obviously I'm no use for you here. If I'm going to be assisting you with *business* abroad, shouldn't I have the basic facts of who I'm going to be dealing with?"

He sighs.

"I have business partners across Europe, our...*relations* are unfriendly at the moment," he explains, avoiding giving away too much information. "You will accompany me on several trips and ensure that what they say to me in *English* is what they say to each other in their *native tongues*. Similar to the unfortunate incident at the bank."

"So, I'm a spy now? Lovely. That always ends well."

"There is always a risk in business. It is inevitable."

I scoff. "*Your* business is a bit riskier; don't you think?"

He ignores me, retrieving a document from his desk. He

holds it out. "I had an employment contract drafted for you in case your family and friends ask questions. You can make copies if you'd like."

"That won't be necessary, Mr. Di Vaio. I don't have anyone to file a missing person's report."

"Your grandmother?" He frowns. "Will she not worry?"

"Well, she's dead so no I don't think she will."

He purses his lips in thought. "You have seen a lot of death."

I blink. "I imagine you have as well."

His gaze flickers to the portrait above his desk as he stiffens. "Yes. I have."

I wonder how many of those deaths were a result of *his* gun.

"Well, at least we have *one* thing in common," I note wryly, getting tired of standing. "So, when do we leave to go.... wherever it is we're going?"

It takes a moment for Milo to recover. His father and brother must have meant a great deal to him. But when you're born into a life of crime, is death really that rare?

"I will be traveling to Sicily for a week on Sunday," he finally says. "In which time you will complete self-defense and weapons training."

My mouth hangs open. "What? Why do I have to learn self-defense?" I toss him a sly smile. "Losing confidence in your ability to keep me safe already?"

"My business partners are dangerous men, Kiara. If I'm unable to protect you, you need to be able to protect yourself."

"Dangerous business partners, hey?" I cross my arms. "Is that a norm in the *hospitality* industry?"

He casts me an unimpressed glare. "I am serious, Kiara.

You will train with Giovanni every day until I deem that you are prepared to enter this world. No sooner."

"I'm a quick learner." I know that I should heed his warning but for some reason, I'm not scared. "I'm sure it'll be a breeze."

"Intellectual acuity will not benefit your physical endurance, Kiara." His lips twist up in a cunning smirk. "This is not a matter of brain—" His hungry eyes dance across my chest. "But of body."

"I know my body, Mr. Di Vaio," I say, instinctively biting my lip as I press my palm against his hard chest. "You'd be shocked by the things it can do."

He grabs my wrist. "Be careful what you say, Kiara," he rasps. "Unless you are prepared to prove it."

My breath hitches, his tight grip sending a wave of heat to my core. "I'm always careful with my words," I whisper, my chest rising. "What does that tell you?"

A barely audible groan escapes the back of his throat as he drops my hand, arousal in his glare. "Do not poke the dragon, Kiara."

"Dragon?" I let out a mocking scoff, turning on my heel to exit his office. Enough fun for one day. "Wow, that is *one big ego.*"

"I will see you in a week," he grunts in a strained tone, his fists clenched as he returns to his desk.

"Mhmm." I twist open the door handle and pause, craning my neck over my shoulder. "Oh, one last question—"

"What?" he snaps, peering up at me.

I tilt my head, tone flirty and coy, "Are you a virgin?"

He smirks, letting out a smoky chuckle. "Goodbye, Kiara." A beat. "And please, do not fuck any more of my guards."

# CHAPTER 7

## A FORCE OF LIFE

CRACKLING FROM THE TAMED FIRE UNDER THE MANTEL echoes through the library as I turn the page on my Kindle, envy thrumming in my veins.

If only Tolstoy could rewrite my life; there'd be suffering, naturally – it's Tolstoy – but there'd also be hope.

Leo was excellent at writing hope.

*"A wound in the soul, coming from the rending of the spiritual body, strange as it may seem, gradually closes like a physical wound. And once a deep wound heals over and the edges seem to have knit, a wound in the soul, like a physical wound, can be healed only by the force of life pushing up from inside,"* I murmur, reading out loud as I take a sip of wine.

Sure, it's only 11 a.m. but I'm in Italy. Who's going to judge me?

"A force of life," I repeat, shaking my head, frustration oozing through my pores.

But what if your life *is* the catalyst of your wounds? What then, Tolstoy? Huh? What happens then? Pierre found solace in love. Is that supposed to heal all too? So, life and love? Those are the only true cures to suffering?

Absurd.

"Kiara, there you are."

I snap my head up, putting the Kindle to sleep as Luisa enters the dimly illuminated library. Out of the *twenty* rooms, she showed me last night, this is by far my favorite. It's more intimate than the other obnoxiously large spaces in the villa.

Really, who needs *three* living rooms?

But at least now I have my footing. She was quite thorough in her tour; even going as far as giving me a hand-drawn map in case I get lost. Milo's bedroom, which is situated down the hall from mine, was circled in red.

Now that I think about it, perhaps *he* drew the map.

"Good morning."

"Indulging so early." She eyes the bottle of Masseto on the table as she takes a step down into the sunken library. "I'll be sure not to tell Milo that you've opened the last of his favorite wine."

"I'm sure he can afford to buy another bottle." I take a sip, the aromatic complexity and tannic structure of the blend whirling around in my mouth. "It's delicious, I can see why it's his favorite."

Luisa casts me a smile, her eyes crinkling from the force. "Yes, it's very exclusive," she says as she approaches the couch. She passes me the copy of *The Divine Comedy*. "Milo said you left this in his office last night."

"Thank you." I gently wrap my fingers around the first edition. "Was he too busy to give it to me himself?"

"He and my father left for Sicily this morning," she explains, gracefully sitting down on the armchair across from me.

"I thought they were leaving tomorrow?" I frown, placing the book next to me, mildly irked that he didn't inform me of his change in plans. Instantly, I scold myself for caring. He doesn't owe me anything.

"Something urgent came up. It happens a lot."

"Right," I hum, unsure of how to continue this conversation.

Luisa is a stranger, someone I know nothing about, someone I doubt I have anything in common with, except for Milo.

And he's a mystery to me too.

An enigma.

A *challenge*.

"I've been meaning to thank you, Kiara," Luisa says, her tone solemn.

I squint in confusion. "For what?"

"For saving Milo's life." A pained frown mars on her brows. "He might disagree, but if it weren't for you, he would most likely be dead. He thinks the Russians would have let him go, code of honor and all that shit, but I know they would've killed him as soon as they got their hands on whatever was in that security deposit box."

Does she *actually* not know it was a USB stick in the box or is she *pretending* not to know? Either way, her interpretation of the events indicates that Milo might owe me something after all.

"You're welcome," I mutter, wildly curious as to what was on that thumb drive. I hadn't given it a second thought until now. It must have been important. Valuable enough to start a war.

"If we were to lose Milo after Sergio and V—" She freezes, glancing across the shrine of oil paintings hung on the wall behind me. I crane my neck and follow her sightline.

Generations of Di Vaio's, I presume, based on the facial structures, the strong resemblance to Milo, the sense of power and superiority. On my tour, I noticed a few empty spaces on the walls where a portrait must have hung, the paint was brighter, preserved, like it was hidden from the elements behind a frame.

This family loves their art.

"His brother and father?" I keep my tone neutral so as to not sound too nosy. "They passed away recently?"

Luisa stiffens, wary hesitation dancing around her face. "Santino, Milo's father, passed away four years ago." She swallows. "Sergio, his brother, nine months ago."

*Nine months.* Fresh.

I take a deep breath as I nod, my heart aching with empathy. "I'm sorry for your loss."

I want to ask how they died but I'm already overstepping. The fact that she's divulging this much information is surprising enough. Soon, I'll have the whole picture but for now, I'll settle for bits and pieces.

I add, "Were you close to them?"

"I was. They were family. We are *all* family."

And I'm not.

It's written all over her face. I don't need to be adept at reading people to pick up on her disdain. It's as clear as the sun is bright.

She doesn't trust me.

Fair.

I don't trust her.

I don't trust anyone.

I only trust facts. And the fact is...I need Milo. And it

seems like he needs me too. So unfortunately for Luisa, and I'm assuming the rest of the *family*, they'll just have to deal with it.

I tried to research as much as I could about *Santi Oscuri* last night, but my efforts were in vain. There is no concrete evidence of any of their illegal activities, just conjecture, speculations.

The Italian government had tried to arrest them several times but to no avail; key pieces of evidence disappeared, recanted testimonies, missing witnesses.

Shady shit.

In the eyes of the law, Milo really *is* just a businessman.

But in these walls, he's *Don* Milo, and his word is final. And if he wants me here, I'll stay here, no matter how uneasy it makes Luisa.

"Well, I'm sure they're in a better place," I say, mimicking her inauthentic sweet smile.

What a ridiculous phrase to say to someone in mourning. Even those who aren't religious use it. It's lost all meaning, all novelty, all genuineness.

It's like saying bless you when someone sneezes, have a good weekend to your coworkers on a Friday, Happy Birthday on a Facebook wall.

It's meaningless. A socially constructed response. A platitude.

But it works.

"They are," Luisa agrees, standing up with a sigh. "Tomorrow we begin your training, yes? I will introduce you to Giovanni and Mateo, your trainers, they will also be your security detail if you ever choose to leave the estate."

I'm allowed to leave? How *generous* of the Don.

"I look forward to it."

"Alright, I will see you later." She tilts her head, lips pursed. "Will you be joining us for dinner tonight?"

She'd be a terrible poker player. Atrocious. Why ask if you don't want me to join? Courtesy? An order?

"I'll take it in my room," I reply, relief donning her sharp features as I turn my attention to the book Milo lent me. "But thank you for the invitation."

"No problem. I will have Teresa bring it up to you," she says and walks away.

I glide my fingers along the textured front of *The Divine Comedy*. I could use a little break from Russian lit. Flipping open the hardcover, my gaze darts to a handwritten note placed against the spine and my lips quirk up into an amused smile.

It's a quote from the poem. I know it well.

*"The devil is not as black as he is painted."*
    *Don't fold the pages, Kiara.*
    *—Milo*

I expel a soft laugh. I suppose even the devil was once an angel.

"*Again!*" Gio commands in Italian. He holds out his fists which are wrapped in boxing gloves, a sheen of sweat on his bald head.

The European Mr. Clean is starting to get on my nerves. We've been training for the last five days; I deserve a tiny break.

"Just give me a minute to breathe!" I snap. Snickers from Mateo and the other men sound through the gym.

My audience has gotten progressively larger in the last week. Even though Gio is almost three times my size, I've managed to get him to his knees...*once.*

When Milo said self-defense training, I didn't think he meant full-on kickboxing lessons. I assumed I'd just learn the basics of how to *fend off* an attacker, not *pummel* them to the ground.

I push back the damp baby hairs sticking to my forehead and tighten my ponytail.

*"Again, Kiara."* Gio grins as he gets in the guard position. *"Until you can't stand."*

"Or until *you* can't stand." I grind my teeth. "For someone who smokes a pack of Marlboros a day, I'm surprised you're not passed out already!"

He shrugs, tossing me a smirk. "I have good stamina," he says in English. "Years of practice."

I roll my eyes.

"Can we go back to the range?" I ask in a cutesy tone, batting my eyelashes. I've learned I much prefer to handle a firearm rather than use my body to fight. Pulling a trigger doesn't result in nearly as many aches and pains as kickboxing does. *"Please?"*

Gio lets out a defeated breath, taking a step closer to me. Perhaps flirting to get my way isn't the most appropriate course of action but a girl's gotta do what a girl's gotta do.

"One more round." His eyes gleam with heat for a second before his gaze darts over my shoulder and he freezes, the fire dying out, replaced by fear. "Don Milo..."

I whip my body around to find Milo leaning against the door frame, his arms crossed over his black t-shirt, light grey sweatpants hanging off his hips, his dark eyes hardened, glaring at Gio.

"I will take it from here." Milo hefts off the door and flicks two fingers in the air.

The gym empties within seconds, doors slamming as his men clear the room.

Shit.

# CHAPTER 8

## THE GAMES WE PLAY

HIS PRESENCE IS LIKE A VACUUM, SUCKING ALL THE musky air out of the room, making it hard to breathe. Making it hard to fucking *see*.

I don't want to be affected by this man, but his energy is undeniable. With a snap of his fingers, he can make the world stop, jump, rollover.

And honestly, that kind of control... it's fucking hot.

"You're back."

My chest rises in my sports bra as he devours my glistening body, his greedy gaze bouncing along my soft curves.

And I like it.

I like it when he looks at me like that. It's like he's bestowing me with some of his all-encompassing power.

And in my position, I'll take all the power I can get.

My conversation with Luisa verified that I'm not welcome here. That I'm an outsider. Sure, everyone has been kind and courteous to me this past week, but they had no choice. But as long as Milo wants me, I hold *some* of the cards. The more power he gives *me*, the less power *he has*.

It's like a twisted game of tug-of-war; as long as my hands are on the rope and I'm still standing, I haven't lost.

I won't lose.

Blinking, I add, "How was—"

"Show me what you have learned, Kiara," he rasps, reaching for the hem of his shirt. He slowly pulls it over his wide shoulders, purposely taking his time, knowing that he's drawing me in, sucking me into his black hole. I bite my lip, my mouth dry as I absentmindedly study his sculpted figure.

With a flick of the wrist, he drops his shirt on the padded floor. He strides toward me, shadows from the recessed lighting bouncing around the hard ridges of his chest, the ripples of his abs, the defined V that leads to the large mass bulging from his joggers. With every step he takes closer to me, a muscle on this perfect body twitches, so tempting, so fucking refined.

He licks his lips, reaching for the boxing gloves in my hands and tossing them aside. "Wha—" I clear my throat. "What are you doing?"

"Taking the training wheels off." Mischief grows in his irises he leans into my ear, his chest flush against my breasts. His stubble grazes my jawline as he whispers, "Hit me, Kiara. I want to feel your hands against my body."

*Power.*

"I don't want to hurt you, Mr. Di Vaio," I say in a taunting tone. "I've learned a few tricks."

His chest rumbles like the beating hooves of wild animals, his baritone laugh reverberating through my body.

"Trust me, Kiara—" He snakes his hand around the back of my neck, tugging it backward, and his black eyes burrow into mine. "I am a *very* difficult man to hurt."

Based on the various scars scattered across his chest and

slicing through his tattooed arms – he's lying. He's made out of flesh and blood, just like me. But I won't argue. I'll let him have this one.

"Have it your way." I detangle myself from his iron grip, roll my neck, and stretch out my arms. "Ready?"

He smirks, widening his stance. "Come and get it, *Kiara.*"

I get into position, praying that I don't make an idiot out of myself. I'm sure he'll be able to block all my punches but the idea of getting to touch him is causing a flurry of excitement to course through my veins.

I cast him a sly smile. "As you wish."

Pointing my thumb to the floor, like Gio taught me in order to not break a finger, I swing my left fist forward to jab Milo's chest. He catches my hand in his palm.

Fuck.

I repeat the action, Milo grinning each time he blocks my throws. He's barely even trying. This is so embarrassing.

"Good form." He drops my hand, my arms already getting tired. "But try harder. *Hit me.*"

"Yes, *sir,*" I say through my teeth, annoyed that he can sense which direction I'll be swinging from.

His eyes light up from the moniker. *Hmm.* He liked that. How telling. Having caught him off guard, I take the opportunity to test out a different approach. My right foot turns inward, my hip following through as I cut my right fist across the air, slamming his shoulder. This time he staggers backward. I smile, pleased with myself.

"Distracted?" I cock my head to the side, clicking my tongue. "Come on now, *sir.* Get your head in the game."

His jaw clenches, evidently furious that I landed a shot but there's a very small trace of amusement tugging on his lips. At least I hope it's amusement.

"Clever." He repositions himself in front of me. "Again."

And so, I do. Over and over and over again until I'm panting and frustrated. It's like he can anticipate my every move.

I grunt, shifting my weight from my left heel to my right. Forming a ninety-degree angle with my elbow, I attempt to pop Milo with a right hook. He side-steps my attack and I stumble forward. My heart races with exhaustion, my fists starting to hurt from the repetitive motion, but his goddamn smug face is pissing me off.

Enough!

With one final swing, I turn my right hip and shoulder, and punch upward, knocking my fist against Milo's chin in an uppercut. *Hah!*

When I land the punch, a fire ignites in Milo's eyes as he drags his thumb across his lips, a smear of blood on the pad.

*Shit.*

"My turn," he taunts, latching onto my forearm. He spins me around, his dick pressed up against my ass.

*Oh, God.*

"What do you do now, Kiara?" He squeezes my body against his, both of my wrists trapped between his one hand. His hot breath blows against my ear as I squirm, inadvertently creating friction against his most vulnerable body part. A groan escapes the back of his throat, but he doesn't acknowledge it, instead he asks, "How do you escape?"

Trying to free myself, I writhe against Milo's body, his cock hardening against me, growing, revealing his cards. Yes. *This* is power. *I* have the power. Well—I inwardly chuckle, based on the sheer size pressing up against my ass and my sudden urge to *grab it,* I guess he has a little power too.

But unfortunately for Mr. Dark and Dangerous, I have *phenomenal* self-control.

With all the strength I can muster, I spin my body around, trying out a release technique Mateo taught me. Clearly, I wasn't paying enough attention because when I twist in his arms, I fumble, my feet crossing with Milo's, knocking me off balance, and I plummet backward on the rubber floors, taking him down with me.

"Get off." I peer up at Milo who's straddling me, the fabric separating our bodies not thick enough, or too thick; depends on which side of my brain is talking. The side that hasn't fucked in six months says it's the latter.

"Make me." He pushes his hips forward and his dick twitches against my sex as he pins my arms above my head, a wicked smile on his face. *Fuck.* I'm losing power. "What's wrong, *gattina? Distracted?"*

Bastard.

"I don't know what to do," I admit in a breathy tone, flexing all my muscles, attempting to move his steel body off me but he doesn't budge. Terrifying realization dawns on me. This isn't good. If this were a real attack, I'd be fucked. "Help me. Tell me what to do."

Milo curses in Italian as he takes a deep breath, loosening his grip on my hands but not dismounting me. "Slide your elbows to my knees. Keep them on the floor. At the same time, thrust your hips up. *Fast."* He wants me to *thrust?* He rolls his eyes, picking up on my hesitation. "Just do it, Kiara."

"Fine!" I expel a sigh and follow his directions. With the combination of movements, Milo jolts forward, bracing himself with his hands.

"Oh my God!" I exclaim, wiggling my fingers. "My arms are free." I pause, frowning. "But you're still on top of me."

"Yes," he says, staying in position, his chest hovering above my face. *Mmm.* He smells sweet. Like vanilla-infused oak. Or sherry cask scotch. "Now, grab my left arm, trap it, and push me off to the side."

"Push you?" I let out a scoff. "You're like one hundred and ninety pounds."

"Kiara, my weight is currently all in my knees. You are simply *distributing* the weight." His tone edges on annoyed. "You can do it. Trust me."

*Trust me.* Hah. Like it's that simple.

"If you say so," I mutter, jerking his arms and almost effortlessly tossing Milo to the side. I roll out, surprised that his technique actually worked. My eyes widen with astonishment as Milo stands up, adjusting the band of his sweatpants, an impressed look on his face. "I did it!"

"You see? Easy." He holds out his hand and helps lift me to my feet. "You did well, Kiara. Not excellent, but well."

"Apologies for not mastering the art of self-defense in five days." I grab a towel and bottle of water off the bench press. "I think I did fairly well under the time constraints."

Milo's gaze focuses on my lips as I pop open the nub of the water bottle with my teeth. "Yes, very well." He rubs his chin. "But I do hope your arms training was more—" He pauses as I wipe the water dripping down the side of my mouth. "Fruitful."

"I think you'll be pleasantly surprised by just how *fruitful* it was," I say, padding the towel on my breasts. I need a fucking shower. He heads to the door. We're going now? "Aren't you forgetting your shirt?"

"If you can walk around half-naked, so can I," he says, exiting the gym. "I'm a feminist, you see."

"I have clothes on," I note with a head tilt. "I'm hardly naked."

"You might as well be." His gaze sweeps across my body as his fingers scoop up the strap to my sports bra. "There is not a lot left for the imagination."

"Oh, but there is, trust me." I let out an amused chuckle when Milo's eyes harden. Smartass. "Are you *sure* you trust me with a gun, Mr. Di Vaio?"

"Do you feel like shooting me, Kiara?" he smirks, leading me toward the range that's across the hall from the gym.

"Always, sir," I coo as we enter a large cement room with an angled backstop on the far wall. Gio explained to me that it's built that way so bullets ricochet up. I'd hate to be the poor bastard that learned that the hard way.

Milo selects a Beretta 92 FS from the armory, his go-to apparently. "You will use this." I watch in awe as he grabs a magazine off the counter, inserts it into the well, and racks the slide; his movements graceful, fast, like it's ingrained into his muscle memory. "Here."

I take the pistol from Milo as he places protection over our ears. I re-grip the Italian-made gun at the base, hovering my index finger over the trigger. The paper targets hang ten yards away.

Milo stands behind me, placing his hands on my shoulders, applying pressure to the blades. "You must relax, Kiara," he whispers and my body melts against his touch. "You need to hold the Beretta with a firm grip but allow for a bounce-back, understood? Anticipate a recoil."

"Okay." I aim at the target, taking a deep breath as I focus my vision on the red dot in the center of the paper. I pull the trigger and shoot off ten rounds, my shoulder jolting back after each fire. It's an exhilarating feeling, cathartic, something I'm scared to grow accustomed to.

"Let's see how I did." I remove the earmuffs and flick on the mechanical rails. The target flies toward us, most of the shots in the center of the target. I spin to face an impressed Milo, unable to hide my prideful grin. "Pretty good, right?"

He shrugs as if I didn't just kick some serious Beretta ass. "Not bad." He walks back to the armory and retrieves two more pistols. "With these now. You must learn to be... *flexible.*"

"A challenge? Fine." I roll my eyes, grabbing the Ruger GP100 revolver from his hand. This one was my favorite to shoot this week. Made me feel like I was in a Western. Reach for the sky.

For the next thirty minutes, I showcase my impeccable talent for firearms. I never thought I'd enjoy firing a weapon, I'm a pacifist, but damn, this shit is fun as fuck.

"I must hand it to you, Kiara," Milo says at the end of the session. "You are a fast learner, not many women can handle the strength and power of a .357 magnum."

"Yes." I shoot him a coy smile. "It appears I like my weapons how I like my men, Mr. Di Vaio. Ironic, is it not?"

Knight to F3. A little Sicilian defense. Why not?

"*Very* ironic indeed."

"So?" I lean against the edge of the counter. "Did I pass your little test?"

Without saying a word, he disappears down the hall, leaving me alone and confused. Was I supposed to follow him? Words, are they that difficult to use? I linger by the post for a few seconds, unsure of what to do. Just as I'm about to leave, Milo returns with a black case in his hand.

"Your graduation gift." He opens the case and he places it on the table. I eye the tiny pistol laid across the foam rounds. Is he fucking with me? "Perfect for you."

I scoff as I pick it up. "You're giving me a *hooker gun?*

Seriously? What about the revolver? This—" I shake my head, offended. "It's a toy."

He expels a melodic laugh. "This is not a toy, Kiara." He takes the miniature gun from my hands. "This is a Ruger LCR .38 special. It is—" He cocks it. "Reliable." Aims at the target. "Concealable." And fires. "Powerful."

"Ow!" My ears ring from the lack of protection. "Fuck, that's loud!"

He's unfazed as he draws closer to me. "It is small but—" He tucks the pistol into the band of my leggings, his fingers sweeping my skin, teasing it, forcing a shiver to seize my spine as he whispers, "You can hide it... *anywhere*." He pulls away, a devilish smirk on his face as he scans my tense posture. "A problem?"

"No," I peep, exhaling a shaky breath. Now I really need a shower. "Not at all."

"Fantastic," he states, knowing quite well that he's rendered me a hot mess. Asshole. "We leave for Spain tomorrow. Luisa will help you pack."

I blink. "And what are we doing in Spain? What should I pack?"

"I will tell you when the time is right." A knowing grin spreads on his face. "As for clothing, cocktail dresses. Nothing too revealing, of course."

I snort. "Is that for my benefit or for yours? Worried about a little competition?"

He stalks toward me and grabs my chin; his thumb coaxing open my bottom lip as his hauntingly intense gaze feasts upon my shaken features. "The only person who should be worried is you, Kiara. You do not want to defy my wishes."

My breath hitches. "Maybe I do."

His grip tightens around my jaw as he drags his large

hand to the base of my throat, applying minimal pressure that sends heat to my core. "No, *sweetheart*," he rasps. "You don't."

But I do.

I really fucking do.

# CHAPTER 9

## A ROAD DIVERGED

WITH EVERY STEP I TAKE CLIMBING ABOARD MILO'S private luxury aircraft, it feels like blood is gushing from the soles of my red-bottomed heels.

How many lives were lost in order to afford such lavish transportation?

My guess is *too* many. Far too many.

The jet is packed with rich ivory leathers, fine walnut veneers, and stylish marble stonework. Disgust and astonishment battle for supremacy in my mind as I roam through the cabin. Milo, Marchello, our guards, and the others take their seats on the pristine divans.

"Sit." Milo gestures to an empty seat in front of him, a sleek glossy wooden table dividing the two chairs. "You can explore once we are in the air."

I slump into the off-white leather loveseat, placing the brown monogrammed tote bag Luisa purchased for me on the ground. It's too flashy for my liking, I much prefer a handbag that doesn't scream privilege; I'll have to do some shopping in Spain. Prior to leaving the estate, Luisa presented me with an infinite visa card to do with what I please. No limit.

That seems to be a recurring theme with Milo. Nothing is off-limits.

"I would've been able to explore it the first time around if someone didn't drug me," I mutter, gazing out the window as the crew prepares for liftoff.

"It was not intentional." He adjusts the cuffs of his black button-up shirt before fanning open today's edition of *Il Corriere Della Sera*. The headline reads: *Two Unidentified Bodies Found at the Port of Palermo.*

I squint suspiciously at Milo. That can't be a coincidence.

"How was your trip to Sicily?" The plane takes off and I grip the armrest, taking a deep breath. *Please let there be no turbulence.* "Anything interesting happen?"

"No." He keeps his eyes affixed on the daily Italian newspaper, not bothering to look at me. "It was uneventful."

"Really?" My heart skips a beat as the plane ascends into the sky. "You didn't, I don't know, murder two people or anything?"

This grabs his attention.

"What?" A frown mars his groomed brows as he closes the paper, lowering it to his lap.

I point to the front page, tilting my head as I perk up an accusatory brow.

"This?" He lets out a small laugh, looking at me like I'm a clueless child. "Please, Kiara, do not offend me so early in the morning."

I cross my arms. "That wasn't you? *Really?*"

He places the newspaper on the table, hiking his ankle over his thigh, his black loafers bouncing up and down as he grins.

"If it *were* me, Kiara, there would be *no* bodies," he says with twisted humor as he scans the front page again. "And I would certainly not dispose of said bodies in such an unimaginative location. A dock? How amateur."

There's nothing in his tone or posture that indicates he's lying, if anything, he truly is offended by my accusation.

My knowledge of the mafia world is limited to what I've seen on television or read in books, but discretion *does* seem to be of vital importance to the preservation of criminal organizations.

That being said, my suspicions are still completely warranted.

"Okay, well then how would a professional, such as yourself, dispose of a dead body?" I cross my legs, mirroring his body language. "Give me a mini-Masterclass in the art of — how did you put it before?" I pause, biting my lip. "*Clean up.*"

"Kiara," he hums with amusement. "A woman should never be burdened with the knowledge of such gruesome matters."

I cock my head to the side. "I thought you said you were a feminist, Mr. Di Vaio? Believe me, I think I can handle it."

"Perhaps." His gaze drifts over to a flight attendant near the galley. He waves two fingers in the air before snapping his focus back to me. "But I would hate to strip you of your innocence. Some things are better left unsaid."

"My innocence?" I blink, an incredulous scoff escaping my lips. "I think that ship sailed when you shot two men right before my eyes, don't you think?"

He sighs, a pensive look on his face. "There is innocence of the eyes and innocence of the soul, Kiara. It is important not to confuse the two. And believe me, there are far worse things to witness than a bullet entering the brain."

"How very poetic. But everything is connected. Your eyes, heart, mind, soul. It makes one being. What the eyes witness seeps into one's soul. You can't compartmentalize morality, Mr. Di Vaio."

His jaw tenses. "In my line of work, Kiara, it is required."

"Perhaps you should rethink your line of work then." I rest my head against the wall of the plane, my brain buzzing from the vibrations. "It seems like a steep price to pay for eternal damnation."

"Eternal damnation?" He lets out a boisterous laugh, drawing perplexed glances from his associates. "Oh, Kiara, what is it that you think I do? Murder children? I can assure you, in the hierarchy of evil, I'm nowhere near damnation."

"I don't think that's your call to make."

His eyes harden. "Nor is it yours."

I scowl at him, my blood pulsing with irritation. Who does he think he is? Does he expect me to waver on my stance? Accept that murder is just an unfortunate byproduct of his chosen profession?

No. I won't.

There are universally accepted notions of right and wrong.

And he's wrong.

For the next hour, we sit across from each other in silence. He reads the newspaper and I read Dante's Inferno.

Hell.

Based on the headlines of worldwide newspapers and the political and social turmoil across the globe, perhaps Hell is not such a foreign place after all.

Although Mr. Alighieri's prose is quite thought-provoking, it's also emotionally draining. When I reach my daily limit for allegorical narrative, I shove *The Divine Comedy* back into my purse, opting to switch to a lighter tale, perhaps *Cold Comfort Farm*— Nana's favorite.

As I attempt to fish out my Kindle, my fingers glide across the pistol at the bottom of my bag. It's unnerving that something so small holds so much destructive power. I pull the gun out of my purse, twisting it in my fingers, examining it carefully.

"I would prefer if you did not point a loaded weapon in my direction when we are thirty thousand feet in the air," Milo says, peering over his newspaper.

I frown. "How do you know it's loaded?"

"A party trick," he smirks, mocking my words as he lowers the paper.

"Hilarious." My frown deepens. "But, seriously, how? I'm curious."

He sighs, clicking his tongue. "I can tell by the way you're holding the gun, Kiara. The tiny muscles in your wrists are a dead giveaway."

"Oh." I twist my wrist around, the gun waving back and forth as I examine how my hand clenches. This doesn't make sense. How can he—

"Kiara! Put down the fucking gun. This aircraft is not bulletproof. You shoot, we die."

"Don't worry. The safety is on." I roll my eyes, lowering the pistol. He shoots me a dubious look. "Yeah, that's right, I know what a safety is now. Thank you very much."

If only I knew sooner, then *maybe* I wouldn't be here right now.

He expels a low chuckle. "Still, put it away." He pauses. "When *did* you load the gun? I don't remember inserting a clip when we left the range."

*The range.*

I shiver, tracing my fingers along my neck, remembering

Milo's strong grip, his touch, the way my insides knotted from his warning, the way every fiber of my being wanted to revolt against it.

"I couldn't sleep last night so I went back. I loaded it before going to bed." I let out a small laugh, banishing all thoughts of Milo's lithe body ravaging mine out of my head. *Not today, Satan.* "Honestly, it's trickier than it looks. It took me a few tries to figure it out."

"'There is a learning curve, that is true." Milo takes a sip of red wine, a faint grin on his face. Why is he smiling? "It will get easier over time."

"I don't know..." I glance at the flight attendant. I could go for a glass of wine. Or ten. It's nice to see that I'm not the only one who drinks before noon. "You make it seem so effortless."

Milo snaps his fingers, catching the immediate attention of the blonde woman. "Another glass of Chianti," he states, silently verifying the order with me. I nod. I guess he's *somewhat* useful. "You must understand, Kiara, I was taught how to load, take apart, and reassemble a gun before I learned how to ride a bike."

"*What?*" I blink at him as a wine glass appears in my hand. "How *old* were you?"

"Six, I think. It was a long time ago." He shrugs, unbothered. "My father ensured that my siblings and I received the proper training from an early age."

"Wow," I hum, shocked by how casual he sounds, as if children handling firearms is normal.

But maybe in his world, it is.

"Kiara," he says softly, "this was the life I was born into. It is all I have ever known so do not look at me with sympathy. I do not need it."

A child. He was just a child. An innocent, pure soul.

How can I not feel sympathy? How can my heart not ache for him? When other kids were going bowling, riding skateboards, he was learning how to shoot. How to kill. How to carry on the legacy of his family's name.

But I get it. I do.

Some things are not up to us. They're above our pay grade.

Our families. Where we're born. When we die.

*How* we die.

In our sleep. From cancer. Murder.

Black ice on the road.

"I guess we can't choose our fate, right?"

"*Do not be afraid; our fate cannot be taken from us; it is a gift,*" Milo says in Italian, reciting a portion of a Canto from Dante's Inferno. "We are all given a path to walk, Kiara. Mine is simply different than yours. But our destinations are the same."

"Yeah..." I nod, sipping on my wine, confused yet relieved by his words. *The same.* Is that possible? "I guess you're right."

Milo takes a deep breath, a gentle smile on his face. "So, with all of that being said, do not feel discouraged with your training, I have twenty-five years of experience. For a novice, you are excelling."

"You're thirty-one?" I calculate his age in my head. "I thought you were younger."

Not by a lot, but I didn't think he was eight years older than me. Maybe five years max.

Okay...maybe four.

"Really?" he smirks. "Thank you."

I roll my eyes, tossing him a sly grin. Such arrogance. "That was not a compliment."

He lets out a dissatisfied humph. "Tread lightly, Kiara. I can be quite sensitive at times."

I laugh at the absurdity of his statement. "Apologies, I momentarily forgot how fragile a man's ego can be."

He glares at me. "That is the opposite of treading lightly. You are not very obedient, are you?"

I tilt my head. "I can be *very* obedient, Mr. Di Vaio. Depends on the circumstance."

His lip twitches, his pupils dilating as he lifts up his wine, methodically twirling the red liquid around the curved orifice of the glass. "And what types of circumstances would those be?"

I shrug, casting him a knowing smile, refusing to satisfy his oozing curiosity. "I guess you'll have to find out."

His tongue delicately laves against the sharp edge of the wine glass before he takes a slow sip of Chianti.

"I intend to."

I swallow, sinking my teeth into my bottom lip. "I'd like to see you try."

"In that case—" A puckish grin clips his lips as he lifts up his glass. "To challenging oneself."

"And to knowing one's limitations."

# CHAPTER 10

## IN THE DETAILS

FOR THE FIRST THIRTY MINUTES OF THE DRIVE FROM THE airport to Hotel Di Vaio Madrid, I'm so entranced by the beauty of this foreign city that I forget I'm in a Rolls Royce, sitting next to a man with questionable ethics and a murky moral compass.

Madrid is mesmerizing, with the combination of renaissance architecture and flares of tasteful modernization, it's not surprising this city was a muse to so many great poets and artists.

"Over there is *Casa Botín*," Milo hums, drawing my attention. He gestures toward a building in the distance with a wooden caramel exterior. "It is the oldest restaurant in the world. Ernest Hemingway—"

"Wrote about it in his novel *The Sun Also Rises*," I interject his factoid with a smug smile. "Yes, I'm aware."

"Are you also aware that it is quite rude to interrupt someone when they are speaking?" He scowls at me as he pulls out his cellphone from his pants pocket and types out a message. "Did your parents not teach you any manners?"

My cocky smile contorts into a pained frown, my jaw

tightening. "They taught me as much as they could in the short time that they had."

He peers up from his phone, wincing apologetically as if realizing the tactlessness of his question.

"Forgive me. I forgot that they passed away when you were young."

"It's fine. I don't expect you to remember every minute detail of our conversations."

"That is hardly a minute detail, Kiara." Milo takes a deep breath as he gazes out of his window. "I should have remembered." He pauses, adding, "It is not easy to lose a loved one."

His mournful tone pricks at my heart. He's speaking from experience. *Recent* experience.

A pang of empathy stirs in my stomach. "No, it's not."

He clears his throat, his discomfort on the subject palpable as he faces me.

"You mentioned earlier that you would like to go shopping, correct?" he asks, changing the topic. "You will have several hours before we are expected at Aria. Gio and Mateo will escort you wherever you'd like to go."

"Aria?" I ask, grateful that I'll finally have some time to myself. Well, that is if my guards don't breathe down my neck the entire outing. I might have to set some parameters with them. "What's Aria?"

"A club I own. We'll be meeting several of my business partners there later tonight." He gives me a quick once-over. "You will need to dress *appropriately*. I can recommend a few boutiques if you would like."

"Thanks, but I think I can handle *shopping* on my own." I cross my arms, still not entirely sure of what my role is. "What do you expect me to do tonight? Other than eavesdrop on your Spanish friends. I need context, Mr. Di Vaio, if I'm to report anything of actual value."

With a resigned sigh, Milo offers, "You are an intelligent and intuitive woman, Kiara. You will know if something is of value or not."

I roll my eyes at his compliment even though it fills me with an odd sense of accomplishment.

"I need details. Why are we meeting with these people? Who are they? What kind of *business* do they do for you? Does it have anything to do with the Russians? Do they—"

Milo raises his hand and I stop talking, hoping he'll answer my questions.

"Oh," he smirks. "Perhaps you *are* obedient."

"Only when I want something. So? Tell me what I want to know."

Milo licks his lips, scanning me with guarded eyes before finally revealing, "What happened in Hawthorne, at the bank, has not been made public, and I intend to keep it that way. My associates here cannot know that we are at odds with the Russians. It would be bad for business. We are here to ensure that their confidence in my... *organization* has not wavered, understand?"

"Yes," I hum. "Basically, we're here because you're worried that they know you were *kidnapped* which makes you look weak, and you don't want that. Right?"

His twitching right eye indicates that he's not entirely impressed with my interpretation. "In layman's terms, yes. That is why we are here."

I shoot my shot. "So why *were* you kidnapped? I mean, you're constantly surrounded by guards – how did that even happen? And why do you bank under an alias? And why Hawthorne and not Manchester?"

"You ask too many questions." Milo closes his eyes,

letting out an exasperated sigh. "There are things you do not need to know. Just focus on the task at hand."

"Why are you so hesitant to tell me? What do you think I'm going to do? *Tweet* about it?" I ask, getting irked by his lack of cooperation. "Just give me something. Anything. A little crumb will do."

I've already established that he traffics drugs and funnels the funds through his hotels. I assume his international *associates* are dealers? Maybe distributors? But the Russians? I'm lost.

He mulls it over for a few seconds before sighing in defeat.

"We use smaller banks because the staff is easier to control. I was in Manchester visiting an old friend when the Russians found me. Only a few members of my team knew where I was going. I was alone for only two minutes. They caught me off guard which *rarely* occurs."

That kind of precise knowledge takes insider information.

"Seems like you have a rodent problem. Might need to set a little mouse trap back in Genoa."

He casts me a devious smirk. "*Had* a rodent problem. It has been taken care of, believe me."

I suck in a sharp breath, shocked by how unaffected I am by his comment. "You killed him?"

"He killed himself. He was foolish to think he could betray my family and live to grow old and grey."

"You're not very forgiving, are you?"

"There is no room for forgiveness in my world, Kiara," he says, pressing me to heed his warning. "It is best that you remember that."

"I'm not a fool, Mr. Di Vaio. I would never—"

The screeching of tires cuts me off, the car swerving back and forth, our bodies swaying side-to-side.

With a vice-like grip, I latch my fingers around Milo's forearm as my heart drops to my stomach, an all too familiar fear overpowering my senses, blurring my vision.

The car levels out in seconds, but I'm still frozen with trepidation. Our driver rolls down the window and screams profanities into the symphony of honking cars.

"Kiara." Milo's soft voice fills my ears as I stare into nothingness. "Kiara, are you alright?"

"Uh-huh," I murmur between ragged breaths, unable to fill my lungs with enough oxygen.

His warm palm covers my hand, squeezing it gently. "Close your eyes," he whispers. My eyelids flutter shut. "Take a deep breath, Kiara—" And I do. "Good, now hold it for seven seconds. Six, five, four, three, two—" I exhale. "Now inhale for four seconds."

I repeat this process for what feels like hours until the panic fades away, until I can move my limbs, until my mind is clear.

With his large hand still enveloping mine, Milo asks, "Better?"

I swallow, embarrassment washing over me. "Yeah," I mutter. "Thank you. I don't know what happened, I haven't —" I expel a shaky breath. "How did you know what to do? How did you—"

"My older sister." His fingertips tickle my palm as he slowly drags his hand away from mine. "She is a psychologist, she's g—" He pauses. "She specializes in panic and anxiety disorders; she sends me a lot of articles."

"Sister? You have a sister?" I frown. "And she's a... *psychologist*?"

This is the first I'm hearing of her. There are not a lot of portraits of women hanging on the walls of his villa. Granted, I haven't memorized all their faces, but I didn't see women who resembled Milo. Perhaps she was excommunicated. Are mafia women even allowed to have jobs? Maybe that's why there are empty spaces on the walls.

No. Enough. I need more information before I jump to conclusions.

"Yes, I have a sister. She lives in Monaco with her husband and my mother."

"Your mother doesn't live in Italy?" This doesn't make sense. Aren't these types of *families* supposed to stick together? Or has TV ruined my perception of the real world? "Why?"

"She moved in with Julia after my father passed away." His body stiffens. "It was too painful for her to be in that house. Too many memories."

"Oh, that makes sense. And your sister, Julia? When did she move to Monaco?"

Milo lets out a cynical scoff. "As soon as she could."

"And that was allowed? Aren't there...rules or something?"

Milo cocks his head to the side. "Of course, she was allowed. She was not a *prisoner*."

"And she's a psychologist? Why did she go into psych?"

Milo grunts something inaudible in Italian as he closes his eyes, evidently tired of my onslaught of questions. "You can ask her yourself when we go to Monaco in a few days."

We're going to Monaco next? When was he planning on telling me?

I purse my lips. "You know, I wouldn't have so many questions if you just told me things from the get-go."

"Do you know the saying; curiosity killed the cat? It

might be an overused adage, but it holds some merit, don't you think?"

I roll my eyes as the car rounds a corner and pulls into a driveway surrounded by lush greenery and spurting fountains.

"Holy shit..." I peer out of the window, my gaze traveling up the length of the stone-arched white Hotel; mystique and grandeur captured in all the fine details of the design. An attendant opens the door for me and I step out, the warm autumn sun soaking into my skin. "You own this?"

"Yes," Milo says with a casual shrug. "Come."

I twist my head toward the other SUVs. Marchello hops out of the car and immediately lights up a cigarette. He really shouldn't smoke at his age. I'm sure Luisa wouldn't want to lose her father prematurely.

"Kiara, come." Milo taps his foot impatiently. "They will join us later."

I follow Milo through the glass doors, gripping my purse as employees greet us with polite smiles; their respect and admiration for Milo evident in their body language, the way they bow their heads as he passes like he's a king, a god.

"Don't we have to check-in?" I ask as we pause in front of the elevators.

He lets out a small chuckle, Gio and Mateo joining in. "No, we do not." He pulls out a keycard from his wallet. "The top floor is always reserved."

"Right..."

It's his palace, after all.

We ride the elevator to the thirty-first floor, my ears popping from the elevation and speed. The door opens into a lavish suite; sophisticated furniture sprawled around the room, avant-garde design in the fine details of the decor, floor-to-ceiling windows that overlook the city center,

French doors that lead to a rooftop patio with a sunken pool in the center, a hot tub just off to the side.

*Wow.*

"Your room is over there." Milo gestures down the ash-grey hallway before handing me a key card. "You have five hours to explore. I expect you to be ready at eight."

"Thanks." I slip the keycard into my wallet next to the visa card as I glance over to Mateo. "I need a few minutes to freshen up and then we can go, okay?"

"Sì," he says, keeping his expression neutral. "*I will get the car.*"

"No, I want to walk. It's a nice day."

Mateo's eyes drift to Milo for approval.

"Whatever she wants." Milo checks his phone, frowning. "I must go now."

"Is something wrong?" I ask, pulling items out of my purse to make it lighter.

"No." He looks at me, expression softening. "Everything is fine. Enjoy your afternoon."

I wave his visa card in the air. "Oh, I will."

Taking two strides toward me, Milo leans down and pushes my chestnut brown hair off my shoulder. His intoxicating cologne permeates the small space between us as he whispers in my ear, "Wear something red."

"Red?"

"Yes," he smirks. "It would please me."

I toss him a sweet smile. "Of course, Mr. Di Vaio. I aim to please."

I'm wearing fucking black.

# CHAPTER 11

## SMOKE AND FIRE

MILO GLARES AT ME AS HE SLIDES INTO THE SUV, HIS judgmental gaze taking in the itty-bitty scrap of luxury fabric wrapping my body, hugging all the right places. I don't say anything, instead simply flash him a small smile, my combative eyes doing *all* the talking for me.

*Make a comment. I dare you.*

Since he refuses to elaborate or explain *anything* in detail, the phrase *dress appropriately* was *far* too vague for me to interpret with any certainty, so I opted to wear a dress I deemed appropriate for a nightclub setting.

His mouth opens for a brief second but then snaps shut like he knows I'm waiting for it, anticipating his displeasure, and he doesn't want to appease me.

He doesn't want to lose.

*"Drive fast,"* Milo tells our driver in a clipped tone, his attention focused on his phone. *"We are late."*

Because *you* were late, I want to add but decide to keep my remark to myself. I'm sensing he's already in a foul mood, I wouldn't want to poke the self-proclaimed dragon.

At least not yet.

I cross my legs as the car hums to life, running my fingers over the hem of my charcoal halter dress that reaches mid-thigh. The seven gold chains attached to the back of the couture garment press against my bare spine as I lean back into my seat: the icy sensation from the precious metal cutting through the dizzying heat of Milo's presence.

I tilt my head, my mouth dry as my greedy gaze skims his ensemble. So understated. So simple. So *goddamn* enticing. He's wearing what he usually does – black slacks and a black dress shirt with the top two buttons undone. His sleeves are rolled up to his forearms, showcasing his black and grey tattoos; the scars on his arms evidence of his strength, his vigor, his power and...and I'm suddenly overwhelmed.

I'm overwhelmed by the tugging ache just below my stomach, the primal urge to rip the silk shirt off his perfect body, dig my nails into his flesh, touch him, mark him, taste him, *consume* him.

*All* of him. Every wicked inch.

*Oh, fucking hell.*

I expel a small breath, squeezing my thighs shut as I command my treacherous eyes to stop gawking at him but they're disobedient, bratty, *rebellious*.

They don't care that we're losing a battle. They don't care about the consequences. They don't care about logic or reason or strategy.

They just want to stare and admire and *undress*.

*Fucking hedonists.*

I pull a tube of red lipstick out of my clutch and touch up the corners of my lips, distracting myself from the magnetic pull of his aura. "How far is the club? Are we close?"

Milo doesn't bother to look up from his phone. "Not far."

"Oh." At least he can't see how affected I am by his proximity.

For fuck sakes. Get it together. This is *not* part of the plan.

*At all.*

The drive to the club is silent, the type of silence that speaks thunderous volumes. He's pissed, anger diffusing from his pores, thickening the air in the Rolls Royce, making me flustered, hot.

So *very* hot.

He steals glimpses at me when I'm not looking. I can sense it. I can *feel* his leering gaze on my legs, my slender shoulders, my breasts. *Everywhere.* And I want him to look. I *want* him to study my body, remember it, crave it, do *anything* to have it.

Because that's power. And I have no qualms with letting power corrupt me *absolutely.*

The car abruptly stops, and Milo gets out in a rush, holding the door open for me as I slide to his side. As I hop out of the vehicle, my phone falls from my lap onto the sidewalk.

*Shit, I thought I put it in my purse.*

Crouching down in an elegant manner so as to not flash any bystanders, I rest my palm against Milo's upper thigh, steadying myself on my heels as I pick up the cellphone.

Milo clears his throat, drawing my attention. I peer up at him, his body towering over me.

He casts me a debased smirk as he cups my jaw, tilting it, his thumbs grazing my bottom lip. "You look good on your knees. But perhaps now is not the time, Kiara."

*Fuck.*

With shallow breaths, I trail my hand up the length of his body and stand up, leaning into his ear. "What a shame... Because you'll *never* see me in that position ever again."

Milo's eyes darken as he snakes his arm around my waist, yanking me flush against his firm body. His large hand weaves through the gold chains decorating my back. I stifle a contented whimper.

His touch is hot, scalding, *possessive* as he grunts, "You cannot even *begin* to fathom the kinds of positions I want to see you in, Kiara." He twirls a tendril of my hair between his fingers and adds, "Soon, you will be *begging* me to fuck you. It's written all over your face. You want me. So *so* bad."

*Double fuck.*

I let out a ragged breath, unable to form a coherent sentence as his fingers ghost down my spine and force a shudder. "No—" I stammer, wriggling in his arms. "I—I don't."

I can't.

"Yes. Yes, you do." His chest rattles against my shoulder as a low knowing chuckle spills from his lips. He releases me from his grasp and gives me an appreciative once-over. "Nice dress by the way," he hums, reaching for my hand. "But I told you to wear red."

I swallow as his fingers lace through mine. *What is he doing?* "I *am* wearing red," I whisper, attempting to gather my wit. I'm not going to suffer alone. "You just can't *see* it."

His gaze darts to the part of my body that's screaming to be touched, to be ravaged. "Fuck..." He tightens his grip around my fingers, his eye full of restraint. "Kiara..."

Satisfaction spreads across my face. I won't lose. Not today. "I'm getting cold. Let's go inside."

Milo shakes his head, looking at me like I took away his favorite toy. "You will regret teasing me like this," he states as he leads me into Aria. "We will continue this conversation later. For now, I need you to smile and not talk, understand?"

Thumping electro house music sounds around us, the deep harsh bass vibrating my heart, my teeth. "What is our relationship?" I ask as he adjusts his grip on my hand.

"You are my date." Red and purple strobe lights blind me as we maneuver through a labyrinth of tables, Gio and Mateo on our tail. "Do not react when they speak Spanish. For all they know you're just an American."

"Okay," I mutter as we enter an area of the club that's littered with private alcoves. It's secluded here, slightly fewer people but it feels just as dirty, just as sinister.

I find myself squeezing Milo's hand as we approach the last tented seating area. Anxiety creeps into my chest as two men in black stand guard outside the table, their arms crossed, their expressions menacing.

I got this. This is easy. Don't talk. Only listen. I'm good at that.

Once they notice Milo, the two guards step to the side, nodding at him with respect as one of them gestures for us to enter the dim room. It's bigger than I thought it would be. My gaze bounces from the three men lounging on the plum velvet chairs in the middle of the room to the scantily dressed women perched on their laps. On the far side of the alcove, there are more people drinking, laughing, snorting cocaine off silver plates.

"Milo!" One of the men stands up, his voice deep, rough, like he's smoked his whole life. "Welcome, welcome." Milo detangles his fingers from mine to shake the hairy hand of the man who's wearing far too much cologne. "It's nice to finally have you back in Madrid, it's been far too long. Please sit."

"It is good to be back, Manuel," Milo says in a cool tone

as we sit down on a chaise across the table from the three men. Two of the men stare at me, their grins causing me much unease.

"Ricardo," Manuel says, looking at the greasy man to his right, whose face is shoved inside a blonde woman's tits. *Classy.* "A drink for our friends." He faces us, and asks, "Mezcal is, okay? It's a twelve year from Oaxaca. Very good."

"Kiara?" Milo asks me in a whisper. "Will you have a drink?"

"Mhmm." I sidle closer to Milo. I don't belong here. He places a reassuring hand on my thigh as if sensing my discomfort.

"Hey!" Manuel shoves Ricardo who's in his own little world. "Get the fucking drinks."

"Relax, Kiara," Milo hums into my ear. "They are harmless."

"I'm not scared." And I'm not lying. My discomfort is not stemming from fear. I know I'm safe. I have Milo. *And* I have a gun in my clutch.

Ricardo comes up for air, pushing the blonde girl off his lap as he wipes his mouth on his sleeve. His gaze lands on me for the first time as he grabs a bottle of liquor from a small side table, pinching two shot glasses between his fingers.

"It's strong," he says to me with a grin. "Be careful."

I take the shot from his grimy fingers, tossing him a forced smile as he hands Milo a drink.

"To friends." Manuel holds up his drink in the air before all the men down their shots in one fluid motion. I take a small sip. I probably shouldn't get drunk. I need to stay focused. Coherent. Manuel frowns at me. "You don't like it?"

"I do," I say, taking another sip. "It's good."

Manuel purses his lips, his gaze darting between me and Milo. "She's a quiet one. Not like—" He blanches immediately. Milo stiffens beside me and Manuel clears his throat.

"How's business?" Milo asks in a harsh tone. "Update me."

Milo and Manuel begin chatting about *business*. Not like who? No. Not important. *Focus.* Two more of Manuel's men join him on the couch. I stay silent as I listen to them talk numbers and shipments and money. So much fucking money. Hundreds of millions of euros. And they're unfazed, speaking about such wealth as if it's pennies.

A fat smile spreads across Manuel's face as someone passes him the platter of cocaine, a glass straw rolling on the curved surface.

"It's good shit." He shoves the tube up his nostril and snorts a line, letting out an ecstatic exhale. "Have some." He holds out the plate in front of me. "Have some fun."

"No," Milo shoots Manuel daggers, "none for her."

I eye the plate warily. "I'm good, thank you."

A greying man to the left of Manuel snickers, muttering in Spanish, *"He probably gets pussy on demand. She's a good little dog."*

I clench my teeth together. Don't react. Don't react. I am not a little dog.

Another man adds with a chuckle, *"I'd fuck that dog dry."*

Sucking in a sharp breath, I crane my neck toward Milo. "Maybe just a taste?"

He studies my expression, attempting to ascertain my intentions. I'm not opposed to drug use. I've never *done* drugs, but I don't like to judge those that do. I drink alcohol, technically that's also a drug. Also addicting.

Honestly, aside from not wanting to look like a weak submissive woman, a part of me is actually curious what it feels like, why it's so popular, why Milo makes millions off this fine white powder.

"Just a little?" I ask again.

"Open your mouth." Milo lightly dips his pinky into the pile of cocaine, white dust falling on his pants as he brings it toward me. "Give me your tongue, Kiara."

I hesitate for a second before opening my lips, giving him access to my mouth. Milo smears the coke on the tip of my tongue; the taste is awful, horrendous, like acid and bleach.

Fuck, that's gross.

Milo stares deep into my eyes, his pinky still coating my taste buds. "Do you like it?"

"Mhmm," I lie, closing my lips around his finger as he pulls his pinky out of my mouth. His pupils dilate— hungry and surprised. "I love it."

"*Lucky bastard,*" someone says in Spanish.

This time I smirk, swallowing down the bitter taste of a drug I never want to try again. My throat burns as it flows down my esophagus.

"Are you going to have some?" I take a sip on the Mezcal, hoping it washes out the disgusting taste in my mouth.

"No." Milo shifts his body toward me. "I do not do drugs, Kiara."

I blink. "You don't?"

He subtly shakes his head, a hint of amusement in his weak smile. "No."

"Oh. Good to know."

Well fuck. I thought he was going to do it too. Oh my God, that sounds so pathetic. *Oh my God, I just did cocaine.*

Okay. No need to freak out. It was just a little dab. Not even up my nose. It won't work. Nothing will happen.

Right?

Milo continues talking with his *friends,* glancing at me periodically, probably making sure I'm still alive. With every minute that passes, my body relaxes, their voices become clearer, sharper, everything turns brighter, vibrant. My fingers tingle, my heart rate increases, the Mezcal tastes *so* good, the smell of cigarettes is pungent and strong, and I want some.

I *need* some.

"Can I?" I ask Milo who has a Marlboro tucked between his index and middle finger.

"Only a little." He cocks his head to the side, holding the smoke in front of my face. I latch on to the end of the cigarette and suck, smoke filling my lungs, the combination of stimulants jolting me awake.

I can't sit any longer. I need to stand. I need to move.

"I want to dance," I say, exhaling a smoky cloud into Milo's face as I stand up. My knees feel weak, wobbly, but I don't care. Everything feels so good, so light. "I'll be on the dance floor."

His jaw tenses. "Five minutes. You can dance for five minutes."

"How generous of you, Mr. Di Vaio." I down the last of my drink and traipse out of the alcove. Gio follows behind me, not too close, but he's there, watching me, making sure I don't do anything reckless.

I close my eyes when I reach the center of the crowded dance floor, the carnal beats filling my ears, thumping in my blood as I move to the sensuous pounding music.

The air is moist and humid and thick, and I'm flying,

running my hands through my hair, down my body, my curves. I become entranced in the dark melody.

Song after song, I dance, forgetting about everything. My past, my present, my future. None of it matters. Not now. Not when I feel like a fucking queen.

A hand grabs my waist and tugs me backward. *Milo.* His intense oaky cologne smells *so* fucking good, musky and spicy and masculine, and so goddamn sweet.

I don't stop moving to the music as he wraps his arms around my hips. No. I move more. I sway faster, harder, with more urgency.

"Mmm..." I lean back against his sculpted chest, winding my arms around his neck, my fingers tugging on his hair as my ass grinds against his pelvis.

"The things I want to do to you," Milo breathes, dragging his nose along the shell of my ear. He cups my breasts, rolling my nipples between his fingers.

I let out a moan, arching into his chest. "Like what? Tell me what you want to do to me, Mr. Di Vaio."

His hand coils around my neck, caressing my jaw, my chin, my lips. "Unspeakable things." He spins me around, raking his hands through my sweaty hair as he adds in a growl, "But not when you're fucking high."

"Do you want to fuck me right now, *sir?*" I click my tongue. "I thought *I* was the one that was supposed to be begging, hmm?"

He doesn't like that. Not one bit. I knew he wouldn't. But that's why I said it. Why I poked the dragon. I want his fire. I want him to burn me. I want to feel something.

Anything.

"You're leaving." He snaps his fingers at Gio who rushes toward us. "Take her back to the hotel. Watch her."

"Why?" I whine as Gio hands me my purse. "I don't want to leave."

"Go," he hisses, running a frustrated hand through his hair. "Now."

I roll my eyes, following Gio out of the club. There's no use in fighting. He always gets his way. Always.

I hate him. God, I hate him. Am I not allowed to enjoy myself?

My euphoric state dwindles on the ride back to the hotel.

Asshole.

Slamming my bedroom door shut, I strip out of my dress and slip under the covers, my body still thrumming off the last remnants of drugs in my system.

Closing my eyes, my hand travels down my stomach toward my sex.

Fuck Milo.

I can be my own dragon.

# CHAPTER 12

## PRICE TO PAY

I SIT PERCHED ON THE EDGE OF MY BED, ANXIOUSLY fiddling with a fraying thread on my white linen dress. I stare at the light grey door that leads straight into the second circle of hell.

*Don't be such a baby. Just go! Rip the damn band-aid.*

Closing my eyes, the faces of all the great women that came before me and fell victim to lust in the midst of a power struggle pop into my head.

Cleopatra wouldn't lock herself in her room after an embarrassing encounter with Caesar. No. She would march out, head held high, and grab a fucking cup of coffee from the kitchen.

Helen of Troy wouldn't be humiliated after grinding against Paris in a Trojan nightclub. No. She would play it off as if it were a part of her strategy, a part of her plan.

I wince, remembering that both of these women died horrible deaths; on second thought, perhaps they're not the best role models.

*Damn it.*

It's almost 12 p.m., I've been awake since 8 a.m. I'm

hungry. I'm thirsty. And I'm in desperate need of a fucking ibuprofen. There's a dull ache pulsing against my temporal lobe, my mouth is dry, my throat is sore, and my stomach is grumbling.

*Just go. Move your dumb ass and deal with the consequences of your stupid actions. You want to act like a horny teenager? Well, this is the price you have to pay.*

I want to blame the cocaine for my recklessness last night, but I can't.

It was me. All me.

I let out a groan, sucking in a deep breath and straightening out my shoulders. Confident. Just act confident. Act like last night didn't happen. Nothing happened. I just won't bring it up. It's just a *regular* Sunday.

I grab my Kindle off the nightstand and unlock it, pretending to read as I twist open the door handle and saunter down the hallway toward the main living area of the suite. The faint smell of espresso beans permeates the air.

*So close.*

In my peripheral, Milo and Marchello sit around the dining room table, engrossed in what appears to be a serious conversation. Good. He's distracted. Just don't look up. Keep walking, the heavenly nectar is almost in reach.

*"Buongiorno,* Kiara," Marchello calls out in a casual tone just as I'm two seconds away from the kitchen. *Damnit.* "Did you sleep well?"

I force a smile, swallowing my pride as I turn to face the two Italians who are huddled in front of a computer. I can't gauge from Marchello's facial expressions if Milo told him about my behavior last night. He's hard to read, and that irks me.

"Good morning." I keep my gaze on Marchello and

Marchello only. I fear that if I take one glance at Milo I'll spontaneously combust. "I slept great, thank you."

"Really? The *cocaina* didn't keep you up?" Marchello perks up a salt and pepper brow.

Shit. He knows. But...how *much* does he know?

I blink. "Nope. I guess it wasn't that potent."

Milo scoffs, drawing my attention, his full lips twisted up in a dubious scowl. "Not potent? I would beg to differ."

Channel Cleo. We are channeling Cleo-*fucking*-Patra.

"Beg all you want, Mr. Di Vaio," I say, tilting my head. "But that doesn't change the fact that I slept like a baby." Courtesy of my fingers and a *very* vivid imagination but he doesn't need to know that. "How was the rest of *your* night with Manuel?"

"Useless," he states curtly. "I left shortly after you did. There was no reason for me to stay behind without my translator."

I cross my arms. "You're the one who forced me to leave. *I* wanted to stay if I recall correctly."

His lip twitches. "You were not in the right state of mind to be of any use if *I* recall correctly."

"Maybe you shouldn't have given me so much coke then. Your fault."

"My fault?" He lets out an incredulous scoff. "Your non-existent tolerance for drugs is *my* fault?"

"Yes, your fault. You were the one who gave it to me."

"Because you *asked* for it. Twice, might I add."

"And you could've said no. *Twice.*"

"Fine." His eyes harden as he wets his lips. "I'll remember that the next time you want something from me."

I stifle a whimper. I am digging myself into a hole right now. I am *literally* telling him to say no to me more often.

"Fantastic. You do that. I'm going to get some coffee now. It was nice chatting with you two."

"Not so fast."

*Shit.*

I gaze heavenward before spinning back around. *I just want some coffee.*

"What?"

Milo nods toward the laptop, a devious grin capturing his face. "Since you decided to get high instead of doing your job last night, I had to resort to... alternative measures."

"Alternative measures?" As much as I hate to admit it, he has somewhat of a valid point. In my efforts to not look like Milo's little...*dog*, I did sort of mess up the purpose of my being there. "What did you do?" I glare at him. "Did you kill him?"

Marchello and Milo exchange an amused look before they both start laughing. Like *really* laughing, as if the idea is preposterous, which it's not.

"No, Kiara," Milo says between chuckles, "I did not *kill* Manuel. How absurd."

I roll my eyes. I am *not* caffeinated enough to deal with this man. "So, what *did* you do?"

Milo casts me a sly smile. "I planted a listening device in Manuel's pocket."

"A listening device?" I glance at the laptop. Oh, God.

"Yes. I had it embedded into a lighter." He turns the computer toward me, an audio file pulled up on the screen. "This will be your task today." He pauses as Marchello suppresses a knowing grin. "Manuel enjoys a good time. He was awake until 6 a.m."

My jaw drops. "You want me to listen to *six hours* of audio? Seriously?"

"Yes." He shrugs, unbothered. "Perhaps this will teach

you to refrain from indulging in narcotics while working."

I grind my teeth together. "And you just happened to have a listening device ready to go? How convenient."

"I brought it to him after you left," Marchello explains as he stands up, polishing off his tiny cup of espresso. He's taunting me. "I will take my leave now." He faces Milo, whispering something to him under his breath. "*Si?*"

Milo nods. "*Be careful.*"

"*I am always careful.*" Marchello grins, knocking twice on the wooden table. "Goodbye, Kiara. See you tomorrow."

I toss him a lazy wave as he exits the suite. "Why does he need to be careful? Russians?"

He shakes his head, not answering my question as he points to the computer. "You should get started soon, Kiara. You have lots of audio to comb through." He expels a low laugh. "I hope you don't mind porn. Manuel...he is how you say... a lady's man."

I blink rapidly. "Sex? I'm going to have to listen to him have sex?! Can't I just skip that part? How is that relevant?"

Milo smirks, pushing himself off the tan Parsons chair. "A man is very boastful when he *wants* to *fuck*, Kiara," he says, stalking toward me with determination. "Even more so when he *is* fucking." He stops in front of me and pushes a strand of hair behind my ear, his dark eyes glimmering with insinuation. "And when he's *done* fucking—" He clicks his tongue. "That is when all the secrets come pouring out."

My back presses up against the kitchen island. "Does that apply to *all* men? You included?"

"Why don't you fuck me and find out?" He raises a challenging brow. "Maybe I'll tell you *everything* you want to know." He draws nearer, his scruffy stubble brushing against my cheek as his lips wisp across the tip of my ear. "Every *deep, dark secret.*"

"Is that all it takes to break down the Berlin wall?" I breathe, my breasts rising, pushing against his chest as he grips the counter behind me, caging me between his arms. "A little pussy power?"

He grins. "What can I say? I am merely a mortal man, Kiara. Some things are universal."

I place my hand on his chest and bite my lip. "You know what else is universal, Mr. Di Vaio?"

"What?"

I cock my head to the side. "Liars."

"You think I'm bluffing? I can assure you I am a very honest man."

"*Please!*" I snort, releasing a melodic laugh. "You're the head of *Santi Oscuri*. If you were an honest man, you'd be dead by now." I cover my mouth at the ridiculousness of his statement, my eyes watering from the humor of it all. "An honest man? God, you're funny."

Milo crosses his arm, peering down at me with irritation. "Are you done?"

"Mhmm." I wipe a tiny tear from under my left eye and take a stabilizing breath. "I'm done."

"Good," he states flatly. "Get to work. I expect you to be finished with the recording by the time I return. Do not skip anything."

"Where are you going?"

He smirks. "I would tell you, Kiara, but I would probably be lying, right?"

I roll my eyes when he's not looking. "Most likely."

"There are headphones on the coffee table," he informs me as he grabs his jacket. "Have fun, Kiara." He pauses. "Try to not get too turned on, okay?"

"I'm sure that *won't* be an issue."

Okay. It's an issue.

I'm currently on hour five of Manuel's Marvelous Night Out and things...they're heating up. Really heating up.

Over the course of the day, I have learned three facts about this man.

1. He talks about himself. A lot. The cars he drives, the number of properties he owns, his obsession with David Villa, and his damn dog.

2. He does far too much cocaine. The number of times I've winced from the screeching sound of him snorting a line, it's insane. I was under the assumption you're not supposed to get high off your own supply. Evidently, he doesn't follow that rule.

And lastly,

3. Manuel has a wife. A wife that he uh—shares other women with. A wife that likes to fuck his girlfriends. Plural. He has two girlfriends *and* a wife.

An orgy. They are having a fucking cocaine-infused orgy.

I sip on my wine as I listen to the audio, my cheeks burning up from Manuel's dirty ass kinks. I could turn it off. I could just fast forward. Yet...I don't.

I listen.

With my goddamn eyes closed.

*"Lick her pussy, Maria,"* Manuel grunts. Moans blare into my headphones. *"Yes, just like that. Faster, Maria. Make her come, make her our little whore. Yeah, that's right baby."*

*"Harder, Manny,"* Rosa begs. Rosa is very vocal, I've learned. *"Please, fuck me. Don't stop. Oh god. Yes! Yes!"*

*"Come inside her, my love,"* Maria coos. His wife. Freaky

woman. *"Fill her pussy with your cum. Do it for me. Fuck her until she can't walk. Fuck her!"*

More moans. Panting. Screaming. The slapping of flesh against flesh. Wanton mewls from his girlfriends, his dominating wife.

I bite my lip, squirming on the couch, my panties, despite my best efforts, soaked. The pressure in my core is building up, begging to be touched, dying to be released.

"Enjoying yourself?"

My eyes spring open, the stem of the wine glass in my hand nearly snapping in half.

*Fuck.*

Milo stands on the opposite end of the coffee table, arms crossed, the setting sun reflecting off his aviators. "You look —" He slides his sunglasses to the tip of his nose. "Uncomfortable."

Setting the wine on the table, I pause the audio. Remain calm. He knows nothing. "I'm fine. Just uh—doing my job."

"Oh?" Milo smirks, circling the table toward me. Oh no. Oh god, what is he doing? "Anything to report?"

I shake my head and cross my legs, moisture spreading between my thighs. "Nope. Nothing to report. He hasn't mentioned the Russians at all."

"Interesting..." Milo lowers himself onto the couch beside to me, nodding toward the screen. "Let's listen to the rest together, yes?"

My heart rate accelerates. Together? He wants us to listen to *that*...together? No way. Not happening. I'll die. I will literally drop dead.

"I'm almost finished." I tilt my body away from Milo but he sidles closer to me, the gritty texture of his jeans rubbing against my bare thigh. "It's not a two-person job. I got it. You —" I clear my throat. "I don't need you."

Milo expels a dark knowing chuckle. "It was not a request, Kiara." He unplugs the headphones, his index fingers hovering over the spacebar. He licks his lips. "What's wrong, Bella? You look nervous."

"Me?" I take a giant gulp of red wine. "Nope. Not at all. I'm fine."

"Good." He holds my gaze as he slowly, so fucking slowly, presses play on the recording.

Instantly, needy panting mixed with Spanish pleas fills our ears.

We sit there for several excruciating minutes before Milo opens his mouth.

"What is she saying?" Milo asks in a husky tone. "Translate for me, Kiara."

This conniving little bastard.

"Use your imagination."

"I'm afraid I'm not a very imaginative person," he says, a cunning smile on his face, "tell me what she's saying, Kiara." He pauses. "*Verbatim.*"

I press my lips into a thin line. "I can't..." My entire body burns up from the erotic noises booming from the speaker. Corrosive sexual magnitude radiates off Milo's body, fueling my desperate desire to be touched. "I—"

"This is your job, Kiara." He grazes my cheek with the back of his hand. "This is why you are not dead yet. Tell me what she is saying."

Why do they talk so much during sex? Why can't they be those silent couples that barely say a word? Fucking chatty Europeans.

"Translate, Kiara. *Now.*"

I close my eyes. I hate him. I fucking hate him.

"Fuck me," I whisper in a monotone voice. "Harder. Yes, oh God, yes."

"Keep going, Kiara. More."

"It's so big. Your cock is so big. Yes. Fill me, *Manuel*—"

"Stop." The audio disappears. I open my eyes to find Milo leering at me, his chest rising, jaw clenched. "That's enough."

I frown. Why did he— Realization dawns on me. Oh... He didn't really think that one through, did he?

"What's wrong, Mr. Di Vaio?" I ask innocently. "Did I do something wrong?"

He slams the laptop screen shut. "You are finished."

I blink. "Don't you want to hear the end? I think that *Manuel* was just about to—"

He grabs my chin between his fingers, his eyes opaque with fury. "Do not finish that sentence, Kiara."

"Whatever you say, *sir*." I smack his hand away and stand up. "I'm going to go take a shower. If you'll excuse me."

"We are leaving tomorrow," Milo calls out as I push past him. "Be ready on time, yes?"

I crane my neck over my shoulder and lock my scheming gaze on Milo. "Yes!" I exclaim in a wanton tone, pouting, contorting my face for the ultimate effect. "Yes! Oh my God, yes! Yes, Milo! Fuck! Yes!"

Milo jolts up from his seat, clenching his fists. "Kiara..."

I bat my eyelashes. "Mr. Di Vaio."

He sucks in a sharp breath. If looks could kill. "You are—"

"Perhaps you need a shower as well."

"Is that an offer?"

"No. Just an observation. Have a good evening, sir."

And I walk away.

There is not enough soap in the world to clean off the filth I've had to endure today.

And a part of me, a small part, doesn't want to.

# CHAPTER 13

# THICKER THAN WATER

"KIARA, WAKE UP." MILO'S SMOKY VOICE FILLS MY EARS, his hand rattling my shoulder. "Kiara."

My eyelids flutter open, my neck slightly sore. "What?" I croak, my vision adjusting to the late autumn sun beaming through the window. "We're here already?"

"I truly marvel at your ability to fall asleep so easily," Milo notes, getting out of the SUV.

"Well, I wouldn't be so tired if you didn't *force* me to wake up at 7 a.m. and then make me wait *four hours* before we even left the tarmac."

I look around, the picturesque beauty of Monaco instantly zapping me awake. The scent of the ocean fills my lungs as I take in the lush palm trees, the meticulously trimmed hedges, the narrow coastal skylines, and the sharp colossal mountains that surround us.

"You seem agitated, Kiara." His top lip curls up into a smirk as he offers me his hand. "Perhaps next time I will wake you with a kiss."

I narrow my eyes at him as I slip out of the car, ignoring his assistance. "I'm fairly certain that if Aurora was a *modern-day* princess, she'd sue the shit out of Prince Phillip for sexual harassment."

Milo chuckles. "It is a risk I am willing to take."

"A gambler, I see."

"Naturally." Milo gestures down the sandy stone path that leads to an idyllic villa several stories high. "This way."

"Where are Marchello and the others?" I ask, craning my neck over my shoulder. Gio and Mateo trail behind us, luggage in hand. We walk up the steps toward the estate, the Belle Époque influenced architecture simply breathtaking.

"They are staying at a hotel." Milo pauses in front of the peach-colored double doors with golden accents on the trim. "My sister cannot accommodate everyone."

"Really?" I hum as he rings the doorbell situated inside a wooden carving of a lion's mouth. I tilt my head back to survey the grand villa. "*Looks* big enough."

Milo expels a low chuckle. "Let me rephrase. She does not *wish* to accommodate everyone."

"Is she not a fan of your...*friends*?"

"Not entirely," Milo confesses, knocking on the door.

So impatient.

"I like her already."

The front door swings open. An adorable blonde child wearing a pink tutu and a sparkling crown grins up at us. *Are those real diamonds?*

"*Zio!*" She waves her arms in the air. "*Zio!*"

Uncle?

Milo swoops his apparent niece into his arms, the uninhibited smile plastered across his face throwing me off.

"*Principessa Natalia.*" He adjusts her falling tiara. "Why are you opening doors? Didn't *mamma* tell you it's not safe?" He pinches her rosy cheek. "I could have been a *monster*."

Natalia giggles, squirming in Milo's embrace, her chubby face scrunching up. "Monster's not real. And my *mamma* say I can open the door."

"She *did?*" Milo gasps, his tone light, playful, *happy*.

Who *is* this man?

Milo's niece nods her head feverishly before snapping her round eyes over his shoulder, looking at me with a curious gaze. "Who are you? Why you here?"

I stifle a laugh. Adorable *and* blunt.

"I'm Kiara." Milo leads us into the home, the colorful aesthetic of the estate a stark contrast to his Ligurian property. "I'm your uncle's uh—"

"Kiara is my friend," Milo chimes in, setting Natalia on the ground as Gio places our suitcases against the coral walls of the foyer. "She's here for your party."

Party? There's a party? I'm always left in the dark. Always.

Natalia blinks as she stares at me. I swear she's judging me right now. The little girl pushes her lips into a pout as she crosses her arms.

"You pretty."

In my peripheral, I catch Milo rolling his eyes.

"Awe, thank you," I reply to Natalia, subtly tossing Milo a boastful scowl. "You're pretty too."

"Oh, I know," Natalia says with absolute certainty as she taps her ballet slipper on the ground. "What's your favorite color?"

Milo crosses his arms, sidling up next to Natalia, mimicking her diva stance. "Yes, Kiara," he says playfully, "what *is* your favorite color?"

I bite my lip, my gaze fluttering across Natalia's costume. "Pink?"

Natalia's eyes widen, her tiny body about to explode

from glee. "Me too!" She jumps up and down. "I love pink! I have pink shoes and pink dresses and pink walls and pink pants and pink shirts and pink toys and pink—"

"Basically, her entire room looks like cotton candy," a perky feminine voice with a thick Italian accent calls out from behind us. "Milo! You're here, and look, no blood on your clothes. I am so honored."

"Julia." Milo frowns as we turn around. His sister saunters toward us wearing a flowing red sundress, her ashy blonde hair pulled up into a cascading ponytail. "Not in front of Talia. *Please.*"

"Go play," Julia says to her daughter who dashes out of the room without a word. *So well behaved.* Julia purses her lips before giving Milo a hug and two pecks on the cheek. "I see you still dress like the grim reaper. Mocking death, ah?"

"Not everyone wants to walk around looking like a rainbow, Julia," Milo grumbles as he pulls away and lethargically gestures toward me. "This is Kiara, she's—"

Julia grins, opening her arms. "The woman who saved your ass from the Russians, of course!" She plants kisses on both of my cheeks. "Welcome to Monaco, *cara*! It is so nice to finally meet you." She holds me at arm's length, giving me a once-over. "Well, now I know why my idiot brother didn't kill you. *Bellissima!*"

"Oh, thank you," I hum, slightly taken aback by her friendliness *and* the fact Milo's already told her about me. "It's nice to uh—meet you too."

"Let's go and have some drinks, yeah?" Julia's gaze snaps over to Gio and Mateo who've been silently creeping in the background. She glares at the two guards, crossing her arms under her generous chest. "Smile for fucks sake, you're in Monaco! Why you look so sad?"

Milo closes his eyes, letting out a sigh. "Julia, please—"

"What? They are standing there like two brick walls!" She tosses them a scowl. "Do you walls want a drink or?"

Gio's head snaps to Milo for approval and Julia slaps her hands against her thighs, mumbling in Italian under her breath. "You have them trained better than *papa*. Do they need to ask your permission to take a shit as well?"

Milo sucks in a deep breath, keeping his composure in check despite the fact there's a very large vein popping out of his forehead.

"Oh, relax, little brother." She expels a dramatic sigh. "I was joking." She casts me a side-eye. "He is so sensitive sometimes, no?"

"Sometimes," I grin as Julia loops her arm through mine.

"*Fucking women,*" Milo murmurs under his breath and trudges behind us as we step onto the terrace that overlooks the white sand and glistening teal ocean of Lorvotta beach.

"Paolo! Baby! Look who's here!" Julia sings, addressing a man who's sitting on a contemporary grey sectional at the far end of the patio.

"Milo!" Paolo adjusts his light linen attire before standing up. He holds out his hand. "It's been too long. How are you?"

"Alive," Milo chuckles, shaking Paolo's hand. The two men grin at each other as if they're in on the same secret.

"Poor bastard," Paolo laughs, gesturing for us to take a seat. "He was a moron, even as a child."

"If only he outgrew it," Milo states as a young man carrying a tray of cocktails approaches us. Milo picks up two glasses and hands me one, nodding at the server. "*Grazie.*" His attention shifts back to Paolo. "This is Kiara, Kiara this is Paolo, Julia's husband and my—"

"*Business partner?*" I tilt my head and take a sip of the sweetest cocktail I've ever tried. *Holy hell.*

Julia claps her hands, a boisterous laugh escaping her red lips. "She's a quick learner, I love it."

"Yes," Milo says flatly. "It is truly a gift."

"*Allora*, Kiara," Paolo begins, reclining against the plush throw pillows on the sofa. "How is it working for Milo? Is he treating you right? This man, he is a bit—" He pauses. "*Temperamental.*"

Temperamental? That's putting it lightly. Milo is arrogant, callous, infuriating, stubborn, but fuck—he's the most alluring man I've ever met.

Even now, sitting six inches away, all I want to do is fist his goddamn shirt, pry his full lips open with my tongue, anger him, feel his fingers coiled around my neck, show him *exactly* how obedient I can be.

But of course, I don't.

"Well, he hasn't killed me yet..." I dismiss the treacherous thoughts out of my head. "So, I guess... so far so good."

Paolo laughs. "That is a very good attitude to have, Kiara. Very positive."

Milo snorts, stating in a sardonic tone, "Don't let that smile fool you, Paolo. She is as positive as an electron."

I shoot Milo a glare. "I think under the *circumstances*, I'm pretty fucking positive. Don't you think?"

"Circumstances can *change*, Kiara," Milo says, a raspy timbre in his voice. "Don't forget that."

Julia expels a sigh. "Please, Milo, do not threaten young women in my house. So fucking rude!"

Milo closes his eyes, his body language stiff, annoyed. "I was not—"

"Enough from you," Julia says, waving him off. Milo reluctantly stops talking. Fuck Cleopatra. Next time I'll channel Julia. "I'd like to learn more about Kiara. Milo said you speak seven languages, yes?"

"Mhmm."

"Fascinating," Julia gawks, resting her chin on her palm as she leans over her crossed legs. "And you're how old?"

"Twenty-three."

Julia pouts. "So young." She tilts her head to her husband. "Do you remember when I was that young? Do you miss it?"

"Oh, I remember." Paolo wiggles his groomed brows. "But you are like wine, baby, every year more delicious."

Julia tosses her husband a flirty wink. "Ti amo, Paolo. You are too sweet."

"How did the two of you meet?" Maybe they'll be more forthcoming than my brooding travel companion.

Paolo sets his drink on the oval woven table. "We met when we were kids, our families they—" He mulls it over. "*Worked together*."

Julia clicks her tongue, expelling a scoff. "She is a smart girl, Paolo, she knows what that means. Just say it for fuck sakes."

"Milo?" Paolo asks. "Do we trust her?"

"No." Milo shifts his body, draping his arm over the sofa, the taut muscles under his dress shirt flexing as he stretches. He licks his lips, his gaze combative. "But I suppose there is no harm in telling her the history of *Santi Oscuri*."

Progress. I'll take it.

"If you say so," Paolo hums, uncertainty dancing around his features.

I listen attentively as Paolo discloses how *Santi Oscuri* came to be. Apparently, in the '70s Italy was primarily ruled by two mafias, the Di Vaio family and the Casellati family. After decades of bloodshed, wars, and deaths, the two Dons, Milo and Paolo's fathers grew tired of the feud and agreed to blend the families, ensuring total domination over the entire country.

With caveats. Obviously.

"So, you were forced to marry each other?" I ask, sipping on my second cocktail. "And you were okay with that?"

"Of course not!" Julia says. "I was furious with *papa* when he told me. Sergio, our brother—" She pauses, swallowing as Milo tenses beside me and winces at the sound of his deceased brother's name. "He um... he was supposed to wed the oldest Casellati daughter, but she got pregnant from another man and the entire arrangement fell apart."

"I only have one sister," Paolo elaborates. "When that didn't work out, well—here we are."

I purse my lips, processing all this new information. They were forced to marry yet...

"But you seem so happy together."

"It took time, Kiara," Julia says. "We had to learn to love each other and set limits."

"Limits?"

"Yes," Julia says, downing her drink. "For example, Paolo and I do not ever talk *business*. Ever. It's not allowed."

I blink. "You don't?"

"No, I don't want to know all that crazy shit," Julia says. "It causes me a headache."

"Don't you get curious?" I ask, thinking out loud.

Julia shrugs. "No, I don't care. Paolo and I, we do three things."

"Julia..." Milo hums, his voice strained, pleading. "Please."

"What do you do?" I ask tentatively. Milo drags his hand down his face as if he knows what's coming.

Julia smirks. "We fuck, we fight, and we eat."

"*Allora—*" Milo claps his hands, standing up, clearly not

happy to hear about his sister's sexual escapades. "I think it is time for Paolo and *me* to talk business... *inside.*"

Julia sighs dramatically. "Such a prude."

I snort, choking on my drink. *A prude?* Now that is one word, I would *never* use to describe him.

Milo snaps his mischievous eyes at me. "Something to say, Kiara?"

I press my lips into a thin line. "Nope," I peep as Paolo joins Milo's side. "Nothing at all."

"We will go too," Julia says to her husband as they make their way back inside. "I will give Kiara the tour and show her the bedrooms." She winks at me. "Don't worry, you get your own."

"Oh, good..." A slight wave of disappointment washes over me as I polish off my drink.

Milo lingers by the French doors waiting for me, his arms crossed over his chest. He leans against the frame, his lithe silhouette drawing me closer, pulling me toward him.

"It seems as though my sister has taken quite the liking to you."

"The feeling is mutual." I pause a couple of inches away from him, afraid to get any closer. "Honestly, it's hard to believe that the two of you are related. She's very—"

"Loud?"

"No..." I cock my head. "I was going to say *pleasant.*"

"And I am not pleasant?" He takes a stride toward me, closing the distance between us. His hand curls under my chin as he asks, his voice low, husky, debilitating, "Do you not enjoy my company, Kiara?"

"Do you enjoy *mine?*" I raise a brow, my pulse quickening from his faint touch.

"Yes," he whispers, the scent of tropical fruits escaping

his mouth as he leans into my ear. "Especially when you are *asleep*."

"Good thing we're in different rooms." I meet his suggestive gaze. "I guess you'll have to find yourself another sleeping beauty."

Milo chuckles. "There are no locks on the doors, Kiara. Keep that in mind."

My chest rises, the alcohol from the cocktails hindering rational thought, making his acute observation moderately enticing. "Do you plan on sneaking into my room?"

"No," he grins with wicked confidence. "You will come to mine. I guarantee it."

"I—"

"Kiara!" Julia hollers. *Oh, thank God.* "Where are you? I changed my mind! We're going shopping! Let's go now before the stores close! I still need to buy a dress for Talia's party."

"Go," Milo says in a defeated tone, dropping his hand as he nods down the hall. "You do not want to keep her waiting."

I readjust my purse, casting Milo a smile as I attempt to look normal, unaffected. "Maybe I'll buy some *locks* while I'm out."

"Are you afraid you won't be able to resist me?"

I expel a soft laugh. "The locks are for *you*, Mr. Di Vaio. Not for me."

"Kiara!" Julia shouts, annoyed. "*Andiamo!*"

Milo is right.

His sister *is* loud.

...And the locks *are* for me.

## CHAPTER 14

## NEARING THE EDGE

IT TOOK ME LONGER TO FALL ASLEEP LAST NIGHT THAN I'd care to admit. With the covers pulled up to my chin, anticipation rose in my chest as I waited for Milo to come into my room and slither under the silk lavender sheets.

I wanted him to take me, do unspeakable things to my willing body, show me just how powerful he can be. I wanted him to corrupt me, destroy me, put us both out of our goddamn *fucking* misery.

But he didn't. He never came.

*Bastard.*

It would seem that we're at a stalemate, neither of us willing to admit defeat, to give in to temptation, to lose.

Well, that will change... *today*. I'm sure of it.

After spending the afternoon gallivanting through Monaco with Julia, I've come to realize that she and Milo have more in common than I originally thought; they both don't take no for an answer and they both have *very* expensive taste.

I know that a child's fourth birthday party is not the ideal occasion to try out seduction techniques, but the dress

Julia forced me to buy yesterday might just drive Milo over the edge.

The mauve long-sleeved mini-dress features a deep V, a knotted neckline, and an overlap-style hem that showcases a high leg slit. It's not a garment *I* would personally consider appropriate for such an event, but if Julia has no qualms, I say eat your heart out Mr. Di Vaio.

My only hesitation with wearing something so skimpy before 7 p.m. is that Julia informed me their mother would be returning from Paris today for the festivities.

Do I want an ex-mafia queen's first impression of me to be that I'm a tramp? No, of course not. But after getting a glimpse at what Julia herself is wearing, I think I'm dressed quite modestly, well, aside from my spilling breasts.

When my chestnut brown hair is perfectly curled into large cascading ringlets and I've coated the last of my lashes with charcoal mascara, I complete the mirage with a single spurt of Coco Mademoiselle.

I've got to cover *all* the senses if I'm going to bring Goliath down.

Julia greets me at the bottom of the spiral staircase, and we make our way to the gardens at the back of the estate. As we pass the many unfamiliar faces, the vibrant scent of roses engulfs my lungs.

"That dress! It's amazing on you. I have such good taste, no?!" Julia gushes, picking up a glass of champagne from the floating servers.

"It's a little revealing..." I peer down at my chest, making sure everything is still in place. This is my first-time using tape to secure the ladies in place. Julia has *lots* of tape.

"God gave women breasts for two reasons, Kiara," Julia muses as we push through the guests toward the high-top tables scattered across the trimmed green grass. "To feed our children and to wear slutty dresses."

"True," I stifle a laugh.

Surveying the crowd for Milo, I admire the muted string lights laced tree to tree, the whimsical slides, bouncy castles, and balloons filling the garden. My birthdays have *never* been this glamorous.

My gaze lands on the tiny white benches set up next to a rose floral backdrop with *'Buon compleanno, Natalia'* written across the top with shimmering gold cut-out letters. Giggles stream from the benches, a handful of children decorating tiaras; gems, glitters, and glue spread across the table.

"Who are all these people?" I ask, taking a sip of bubbly. The only faces I recognize are Milo's associates— Mateo, Gio, Marchello, a few others. "Are they friends of the *family?*"

"No, thank God." Julia snatches an hors d'oeuvre off a passing plate and shoves it into her mouth, releasing a small moan of satisfaction. "These are mostly our friends and their children. Obviously, they are unaware of who we are, so please—"

I wave her off immediately. "Oh, don't worry about it. My lips are sealed. Milo has hammered home the importance of discretion more than once. I value my life more than I value gossip."

Julia rolls her eyes. "Milo has never hurt a woman before. I doubt he will start now. He is like a Rottweiler, barks and growls, but if you throw him a bone he'll go away."

I set my drink on the table. "Yeah? What's his version of a bone? This information might be of some use in the future."

Julia flips her blonde hair over her shoulder, casting me

a knowing grin. "He is a man, Kiara. Unfortunately, his bone *is a bone.*"

"I figured," I sigh, hoping I'd get a different answer. This really is the only card I hold. So annoying. "There's nothing else?"

Julia purses her lips. "I love my brother but even *I* don't know him that well. But whenever he used to get upset with —" she freezes, wincing before recovering quickly, "A Gurkha Black Dragon cigar calms him down. It's a Milo sedative. I actually have a carton I can give you."

"Thanks..." I narrow eyes suspiciously. "Who were you talking about?"

"Hmm?" Julia blinks. A horrible actress, really.

"You said he used to get upset with someone? Who?"

Julia's lips stretch into an apologetic smile. "I am sorry, *cara*. It is not my place to say. Milo, he—he will tell you when he is ready, if he ever is."

My mind runs wild with theories. Wife? Girlfriend? Cousin? Friend? Who is this person? Why the hell is everyone so afraid to mention her? Or maybe it's a *him*. A boyfriend?

Husband?!

"Relax, Kiara," Julia says, catching my perplexed expression. "It is in the past."

"Okay."

Julia's face lights up as she peers over my shoulder. "*Mamma!*"

Shit.

Turning around, my gaze lands on an older woman in her late fifties, her jet-black hair pinned up. She's wearing a gorgeous figure-hugging emerald gown with golden embellishments. She links her arm through Milo's as they approach our table.

I blink, mesmerized by the beauty of their mother. Her sharp dark features, rouged cheeks, and plump lips make me feel slightly insecure. She looks like Sophia Loren – classy, elegant, graceful.

And Milo. Well—he looks like the devil, a sinful master-piece wrapped in couture and strapped with a Beretta; tantalizing, refined, *deadly*.

"Mamma, how was *Paris*?" Julia asks, giving her mother two kisses as they pause in front of us. A tingle of nervous-ness pricks at my fingertips.

"Crowded." Her mother eyes me carefully, her expres-sion neutral, unreadable, like she's had practice disguising her emotions. *Years* of practice.

"Mamma, this is Kiara," Milo says, gesturing toward me. His gaze pauses briefly on my chest. His tongue darts out of his mouth and wets his lower lip. So far, I'd say the dress is working. Milo clears his throat. "Kiara, this is my mother, Antonia."

"It's a pleasure to meet you, Antonia," I say, smiling through the anxiety.

The ex-mafia queen is silent for a beat before taking a dainty step forward. She leans forward and presses her cheek against mine as she graces me with kisses.

"The pleasure is all mine, Kiara," she says. "My family owes you a great debt."

"*Mamma—*" Milo begins to say but his mother holds up an authoritative hand.

"Quiet," she says, trapping me in her serious gaze. "If it were not for this girl, I would have lost two sons this year, Emilio! You need to acknowledge that or else you are a fool."

The atmosphere around us drastically changes as Milo swallows, softly stating, "I am aware of the gravity of the situation, Mamma, and I will ensure that Sergio's death will not have been in vain."

Antonia's head snaps at her son. "Not in vain? Greed, Emilio, that is what caused his death. I would hope you have learned from his mistakes."

"*Mamma...*" Julia places a careful hand on her mother's shoulder. "It is Natalia's birthday; can we please not talk about this right now? It is a happy occasion. Please?"

Antonia sucks in a small breath that relaxes her tensed features and she cranes her neck to look up at her son. Milo's pained expression sends a pang of unease to my heart.

"Julia is correct. This is a celebration. We will talk about this later," she says then faces me, tone softened, sincere. "Kiara, I thank you, as a mother. Not many people would have been as brave as you." Her attention is drawn away by Natalia's joyous laughter. "I will go see my granddaughter now."

"Yes, let's go play with Talia," Julia agrees. "Kiara, you enjoy yourself, yes? My friends are all very kind, I promise."

"I will." I nod as Antonia and Julia waltz away, leaving me with a sulking Milo. "Are you alright?" I ask him, attempting to gauge his mood.

No matter one's age, scolding from a parent is never fun, especially when the subject matter is that of your deceased sibling. My plan to seduce him might need to be put on hold until he lightens up.

"I'm fine." Milo runs a hand through his hair and lets out a deep breath. "It is none of your concern."

"Okay." He's clearly quite irritable right now, and I don't wish to provoke him even further. I eye my empty flute. He doesn't seem in a very talkative state either. "I'm uh— going to get another drink. Do you want one?"

"No." He closes his eyes, shoulders relaxing. "I should spend time with my niece." After a beat, he asks in a warmer tone, "Would you like to join me?"

I contemplate his invitation, nibbling on my bottom lip. I don't want to insert myself into his family bonding time. He's mentioned he doesn't get to see Natalia often.

"I'll find you in a bit. Go be with your family."

"Alright." Milo nods, not pushing me to come with him. "Will you be okay by yourself?"

I cast him a weak smile. "Yes, I'm used to it."

Milo tilts his head. "Kiara..."

"Go," I say, forcing a bigger smile. "I'm fine."

He hesitates for a second before striding toward the arts and crafts area. I purse my lips, looking around at all the strangers surrounding me. I don't remember the last time I've had to mingle. Back in Hawthorne, I had one friend, Noelle, who would drag me out to events and bars, but she moved away a year ago and my social life ceased to exist.

After getting another glass of wine, I saunter from group to group, like a sad little nomad, searching for a table that's discussing something I care about, something I can contribute to.

With the mix of Italian, English, and French being spoken, my brain struggles to decipher the topics being discussed, hindering my ability to choose a clique.

I walk aimlessly around the vast gardens, catching tidbits of broken conversations. Instead of partaking in a meaningless discussion with people I don't know, I chose to admire the landscaping of the estate and take solace in the time I get to spend with myself, with my own thoughts. No pandering, no fake smiles, just me.

Or so I thought.

"Kiara," Marchello's voice calls out in the distance, startling me.

"God." I grab my chest as he emerges from the shadows of the rose bushes, cigarette in hand. "You scared me. What are you doing out here?"

"Milo doesn't let me smoke in front of the *bambini*." He takes a long drag of the Marlboro red. "So, I come here."

"Oh." At least he has some boundaries. "That's very...responsible of him."

"Yes." He expels a hoarse cough before smiling at me. "Milo is very fond of children."

"I can tell." He looks so natural and happy around his niece.

Marchello tosses the butt of his smoke on the ground, stomping on it with his boot. "Enjoy the party, Kiara. Try not to get too drunk. We have an important day tomorrow."

I frown. "What's tomorrow?"

Marchello chuckles, his wrinkled forehead creasing. "We are playing poker with some friends at Monte Carlo then we go to Sezza Lounge. Milo didn't tell you?"

"He doesn't tell me a lot of things." I tap my nails against the wine glass in my hand. "Do I have to play too?"

"You will be there to listen and watch. This time maybe no *cocaina*, okay?"

I suppress the urge to roll my eyes. "No coke, got it."

"Good." He looks at me warily before walking away. I can't tell if he likes me or not, but I don't really care. His opinion of me is the least of my concerns.

When I've explored as much of the acreage as these stilettos will allow, I find myself approaching the white benches. Milo sits at the small table surrounded by three children, Julia and Antonia nowhere to be seen.

"Hey." I tap his shoulder. "When were you going to tell me—"

Milo turns his head toward me, and I burst out laughing, wine nearly spilling out of my nostrils as I take in the pink monarch butterfly painted on his cheek. "Oh my God. Wow."

Milo grimaces. "Do not say a word, Kiara."

I press my lips into a thin line, suppressing a stream of chuckles. "It's a good look on you. Very...*colorful*."

"My niece," he sighs. "She is very convincing."

"Kiki!" Natalia coos, jumping out of her seat. She runs toward me and grabs hold of my hand. "Come bounce with me." She latches onto Milo's hand as well. "Let's go now, okay?"

I blink, my gaze darting to the inflatable castle in the distance and then down to my chest.

"Bounce?"

Milo stands up, a smug smirk on his face. I would think that a man with a pink insect painted on his cheek would lose some of his sex appeal but he's just as attractive, perhaps slightly less scary, but attractive.

"Kiara would *love* to bounce with you, Talia," Milo says as his niece drags us to the castle. He lowers his voice so only I can hear him, "Perhaps it is *my* birthday today as well."

I roll my eyes as the attendant tells us to take off our shoes.

"I would think this would be more of a punishment than a gift."

We climb into the wobbly purple interior, the trapped heat instantly boiling my skin as Natalia and two of her friends begin prancing around us. Our bodies teeter up and down from the motion.

Milo frowns, realization dawning on him as I bend my knees and start jumping. I keep my gaze locked on his darkening eyes as gravity becomes my best fucking friend.

Oh. Yes. Definitely a punishment.

"You not bouncing!" Natalia shouts at her uncle. "Zio! Bounce."

Milo shoots his niece a warm smile laced with undertones of annoyance as he matches my rhythm.

"You are an evil woman," he says, my heart rate climbing from the repetitive jumps. "This is worse than torture."

I smirk, pleased that he's suffering. "Maybe you should close your eyes. Ease the pain."

Milo's expression hardens. "I never believed in nominative determinism until I met you, Kiara. But it seems as though your only job is to cause me great pain."

His breadth of knowledge impresses me. "Funny. Maybe you're right."

"I am seldom wrong," he says as Natalia grabs his hand and pulls him away from me, forcing him to jump around in a circle with her and her friends.

I'm sure Milo's niece would've stayed in the bouncy castle all night long if she could, so when Julia hollers into the tent, saying it's time for cake, I'm relieved to finally get out of this sweat infused sauna.

All the guests crowd around the head table, smiling and clapping as Natalia blows out her candles, the smoke floating up into the star-infested sky. The night wraps up shortly after Natalia opens all her lavish gifts: luxury electric toy cars, jewelry, life-sized stuffed animals.

"Natalia," Julia begins, looking down at her sleepy daughter as the guests trickle out of the gardens. "It is time for bed now. Do you want to walk to your room, or do you want me to carry you?"

"Carry," Talia yawns, holding up her arms.

I blink, surprised that she didn't protest. "You're good."

"Psychology, *cara*," she whispers, lifting her child into her arms. "Useful in many respects."

"Milo told me you're a psychologist." I follow Julia up the stairs to Natalia's bedroom. "What made you choose that field?"

Julia pushes the hair out of her daughter's face, Natalia's eyes closing. She's a trooper for staying up this late.

"I wanted to help people. When you're raised in a family like mine, it is hard to see the good sometimes. I just wanted to do something that might balance all the evil."

"Do you practice?" I ask in a quiet tone as we enter Talia's room. She wasn't lying. Everything is pink. Julia lays her daughter on the bed, draping the princess comforter on top of her tiny snoozing body.

"I have a couple of patients." She presses a kiss on Natalia's forehead. "It is not a full-time job but it's rewarding."

"I think that's very admirable." Julia flicks off the lights and slowly shuts the bedroom door. She clearly doesn't *need* to work yet she does.

Julia smiles, suppressing a yawn. "Thank you, Kiara. I think I will go to sleep now. Too much champagne."

"Goodnight, Julia," I say as she gives me a parting hug.

I guess I'll go to sleep too.

Climbing the stairs to the top floor of the estate, I round the corner and head down the hallway. Just as I'm about to reach my room, Milo emerges from the powder room, the butterfly on his cheek washed away, reverting him back to his old dangerous self.

"Hi," I whisper, lingering in the middle of the dimly lit

hallway. My nerve endings buzz at the sight of the gorgeous man in front of me. "You disappeared."

Milo stalks toward me, spearing me with his sharp gaze. Chaos stirs in my chest as he gets closer and closer and closer—until he's too close.

Much too close.

"Were you looking for me?" His merciless gaze sweeps across my face and outlines the curves of my body. Flushed. I feel so damn flushed. "Did you miss me, perhaps?"

"No..." My chest rises from the malignant desire bubbling in my blood.

Milo lifts his hand up to my cheek, his long fingers tracing down the slope of my neck, down my collarbone, my chest, over the heaving swells of my breasts.

"There are sculptors around the world, Kiara," he rasps, his fingers stopping at my nipples, circling the stiff, desperate peaks. "That would die a thousand deaths just to have you as their muse."

I bite my lip as he continues his tortuous ministrations. "Any of them in Monaco? Maybe I'll reach out to a few. I seem to have a lot of free time these days."

Milo's dark eyes narrow in controlled frustration as he drops his hand, leaving me longing for his touch. "I can think of several ways in which we can fill your empty days." His voice is low, gruff, infuriatingly seductive. "All you have to do is ask."

"Is that what you want, Mr. Di Vaio? To fill my...*days?*"

"Kiara..." He drags his rough thumb across my parted bottom lip, his muscles tensed, full of restraint. "It is what you want as well. Come to me, *bella*. I will make you feel *so full*."

My insides constrict with debilitating need as I place a covetous hand on his chest, my conflicted heart thrumming between my lungs, lust and logic jousting for reign in my mind.

I trail my fingers down the length of his suit, my lips parted, parched, as I look up at him. "If you want me, you know where to find me."

Milo coils his fingers around my wrist, holding me with a firm grip, his gaze glinting with violent hunger.

"Why must you be so difficult, Kiara? This is a war you will never win."

With subtle defiance, I arch into Milo's chest, melding my body against his, his semi-hard-on pushing against my core.

"That seems uncomfortable." I rock my hips in tiny circles, the friction inching me closer to surrender. "If only there was a way to remedy your *unfortunate* situation."

"You will break, Kiara," he growls, his jaw twitching. He takes a step back, a guttural groan escaping the back of his throat, his expression glowing with disdain, *torture*. "I will break you."

"I'm already broken, Mr. Di Vaio," I whisper, my stubborn resolve almost melting. *Almost*. "Yet here we are."

"No, Kiara, you are simply bent. But when I'm done with you, you will be shattered, broken beyond all recognition."

"I'm not fragile like glass, Mr. Di Vaio," My pulse quickens, "I'm fragile like a bomb."

"In that case," he smirks, turning on his heel. "I can't wait to make you explode."

"Me too."

Me *fucking* too.

## CHAPTER 15

# LUCK BE A LADY

MY GRANDFATHER WAS A DIE-HARD FAN OF JAMES Bond. I've seen every single movie in that franchise dozens of times. I know *Golden Eye* scene for scene. I know *Never Say Never Again* like the back of my hand. I should have been prepared for what I was about to witness. Yet, stepping into Le Casino Monte Carlo, a white fur stole wrapped around my shoulders, I nearly collapse from the striking glamour and prestige of such an iconic establishment.

Gripping my ruby red clutch, I follow Milo through the grandiose rooms, my footsteps silent against the warm-toned carpet. Luxurious chandeliers hang from the vaulted ceilings, intricate designs carved into the cream archways, impressionist paintings thoughtfully tucked in the corners of the golden-hued *salle*.

I really wish Julia and Paolo could've come with us tonight, but residents of Monaco are forbidden from stepping foot into the gaming rooms of the casino: A royal decree issued by Princess Caroline on the basis of morality.

Apparently, the monarchy has no qualms with

foreigners gambling away their life savings just not their own citizens.

"Do you have any experience playing poker, Kiara?" Milo asks, maneuvering through the roulette and craps tables to the private gaming rooms.

Marchello hovers by Milo's side, his gaze guarded, watchful. The other men in black surround us in a protective semi-circle. Despite their best efforts to blend in by wearing designer tuxedos, they're not very inconspicuous.

"Does watching poker tournaments on TV count?" I ask as a sharply dressed young man greets us in front of a wooden door that leads to our ominous destination.

"For most people that would be insufficient experience." Milo hands the attendant several hundred Euros. "Yet for you, Kiara, that seems plentiful."

The young man pockets the generous tip and smiles with gratitude, "Your guests have already arrived, Mr. Di Vaio." He ushers us inside.

A single poker table sits in the middle of the otherwise sparsely decorated room. Three out of the six chairs surrounding the game are occupied by men ranging in age but not in status.

"Why are there three empty chairs?" I ask. "I thought only you and Marchello were playing?"

Milo grins, his softened yet scheming eyes studying me as he casually says, "Me, Marchello, and *you*."

"Milo," Marchello protests with a frown as we approach the velveted green table, thick brown leather cushioning the perimeter. "I don't think that's a good idea. What if she loses? This is a high stakes game; she knows nothing."

Milo glares at his underboss. "If I wanted your opinion, Marchello, I would have asked." He glances at me, tilting his head. "You will play, yes?"

I purse my lips, faded memories of my father playing poker with his friends whirling through my mind as I try to remember the rules. Pairs, three of a kind, four of a kind, full house, flush, straight, royal flush. Aces are high.

*Poker face.*

How hard can it be?

"Are you sure?" I ask, hesitant knowing the buy-in must be in the thousands. Even though I'll be playing with Milo's money, I don't want to be careless and lose it all. I don't need another thing hanging over my head, waiting to crush me when the time is right. "Marchello is right. I've—I've never played before. I don't think I should—"

Milo smirks. "Poker is all about emotions, Kiara. You seem to be very good at reading people." He nods at the three men who are sipping on martinis and scotch, getting impatient as we linger several feet away. "I think you can take them, no?"

"Who are they? Friends or foes?"

Milo expels a quiet chuckle, waving two fingers at the dealer. "I guess we will soon find out." We approach the table, Milo's posture tall, confident as he pulls out a chair. "Good evening my friends, I hope you were not waiting long."

The middle-aged bald man with a martini in his hand casts us a small smile as Milo and Marchello sit down.

"We arrived mere minutes ago," he says in a French accent. "We were thrilled to receive your invitation. Paris is swarming with tourists right now, a trip is just what we needed."

"Yes, my mother was just complaining about the same thing," Milo says, looking up at me. "Kiara, please sit down."

Tentatively, I shrug the stole off my shoulders, the nerves from the impending game warming my body as I take a seat beside Milo. Across the table, the three Frenchmen leer at me like they've never seen a woman before. These must be his associates from France.

A part of me is disappointed, I would have rather gone to Paris to determine their loyalty. Maybe he has more *friends* we could visit in the city of love.

"Henri," Milo addresses his associate, the other two men on Henri's side silent as they listen intently. "This is Kiara, she will be joining our game. I hope you don't mind."

Henri's sunken green eyes widen with intrigue as he gives a once-over. "Did you bring her to distract us, Milo?" He lets out a rough chuckle. "It's a good strategy in theory but perhaps you underestimate our skills."

"Or maybe he overestimates her beauty," the younger man to his right adds, his thin lips twisting into a grin as his blue eyes glide across my shimmering floor-length gown. "All that glitters is not always gold."

Milo's lips curl up into a controlled and cool smile. "Even the Bard himself would find that statement to be sheer folly."

He knows his literature. And his beauty. Smart man.

Poker chips are placed in front of each player and the dealer begins shuffling. Servers offer Marchello, Milo, and myself a drink and I glance over to Milo, unable to hide my grin as I take a martini off the tray.

"The who?" the young man asks, his accent throwing me off. Whereas Henri has a definite Parisian flair to his tone, this man sounds like a foreigner.

"Andre," Henri snaps, his deep voice issuing a warning as he meets Milo's cold gaze. "He is new, I apologize."

Andre grimaces, taking a peek at the cards placed in front of him. His left eyebrow rises just a millimeter, the corner of his lip twitching. Not a good hand, I'd guess.

"Think nothing of it." Milo glides his two cards between his fingers, his expression neutral as he scans his hand. *Hmm.* I can't get a read. He must be a seasoned player.

Before looking at my own cards, I carefully and discreetly examine the reactions from the five men sitting around me. None of them possess overtly strong reactions, other than Andre; his frustration is almost laughable.

Sucking in a sharp breath, I take a gander at my own hand. Jack and a 3. Both Spades. Could be worse. I could have whatever Andre's cards are.

With an ante of ten thousand euros, my competitive side emerges as we begin playing. Milo and Henri chat as if there are not thousands of euros in the pot. Although I suppose for them, this is the equivalent of playing penny slots.

The flop is kind to me, allowing for a pair of Jacks, the other two cards an Ace of clubs, and Queen of spades.

"Kiara? Call or fold?" Milo asks, giving me a sly smile.

"Call." I toss red chips into the middle of the table. "Maybe I'm a gambler as well."

Andre takes a minute to mull over whether he should call or fold which surprises me. He clearly doesn't have a good hand.

Why risk it?

"Call," he states in a self-assured tone. I let out a small chuckle, covering my mouth. Five sets of eyes dart toward me, all of them amused except for Andre's. "Did I miss something funny?"

I clear my throat, taking a sip of my vodka martini. "No, not at all. I just remembered a joke, that's all."

The game continues. The turn is a 7 of spades. Oh, one more spade, and I have a flush. I keep my expression muted.

"I enjoy a good joke," Andre says, leaning his forearms on the playing table. "Care to share, *Kiara*?"

"Um..." I hum as Henri's more silent associate raises. "It's more of an inside joke. You had to have been there."

"Of course." Andre reclines back into his seat, studying me intently before his gaze darts to Milo. "You must have *many* inside jokes. I hear *Santi Oscuri* is full of comedians."

Wow. He must be super new. I'm fairly certain that name is to remain unspoken.

"Yes," Milo replies in a flat tone, calling the raise as I do the same thing. Fuck it at this point; go big or go home. "But we are nowhere near as comical as you Frenchmen."

Henri lets out a deep laugh, cutting the building tension. "You are not wrong, my friend. Laughter feeds the soul and we Parisians, we are full of soul."

"Are you full of soul as well, Andre?" I ask casually, using this as an in. "How long have you lived in Paris?"

Milo keeps his expression neutral, his eyebrows perking up just a smidgen but not enough to insinuate he's skeptical of our lanky friend.

"I was born in Germany, Kiara," he replies in a smooth tone. "But I grew up in Paris, so yes, I would say my soul is quite full."

"*Where in Germany were you born?*" I ask in his native tongue, cocking my head to the side, instantly regretting the decision to show my cards.

Shit. They're not supposed to know. Fuck fuck fuck.

Andre's eyes light up as Milo shifts in his seat, his displeasure emanating off his stiff body. I avoid my employer's gaze. He's going to be pissed. I need to lie the shit out of this one.

"You can speak German? I'm impressed." A smile creeps up on Andre's hollow face. "Do you have German heritage?"

I was expecting Andre to be dubious about my knowledge of his language, but he looks genuinely impressed, relaxed almost. I'll just have to remember not to start spewing out French words then maybe I'll survive this evening unscathed.

I don't miss a beat, keeping my tone level, calm. "My great grandmother was born in Germany but fled to the UK after the Second World War. I know a few phrases here and there, not too much though."

"Where in Germany was your great grandmother born?" Andre asks, pursing his lips, mirroring my original question.

"Berlin."

"Beautiful city, is it not?" Andre rubs his chin. "That's where my family originates from as well."

"Oh."

Henri lets out an exhausted sigh as he glances at the dealer who's been ready to flip the river for some time. "You're German, she's German, fantastic. Can we get back to the game now?" He taps his fingers against his cards. "I am one card away from bankrupting Milo."

Milo fakes a laugh; no emotion is his tone. "This game would need to last one hundred years, Henri, for you to bankrupt me. But I would like to see you try."

"And try is what I'll do," Henri grins, downing his martini and waving for a new one.

Andre's lip twitches. "In France, it's frowned upon to flaunt one's wealth. It can be interpreted as arrogance."

Milo shoots daggers at Henri's third in command, his mouth opening to say something, but I interrupt him, my tone light as I quip, "Well good thing we're in Monaco, right? I think the motto of this sovereign state is—" I tap my fingers playfully against my lips. "If you got it, flaunt it."

Henri's boisterous laugh fills the frigid silence of the

room, "Excellent point, Kiara! Excellent!" He nods at the dealer. "We're ready now, flip the card."

The dealer discards the top card from the deck before flipping the next card over and sliding it toward the others on the table. 10 of spades.

"*Merde!*" Henri smacks the cushioning around the table, Marchello also letting out a frustrated grumble.

After one more round of bets, I grin as everyone turns over their cards. No one folded. And looking around the table at the abysmal display of poker talent, most of them should have thrown in the towel at the flop.

Except for Milo, who has a straight of 8, 9, 10, J, Q, and the man on Henri's left side who has three of kind and a high Ace.

"You bastard!" Henri shoots Milo a friendly glare, slapping his friend's back. "Antoine almost had you! But I guess the house always wins."

"Actually..." I clear my throat, a smug smile on my face as I reveal my hand—a flush of all Spades. "It would seem that *I'm* the bastard."

Milo's head whips toward me, his lips curled up into a smirk. "Beginner's luck, perhaps?"

I shrug coyly as the dealer pushes my winnings toward my growing pile. "I guess we will soon find out."

He shakes his head, a glimmer of amusement in his eyes. "You are full of surprises, aren't you?"

"Maybe all that glitters *is* gold," Andre mutters, not even bothering to turn over his cards.

For the next three hours, hundreds of thousands of euros are exchanged between the six of us, the game getting sloppier as the night progresses. Binge drinking and snorting lines of cocaine do nothing for the Frenchmen except make them sore losers.

"Fuck!" Antoine roars when the last card is flipped. He runs his hand through his mousy brown hair. "I'm out. My wife is going to kill me!"

Marchello laughs, scooping up his winnings. "I think it's time to go to Sezza." He grabs the attention of one of our many bodyguards. "Cash out for us."

Luigi nods as the six of us get up and stretch, everyone slightly wobbly and off-kilter from drinking excessively and sitting down for so long. Even with bathroom breaks, the muscles in my legs feel tense.

"Can we walk there?" I ask Milo, grabbing my fur stole off the back of the chair and wrapping it around my body. "Is it close?"

"Yes, it is only a five-minute walk."

Milo leads me out of the private room, our broke friends in tow.

# CHAPTER 16

## TWIST OF FATE

"You played well," Milo notes as we stroll through the casino toward the front doors. "How much did you win?"

"I don't know." I shrug, stifling a yawn. Maybe I should order an espresso at the lounge. I'm starting to see why these men do so much coke. They'd be zombies if it weren't for the illegal pick-me-up. "I didn't count it. It's your money, not mine. I was just playing for fun."

"You can think of your winnings as a bonus on top of your salary." Milo opens the front door and the star-speckled sky greets us. It's fucking late. I can't believe the night isn't over yet.

"I have a salary? Really?" I cross my arms to retain body heat, the wind nipping at my skin as we walk to Sezza. "And I didn't even get a chance to negotiate it."

"Your salary is the gift of life, Kiara." He gives me a lopsided smile. "You should be pleased."

I roll my eyes as we cross the street toward the water-front. "Julia said you've never hurt a woman before. I'm starting to think you wouldn't have actually shot me."

"Julia knows only what I want her to know." Milo places his palm on the small of my back as we round a corner. It takes all my willpower not to lean back, further and further into his warm touch. "This way."

"So, you have?" I raise an eyebrow. "Shot a woman?"

Milo cocks his head to the side, humor flickering across his strong features. "A gentleman never tells."

I give him a scowl. "I think that applies to kissing not shooting."

He smirks. "Both acts can be quite life changing depending on the source. Should I show you?"

I bite my lip as we approach the bar and lounge. "You want to shoot me, Mr. Di Vaio? Still? I thought we were past that."

"Kiara," he rasps, his vicious gaze landing on my mouth. "We both know I was not talking about shooting."

Before I can reply, Marchello sidles up next to Milo. "We need to talk numbers with Henri before he's too fucked to stand." He cranes his head toward me. "Andre will keep you company." I frown which makes him add, "Gio and Mateo will also be there."

"Great."

I let out a weary exhale as we enter the upscale lounge. The hostess ushers us to the backroom. The lurid red lighting creates an atmosphere of depravity that starkly conflicts with the overall elegant aesthetic of the bar.

The Frenchmen are already scattered among the glass top tables. Several gorgeous women circle the room, their eyes full of dollar signs as they scope out the pool of potential targets.

Milo nods at his business partner at the far end of the room. Henri stands up and struts toward us, the sway in his gait indicating he's had one too many cocktails.

"I won't be long," Milo says to me as I take a seat on the white leather bench. His gaze snaps to Gio, Mateo, and Andre who are conversing two tables over. "Have a drink, Kiara. Enjoy yourself." He pauses and adds in a whisper, "Try not to speak any French."

"Yeah, yeah." I place my clutch on the table. The heaviness of the Ruger in my purse sends vibrations rippling through the glass. Whoops.

"Don't wander." Milo shoots me a glare before he, Marchello, Antoine and Henri saunter away from the inebriated group of men toward a private room to discuss business.

A server approaches me and quickly takes my order, not bothering to make eye contact. I recline into the built-in booth, taking in the chaos that ensues before me.

Drugs, drinks, debauchery.

This seems to be my new normal. I feel like an anthropologist, studying the mating behaviors of Europe's most deadly elite. If I were a bystander, I wouldn't think these men were capable of any harm; they all just look like intoxicated businessmen who got quarterly bonuses and decided to spend their money on hookers and blow.

My gaze lands on Andre who tosses me a grin. I smile back.

A mistake.

Taking my friendly smile as an invitation, Andre strides in my direction, his bowtie loosened, his pupils the size of saucers as he slumps down beside me, spreading his legs and angling his body toward me.

"You look lonely, Kiara," he muses, taking a sip from his frothy amber ale.

"Just because I'm alone doesn't mean I'm lonely." I shift

my body away from his perched-up knee which is almost grazing my thigh.

So much for personal space.

The server returns with one out of the two drinks I ordered. She hands me the double espresso. "And the martini?" I ask politely, placing the liquid cocaine on the table.

"It's coming," the server murmurs, her attention focused on all the men in the room and the cash sprawled across the tables. "It won't be long."

"Thank you," I say but she's already moved on to the next table. Girl's hungry, who am I to judge? I pick up the espresso by the tiny handle and bring it to my lips, taking a sip.

"So, Kiara..." Andre's speech edges on slurred, his Eastern European accent more evident, "How long have you known *Milo*?"

Clearing my throat, I wipe the crema off the corner of my lip as I set the espresso on the table. "A few weeks."

Andre hums, nodding his head. "And what is your relationship to the *Don*? Are you his girlfriend?"

Shit. Milo didn't give me instructions this time around.

"My relationship with *Don Milo* is none of your business." I emphasize his title, hoping Andre takes a hint. His mouth opens. Oh God, he's going to pry. I quickly add, "How long have you worked for Henri?"

Andre purses his lips. "Under a year. But don't think that makes me any less important to our organization."

"Oh, I would *never* think that. You're clearly a very valuable member of the team."

"I am." He puffs out his chest like a fucking peacock. "I'm glad it shows."

"Yes, of course. That's why Henri left you out here to

stand guard while he and *Antoine* discuss business with Milo. He *clearly* trusts you the most."

"Exactly." He grins at me, greasy and proud. His demeanour makes me uneasy. "Where did Milo find someone like you?"

I blink. "What?"

"Well–" Andre slides closer to me on the bench. "You are beautiful, intelligent, and charming. A hard combination to find in our line of work."

A shiver courses down my spine, an instinctual warning that he's getting too close for comfort. "Maybe you're not looking hard enough."

"Or maybe I don't have time to look." He lets out a chuckle, exposing his yellowing teeth. "But sometimes...things just fall into your lap."

Ew.

"My martini is taking too long." I grab my clutch off the table and down the espresso. "I'll get it myself. If you'll excuse me."

Turning on my heel, I head to the closest bar at the back of the lounge. Wow. That man has some serious bravado. I'm all for confidence in a man, the more the better, but Andre's confidence lacks any substance.

"Hi," I greet the bartender. "May I please get a vodka martini, onion instead of an olive."

"*Oui.*"

I wish I brought my Kindle. Without Milo to entertain me, I'm ready for this night to end.

In my peripheral, I see Andre stumbling toward me. Good God. There's nothing worse than misplaced confidence and drunken courage. He's determined, I'll give him that.

Andre stops beside me, resting his elbow on the edge of the bar, a grimy grin on his face.

"Let me buy you a drink, Kiara," he says, reaching for his wallet.

"No." This time my tone is stern, serious. I'm done playing polite. He's starting to irritate me. "I can buy my own drink, thank you though."

He feigns a frown. "Nonsense, I insist."

I scoff, cocking my head to the side. "Maybe I wasn't clear. I'm going to buy my own drink with my own money so put that away." I smile. "Plus, seeing as you lost almost two hundred thousand euros tonight, perhaps *I* should be buying *you* a drink. Another beer?"

His beady blue eyes harden, his posture stiffening. "When a man offers to buy a woman a drink, Kiara, she should graciously accept it."

I blink, expelling an incredulous laugh. "Is that so? Well, when a woman is clearly turning down a man, he should accept it." I pause, shooting him a blatant glare. *"Graciously."*

Andre steps toward me, his features cold and deadly as he grabs my arm. "Listen to me you little *whore*." His fingers coil around my wrist like a boa constrictor. Pain shoots up my arm and my heart races. *Shit.* "If only you knew who I was, you wouldn't be running your—"

"Say that again."

Like a fallen angel, Milo appears out of the shadows, slamming Andre into the side of the wooden bar, his menacingly frigid gaze burrowing into Andre's pathetic little eyes. Milo bends his right arm ninety-degrees, the recessed lighting on the ceiling reflecting off the silver blade pressed into Andre's stomach. "What did you call her?"

"Oh my God!" I gasp. "Milo stop! What're you doing?"

He ignores me, leaning closer to Andre who's grinding his teeth. "If you ever *look* at Kiara again, I will cut out your kidney, understand?"

"Milo! Stop!" I plead as he pushes the tip of the switchblade further into Andre's side. His dress shirt dips from the force, blood seeping into his white button-up. "Milo!"

Nothing. No acknowledgment of my presence. Fuck this. He can do whatever the fuck he wants.

I whip my body around and march toward the emergency exit at the back of the lounge. My blood thrums with irritation as I swing open the doors that lead to the loading bay.

That's his solution for everything? Violence? Is there no in-between? Yes, Andre deserved to be put in his place but a knife?! Is he crazy?

"Kiara!" Milo's voice calls out from behind me a few seconds later. I pick up my pace, storming through the cars parked in the dimly lit lot. I need fresh air, distance from the insanity. "Where are you going?"

"Home!" I pick up the bottom of my dress that's trailing on the dirty ground as I look around. How the fuck do I get out of here?!

"Kiara, stop!" Milo demands, catching up with me. He grabs my forearm, and spins me around, his chest heaving from adrenaline. "Why are you so upset?"

My jaw drops. "Are you seriously asking me that question?"

"He called you a whore." His jaw tightens. "That is unacceptable."

I flap my arms. "So, your solution to him acting like a little boy and calling me a *mean name* is to harvest his fucking organs?! Don't you think that's a little excessive?"

"Andre disrespected you," he snaps, running a hand

through his hair. "If he disrespects *you* then he disrespects *me*."

"So that was for *your* benefit then?" Frustration courses through my body. "Nothing to do with me?"

"That's not what—" The sharp edge of his stubbled jaw twitches. "Just come back inside, Kiara."

"No!" I yank my arm out of his hand. "I'm leaving! It's late, I'm tired, and you *clearly* don't need me anymore. I'm going back to Julia's."

"Kiara!" Milo follows me further into the parking lot, the streetlights fading away. "You cannot walk around by yourself. It's late."

"I have an excellent sense of direction." I let out an annoyed sigh. "I just need to find the exit first then—"

"Emilio!" A deep voice calls from several yards away and my head snaps toward the emerging silhouette.

Oh, for fuck's sake!

"Leave." Milo meets Andre's icy glare. "Now."

"Fuck you." Andre's nose wrinkles, his top lip curling up into a scowl as disgust flashes in his eyes.

*Oh, shit.*

"Milo," I whisper, trepidation creeping up my spine as I examine Andre's expression more intently.

He's not just angry, he's livid, a deep-seeded contempt clipping his mouth, oozing from his pores.

"Get the fuck out of here." Milo takes a step forward, asserting his dominance but Andre doesn't flinch, instead, superiority flashes across his face.

*No...*

His hand slowly snakes around his body like he's reaching for a—

"Milo!" My heart drops to my stomach, legs trembling. "Gun!"

It happens so fast.

Milo whips out his Beretta that's tucked into the back of his pants.

But he's too slow.

Just a second too slow.

By the time Milo's pointing his pistol, Andre's already fired a silent shot. The bullet grazes Milo's right shoulder. He falls backward, slamming against the cement. The Beretta flies out of his hand and skids under a parked car.

"Milo!" I scream, my heart racing, my hands shaking as Andre strides toward us, his maniacal laugh filling my ears, weakening my knees.

Milo's six feet away from me, gripping his shoulder, groaning in pain.

"Kiara, go!" he demands, keeping his gaze on Andre. "Go!"

"She stays." Andre stops a few yards away from Milo. He tilts his head as an evil grin spreads on his face. "I don't know why everyone is so scared of the great Don Emilio. You are not as indestructible as some chose to believe. You are made of the same flesh and blood as everyone else. Look at you—" He lets out a scoff. "Pathetic, just like your brother."

"Do not talk about my brother like you knew him," Milo spits, attempting to get up.

"Stay down." Andre points the gun at him, clicking his tongue. "I'm not sure how such a weak man managed to cause my boss so many problems." This accent gets thicker, less controlled. "I wasn't supposed to kill you tonight but—" He shrugs. "Plans change."

"Who are you?" Milo asks, his voice deep, even. No hint of fear. Nothing. "What do you want?"

"We want our guns back." His gaze jumps to my frozen

face. "But since you've been so unwilling to cooperate. I'll gladly take your life instead."

"You work for Igor," Milo deduces.

No. This isn't happening. He's going to kill him. He's going to shoot him. I knew something was off. I knew it. I felt it. German? He's not fucking German.

"Say hello to Sergio for me." Andre smiles, regripping his pistol. "Any last words, Emilio?"

My brain buzzes with fear as I glance down at Milo, my heart clenching as his face morphs into Natalia's, into Julia's, into Paolo's, into his mother's, into Marchello's.

Into *mine*.

No. Please. No.

Fighting back tears, terror fills my body as I grip my purse. My hands clutch onto the outline of the Ruger.

My breath catches in my throat.

"Well?" Andre takes a step closer to Milo, his gun pointed directly at his heart. His heart. He has a heart. It's still beating. He's alive. He's human. He's just a man. A person. "Anything to say?"

Milo was right.

There is innocence of the eyes.

I've seen death. Lots of death. Like a ghost, it's followed me my whole life. Its claws have been dug into my flesh since I was thirteen. It's become a part of me.

I've only seen death.

Until now.

"Andre!" I grip the pistol tightly in my hand, my finger on the trigger. "...I'm sorry."

And then there's innocence of the soul.

The good. The pure. The holy.

The human.

And as the lead bullet leaves the chamber and travels

through the air, the soul that I've tried so hard to preserve, to nurture, to hold sacred—it vanishes, disappears, fades away.

Then the innocence is gone.

And only darkness surrounds me, fills me, devours me.

Renders me immobile.

# CHAPTER 17

# WHITE FLAG DOWN

*Our Father, who art in heaven, hallowed be thy name.*

"Kiara, can you hear me?" Milo kneels down in front of me. Blood gushes out of his right shoulder, staining his clothing, dripping on my dress, on the filthy cement that I've collapsed on. "Kiara."

*Thy kingdom come; thy will be done; on earth as it is in heaven.*

"Kiara..." His voice is like the wind, howling in my ears, so quiet, so calm, yet so fucking destructive. "Kiara, please say something."

*Give us this day our daily bread. And forgive us our trespasses, as we forgive those who trespass against us.*

"It's okay, Kiara." His warm hand encircles mine, prying the murder weapon out of my rigid fingers. "It is over. You're okay."

*And lead us not into temptation; but deliver us from evil.*

"Milo!" Marchello roars, his heavy footsteps followed by many *many* others, like the thundering of a pack of wild horses, their hooves beating on the ground, matching the frantic rhythm of my heartbeat. "What the fuck happened? You are bleeding!" A pause. "Is that fucking *Andre*?"

*For thine is the kingdom, the power and the glory, forever and ever.*

I blink, my gaze focused on him. Only him. No one else.

So still. He's so still. Like an abandoned toxic lake on a summer's day when there's no breeze, no sound, no ripples on the water.

Nothing.

Motionless. He's just an empty vessel. No life. There's no life in him.

I took it.

I took his fucking life.

Milo's voice is deep and muffled, like echoes in an underwater cave. "Gio, get the fucking car. Now!"

*Amen.*

"Milo." Marchello squats down beside my victim. "Milo!"

"Kiara..." Milo's face is so close to mine but I can't see it, it's invisible, non-existent, a blur. "I'll be right back. Just breathe."

Breathe.

I *can't* breathe. It *hurts* to breathe. Every breath I take feels like knives are spearing my throat, my lungs, my heart.

I shouldn't breathe. I should stop. If I don't breathe then it won't hurt. Then it'll go away. It'll *all* go away.

But—

But I deserve the pain. I deserve the agony. The suffering.

I deserve it all.

I inhale, sucking in the cold air around me, filling my body with torment, with evil.

Andre's evil.

It's inside me now. A part of me.

His hatred, his contempt, his life.

It's a part of me.

Marchello places two fingers on Andre's pulse point, craning his head up to meet Milo's eyes. "He is—"

"I know," Milo says. "Handle it. Tomorrow we leave for Genova."

"You need a doctor," Marchello notes as he brings himself to his feet. "She will meet you at Julia's. Leave the rest with me."

Screeching tires. Headlights. Commotion. Italian. French. Everything is jumbled. Nothing clear. Static. Torturous static.

*The Lord is my shepherd, I lack nothing.*

"Kiara, we need to leave," Milo says. "Can you stand up?"

*He makes me lie down in green pastures; he leads me beside quiet waters.*

Milo winces, snaking his right arm around my paralyzed body. He lifts me to his chest, every movement gentle, controlled, tender. "Gio, get the door."

*He refreshes my soul. He guides me along the right paths for his name's sake.*

Leather. Fresh leather. The scent is nauseating, sickening, dizzying.

Milo pulls his cellphone out of his pocket and dials a number. "Julia, something has happened."

*Even though I walk through the darkest valley, I will fear no evil, for you are with me, your rod and your staff, they comfort me.*

Comfort me.

Comfort.

*No.*

*No!*

I'm sorry, Nana. I can't. I just can't. It's not enough. These words aren't enough. These verses, these passages, these testaments of good and hope and faith.

It's not enough.

There's no point. I don't fear evil for it has conquered me. It has tainted every fiber of my being. It has seeped into my skin, spread through my body like a cancer.

Malignant. Malevolent. Malicious.

I don't fear evil anymore.

Because I *am* evil.

I'm so sorry, Nana. I'm so fucking sorry. I wanted to see you. I wanted to give you a hug. I wanted to dance through the heavens hand in hand, to see Grandpa, to see Mom, Dad.

But I can't anymore. It's not possible. I'll never see you again. You must be so disappointed in me, Nana. You have every right to be.

I was weak. I was scared. I was wrong.

A life is a life. You taught me that. I played God. I played God, Nana.

And now my punishment is to play with the devil for all of eternity.

The car door opens and I'm in Milo's arms again, the metallic odor from his wound permeating the air around me, coating my tongue, filling my nostrils.

"Fucking hell, Milo!"

*Julia.*

"Oh my God, she's freezing." Julia caresses my cheek with the back of her hand. "Paolo, take Kiara to her room."

"No!" Milo's grip tightens around my body. His nails dig into my shoulders, my thighs. "I will take her."

"You're fucking bleeding, you idiot!" Julia snaps. "You

need stitches. Dr. Romero is in the kitchen waiting for you. Paolo will take her."

"Stitches can wait." Milo cradles my limp body as he walks up the stairs, faint grunts of pain escaping the back of his throat. "Kiara, please say something." He pushes a strand of hair out of my face, his thumb grazing my temple. "Please."

"Put her down," Julia says. "Now go, Milo. You're getting blood on my fucking carpets."

I fist the silk lavender fabric of the duvet as I perch on the edge of the bed and stare at the wall, my head light, fuzzy, *disoriented*.

"Will she be alright?" Milo paces back and forth in front of me, running a hand through his hair. "She hasn't said anything since—"

"She's in fucking shock, you idiot. Paolo—" She looks at her husband. "Take him downstairs. Now!"

"But—"

"Baby brother," Julia says, her tone gentle. "I will stay with Kiara, please go and see the doctor. You're pale, you've lost a lot of blood. Don't be foolish. Please, Emilio. *Go*."

Milo kneels in front of me, concern filling his dark eyes as he curls his fingers under my chin. "Tesoro," he whispers. My eyelids flutter closed as he brings his soft lips to my forehead. "I will be back."

And he leaves.

"Cara..." Julia rubs my hands between her palms. "We need to warm you up. I will draw you a bath, okay?" She pauses, scanning my face. "Can you nod if you hear me?" I move my head. Barely. "Good, *cara*, good. I'll be right back."

Julia opens the door to the ensuite bathroom and turns on the bathtub faucet before returning.

She removes my shoes, one by one, tossing them off to

the side. She stands up and removes the stole off my shoulders. Scarlet blotches of blood stain the white fur, tainting the material, ruining it. It won't come out. It's permanent.

"Can you undress yourself?"

"Mhmm," I hum as she lifts me to my feet. "Zipper."

Julia unzips the golden gown, and it falls to the floor around my ankles. I step out. "Take my hand, Kiara." Her motherly touch relaxes me as she walks me to the clawfoot tub. Bubbles float on the surface of the steaming water. "I'll give you some pri—" I remove my bra and panties before she can finish her sentence.

Julia dips her finger into the tub. "Let me know if it's too hot."

I lower myself into the scalding hot suds, my skin burning as I sink into the bath. I bring my legs to my chest, resting my cheek on my knees.

Julia pulls up a stool next to the tub, a shampoo rinser in her hand. *Probably Natalia's.* "Kiara, how are you feeling?" She submerges the pink cup into the water and pours the contents over my head. "Talk to me, cara."

I close my eyes, the soapy water cascading down my face, over my eyelashes, down my nose, my lips, into my mouth.

"Numb."

"That is a normal reaction when a person experiences something traumatic." She drags a loofah over my shoulders as she scrubs away Milo's dried blood.

"I know," I breathe.

I know it all too well.

"Milo, he—um...he explained to me what happened," Julia hesitates. "What you did—"

"I killed someone... I killed someone, Julia."

She swallows, her eyes welling up with tears. "And if

you didn't—" Her breath hitches. "My little brother would be dead."

At this moment, that fact shouldn't matter. It shouldn't justify taking a life. Even a bad one. I have blood on my hands. Literally and figuratively. And that's not okay. It's not acceptable. It can't be acceptable. There is good and there is evil. There is wrong and there is right.

I was wrong.

Wrong. Wrong. Wrong.

Yet.

Seeing the gratitude in Julia's eyes, the heart wrenching appreciation glowing in her irises, it doesn't seem so wrong, and that, that kills me, destroys me, *decimates* me.

I don't say another word as Julia washes my hair and scrubs my body. She can cleanse my exterior, make it shiny and new, but she can't cleanse my soul. She can't wash away the dirt, the grime, the mildew of my actions, of my decision to play judge and jury.

"Here—" Julia holds out a cotton robe as I climb out of the tub and slip my arms into the warm clean garment. "Do you want anything to eat, Kiara? Drink?"

"No."

I look at my reflection in the semi-fogged-up mirror. The woman staring back at me is a stranger. I don't know her. I don't *want* to know her.

I hate her.

I hate her so fucking much.

"Why don't you get some sleep." Julia lifts the drain plug out of the tub, the once clear water now a rosy hue. "We are leaving early for Genova tomorrow."

I blink. "You're coming?"

She smiles. "Yes, *cara*. Paolo and I are going with you. My mother will stay here with Natalia."

"Okay." I amble toward the king-sized bed, curling myself in a ball on top of the covers. "Goodnight."

"Sleep, cara." Julia flicks off the lights.

It's too dark. I switch on the lamp on the nightstand. I can't handle any more darkness.

For what feels like hours, I lay on my side, not moving a muscle as the shadows of trees dance across the white walls, jagged branches swaying in the wind like terrifying puppets.

"Kiara, are you awake?"

I crane my neck toward the door, a sense of calm washing over me. "Yes," I whisper as Milo strides toward me, a black T-shirt wrapping his torso. White bandages peek out from the collar, the sleeve.

The mattress dips as he sits down on the edge. He sweeps my dampened hair behind my ear, his rough thumb trailing across my cheekbone. His gaze flutters down the length of my curled-up half-naked body.

"Kiara..." His voice is like a soothing lullaby. "*Thank you.*"

I bite the inside of my lip, my tear ducts trembling, my cheeks burning from his gentle touch. He's thanking me for killing someone. I'm getting praise for being a murderer.

I can't form words. A sentence. I don't know what to say. *You're welcome?* How can I say something like that? How can I tell him that I'm also thankful?

"I—" Milo expels a labored sigh, his jaw tightening as I stay silent. "I will let you sleep." He pushes himself off the bed.

Panic fills my heart.

"No—" I fist the fabric of his shirt, my tone pleading, *desperate.* "Don't leave." I pause, meeting his pensive gaze. "Please don't leave me."

I don't want to be alone. Not now. I need him. I need someone beside me. I need someone to keep the shadows at bay.

To keep the demons away.

"Stay... just for a bit."

*Only a bit.*

Hesitantly, Milo dwarfs my hand with his as he lowers himself back down on the silk sheets, his body full of tightened restraint, the veins in his forearms like stripes on a zebra, mesmerizing, beautiful. I inch backward as my heart races, making room for him, the cool fabric of the covers like ice underneath my legs.

"I will stay with you for as long as you want."

He winds his left arm around my neck, raking his fingers through the wet strands of my hair. He brings my head to rest on his rising chest, the cotton robe slipping off my shoulders as I melt into his warm embrace, my palm resting on his stomach.

*Oh, God.*

My insides stir from the proximity, from the heat emanating from his body, from the rough texture of his jeans against the inside of my thigh. My breathing is shallow as his increasing heartbeat echoes into my ear, so loud, so deafening; it cuts through the charged silence that encapsulates us.

He idly draws tiny circles on my bare shoulder, slowly pushing the robe further down my arm. His faint but scorching touch sends shivers through my whole body. He conjures goosebumps, desire, *need.*

"Are you cold?" The husky timbre of his voice reverberates through my body like a fucking earthquake, crumbling walls into dust, shaking my very fragile foundation.

I let out a shaky breath, tilting my head to meet his darkened eyes, my mouth dry, *parched*. "Are you?"

He shifts his position, angling his body toward me. The pad of his thumb floats over my parted lips, his strained gaze locked with mine.

"No." He draws closer to me, his heady breath fanning my skin. "I'm not."

"Good." I squirm restlessly against him. Conflict stirs in my heart, the repressed emotions of today bubbling to the surface, filling my eyes with tears as images of Andre's dead body flash across my mind.

*What is wrong with me?*

"Kiara..." He wipes the rolling tears from my cheek. "Do not cry. *Please*."

My teeth clench together as my eyelids flutter shut. I can't hold it in anymore. I can't push it down. I can't.

"I killed someone," I whimper, unable to contain the sorrow. "I—"

"*Shh*," Milo hums, holding me tight against his chest. "It's okay. You are okay."

The warmth of his body heat absorbs into my shattering skin. "I want to forget."

Comfort.

In this moment, he is giving me comfort. He's holding me together. Literally. But I need more than comfort. I need more than to be held. I need to forget. I crane my neck up, my gaze piercing his.

"Make me forget, Milo," I whisper against his lips as I inch closer, his sweet breath filling my drowning lungs. "Please."

Milo stiffens, tightening his arms around my body as he says in a retrained, almost pained tone, "Not like this, tesoro..."

"Milo," I breathe out his name, desperation in my voice. "Please."

Milo's jaw tightens as he studies my face. He sees it. Sees me. And he's conflicted. Just like me. But we both want it. We've wanted it for so long. We wanted it. But now...now I *need* it.

"Are you sure, tesoro?" he asks in low murmur.

"Please..." I slowly drag my hand down his torso toward his cock. "I'm sure."

"No." He pushes my hand away as he shakes his head.

"No?" I frown. "Why?"

"Because..." He's silent for a moment before he whispers, "It is *you* that needs to forget, not *me*."

"Wha-" My words are trampled as he drags his hand down my neck to the base of my throat. He glides his fingers underneath my robe, edging it away, making me shudder.

*Oh, God.*

"I will make you forget—"

My breath hitches as his warm palm finds my breasts, his fingers rolling my nipples. Heat erupts in my core, my legs clenching from the ache.

"Everything."

I let out a moan, writhing under his touch as he rolls on top of me, pinning my hands over my head. He peers down at me like I'm his prey.

And I am. *God, I am.*

I am at his mercy, and I want him to be merciless. I need him to make me feel. Feel something other than grief. Other than numbness. I want to feel alive, in the sickest, most twisted way possible. I want him to burn me, destroy me, make me forget.

"Close your eyes, tesoro," he rasps. And I do. "Good girl."

He's letting me win, and God knows I need a fucking

victory right now. But did I win the war? Or simply the battle?

I whimper as he plants open mouth kisses on the underside of my jaw, my neck, my shoulders. His palm assaults my breasts, blissful pain spearing my nerve endings as he twists, gropes, squeezes. Neurons fire in my brain.

"Milo—" I cry as he nips at my neck, his sharp teeth grazing my throat. He peppers kisses in the valley between my breasts, his stubble rough against my skin, his taunting hand feathering down my stomach, past my mid-section, to my thighs, parting them, stopping at my pulsing sex.

*Fuck.*

"You are so wet for me, Kiara..." he growls, swirling his fingers against my slick slit, pressure building between my legs. My hips buck as he plunges two fingers into my soaking wet pussy, his thumb stroking my clit. His mouth latches onto my stiff nipples— biting, licking, savoring.

Buzzing. My body is buzzing from his expert touch, my toes curling from the pleasure, my lungs panting, quivering.

I expel wanton gasps as he whirls his fingers inside me, pushing in and out. His lips trail further down my belly, his tongue coating my skin with sloppy wet kisses as he settles himself between my legs. His strong hands coil around my thighs, spreading them apart like the red fucking sea. His balmy hot breath blows against my sex.

And then I die a sweet, torturous death.

"Fuck!" My breathless cries fill the room as his mouth crashes down against my clit, his impure tongue flicking, sucking, *biting* my sensitive nub as his fingers pillage me, annihilate me, send me to another fucking realm.

A realm of pleasure, depravity, greed, *lust.*

No consequences, no moral dilemmas, no right, no wrong.

Just pure fucking debilitating ecstasy.

I wind my fingers through his dark hair, tugging at his roots as I undulate my hips around his sordid mouth, needing more friction, more pleasure, more everything.

The pressure builds inside me, twisting my uterus, his fingers relentless in their assault. My walls tighten around him, my breathing wild, raw, unfiltered as I bite my fist to stop myself from fucking screaming.

"You're so close, Kiara—" A roaring, animalistic growl leaves the back of his throat as he commands, "Come for me, tesoro. Come for me."

His tongue fucks me like I've never been fucked before. My hips buck forward as a tidal wave of dirty releases gushes from my sex, soaking his face, spraying his fingers, dripping down my thigh like a broken fucking dam.

He holds down my quivering legs as another orgasm rips through my body, the intensity nearly blinding me.

I pant, my legs shaking as he finally withdraws his devilish fingers. My heart races, my mind blank, stars in my fucking eyes.

"Oh my God," I breathe as Milo dismounts me, the mattress bouncing as he gets off the bed. "Holy shit."

"Goodnight, Kiara." Milo's voice is so faint, so quiet like he's not even here. "Go to sleep."

I hum, my body exhausted, drained, defeated as my eyes flicker shut.

And I sleep.

I sleep like the fucking dead.

Until I wake up.

And the pleasure is gone.

And the only thing I feel...

Is anger.

# CHAPTER 18

## TORN AND TROUBLED

LAST NIGHT, HE GAVE ME EVERYTHING I WANTED.

But took everything I had.

Before him, my life was in black and white. It was boring, average, nothing special.

But now it's red.

Just red.

The line between passion, pleasure, pain, and persecution is thin. So *fucking* thin. It's a dangerous tightrope to walk, and there's no net at the bottom to catch me if I fall; there's only fire, flames, fury.

*Fury.*

It's stewing inside my stomach as I get dressed. It's coursing through my veins as I apply my cosmetics. It's eating away at my heart as I curl my hair.

It's glowing in my eyes, spreading through my limbs like an out-of-control wildfire; chaotic, destructive, deadly.

But I can't let it kill me. I can't let it win. I made my bed, and I will lay in it. Like a dog, like a flea-infested mutt who has nowhere else to go, no one to go to, no one to care, no one to save me, no one to put out the flames.

I am alone in my rage.

And that's okay. It truly is. I've had years of practice to deal with it. I have learned how to put out the fire, how to tame it, how to dwindle it into a steady burning ember.

How to conceal it. How to hide it from the world.

And in this world, the one I've been thrust into, emotions can cost me my life. A life that I hadn't ever envisioned for myself. A life of guns, drugs, murder, death. But it's mine. The only one I have. And in this life, those things are normal.

Mundane. Acceptable.

And so, I will conceal. I will hide. I will be strong. I won't let them see me falter.

I won't let *him* see me cry.

*Never again.*

He made me into a monster. And a monster I shall be. I'm not scared of this life anymore; I've been hazed, initiated, granted access into his wicked underworld.

With the pull of a trigger, I've become one of them.

And despite the fact that everything hurts. Despite the fact that every time I look down at my hands I see blood—I am safe now.

Safer than I've ever been before.

Because this time, I *did* save him.

I saved Don Emilio of *Santi Oscuri*. And they owe me. They owe me a *lifetime* of protection.

And after killing a supposed member of the Russian Mob, that protection is priceless.

Now only if I had protection against Milo the man, not Milo the boss.

And shit, what a man he is.

I can still feel his hot lips dancing across my body, his

skilled fingers curling inside of me, and his tongue, his goddamn magical tongue is engraved into my DNA; it's marked me, ruined me for anyone else. He made me feel like a goddess, like Aphrodite on fucking steroids.

But he left me. He fucked me lifeless and then left. A power move, I'm sure. He wanted to show me just how good he could make me feel, give me a little taste of what could be, what I'd be saying yes to if I took the next step.

I'd be lying if I said he didn't convince me. He did. He showed me everything I needed to see. Needed to feel. To experience.

But unfortunately, the simmering rage I feel toward him right now overpowers my carnal desire to fuck his gorgeous brains out.

Hatred.

That's *my* power move.

That's what will keep me going. That's what will keep me sane, safe, secure, *stable*.

Time to start my new life.

The life of a murderess.

With one final coat of ruby red lipstick, I make my way downstairs toward the kitchen, the early December sun shining through the mosaic tiles of the floor-to-ceiling windows.

*"He's clean,"* Marchello says in Italian, his harsh tone bouncing off the walls as I approach the kitchen. I pause outside the archway, pressing my body against the coral wallpaper, my ears on high alert. *"Henri swears he had no idea Andre was a foot soldier for Igor."*

So, Andre *was* working for the Russians. Confirmed. I knew his accent wasn't German. I should've caught on sooner. If I did, none of this would have happened. Andre might still have ended up dead, but it wouldn't have been by my hand.

Idiot.

*"And you believe him?"* Milo asks. My teeth clench at the sound of his smoky voice. *"How can we be sure?"*

Good point. Henri might just be telling them what they want to hear. I wouldn't trust the balding Frenchman either.

*"He is not lying, Milo."* Marchello spills a rusty laugh. *"No man is that strong. And Henri, he has been faithful to our family for years. I do not doubt his loyalty."*

I wince at what Marchello is insinuating. Not that strong? Poor bastard must have spent the night at an Italian black site.

*"Very well,"* Milo hums. *"And what did you do with Andre? Did you—"*

My heart drops.

*"What we always do,"* Marchello replies, his tone eerily chipper. *"Once we are back in Genova, we can talk more, yes?"*

Milo chuckles. *"Yes, Marchello, we will talk."*

No. Talk more now. I need to know mor—

"Kiki!" I grab my chest, startled by the honey-sweet tone of Natalia's greeting as she runs up to me. Her puffy purple dress bounces as she skips. "Goo' morning!"

I clear my throat, putting on a friendly smile. "Good morning, Natalia. How's it going? *Pretty dress.*"

"I know!" She gives me a twirl. "I want juice."

I blink. "Juice? Um...sure. Let's get some juice."

Natalia squeals, grabs my hand, and drags me into the kitchen. Milo and Marchello's heads snap up at me.

"Kiara." Milo studies me warily as Marchello tosses me a respectful nod before exiting the room. Not even a verbal thanks for saving his boss? *Rude.* "You're awake."

I swallow away the bubbling bile of loathing and lust that's forming in the back of my throat. "Natalia wants juice," I say, my tone calm, collected as if I'm unaffected by his piercing gaze. "Is she allowed?"

Milo narrows his puzzled eyes at me for a brief second like he was expecting a different greeting. Well, tough luck. This is what you're getting. Self-righteous fucking dick.

Licking his lips, he looks down at his niece who's running around the island. He scoops her up, planting her tiny body on the granite countertop.

"Did your *mamma* say you can have some juice?" Milo lowers himself to be level with the giggling child.

Natalia nods her head with a cheeky grin. "Mhmm. She did."

Milo hums, pursing his lips. "Are you lying to me, Talia? You should not lie."

I inwardly scoff. *Pot meet kettle.*

"No! She said I could!" his niece whines as I saunter toward the coffee machine and pour myself an espresso. "Please! I want mango. Mango, mango, mango."

"You want *orange juice?*" Milo teases, heading to the fridge. "Okay."

"No!" Natalia exclaims, somehow hopping off the counter and landing on her feet. She aggressively tugs Milo's charcoal grey suit jacket. "Zio! I want mango. Mango!"

I lean against the counter, gripping the mug between my palms, my expression sour. His carefree and relaxed attitude is irking the living shit out of me. He's acting as if nothing happened. Granted, it could be for the sake of his niece, but still. I close my eyes, taking a deep breath, suffocating the flames within.

Milo grins, pulling a juice box out of the fridge. "*Apple?*"

I roll my eyes.

Natalia flaps her arms, stomping her foot. "Mango!" Her shrill voice rings in my ears. Good God, she's got a set of lungs. "I want mango!"

Milo expels a soft laugh, finally giving in to her diva demands and fetching the correct beverage out of the fridge. "Okay, here—" He hands her the juice.

"*Grazie mille!*" she singsongs, humming a sweet melody under her breath as she prances away.

I envy her.

Her innocence.

When his niece is out of the room, Milo strides toward me, his features hardening as his smoldering eyes latch onto mine.

He's back.

"Did you sleep well?" Milo attempts to read my expression. But he can't. I won't let him. Poker face. I've mastered it in a day. A useful skill in *and* out of a casino.

"Yes," I say dryly, gripping the mug so tight it might crack.

"Kiara..." He lifts his hand up to my cheek, but I smack it away before he can make contact.

"Don't touch me." I push past him. He won't corner me. Not this time.

Milo turns around, his lip twitching. "You seemed to have no problem with me touching you last night."

His tone is so bitter it changes the flavor of the coffee in my mouth.

"I wasn't myself last night." Not technically a lie. But not technically the truth either. It's a grey area; Milo's apparent area of expertise. "I wouldn't read too much into it if I were you. You were just a means to an end."

*Milo-tonin.* It would fly off the fucking shelves.

Milo cocks his head to the side. He's not buying a word I'm saying.

"You are upset." He stalks toward me like a lion. "I understand."

I blink, letting out a scoff. "Do you? *Really?* Because that's hard to believe."

"When I gave you the gun, tesoro," his tone softens, "I did not anticipate that you would ever need to use it."

"When are we leaving?"

"Kiara..."

*"When are we leaving?"*

Milo closes his eyes, the muscles in his neck straining. "Thirty minutes."

"Okay, and where's Julia?"

His chest rises as he stares at me through his veil of dark lashes for a second, before answering, "Packing. She and Paolo are driving to *Genova.*"

"Driving?" *Excellent.* "I'm going to go with Julia then."

"No, you will not." He runs a frustrated hand through his hair. "You are coming with me."

"No."

The last thing I want, or need, is to be stuck with Milo in a confined space. I'm either going to kill him or fuck him. Neither option is viable. And the former is far too enticing at this moment. This is for his benefit just as it is for mine.

"Fine," he huffs, pulling out his cell phone. "You may go with Julia."

"Oh, thank you *so* much." Every sardonic syllable drips with disdain. "I'll see you in Italy."

"Where's Paolo?" I ask Julia as she slides into the back of the black SUV, one of her guards in the driver's seat.

"I told him to go with Milo." She rests her Chanel purse by her side as the car hums to life. "I thought this would be a good time to talk."

"Talk?"

The drive from Monaco to Genoa is two and a half hours. That's a lot of talking. I should've taken the jet.

What is there even to say? Am I supposed to tell her that I regret it? That I wish I didn't shoot Andre? The man was two seconds away from ending Milo's life? Her brother's life.

And *do* I regret it? I don't know. It's another grey area. If Andre shot Milo, would he have shot me next? Would I also be dead?

I hate what-ifs. They're toxic. They're draining. They're a waste of time. They fuck with your head. They bring out your worst fears. They eat you alive.

And talking doesn't help either.

Nothing helps.

Julia twists her body toward me. She presses a button on the panel built into the middle console and a partition rises between us and the driver.

Oh, God.

Mistake after mistake.

"How are you feeling, cara?" Julia's clinical gaze burrows into mine like she's trying to crack through the barrier of my brain.

"I'm fine." I shift in my seat, fiddling the pages of the book in my lap. "Really, I am. I did what I had to do."

Julia reaches for my hand, applying a gentle squeeze. "You're not fine, cara. I can see it in your eyes. Talk to me. Please. It will help."

I pull my hand away, crossing my arms. "Are all psychologists this pushy?"

My snippy tone doesn't deter her, doesn't make her frown, doesn't affect her in any way. The deep concern gleaming in her eyes is palpable, but I don't care. I don't want to talk about it. Not to her. Not to anyone.

"With my patients, no I am not. But to my friends? Yes. Always."

I saved her brother. Her affection toward me is inauthentic. It's a result of my evil act.

"We've known each other for a few days, Julia." I look away. "We're not friends."

This hurts her.

And me.

She's silent for a moment before musing, "Time does not determine admiration, Kiara." Her eyes flicker to the Jane Austen novel on my lap. "Sense and Sensibility?"

"An escape." I tap my finger against the paperback book I borrowed from Julia's library a few nights back.

"Have you read it before?"

I tilt my head at her silly question. "Of course."

"Right, so—" A sly smile clips her lips. "Do you remember what Marianne said to Elinor when Willoughby bought her the horse?"

I purse my lips. Oh, she's good. "Yes, I remember."

She casts me a knowing smile. "What did she say?"

I roll my eyes. "That it's not time or opportunity that determine intimacy but disposition."

"And?"

I let out a deep grumble. "And that seven years wouldn't be enough time for some people to get to know each other, and for others, seven days is more than enough."

"Exactly!" Julia claps her hands, her energy almost

breaking through my gloomy reserve. "We are the latter, cara. In just a few days, I have learned everything I need to know about you in order to adore you. So yes, we are friends. Aren't we?"

Her tender words prick my heart. Is she right? Do some relationships transcend time?

"I guess," I murmur, extremely hesitant to open myself up to her.

The more you love, the more you hurt. And she might not hurt me *now*, but one day she will. They all do. Perhaps not from words or actions but from absence. I don't want to grow fond of someone that might not stick around.

"I am not the only one who cares about you, cara," Julia says as if she can read my thoughts. "We are all very grateful that you've come into our lives. Milo—"

"Stop." I shake my head. No. I can't. "Please."

She frowns. "All I am saying is that you have many friends now, Kiara. And we will be here for you in whatever capacity you need us."

I bite the inside of my cheek, the fire igniting inside my body once again. These people are now my *friends*? The ones who take lives? Laugh at the deceased? Commit horrendous crimes? They're my friends?

It's difficult to separate the person from the act. It's hard for me to see the pieces, not just the whole. I hate the whole. It's everything I despise. But the pieces? I'm starting to see the good in the pieces, the tiny flashes of humanity.

I nod, discomfort gnawing at my stomach. "I'm impressed you can quote Jane Austen," I muse, needing a subject change. "Are you a fan?"

Julia smiles. "My father didn't let us watch TV when we were young. Instead, he would read to us every night."

"Every night?" I ask warily. "Even though he was—"

Julia takes a deep breath. "He was always a father first. He always made time for us."

Right there.

Flashes of fucking humanity.

## CHAPTER 19

## BURIED DEEP DOWN

THE PIERCING CHIRPS OF CRICKETS OUTSIDE THE window cut through the ominous silence that surrounds me. I slip on my bathing suit, sighing as I stare at my weathered reflection in the mirror.

I was expecting chaos to erupt once we returned to Italy, but it has been eerily quiet in the villa. It's unnerving. Like the calm before a storm. And a storm must be brewing; there's no way there won't be retaliation for what happened in Monaco.

Absolutely no way.

The phrase 'quia oculo ad oculum' is carved into the stone archway at the front of the estate; it's the first thing anyone sees when they enter.

It's a warning to all visitors. To all employees. To every single member of the family.

*An eye for an eye.*

A war *is* stirring. I can sense it.

I can feel it in my bones.

Thankfully though, whatever sinister scheme is in the works does not require my skill set.

Being left in the dark has allowed me the opportunity to avoid Milo for six days. Six whole days with just three words exchanged between us.

When Julia wasn't whisking me away on sightseeing tours of Liguria, I made myself scarce, invisible, changing my daily routine so Milo couldn't corner me, find me, make me do something I'd regret.

Or enjoy.

Even Gio and Mateo have been giving me space. They haven't been hovering as much as they were before; perhaps because now they know I can take care of myself. That I'm not helpless. That I'm not weak.

That's the silver lining of bagging your first kill; you get clout.

You get left alone.

And just as I think I'm going to make it to day seven in peace, Luisa knocks on my door, a garment bag in hand. A golden clip holds back her ink black hair, a small smile on her slender face.

"Are you going swimming?" She gives me a quick once-over. I cross my arms over the sheer white cover-up that's draped over my body, my black bikini visible through the thin fabric.

"Yes." I grab a navy blue towel off my bed. "Did you need something?"

It's past 10 p.m. which means the indoor pool should be vacant and I can do a few laps undisturbed. I figure if I tire out my body, my brain will follow, and *maybe* I can finally get some sleep. That has been challenging this week.

A lie.

It's been impossible.

"I was told to bring you this." She unzips the matte

black garment bag and reveals a red chiffon floor-length gown.

I roll my eyes. Someone's got a little color fetish.

I run my hand down the delicate material. "What's this for?"

"There is a gala being held in *Milano* on Friday." She strides over to my closet and hangs up the dress. "You are to attend the event with Milo and my father."

I expel an annoyed sigh. "Why? We're in Italy. He doesn't need a translator."

"I am just the messenger, Kiara." She shrugs, her tone kind, careful. "But I believe there will be many international guests in attendance, perhaps that is why Milo requires your presence."

I purse my lips. "What's the gala for?"

"It's an annual fundraiser for the Italian Blood Service," she explains. "Our family is one of their biggest sponsors."

I stifle a snort. The irony is not lost on me.

"If it's just a fundraiser, I don't see why I'm needed."

Luisa tilts her head. "That is something you may discuss with Milo. I am only here to bring you the dress."

Fuck. My volatile emotions are not her responsibility. She didn't do anything wrong. I shouldn't be so short with her.

"Okay." I clench my teeth and force a smile. "Well, thank you."

Luisa smiles, sucking in a small breath before hesitantly noting, "You have not joined us for dinner all week." She pauses, her discomfort palpable. "You are more than welcome at our table, Kiara."

Julia has tried to rope me into dining with the family, but I can't bring myself to do it. I can't break bread and drink wine with these people.

I can't laugh with them as if I'm not crying inside. As if I'm not broken.

Shattered.

"You eat very late," I reply. "Otherwise, I would."

"This is true." A weak laugh tumbles from her lips. "But if you ever change your mind, there is a seat for you."

I've earned a spot at the table.

I'm one of them.

How nauseating.

"Thanks." I slip on a pair of flip-flops and head to the door. "I'll think about it."

We walk down the first two flights of stairs in awkward silence before she veers off toward another room. She's been sickeningly nice to me this week, gentle with her words, smiling all the time. It's creepy. Off-putting. I seem to have gained her respect.

*All* of their respect.

With my hand on the iron railing, I round the corner, booming Italian bickering in the distance.

I freeze on the stairs.

"*You can't, Milo!*" Marchello barks. "*We talked about this. Think about the possible consequences. We can't trust—*"

"*What consequences?*" A loud thump echoes through the halls. "*What is the harm, Marchello? What could possibly happen?*"

"*You are not thinking rationally!*" His baritone voice sends a chill down my spine. "*This is a delicate situation! For once we are one step ahead! You cannot do this.*"

"*I can do whatever I fucking please,*" Milo spits. "*You are not the head of the family, Marchello. I am.*"

"*Then start acting like one,*" Marchello states. "*I am here to make sure you don't make any mistakes. And this, Milo, is a mistake."*

"No, the mistake was listening to you in the first place." His deep sigh fills my ears. *"Fucking hell!"*

*"It is already done."* Marchello's tone softens. *"Everything will be fine. Just give it time."*

"I am not a very patient man. And time has never been a friend to me."

*"It is for the best, my boy. I promise."*

I narrow my eyes. What in the *fuck* are they talking about?

Without context, I'm lost. *One step ahead? Time? Mistakes?* They have information on the Russians? Maybe? But why are they at odds with each other? Don't they want the same thing? What is going on?

Nothing makes sense.

I grind my teeth, irritation flaring my sinuses. Fuck this. I'm not in the mood to play Nancy Drew.

This isn't my problem. I shouldn't even care.

I descend the last stair, craning my head toward the office, the door ajar.

*Shit.*

The moment I come into view, Milo's eyes snap up. His hardened gaze skims the length of my body, his eyebrows furrowed, his lips twisted up with a murky kind of sadness.

My chest rises as our eyes lock, the tips of my fingers buzzing with electricity; the voltage so high that I nearly collapse.

I need to leave. I can't look at him. I can't be around him.

As if sensing my desperation, Marchello's head appears at the doorway. His expression sours as he glares at me for a second before slamming the door shut.

I let out a sigh of relief.

*Thank you.*

The overpowering sensation of nervous energy slowly withers away as I make my way to the indoor pool situated in the west wing of the estate.

The scent of chlorine fills my lungs as I step into the modern-day Roman bathhouse. Warm light from the opulent chandeliers reflects off the crystal-clear teal-hued water.

Tossing the towel on the cream marble tiled floor, I slip the cover-up over my shoulders and drop it by my feet. Dipping my toe into the warm water, I suck in a deep breath and dive in.

Headfirst.

I banish all thoughts, all feelings, all emotions out of my exhausted head as I mindlessly swim laps.

Back and forth. End to end. Swim. Just keep swimming. Focus on the temperature of the water. On form. On speed. On breathing. Nothing else.

Please nothing else.

My arms are weak, tired, almost trembling when I come up for air. My dry eyes burn from the treated water, from the graphic images that flash through my head in my sleep, from all the tears I've shed this past week.

I'm fatigued. So fucking deflated. But I have to keep on swimming.

I *have* to.

Closing my eyes, I inhale the tepid moist air, my muscles relaxing as my fingers coil around the perimeter of the pool.

I'm fine. Everything is fine.

A door slams.

My eyes spring open and I crane my neck toward the

entrance. My knuckles clench, my insides turning as my heart drops into my fucking uterus.

Everything is *not* fine.

With a towel draped over his shoulder, Milo strides to the edge of the pool. My hedonistic eyes soak in every last inch of his exposed, tanned body; his wide shoulders, the defined shape of his lithe abdomen, his strong thighs, the thick trail of dark hair that leads to his massive taunting bulge. His expression is dangerously reserved as he stops at the fringe of the pool, slowly running his fingers through his tousled hair.

*Oh, fuck me.*

My nails dig into my palm, his hauntingly dark gaze locking with mine as he cocks his head to the side, studying me like I'm a mythical creature, a Siren in captivity.

"How is the water?" He peers down at me through his lush veil of lashes, his voice deep, steady, gruff.

"Tainted." I push myself off the wall, floating backward. My heart flutters in my chest, my body tense, *conflicted.*

Space. I need space.

"Kiara..." he rasps, his intense gaze not leaving my face as he enters the pool. He hovers by the shallow end, not letting the water reach his shoulder. "You have been avoiding me for days."

He can't get his wound wet. How unfortunate.

"Take a hint."

With slow, covert movements, I swim backward, pushing myself through the teal water until I'm several meters away from him.

He licks his lips, taking a step closer to me, the water rising over the taut ridges of his pecs. "You cannot ignore me forever."

He's right. I can't. Sooner or later this cycle will have to break. But not now. Maybe by Friday, I'll be better. Maybe by Friday, I'll be calm. I'll heal. I'll recover.

Friday.

"Enjoy your swim." I paddle over to the side of the pool and climb out, my body dripping wet, my hair pasted to my face. I avoid his gaze as I scramble to collect my clothes and wrap a towel around my waist.

"Kiara, please—"

I don't respond. I don't look at him. I don't acknowledge his desperate plea for communication.

Fuck him.

And fuck me too.

Clouds. I'm surrounded by clouds.

Soft. Smooth. *Heavenly.*

I feel light, like a feather, like a whisper, like a summer breeze.

It's so warm. So wonderfully comfortable as I float, fly, *soar* toward a golden gate. It's shiny, beautiful, welcoming.

Bliss.

It's coursing through my veins, it's filling my mind with such joy, such happiness, such serenity.

I'm almost there. Open. Please open.

But it doesn't.

There's a lock on the gate.

I need a key.

Where's my key?

*"Check your pocket."*

Pocket?

I look at my white linen dress. Of course. It's in my pocket.

I slip my fingers into the stitched pouch, my heart dropping.

No.

I can't feel it. It's not here. It's no—

A rough, cold, hard object manifests in my hand.

No. This isn't a key. No.

Please.

My lips quiver as I pull out the pistol, my hand trembling, the clouds dispersing, the gate vanishing, the sun setting.

And I plummet, falling through the sky, screaming, yelling, crying out to the heavens that I'm sorry, that I didn't mean to do it, that I wasn't aiming to kill, that I'm a good person, that I don't deserve this.

I'm a good person.

I'm good.

I am.

I promise.

Please don't.

Don't do this.

I'm so sorry.

Please.

With a thud, I land on dirt, grime, rocks, my body sore, aching, *filthy*.

It's so cold. It's freezing. Darkness. I can't see.

A spine-chilling growl penetrates my skull, *"Welcome home."*

No.

*"We've been expecting you."*

No!

I jolt awake, grabbing my chest. My heart hammers, a sheen of sweat covering my entire body, my breathing ragged, frantic. I check the time. 2 a.m.

*Not again.*

I'm so tired. I'm so tired of this. I just want to sleep. I just want some rest. I want to close my eyes and see nothing.

Taking several deep breaths, my gaze darts to the dresser, to the pistol resting on top of the black cabinet. A foul taste coats my tongue.

I didn't mean to kill him.

I didn't.

I was aiming for his shoulder.

Or maybe his arm. His hand. I don't know. I don't fucking remember. It's a blur. So vague. It happened so fast. One second.

It took a second.

I clench my jaw. This is my fault. I should've trained more. I should've practiced. I should've mastered the pistol before he gave it to me, let me use it, let me slaughter.

I was scared. Shaking. I wasn't thinking. I just pulled the trigger.

Idiot.

Well, never again.

With vengeful determination coursing through my veins, I swing my legs over the bed and slide on a pair of slippers. I grab a satin blue robe and toss it over my nighty, my feet carrying me toward the gun.

Hesitating for a moment, I swallow back the guilt and palm the weapon, pocketing it as I make my way to the range.

I haven't been able to touch the pistol since it happened. It's dirty. It's deadly. But I need to learn how to control it. How to use it. So this never happens again.

I won't let it happen *ever* again.

He's an idiot. He praised me. He told me that I was skilled. I wasn't. I'm an amateur.

Not for long.

Flicking on the fluorescent lights, I march toward the armory, grabbing a handful of bullets and shoving them in my pocket. I lay the gun down on the side table as I slide on ear protection. My gaze darts to the targets at the far end of the range.

I won't leave until *these* bullets hit *that* target in the *exact* locations that I'm aiming.

I need to get better. If I'm going to carry a gun, then I need to be its master, not the other way around.

I let out a shaky breath, yanking the gun off the table. I release the cylinder and load five rounds of .38 special into the chambers.

I snap it shut.

My knuckles are white around the pistol as I position myself in front of the target, my arms extended.

And I shoot.

Round after round blast through the barrel, every shot increasing my heart rate, every rip through the paper target puncturing a hole through my own reserve.

I load, reload, bullet after bullet. The cathartic experience of releasing my fury fills every corner of my being. Each round strokes the fire in my veins, bubbles the lava lying dormant in my heart, fills my bones with a sizzling inferno of rage, regret, *rapture.*

"Kiara!"

I fire one more shot, my muscles shaking from the blinding wrath seizing my body.

"Kiara!"

I whip my body around, my chest rising, my breathing erratic as I point the gun at Milo.

"What?" I spit. "Go away!"

Milo grips a manila envelope in his hand as he strides toward me, his eyes hooded, his expression weak, hurt.

"Put down the gun, Kiara. Go to sleep."

My molars nearly crush one another. "Why? Are you scared I'm going to shoot you?" I let out a neurotic laugh. "Because apparently, I can. I have it in me. I can shoot you right now. I could kill you so easily."

"Kiara, please..." The sharp edge of his jaw tightens, his expression so fucking soft. "Talk to me."

I'm on the precipice of losing my mind, of exploding, of detonating. A time bomb. I can hear the ticking in my brain.

*Ten.*

*Nine.*

*Eight.*

I try to calm myself down, to talk myself off the ledge but then, in a silky tone, four simple words slip out of his idiotic mouth.

"What is wrong, tesoro?"

*One.*

And I erupt.

# CHAPTER 20

## A TECTONIC SHIFT

IT STARTS IN MY TOES, A LOW RUMBLING. THE trembles of psychotic craze vibrates up my ankles, calves, thighs, filling my chest, flowing through my arms, my neck, up to my throat, to my lips.

I've reached my limit. I am no longer in control.

"What's wrong?!" I slam the pistol on the steel high-top table, my hands shaking as I storm toward Milo. My chest heaves as I glare at him. "You're seriously asking me *what's wrong*? Everything! Everything is fucking wrong!"

Milo is silent, the corners of his lips curved down into a frown as he stares at me with those stupid fucking brown eyes. Those wicked, decadent irises that pierce into my goddamn sullied soul.

"I am so fucking tired!" Tears flood my vision, every atom in my body boiling. "I can't sleep! I can't close my eyes without seeing his fucking face!"

"Kiara—"

"No!" I clench my fists. "Do you have any idea what it feels like to experience *every* emotion of the human spectrum but also feeling *nothing* at the same time?! Do you?!"

"Yes, tesoro." His eyebrows knit in profound under-standing. "I know."

"No! You don't! You can't! In order to experience human emotions, you need to *be* a fucking human! And you —" I clench my teeth, shaking my head. "You're a monster, a fucking criminal with no heart, no conscience, no regard for human life!"

His troubled gaze scans my face, his Adam's apple bobbing as he swallows. "You are not a monster, Kiara." He takes a measured step toward me, hesitating for a brief second before caressing my cheek with the back of his large hand. His knuckles catch falling hot tears. "You are *not* a monster."

"I wasn't until I met *you*!" I push against his firm chest with two hands. "You did this! I was fine before you! Every-thing was fine! And now?" I suck in a ragged breath, slam-ming my palms against his torso. "I don't even know who I am anymore! You did this! This is all *your* fault!"

Milo stands frozen, his expression uncharacteristically submissive as I beat my fists against his chest.

"Why?!" I shove him, voice cracking, pained. "Why did you have to come to *my* bank? Why did you have to choose *my* till? Why *me*? Why?! If it weren't for you, I wouldn't feel like this! I wouldn't feel so lost, so empty, so fucking broken! I hate you! I fucking hate you!"

"I am sorry, Kiara." Milo closes his eyes as I continue my assault. "I am sorry this happened, and I am *so* sorry that you are hurting—" He pauses, sucking in a small breath. "But—"

My head snaps up, my fingers scrunching up the fabric of his shirt.

"But *what*?"

"But I did not force you to do anything." His tormented

gaze flickers around my stunned features. "You made those decisions yourself, Kiara. You chose to tell me about the bomb. You shot Andre on your own accord. I did not force your hand."

My mouth hangs open as I blink at him, disbelief gushing through my pores. "Didn't force my hand?! If I didn't meet you, then none of this would have happened! You were the catalyst! It started with you, Milo! You!"

"No, Kiara," he snakes his hands around my wrists, his grip gentle, tender, "It started with *you*."

No. He's wrong. It wasn't me. It wasn't.

"You had a bomb strapped to your fucking chest!" I writhe in his grasp. "What was I supposed to do? Not tell you?! Spend the rest of my life worrying, thinking I could have prevented a possible death?!"

"Why *did* you tell me?" The low tenor of his voice rattles my bones. "You could have stayed quiet. You could have called the police *after* I left. Yet, you told me. Why, Kiara?"

My heart seizes in my chest as I use all my strength to break my wrists free from his tightening grip.

"Because you were in trouble," I choke out, running both hands through my hair as I stumble away from him. "Because I wanted to help you, because—"

"Exactly," he whispers. "Because you are a good person, tesoro. You are a kind, caring woman who *chose* to help a monster like me. Because at that moment, you did not see a criminal, Kiara. You saw a human. And that is *still* what I am."

My lungs expand, our eyes intertwining into a complex labyrinth of craving, grief, confusion, fury, want.

*Hesitation.*

"You kill people..." I hold back tears, polarizing emotions battling in my weary brain. "How can you be human?"

"Because the people I kill, Kiara—" Milo stalks toward me, his chest rising as he stops mere inches away from my spent body. He palms my cheek, his thumb grazing my hairline. "They are the real monsters." He looks so sad, so fucking honest as he peers down at me. "If only you knew what kind of terrible people reside in *our* world, you would not be so quick to judge me for my actions."

Loaded silence hangs in the air as we stare at one another, our breathing shallow, uneven, fucking synchronized.

"Please do not hate me, tesoro." He leans his forehead against mine as I squeeze my eyes shut, unable to respond to his plea. "I cannot stand your silence."

His touch affects me like a slow-burning affliction, an ailment, a malady. It makes me sick. Sick with thirst. Sick with hunger. And with his palm pressed against my cheek, with the heat from his strong hand emanating into my sensitive skin, seeping into my core—I'm starving.

I'm fucking famished.

It's wrong and immoral and twisted but I want him. I need him.

So *fucking* bad.

I need him to touch me, feel me, fuck me until I can't stand. Until I can't breathe. Until all the pain and anger and sorrow are replaced by him. All of him. Only him. Every fucking inch.

The real game is over. The *war* is over. I surrender. I lose. My king is down, trampled, destroyed. And I don't care anymore. There's no point.

He wants me. And I so desperately want him.

So, fuck it.

He wins.

I lurch forward, clutching onto his shirt as I slam my

lips against his. Our teeth crash, scraping against one another as our tongues collide— sloppy, wet, *ravenous*.

He tastes like sin and salvation, a sinister gift straight from the fiery pits of hell, but his lips, his perfect goddamn lips, make me feel, in the purest of forms, like a fucking angel.

A deity. A goddess. A saint.

"Fuck—" A low groan rumbles in his chest as I sink my teeth into his bottom lip. *Hard*. "Kiara..."

I've activated him.

He yanks the satin robe off my shoulders, his possessive hands floating down my bare spine. He pulls me flush against his body, his erection pressing against my core. A moan tumbles from my lips.

"I will incinerate you, tesoro," he whispers across my lips, his breath like honey— succulent, sweet, fucking addictive.

"Do it..." Heat collects in my stomach, coursing through my needy veins, igniting a dormant desire that's screaming to be let out. "I dare you."

"Be careful what you wish for."

His hand grazes down my heaving chest, so light, so delicate, so agonizingly slow.

"Everything I touch turns to ash." His lips flutter against the soft shell of my ear. His hand pushes up my teddy, teasing the hem of my lace panties before sliding his fingers lower and lower and—

*Oh my God.*

"Then burn me." I arch into his fingers as they coax open my slick folds. "Fucking burn me."

"You are not a phoenix, tesoro..." He flicks my sensitive nub, his left hand raking through my tangled hair. He tugs on my roots, forcing my eyes to meet his. My scalp throbs from the pain, the pleasure, the aggression in his touch. "You might not survive."

"You underestimate me." I bite my lip as I grind against his long thick fingers, hoping to create more friction, more movement, more pleasure.

"No, Kiara—" He drags his hand away from my pulsing clit. "You underestimate *me*."

Keeping his hungry gaze locked on mine, he brings his hand to his lips, his tongue swirling around the glistening moisture on his fingertips. My heart batters my chest with need.

"Mmm, *mia dolce ragazza*."

Bastard.

"No—" I drag my palm down the length of his lithe body, stopping at the waistband of his pants. My fingers slip under the thick fabric of his jeans, and I stroke his flesh, teasing him. With a smirk, I sink down on my knees, my heart racing as I unclip the top button and release his erection. His long, thick cock springs forward and I snake my fingers around the base of his shaft. "You really *do* underestimate me."

Milo cups my jaw, his thumb parting my lips, tilting my head to meet his darkened eyes.

"Kiara, there is no going back if you do this." His voice is gruff, hoarse, taunting. "You will be mine. Only mine. Do you understand?"

*No going back.*

It's a warning, a disclaimer. But I don't care. This is it. This is what I want.

Him.

"Yes," I whisper, panting with desire, with anticipation, with uncontrollable lust.

I flick my tongue against his tip, the salty flavor of precum seeping into my taste buds, aching my core, making me hot, flush, *confident*.

His fingers rake through my hair as I drag my tongue across his silky throbbing cock, coating his length with my saliva. I surge forward, taking him in my mouth. His tip slams into the back of my throat, hitting my tonsils. My cheeks concave as I suck the fucking life out of him.

There's something exhilarating about having control over a man's most vulnerable body part. It's like I have all the power. I can make him jump, stop, rollover.

Twisting my hair around his wrist, Milo lets out a deep guttural groan, cursing under his breath, his dick tensing in my mouth.

"You like that?" I tilt my head to meet his hardened gaze. My hand slides up and down his shaft, my palm wet, sticky, my grip tight. "You like it when I suck your cock?"

*"Fucking hell,"* he growls as he lifts me to my feet, his savage lips slamming against mine. My teddy is ripped from my body, his jeans and shirt stripped off in seconds.

Milo grabs me, his fingers digging into the swells of my ass as he hoists me up, my legs wrapping around his waist. He carries me to the steel table, the cold metal sizzling my scolding hot skin as he settles between my legs.

I moan, sliding my hands over his shoulders as he plants open mouth kisses on the slope of my neck, my chin, my jaw.

I glide my fingers over his bandaged shoulder as his teeth graze my neck. "Does it hurt?"

"Yes," he groans, fondling my breasts, pinching my taut nipples. The pressure builds between my legs.

I press my thumb into the center of the wound, wanting him to feel some of the pain I've felt this week. "Good."

"You will pay for that, tesoro," Milo winces, the volatile

gleam in his eyes sending a shiver down my spine as he pushes me back on the table and spreads my knees. His hands coil around the apex of my thighs as he sucks in a deep intoxicating breath.

A primal hunger dilates his pupils as he shreds my panties down the middle like a fucking caveman. He surges forward, his mouth latching onto my swollen clit. His fingers dip into my slickness and my back arches, my toes curling as his serpentine tongue devours me, claims me, makes me fucking scream.

And just as I'm close to exploding, he stops, smirking as he pulls away. I can almost see horns sprouting from his head.

"No," I whimper, resting on my forearms, my face flush, frustrated. "Why'd you stop?"

"Because this time, Kiara—" Milo licks his lips, soaking in every last naked, sweaty, tormented inch of my body. My ass squeaks against the metal as he yanks me off the table. I wrap my legs around his torso. "You are going to come on my cock."

We're surrounded by cement, guns, bullets, casings; everything filthy, dirty, deranged. Like us.

He presses me up against the wall, the tip of his cock rubbing against my clit as he palms my breasts. Desperation courses through my veins as his lips brush against mine.

"Fuck me." I claw his back with my nails, rolling my hips against his dick. The slab of textured concrete scratches my back. The earthy scent of debauchery fills my lungs.

Milo expels a low chuckle, nipping at the soft shell of my ear. "What was that?"

I lick the slope of his neck. "I said *fuck me*."

His hand wraps around the base of my throat, the back

of my head hitting the wall as my breath hitches. The brutality of his touch sets my skin on fucking fire.

"Again," he coaxes, his deep sinful voice making me drip down my thighs. "Tell me what you want."

I squirm, biting my lip as I cup my breasts, rolling my nipples between my fingers. "I want you to fuck me."

"One more time, tesoro," he rasps, his nostrils flaring as his grip tightens around my throat. "Say it."

"Fuck me," I beg, my voice breathy, hoarse, my clit pulsing, needing attention. Needing *him*. *"Please."*

"Good girl," he smirks, taking his hard dick into his hand. He brushes the tip against my soaking folds, teasing me like a fucking criminal. "Is this want you want, tesoro?"

"Please..." I scratch his shoulders, his back, my body on the verge of imploding from discomfort.

Arching down to capture my mouth, he lines up and slowly rocks into me. My walls stretch around him as he fills me with every single inch of his throbbing cock.

"Fuck, Kiara." He slams his hips forward, my pussy clamping around his thickness as he thrusts deeper, harder.

Our tortured, trembling, titillating groans bounce off the goddamn walls as I cry out in relief, in pleasure, in agony, in motherfucking ecstasy.

He's relentless in his movements, an animal, a beast, a fucking creature of the underworld as he hammers me, obliterates me, drags me from heaven to hell and back again. I scream out his name, gripping his hair, his shoulders, the ridges of his biceps.

"Oh my god!" I cry, his thrusts so deep they shake my uterus, my kidneys, my fucking heart as I tighten around him, his cock pulsating inside me.

"Yes," he growls. My eyes roll back, my chest rising and falling, erratic, chaotic. "Come with me, tesoro. Let go."

My legs tighten around his hips, my muscles spasming as we orgasm at the same fucking time. Our brutal moans hang in the muggy, sticky air. My sex drips with his cum, my body tired, sated, satisfied.

Milo rests his sweaty forehead against mine as I grip his shoulders for support. His shallow breaths fan against my lips. "You will be the death of me."

"What a wonderful way to die."

I catch my breath as he lowers me to the ground, my knees shaking as he steadies me. Milo dips down to pick up our clothes, holding out my robe as I absentmindedly slip it over my body.

"Can you walk?" He steps into his jeans and pulls them up. "Kiara?"

"Hmm?" I lean against the cold cement wall, my eyes unable to stay open, my body drained in the most wonderful way. "Okay."

A low chuckle slips from his lips. "Did you even hear what I asked you?"

"Me, walking, yes."

Without any warning, Milo scoops me up into his arms. "You need sleep."

"Are you going to stay with me?" I rest my head on his chest as he grabs the tan envelope off the table.

"Yes," he replies in a soft tone. "I will stay."

"Mmm," I hum breathlessly as he strides out of the range. "What's in the envelope?"

"Tomorrow." He rounds the corner. "I will show you tomorrow."

And if tomorrow never comes.

At least I got to experience heaven.

## CHAPTER 21

## FIFTEEN DOWN

SPOTS OF SOFT YELLOW LIGHT COAX OPEN MY EYELIDS. For the first time in days, I wake up naturally, not from nightmares, restlessness, guilt, but from the sun.

It's refreshing. Odd. And despite the sore and tender ache between my legs – a physical reminder of my wretched deed – I feel rested, relaxed, *rejuvenated*.

Last night, I lost it. I gave into temptation. I crossed a line. A sweet, blissful line that left me feeling on top of the fucking world. The weight that I've been carrying on my shoulders since Monaco doesn't feel as heavy today. It's still there. It'll always be there. But it's lighter. It's manageable. Maybe Julia was right. Maybe I needed to talk about it sooner.

Or scream about it.

In theory, I knew she was right, but I couldn't bring myself to address the storm of emotions brewing inside me. I was naive to think I could ignore it, pretend like it would vanish on its own. I needed to let it out. Expel the pain from my body. I am thankful for Milo. He drove me to the edge.

He helped me set the storm free.

Both storms.

Emotional and physical.

The melody of winter birds fills my ears as I rub my eyes, adjusting my vision to the brightness. Tugging the duvet over my chest, my gaze floats to the armchair in front of the curved floor-to-ceiling window.

I suck in a small breath, unable to suppress a smile. He didn't leave. I would have thought he'd flee once I fell asleep. But he didn't.

He stayed.

Or he came back.

Either way, his presence makes my heart flutter. An electric buzz spreads through my body as I study him carefully, slowly, with mild gratitude and major yearning.

Dressed in a three-piece light grey suit – a change from his usual all-black attire – Milo holds a folded-up newspaper in his left hand, his groomed brows knitted together in concentration. The tip of a fountain pen rests on the corner of his plump lips.

It's hard not to admire the man who somehow managed to bring me back to life.

I trace the curves of his masculine nose, his sculpted jawline, his wide shoulders, his long slender fingers, his ankle that's hiked over his thigh, his bouncing foot.

There is nothing I would change about the unearthly gorgeous man in front of me.

Aside from his profession.

And his spotty morals.

Yet, as he scribbles down answers to what I can only assume is a crossword puzzle, he doesn't look evil. He looks like a man.

A man that's making me question my principles. A man that's shaken my foundation. A man that's shifted the ground beneath my feet.

A man I know I should despise.

But I don't.

Not even a little.

"Are you finished staring?"

His voice startles me, my cheeks flushing from embarrassment as his dark gaze flickers in my direction. Compared to the beast that warped my entire perception of what constitutes good sex, the soft glow of humor in his eyes makes him look so tame, so fucking docile.

When I don't respond, his lips curl up into a knowing smirk. "Good morning, bella."

"Morning." I sit up and rest against the headboard. My belly stirs as he licks his lips. "What uh—what time is it?"

"It is almost 1 p.m." Milo lowers the newspaper to his lap, uncrossing his legs. He twists the pen between his fingers. "I did not want to wake you. I figured after last night...you needed the sleep."

I slept through the whole night? *Wow*. He literally fucked me into a coma.

"How long have you uh—" I swallow, my breathing uneven as fragments of our chaotic, violent, euphoric act flash through my mind. *Holy hell.* I clear my throat, my mouth dry. "How long have you been sitting there?"

"Not long." He expels a rich low chuckle as he cocks his head to the side. "I had several meetings this morning, but I returned as soon as I could."

"Oh." I let out a hum of understanding, a half-smile on my face.

Meetings? About what?

The air between us is charged, heavy with heated memories, with the uncertainty of what happens next. He's guarded. I'm apprehensive. He's cautious. I'm wary.

He's smoldering. And I'm on fucking fire.

Controlling his facial expression, Milo nods to a silver tray on the console table. "Would you like some coffee? It's fresh. Luisa just brought it up."

I blink. Luisa brought it up? To my room? With Milo here? She knows. She must know we—*Oh crap.* This might not go over well with the family. But I mean, it's just sex.

It's not like...

"Kiara?"

"Coffee sounds great." Anxiety thrums in my veins as I slip out of bed, my mangled nightgown rising over my thighs. A tiny breeze blows between my legs. My eyes widen. I am not wearing any underwear. Oh God.

"Is there a problem?" Milo lifts a brow, his covetous gaze dancing around the thin fabric covering my body.

"Not at all," I peep, circling the bed toward the bathroom. "I need to uh—freshen up."

My mind goes into overdrive as I change my clothes, brush my teeth, and attempt to comb the 'I got pummeled into oblivion last night' out of my tangled hair.

I had sex with Milo. A Don. The leader of Italy's most notorious mafia family. Surely, this will have consequences that extend past the bedroom. *If you do this, you are mine. Only mine.* What does that mean? In the moment, the possible repercussions of what I was agreeing to didn't matter, I didn't care. I was too wrapped up in his smell, his overpowering sexual magnitude, my own building desire. But now? Now I'm thinking clearly.

*Sort of.*

What does he want from me?

But more importantly...what am I willing to give him?

Yanking a dusty rose balloon-sleeve cardigan off the hanger, I slip it on, the soft fabric brushing against my midsection. I adjust the leather high-waisted skirt hugging my hips as I give myself an encouraging look in the full-length mirror. *Relax. It'll be fine.* Sucking in a confident breath, I traipse back into my bedroom.

"It might be a little cold now." Milo peers up from the newspaper as I pour myself a cup of tepid coffee from the French press.

"Well, now it's an iced coffee." I glance out the window, the looming grey clouds in the sky grabbing my attention. "I think it's going to rain."

Milo lets out a labored sigh as he scans my face. "Rain is good, tesoro. It is essential to the survival of every living organism. Such as with the sun, without rain, we would perish."

It's all about balance. Rain and sun. Hot and cold. Good and bad.

Right and wrong.

I nod slowly, skimming the top of his newspaper. Interesting choice. "Daily Telegraph? Any specific reason why you're reading a UK paper?"

Milo smiles, the warmth strong enough to thaw every iceberg, flood the earth, drown me.

With a smirk, he gently pats his thigh, inviting me to take a seat. "For the crosswords. I could use some help."

"I'm not good at crosswords," I lie, tapping my nails against the coffee cup.

"I do not believe you for a second." He tilts his head. "Sit, Kiara. I'm almost finished."

"Fine."

I bite my lip as I tentatively perch on the tip of his knee, the texture of his trousers smooth against the back of my thighs. The aromatic dry cedar notes of his cologne drive me crazy as I inhale a tiny breath.

"Relax, tesoro," he chuckles, adjusting his position. He wraps his arm around my waist, pulling me closer to his chest. My skirt rides up. "You are very tense."

"Which one do you need help with?" I whisper as he sweeps my hair off to the side. His stubble brushes against my shoulder as he feathers kisses up the slope of my neck. His fingers glide along my exposed midsection and I shudder, squeezing my thighs together from his all-too-gentle touch.

"Fifteen down." Milo's heady breath blows against my ear, his teeth nipping at the soft flesh. *Holy shit.* "Five letters —" His hand drifts up to my chest, his fingers circling my heaving breasts. "The clue is—" I close my eyes, squirming on his lap as he rolls my nipple between his thumb and index finger. The pressure sends a flood of heat to my lower abdomen. "*Invigorate.*"

Bastard.

"Rouse," I breathe, stifling a moan as he continues teasing, twisting my stiff peaks. "Does it fit?"

"Mhmm." He drags his hand down my chest, past my stomach, his fingers gliding over my thigh— his touch so hot, so meticulous, so fucking *arousing.* "One more—" He slips his fingers up my skirt, curling them under the hem of my panties. My thighs spread to give him more room to explore, to play – to pleasure. "Patience, tesoro."

"Milo," I whimper, rocking my hips against his hand. "Please."

"Twenty-six across—" He expels an airy chuckle, smirking against my skin as he bites my neck. "Six letters—" He pushes past the red lace, cursing under his breath. A guttural growl rumbles in his chest as he swirls my pulsing sex. "So fucking responsive."

I bite my lip, arching into this touch as he slides two fingers into my soaking folds, his calloused thumb flicking the sensitive bundle of nerves.

His lips tickle my ear as he rasps, "The clue is 'covered, as in with chocolate'."

I can barely understand anything he's saying. All I hear is the sloshing of his fingers thrusting in and out of my dripping sex, his ragged breathing, the moans of ecstasy slipping from my lips.

"Dipped?" I offer breathlessly, my walls clenching around his fingers, my toes curling from the invigorating sensation.

Milo stops his ministrations, my needy body tensing. "Try again."

"Fuck..." Frustration courses through my veins. Damn sadist. I can't think right now. "I don't know."

"You do." He whirls his fingers inside of me so faintly that I might die from discomfort. "What is the answer, tesoro?"

"I don't know." Close. I'm so fucking close to climaxing. He increases the speed, the pressure, encouraging me to give him a better answer.

"Think, Kiara. Or I will stop. *Covered, as in with chocolate.*"

"Oh my God!" My belly contracts as he flicks my clit. "Don't stop."

"You are in control, bella. It is in your hands."

I writhe on his lap, his hard-on pressing into my ass. "I don't fucking know! Soaked?"

"Yes, you are," he laughs. "But not the correct answer."

I lied. I fucking despise him. Evil, horrible man.

"Milo," I beg as he slows down again. "Please..."

"Last chance. Think, Kiara. You know the answer."

"I don't know!" I bite my lip, trapped in a cage of literal goddamn torture. "Coated?"

"Good girl."

Milo's grip tightens around my body. His hand snakes around the base of my throat as he dives his fingers deep, *deep* inside me, every movement harder, faster, more aggressive as I shudder, squirm, buck in his grasp.

"Come, Kiara."

And I do, exploding in a wave of rapturous release, my chest expanding, my body blotchy, red, content. I open my eyes as Milo pulls his fingers out of my sex, my heart racing with adrenaline.

He smirks with glowing pride, satisfaction. "See? You *are* good at crosswords. You just need the correct—" He licks his lips. "*Incentive*."

"Funny." I try to scowl at him but my entire being is humming in a sated daze. "You are a cruel man."

"Perhaps." He cocks his head, a lopsided grin on his face. "But you are also a very cruel woman." I sit up, attempting to adjust my skirt, my inner thighs wet and sticky. "Do you know you talk in your sleep?"

His softening erection presses against my hip. Are we not addressing that? "I talk in my sleep?"

"Yes." He curls his fingers under my jaw, brushing his soft lips against mine. "You kept saying my name. It took a lot of self-control not to wake you with my cock. Very cruel of you, tesoro."

My eyes spring open. I said his name? Goddamn subconscious.

I rest my palm against his chest. "I'm shocked you didn't. Seems very out of character."

"All creatures must evolve." He tucks a wayward strand of hair behind my ear as he lifts me to my feet. "Plus—" He smirks. "You deserved an undisturbed sleep."

"Deserved?" In a slight daze, my gaze flits down to a dark blotch on his pant leg, my cheeks immediately blazing with embarrassment. "Oh my God."

He follows my sightline, his lips quirking up into a mischievous grin. "What a bad day to wear grey. I hope no one sees."

My jaw drops. "You better—"

"Kiara," he cocks his head to the side, "don't be shy. It's very natural. Nothing to be embarrassed about."

I close my eyes. "I swear to God, Milo. If you don't change your fucking pants before going out in public, I will literally kill you."

He lets out a low chuckle. "You are radiant when you blush, tesoro. But do not worry. We are going straight to my office."

I frown. "Your office? Why?"

"I need to show you something." He clears his throat, the energy in the room darkening. "It has to do with Andre."

*The envelope.*

My heart drops to my stomach. "What is it?"

"You will see." He holds out his hand, his eyes soft, inviting. "Shall we?"

"I need to use the bathroom first."

A knowing glimmer flashes across his face. "Very well. You can meet me there."

"Okay." Before he exits, I call out, "Milo?"

He cranes his neck toward me, "Yes, tesoro?"

"Do I *need* to see this? Whatever it is."

"I believe it is necessary," he replies with a weak smile. "I will meet you in my office."

"Okay."

Is this what Marchello and Milo were arguing about?

Or something else?

# CHAPTER 22

## THE BURDEN OF TRUTH

WHEN IT COMES TO THE MAFIA, JULIA BELIEVES ignorance is bliss. She set boundaries. She has limits. She doesn't mind being left in the dark. She prefers it. Her Gucci rose-colored glasses are an everyday accessory. She wears them with pride. Ignorance makes *this* life tolerable for her. And that's okay. That's her choice.

But I am not Julia.

Nana raised me to be curious, to question everything, to never stop learning. For me, ignorance is weakness, knowledge is power, and power is confidence. Confidence to make my own decisions, to come to my own conclusions, to feel secure, to feel safe.

But as I sit down next to Milo on the black velvet couch tucked in the far corner of his office, two daunting letter-sized envelopes laid on the glass coffee table, ignorance doesn't seem so bad.

Unease gnaws on my intestines as Milo grabs one of the folders, his eyebrows drawn together with apprehension.

"After what happened in Monaco, I had several of my

private investigators look into Andre," Milo begins. "I wanted concrete evidence that he was indeed affiliated with Igor and the brotherhood."

"And was he?" I keep my expression neutral despite the fact I'm shocked he's divulging information related to the *business*. "Part of Bratva?"

"Yes," Milo confirms, his tone sour. "He was."

I knew he was, but the solidification of facts is disconcerting. I wonder what's going to happen when his boss finds out. What does that mean? What will happen? Will they come after me? After Milo?

Oh, God.

"And Henri didn't know that one of his men was a spy for the Russians?" I already know the answer but I'd like to hear it from Milo. Is he going to be honest with me?

"No, Henri was not aware of Andre's true intentions when he joined his organization." Milo runs a hand through his black hair, his neck muscles tightening. "Earlier this week we discovered that the man who recommended Andre for the position was bribed by the Russians."

I wince. "Did you kill him?"

His shoulders tense. "No, I did not. I trust Henri to deal with *his* employees in the proper manner."

So, *Henri* killed him. Got it.

I flick the tips of my fingernails. "Am I in danger? Did I create more problems for you?"

"As you know, our dispute with the Russians predates what happened in Monaco. It is being taken care of. As long as you are with me, you will be safe."

"Okay." My gaze darts to his hands. *Priorities*. "So, what's in the envelope?"

*Knowledge is power.*

"Andre's real name is Andrei Vasilesvsky." His tone is professional, matter of fact, void of emotions. "He is a cousin of Igor Zharkov, the head of the *Pravda* faction of the brotherhood. He is also—" His jaw clenches.

My heart races. "Also, what? I can handle it, Milo. Just tell me."

*Power is confidence.*

Milo inhales a small breath, his eyes hooded, dark, uncomfortable as he reveals, "Andre is wanted in Moscow for the rape and murder of three women."

*Ignorance is bliss.*

"What?" Knots form in my stomach and my face pales. "He—"

Oh my God. I sat with this man. We played cards together. He flirted with me. He complimented me. He *touched* me. His deplorable, sick, heinous hands were wrapped around my wrist.

And then I killed him. I murdered a murderer. I took the life of a rapist. I saved Milo. I probably saved myself. These are the facts. These facts *should* exonerate me of my crime. They *should* absolve me of my sin. They *should* justify my actions.

But do they? Do they really?

I am not the judge.

"These are the police reports." Milo flips open the flap, removing a thin stack of documents. He passes me the files. My heart clenches as Andre's vile blue eyes stare up at me from the mug shot. "The details are—" A slight head shake. "Disturbing. I would recommend that you do not read the full report."

Too late.

Milo stays silent as nausea, disgust, and anger course

through my veins. My knuckles turn white as I grip the report.

Bound. Gagged. Mutilated. Throats slit open. Their bodies wrapped in garbage bags. Dumped under bridges. The victims were all waitresses. Brunettes. All young women who were just starting their lives. They all had families. Friends. One had a son. A child. This child is motherless now.

Andre was fucked. He was an actual real-life monster. Someone who shouldn't have been given the gift of life.

He was an abomination. An error. A mistake.

My parents weren't religious. We never went to church. Even when I moved in with my grandparents, I never went. But for the last ten years, Nana has preached the word of God. I've listened. I've *tried* to believe. For her sake. It made her happy. I wanted her to be happy.

Nana told me God doesn't make mistakes, but she was wrong. He does. How could God put this man on earth on purpose? Is He *that* cruel? Does He not take responsibility for His children? Is it free will? Is it nature versus nurture? If our lives are predestined, then Andre was destined for *this*? Destined to be a psychopath? And that was, okay? Acceptable? Part of His plan?

I knew there was evil in the world but to be so close to it...it's harrowing.

"Kiara..." Milo places a comforting hand on my trembling knee, his thumb stroking my skin. He gently removes the documents from rigid fingers. "I think that is enough."

"Why did you show this to me?" I suck in a shaky breath. "To make me feel better about killing him?"

Milo swallows as he sidles closer to me on the couch. His thigh presses against mine, heat radiating off his stiff body. "I told you that there are bad people in our world, Kiara." He drags his thumb under my eyes, wiping away the small puddles of frustrated tears. "Men like Andre do not deserve to breathe."

I study him intently. "No, they don't."

"Kiara?" He tilts his head. "What are you thinking?"

"How many men like Andre do you work with? This type of behavior is probably quite normal in your world."

*Our world.*

His features harden, offended. "None. We do not tolerate rape in my family. It is non-negotiable."

"It is?" I ask warily. "Really?"

"Yes. Before *Santi Oscuri* was formed, as retaliation for setting a warehouse on fire—" He falters, his voice hoarse, croaking. "My grandmother, she was—"

*No.*

My troubled heart seizes as I cup his clenched fist, grazing his knuckles with my thumb. "It's okay. You don't have to say it. I'm sorry about your grandma."

"I am too." Milo absentmindedly caresses my fingertips, tenderly, delicately, like he's unaware that he's doing it. "When my grandfather became Capo, he amended the code. Every man under my employ is aware of this rule. And they follow it. They must."

"I'm sorry for implying that—" I swallow, guilt eating at me. "That was insensitive. I just assumed that—"

"It is a normal assumption to make. There are other families who do not abide by our guidelines, but I cannot control those men. I can only control mine."

"Yeah," I whisper, intertwining my fingers through his, creating a web of mutual understanding, respect.

Admiration.

Milo meets my dreary expression. "Kiara, I know this past week has been difficult for you. I am not oblivious to your struggles, but I do hope this new information puts your mind at ease."

My hands tingle from his soft touch. "It does. A little bit, but what about the families of his victims? Don't they deserve justice? It's almost like—" I pause, shaking my head, conflict stewing in my stomach. "It's almost like I did him a favor. By killing him. He should have spent the rest of his life rotting in a Russian prison. He should have suffered. He should've paid for his crimes."

Is that wrong? To wish suffering upon another human being? Even a horrible one? I'm beginning to understand the need for grey areas. I'm beginning to understand Milo.

I just don't know if that's a good thing or a bad thing.

It's quiet for a few minutes, the heaviness of Andre's vicious actions weighing on us.

Both of us.

"Kiara, you di—" he begins to say but stops. "You—"

"What?" I tilt my head, trying to gauge his emotions. I can't. Sadness? Regret? Pain?

"You di—" Milo curses under his breath, expelling a low, almost inaudible grumble as his expression softens. "You did nothing wrong, Kiara. Remember that."

"I know." I nod slowly, trying to convince myself of the same thing as my gaze drifts to the second envelope on the coffee table. "What's in there?"

"Nothing you need to see."

"Why not?" I pinch my eyebrows together, curiosity piquing as I reach for the envelope. "What is it?"

"No." Milo coils his fingers around my wrist. "Trust me, Kiara. Please."

What the fuck is in there?

"Fine," I mutter, pretending to lower the file. Once Milo lets go of my arm, I spring up off the couch with the envelope and round the coffee table.

"Fuck sakes!" Milo abruptly stands up, jaw twitching. "Kiara!"

I open the flap and pull out the contents, my eyes widening in terror and revolt as I scan the graphic crime scene photos. "Oh my God!" I drop the folder, covering my mouth, bile creeping up my throat. "I'm going to be sick."

"I told you not to look, Kiara." Milo strides toward me. He picks up the photos off the floor and slides them back into the envelope. "I need you to start trusting me. One day that trust might save your life."

A foul taste lingers in my mouth as the vivid images of cuts, gashes, slashes, and blood flash through my mind. So much fucking blood.

"Trust is earned," I mutter, calming myself down. "I would be an idiot to blindly trust someone that I've only known for a few weeks."

I immediately regret my words.

Hypocrite. I'm a hypocrite. I'm asking him to trust me yet, here I am, unwilling to reciprocate. Trust requires give and take. I want so badly to give. I do. I just don't want to deal with the repercussion of broken trust. Like a shattered plate, once broken, it's forever changed.

"Have I not *earned* your trust?" Milo frowns, stopping in front of me. "Have I not kept my word? Have I not kept you safe?" He arches down, feathering his lips across my ear. "Have I not fulfilled *all* of my promises?"

His *promises* haunt my skin like a ghost. "You have."

"Then you should trust me, tesoro," he whispers, cupping my cheek.

I lean into his palm, my body relaxing, melting from his delicate touch. "Do you trust me?"

"I am trying—" And he is. I can tell. He's shared more with me today than ever before. He's opening up to me. His shield is cracking. Light peeking through. Pulling me out of the dark. "You and I, we are very similar, Kiara. We do not trust easily, we are both guarded, reserved, but in order for us to work together, we must have faith in one another."

Work together? He couldn't have chosen a more confusing phrase. Work together as boss and employee? Or as something more? I'm scared to know the answer. I'm scared that I'll like it.

"Ever since I met you my faith has been shaken, Milo," I breathe, fighting back tears as I grip his blazer. "Everything I've ever been taught to believe is unraveling before my eyes, one tiny thread at a time."

"Then I shall restore it." He rests his forehead against mine, our noses brushing together. "You simply need to trust me."

*Knowledge is power.*

I inwardly brace myself for destructive impact. "What am I to you?"

He's silent for a beat. The longest ten seconds of my life. I shouldn't have asked. How juvenile.

"I wish I knew." An airy hum flutters across my lips, his hot breath filling my lungs as he laces his fingers through my hair. "I find you to be—" He releases a long exhale. *"Enchanting."*

"What does that mea—"

I'm cut off by his mouth slamming against mine; the softest collision I've ever experienced. His lips have the force of a brick but the touch of a damn cloud, and it's consuming, confusing, and clarifying all at the same time. A dirty trick. A dirty, beautiful, clever approach to put this conversation to rest.

When he pulls away, I'm light-headed, dizzy with delight. "That's not an answer."

"Yes, it is," Milo smirks, reaching for my hand. *What the hell does that mean?* "Let's go have lunch with Julia. She misses you."

"I saw her two days ago," I note as Milo leads us out of his office. "She's kind of needy, isn't she?"

"Very needy." Milo expels a low chuckle. "My father used to call her an orchid. Very temperamental. Needs constant attention."

I grin. "And what did he call you? A cactus? Prickly and never dies?"

"Hilarious." Milo tosses me an unimpressed scowl as we round the corner and bump into Marchello, whose gaze instantly darts to our intertwined fingers. His lip twitches. "Were you looking for me?"

"*Yes,*" Marchello grumbles in Italian, clearing his throat. "*The sparrow is chirping.*"

I narrow my eyes at Milo. "I wouldn't have pegged you for a bird watcher."

Milo's lips stretch out in a forced smile. "I have many hobbies, Kiara." He turns his attention back to his under-boss. "I will come after we eat. Take pictures for me, *si?*"

Marchello's irritation is palpable. "*I think it is better if you come now. The sparrow might fly away.*"

Milo's expression hardens. "It will come back."

"*We do not have the luxury to wait.*" Marchello glances at me for a brief moment. "*I am sure Kiara will be fine on her own for a few hours.*"

Milo lets out a labored sigh, casting me an apologetic look. "I am sorry. I must go."

"Oh," I hum as he drops my hand. "That's fine. I'll just eat with Julia."

"I will find you later tonight."

But he doesn't.

Not that night. Nor the one after.

Who knew sparrows were so time-consuming.

# CHAPTER 23

# DOWN THE RABBIT HOLE

"GET OFF YOUR PHONE," JULIA HUFFS AS I REOPEN MY messages app for the umpteenth time. Still no reply. It takes two fucking seconds to respond to a text. "Am I boring you, Kiara?"

I roll my eyes, flipping my phone face down, the force vibrating all the jewelry sprawled across the dining room table.

Milo's texting etiquette leaves *much* to be desired.

WEDNESDAY

> Where are you?

Apologies, tesoro. I will not make it tonight.

> Why? What happened?

Nothing.

THURSDAY

> Is everything ok?

> Everything is fine.

>> Milo, what is going on? You've been MIA for two days.

Nothing.

THIS MORNING

>> Are we still going to Milan today? Or is that canceled? I'd like to know if I have to pack. Please respond at your earliest convenience. Or never. That works too.

> Pack.

>> I don't want to go anymore. Not really in the mood for a gala. Or in the mood to be ignored.

Nothing.

"I was just checking the time," I grumble. "How is it only 10? I feel like we've been at this for hours."

Resting my elbow on the table, I mindlessly sweep my fingers across all the abandoned necklaces and rings that we're organizing. Half we're donating, the other half we can keep. The ex-mafia queen apparently didn't think these pieces were valuable enough to take to Monaco. One woman's outdated Tiffany's is another woman's... normal Tiffany's.

Julia crosses her arms as she leans back into her chair, her cherry red lips pursed. "Don't lie to me, cara. I can see his name on the screen. What is going on with the two of you?"

I press my lips into a thin line as I add an opal ring with a gold band to my pile of keepers. "Nothing is going on. I just asked him about the gala. That's all."

Seeing as I don't know *what* the fuck is going on between me and Milo, I'm not really lying. He kisses me. He fucks me. He tells me I'm *enchanting*—whatever the hell that means.

And then he drops off the face of the planet.

Am I mad? No. I'm not mad. I'm annoyed. No. I'm not even annoyed. I am simply confused. Mildly irritated. Irked, if you will.

And maybe a little mad.

Just a little.

Julia lets out a sigh, tilting her head. "You can talk to me, cara. You know this. I am not a fool; I can tell that you have been hiding something from me."

Detective Julia.

"Does Paolo ever just... *ignore you?*" I avoid her invasive gaze. God, I sound like a damn teenager. Pathetic. "Like, does he just, I don't know, not reply to your messages for days?"

I am regressing into adolescence.

He is making me into a crazy phone watcher! Every time I get a notification, I jump in my seat. If Apple sends me one more notice to update my iOS, I might actually die from a heart attack.

Julia snorts. "All the time. I could probably fit all the text messages he's sent me over the past year on a single piece of lined paper. The men in this family are not exactly the best at communicating."

"No shit."

"If it makes you feel better, Paolo has also been coming to bed very late the past couple of days," Julia muses, sifting through the necklaces. "Something important must have come up. I wouldn't worry too much about it if I were you."

I narrow my eyes. "They're still *here*? In the house?"

Now I really *am* mad.

"As far as I know they have not left." Julia shrugs, her carefree light attitude making me feel extra pathetic. She glances up at me. "Kiara, if you do not stop frowning, you will need Botox *way* too early."

"You're right, you're right. I just need to let it go. I am *letting it go.*" I expel a deep groan. "Milo can do whatever he wants. Not my problem."

"You had sex, didn't you?" Julia cocks her head to the side. *Oh, shit.* "This is why you are so upset, no?"

I blink. "No."

Julia closes her eyes and takes a tiny, somewhat threatening, breath. "I swear to all the gods, Kiara, if you lie to me one more time, I will cut you in your sleep."

My jaw drops. "I—"

Her eyes flutter open, a hint of humor flashing in her dark irises. "Talk to me, cara." She pauses, cringing. "Not too much detail though."

Fuck it. Maybe she can shine some light on the psyche of Emilio Di Vaio. I sure as hell don't have a clue.

After rambling for thirty minutes, I take a deep breath, my throat dry. Damn, she's a good listener. Too good. If I didn't need a sip of water, I wouldn't have stopped talking.

"So?" I chug back the San Pellegrino, parched from talking. "Thoughts?"

Julia hums, crossing her legs, her gaze pensive, thoughtful, as she mulls over the details. "What is it that you want from my brother? It seems as though both of you are unwilling to define your relationship."

"What?" I choke out. "Relationship? We don't have a relationship. We're just—" I bite my lip. "We're just...having sex?"

This was a bad idea. What an oversight.

Her clinical gaze scans my flustered face. "If you are just having sex then why do you care where he is? Why do you keep checking your phone? Why are we even having this conversation?"

I cross my arms defensively. "Am I going to have to pay for this therapy session, *Doctor* Casellati? Or is the first one free?"

Julia rolls her eyes. "I am asking you important questions, Kiara. You need to decide what you want from him. And once you do, take it. It's simple."

Nothing about this is simple. It's messy, convoluted, potentially disastrous. He's like an electromagnet, capable of generating world-defying power but can also be deathly destructive if not handled properly. And I don't know if I can handle him. There's no manual to follow. No guidelines. No historical data to reference. He's uncharted territory and I don't have a map.

I'm scared of getting lost.

"I don't know what I want," I admit, my tone low, defeated.

And neither does he. We're at a stalemate once again. Except for this time, the stakes are higher. We're not playing with power. We're playing with hearts.

And mine is chained. Locked. Guarded.

Terrified.

Julia smiles, placing her hand on mine as she whispers, "Then first, you must figure out what you want Kiara. Everything else will fall into place."

"Or it'll all fall apart."

Footsteps sound in the distance and I snap my head toward the entryway.

My face falls.

"*Buongiorno, Signora,*" Marchello nods, greeting Julia as

he approaches the table. His eyes are sunken, bloodshot, glazed over as he glances at me. *"Kiara."*

"Good morning, Marchello. How are you? How is my *husband*? Alive, I hope?" Julia glares at Marchello who stays silent, his inquisitive gaze scanning the jewelry on the table. "Well?"

I blink, shocked by her combative attitude and Marchello's sheepishness. What is happening right now?

"Yes, Signora, he is alive." His lips twist up in contemplation. "I believe he went to your room."

"Oh, is your three-day long meeting over? So soon? Are you sure that was enough time to *'talk'*?"

Oof. She might care just a little.

"For now, it is over." Marchello tosses Julia a tight smile. "Paolo is all yours."

"And my brother?" She crosses her arms. I jerk up in my seat. Bless you, Julia. "Where is he?"

"He is in his office." Marchello glances toward me. "Waiting for *you*."

"Me?" I clear my throat. At least he hasn't forgotten that I exist.

"Yes, he told me to get you." Marchello takes a deep breath and checks his watch. "You should go now. We leave for Milan in an hour."

"I can finish sorting the rest by myself," Julia smiles at me then whips her head back at Marchello, snapping at my pile of jewelry. "Take this to Kiara's room."

"No, it's fine," I protest. God, she's on a rampage. "I can do it."

"It is no problem, Signora," Marchello says to Julia, ignoring me completely as he scoops the pile of necklaces and rings into a silver bowl. "It is on my way."

"Excellent." Julia tilts her head as Marchello lingers.

"Was there something else you needed?"

"No."

Once he's out of sight, I gawk at Julia. "What the fuck was that?"

Julia smirks. "That is how you deal with mafia men."

Yeah, maybe that approach works if you're related to the boss. Not just fucking him.

Milo is perched on the edge of the desk, veins protruding from his forearms as he grips the sleek wooden top. I lean against the door frame and cross my arms, taking in the tired man in front of me. His head is hung low, his shoulders slumped, his black hair completely disheveled. He's a mess. A beautiful tantalizing mess.

How unfair.

"You look like shit."

Milo's head snaps up, our eyes locking. A deadbolt. Unbreakable. "I have not slept," he says with a weak smile. "Come in, tesoro. Close the door."

I attempt to stand my ground. "I'm good over here. What do you want?"

"Kiara—" His chest rises with exhaustion. "Come inside and close the *fucking* door." He pauses, peering up at me, his gaze darkened, serious. "*Now.*"

I inwardly roll my eyes, taking a step forward and slamming the door shut. "Happy?"

"You are angry with me." He frowns, rubbing his chin methodically as he gives me a once over. "Why?"

"Really?" I scoff, walking toward the aloof bastard. "You disappeared for three fucking days, Milo. That's why."

"I had to take care of an emergency." He licks his lips as

I approach and stop a foot away from him. *Shameless.* "It was not my intention to upset you, Kiara."

"What was the emergency?"

"I do not wish to burden you with the details, tesoro. It is over now." He expels a defeated sigh. I thought he trusted me. "Kiara, please try to understand. There are many things I wish I could share with you but for the safety of my family, *and* you, I simply cannot."

His velvety voice is so hypnotizing that all the resentment thrumming through my veins dissipates, disperses, dissolves into nothingness. I want to be upset with him. I *am* upset with him. But that particular emotion seems to be overpowered by my need to be touched by him, to be close to him, to feel the warmth of his intoxicating body.

"You could've at least replied to my texts. I was worried something bad happened. That you were hurt."

His plump lips curl into a smile. "I *did* reply, tesoro. Were my responses not adequate enough to verify proof of life?" He reaches out, curling his fingers under my chin. His thumb strokes my jawline, sending shivers down my spine. "A dead man cannot text, Kiara."

"You know what I meant." The gritty texture of his knuckles brush against my skin. I grab his hand and glare at the bruises and dried blood sprawled across the top. I frown. "What happened to your hand? Did a *sparrow* attack you?"

"No." He lets out an amused chuckle, "Just a mild disagreement." He snakes his hand around my waist, my body settling in between his legs.

"Mild?" I tilt my head, my entire fucking body melting into his arms. "That's mild?"

Milo smirks. "It is merely a scratch."

I scowl at him. "Right. I suppose compared to gunshots and murder, that's pretty mild."

"Do you know what I think, tesoro?" Milo pulls me flush against his chest, his large hand gliding up and down my spine as he arches forward, his balmy breath fanning my ear. "I think you are trying *very* hard to find reasons to be mad but in reality—" He threads his fingers through my hair, tugging it gently. "You've simply missed me."

"No..." I squirm in his arms as he drags his thumb along my parted lips. "I didn't."

"Yes, Kiara. You did. " He brushes his nose against mine. "And I have also missed you. I've missed—" He takes a deep breath, inhaling the muggy, heated air swirling around us. "*Le tue belle labbra.*" He feathers his lips against mine, his teeth nipping at the soft flesh. *Oh, God.* "*Il tua pelle morbido.*" His tongue flicks out, leaving wet trails of salvia against my neck. His hand cups my breasts, applying just the right amount of pressure to make my insides burn. "*I tuoi fottuti seni.*" *Holy shit.* "But mostly—" His hand slides up my pleated skirt, two of his fingers stroking the thin fabric of my panties. "I've missed this."

"Milo—" I breathe out a small moan as he rolls circles across my clit. My arms wrap around his neck and I fist his hair as he pushes my panties to the side. Anticipation buzzes through me. "I still need to pack."

"We have time," he growls, pushing two fingers past my dampened folds. He coils his hand around the base of my throat as his lips ambush mine— demanding, ravenous, hungry.

And fuck it if I have any control, I want him too. Like an addict, I crave him, so desperate, so needy, so fucking help-less. He's a drug. A narcotic. A life ruiner. And I want him to ruin me. I need a hit. I need something. Fucking anything.

My hand travels down his chest to his pelvis, stroking

the growing hard-on under his pants. "You really *have* missed me," I whisper against his lips, gasps of airy arousal escaping my lungs as I undulate my hips against his wicked fingers. I unzip his trousers and free his throbbing erection, nearly salivating at the sight of his long, thick cock just waiting to be sucked.

I begin to lower myself to my knees but in one swift motion, Milo flips me over. My chest slams against the cold wooden desk, my ass sticking out. He arches over me, pushing my skirt up, tearing through my panties like a wild animal.

"We don't have *that* much time," he rasps, teasing my slit with a tormenting touch.

"Fuck!" I let out a startled yelp as he slaps my ass, pain shooting up my spine but quickly turning into pleasure. I crane my neck toward him, the electric glimmer of dominance dancing around his face makes me excited. So fucking excited.

With his hand on the base of his shaft, Milo grazes the tip of his cock against my folds. A needy wanton moan slips from my lips. "Please..."

"You are so fucking sexy when you beg." A guttural groan thunders in his chest as he surges forward, filling my pussy to the hilt. "Christ, Kiara..."

I whimper in ecstasy as he loops my hair around his wrist and pulls me backward. I arch my spine, his hand coiling around my neck as his unyielding cock fucks the living shit out of me.

With every thrust, my eyes roll to the back of my head; agony and bliss flooding every corner of my mind.

"You feel so fucking good." He bites my ear lobe, his right-hand tightening around my throat, constricting airflow in the best possible way.

"Oh my God!" I moan as he strokes my clit with his left hand, my walls contracting around his dick, forcing a howling roar to tumble from his lips. "Don't stop!"

I grip onto his muscular forearm, holding myself upright. My minds spins from the earthy scent of sex and sweat and savagery.

"Fuck," Milo hisses as I near nirvana, my legs shaking, quaking, vibrating from violent rapture.

When my orgasm tears through my body, he pulls out, swiftly turning my body around. He lifts me on top of the desk, my legs spreading, inviting him in.

I curl my fingers around his shirt, his shoulders, his hair. My chest is heaving, panting, contorting in breathlessness as he arches over, his lips owning mine. Unrelenting utopia courses through my veins as he punishes me with his cock.

I scream his name, another wave of climax seizing my organs, ripping through my entire being, sending my essence flying to another dimension.

He growls, biting my lip, a metallic taste lingering in my mouth as his whole body convulses. His grip tightens around my hips as he spills hot cum inside of me.

Panting, our bodies fold against one another, our breathing ragged, harmonized. He laces his fingers through my messy hair and rains kisses all over my satisfied face.

He pulls out of me and helps me off the desk, his eyes glazed over, softened, so fucking delectable. "You are a goddess. *Un angelo mandato dal cielo.*"

*If only.*

"I'm hardly an angel," I breathe as we both clumsily attempt to redress. If he keeps shredding all my underwear, I'm going to have nothing left by the end of the year. "And I'm certainly not from heaven."

That's a pipedream now.

Milo wraps me in his arms, stroking my hair, his touch so delicate that I can barely feel it. "You are *my* version of heaven, tesoro. And that is all a man needs."

I'm too comatose to overthink his words. I'll do that later.

His fingers lace through mine as we head out of the office, my gait unsteady. "I still need to pack."

"Luisa should have packed most of your belongings already," Milo says as we climb the stairs to our floor. His hand never leaves the small of my back. Whether it's out of affection or safety, I don't know.

"Did she pack the red dress?" I ask in a playful tone as we round the corner to our rooms. "You really need to expand your color horizons."

Milo lets out a melodic laugh. "The gala we are attending is also referred to as The Scarlet Ball. Everyone will be wearing red, tesoro."

I toss him a coy smirk. "That must be a fantasy come true for you then. It's like your own personal version of Viagra."

Milo narrows his bloodshot eyes at me. "You are all the Viagra I need."

"Charming." I roll my eyes, concealing the grin that's threatening to expose me. I clear my throat as we pause outside my room. "I'll meet you at the car?"

Milo nods, lifting my hand to his lips. "Don't be late."

"I'm never late."

Hurriedly, I give myself what can only be described as a whore bath before I pack a small travel bag and shove make-up, a Kindle, and my phone into a purse.

At this point, I'm giving up on trying to understand Milo. He is who he is and for now, that's okay. Julia might have a point. Eventually, a clear definition of what our relationship is might be helpful, but right now? I don't fucking care.

Right now, I'm on cloud fucking nine.

Before heading out of my room to the parkade, the silver bowl of jewelry on my vanity table catches my eye. I need something to wear with the dress tonight. I pick a couple of necklaces off the top. One diamond-studded choker, the other a ruby heart on a simple chain. We went through so many pieces today; I can't remember if there's something better on the bottom. Doesn't matter, I don't have time to look anyway.

When I get down to the garage, Milo is already in the backseat of the SUV, his clothes changed, his hair damp from a quick shower. He looks refreshed. Still deathly tired but refreshed.

He casts me a playful scowl. "I told you not to be late."

"I'm a woman, we need time."

The driver starts the car and pulls out of the six-car garage.

"Mmm." Milo suppresses a yawn. "That is true."

I tilt my head, getting secondhand fatigue. "Why don't you take a nap? It's a two-hour drive."

His weary eyelids flutter. "I would much rather talk to you, tesoro. I am fine."

I sidle closer to him. "I'm not going anywhere. Just sleep."

And for once, he doesn't protest, doesn't argue. He lowers his head on my shoulder and within seconds drifts off into a deep sleep.

I smile, glancing down at his peaceful face as I pull up *Pride and Prejudice* on my Kindle.

I'm in the mood for a romance.

And this time, it's not for an escape.

# CHAPTER 24

## CRACKING THE SURFACE

"Hey," I whisper, tapping Milo's shoulder as the SUV pulls up in front of Hotel Di Vaio Milan. "Wake up. We're here."

Milo stirs, slowly sitting upright as he pinches the bridge of his nose. Once he's adjusted to the soft light beaming into the car, he stifles a small yawn, his dreamy gaze flickering around my face.

"Already? I could have slept years if you did not wake me, tesoro."

"Unfortunately, yes." I slide my Kindle into my over-the-shoulder purse as he opens the car door. "Do you feel a little bit better?"

"Much," he says, his tone warmer than the early December sun. He offers me a hand getting out of the vehicle. I roll my shoulders, attempting to loosen the kink in my right blade. He notices. "Are you sore?"

"I mean I *did* have the weight of your inflated ego resting on my shoulder for two hours," I tease him as Marchello, Gio, and Matteo approach us. "So yes, a little sore."

He casts me a playful scowl. "You could have woken me up, Kiara."

"I know." I toss him a coy shrug. "But you just looked so...*tame*."

He raises an amused brow. "Tame?"

"Ye—"

"Milo," Marchello cuts me off as he stops in front of us. He holds out his phone, tilting the screen away from me as Milo reads a text. Or is it a photo? I can't tell. "We should go call Nico immediately."

"No, you can call by yourself." Milo surprises me by linking his fingers through mine, his thumb idly drawing tiny circles on my wrist. "We have several hours before the fundraiser. I want to take Kiara to the Piazza del Duomo."

"What?" I blink, excitement vibrating my body. I didn't think we'd have time to sightsee. Let alone *together*. Maybe he's making up for the three days he was MIA. Whatever his reason, I'll take it. "Really?"

"Gio and Matteo will accompany us." Milo nods at our guards. "Not too close, si?"

Marchello's jaw tightens, disapproval flashing across his face. "Milo, this is important. The Duomo can wait until tomorrow."

"It is a phone call, Marchello," Milo sighs, narrowing his eyes at his underboss. "Are you incapable of pressing keys on a pad by yourself? This is quite worrisome if true."

Marchello stiffens. "Of course, I am capable, Milo, however, I am certain Nico would want to talk to *you* not *me*."

"Nico will talk to whoever I tell him to talk to," Milo states, his voice deeper, commanding. "I trust that you can handle this by yourself. If something went wrong on his trip, then call me. If not, I will see you in several hours."

"But—" Milo glares at Marchello who snaps his mouth shut. "Understood."

"Excellent," Milo murmurs, nodding at the car. "Make sure our luggage gets brought upstairs." He pauses, shooting me a subtle smirk. "Same bedroom."

*Define your relationship.*

I shake my head, banishing Julia's voice from my mind. When the time is right, we'll talk about it. That time is not now. I just want things to be relatively simple. Even if it's for a few hours. A few hours of normal.

"Right away." Marchello glances at me with a tight-lipped smile. "Enjoy the cathedral, Kiara. It is spectacular."

"I will," I say, crinkling my eyes, attempting to exude a friendly vibe. "Thanks."

"*Andiamo,*" Milo says as Marchello stomps away, muttering in Italian under his breath. That man needs a hefty dose of serotonin. So fucking grumpy. "This way."

"Are you sure you're not too busy to do this?" I ask hesitantly as we stroll through the streets of Milan, every single building snatching my attention. I will forever be amazed by European architecture. It's awe-inspiring. "Marchello seemed pretty bothered that you left."

Milo chuckles, weaving us through the sparse crowds of tourists. I suppose December isn't the most popular time of the year to visit Italy.

"That is just how he is, Kiara. I've known Marchello since I was born. If he could go without sleep and solely focus on business operations, he would."

"Everyone needs a break every so often," I muse, taking in the quaint cafes, street performers, and the various Christmas market kiosks. "He's going to burn out if he doesn't relax."

"I believe the word *relax* is not a part of Marchello's

vocabulary," Milo says as we cross the street toward the piazza. "He means well but sometimes even I find him to be overbearing."

"Overbearing is one way to put it," I mutter to myself, a wide grin spreading on my face as the Duomo di Milano comes into view. "Wow. It's so big."

Milo tosses me a sly smirk. "I know."

"Cute." I roll my eyes as we stop in front of the largest church in Italy.

The cathedral is a magnificent feat of gothic engineering. The historical stone structure is wrapped in faded pink Candoglia marble, bright stained-glass windows, and vertical towers and vaults. For such a menacing design, with its sharp edges and ridged points, it conveys an airy sense of light, hope, and beauty.

The parallel isn't lost on me.

"Are we going inside?" I bite my lip. "Do we have time?"

"Whatever you want, tesoro," Milo whispers, sweeping a wayward strand of hair out of my face. "But we cannot stay too long. I want to show you something at sunset."

I cast him a suspicious grin. "What?"

"You'll see," he smirks, motioning to my hip. "Gio will hold your purse."

I narrow my eyes. "Why?"

"They check for weapons," he whispers. "I presume you have your pistol."

Right. This is part of my life now.

"Oh shit, that would have been really bad," I murmur, passing my bag to Gio as Milo discreetly hands Matteo his Beretta. Gio sighs, holding my black leather satchel like it's a bomb. I inwardly roll my eyes. *Men.*

"Ready?" Milo gestures to the cathedral. "Lead the way, Kiara."

I eagerly tug on his hand and drag him to the entrance. I stop in front of the paired door, awing at the bas-relief sculptures depicted on the quatrefoils— the crucifixion, Mary and Jesus, the Annunciation. "Ho-ly shit. This is incredible. I can barely make a sphere out of Play-Doh."

Milo snorts. "Perhaps it is best to avoid such language once we are inside." He cocks his head to the left. "It is a church, Kiara."

I cringe, glancing at the attendant standing by the door. "Did he hear me?"

"I think you are safe." Milo places his hand on the small of my back as he fishes out two tickets from the pocket of his black peacoat. He hands them to the older gentleman manning the entrance. "Grazie."

The fact he already had tickets does something utterly annoying to my heart.

It skips a beat.

*Shit.*

The attendant gives me a careful once over, staring a second too long at my legs.

*How inappropriate.*

"Go ahead," he says after a moment's hesitation. "Enjoy."

"Did he just check me out?" I ask quietly. "Isn't that against their code or something?"

"No, your skirt was *almost* too short, tesoro," Milo hums in my ear as we enter the silent cathedral, only the shuffling of footsteps audible. "There is a dress code."

"Oh," I wince. Awkward. "Right."

The interior of this church is almost too much for the human eye to handle. Endless stone carvings, paintings, and golden statues fill every corner. I could spend hours here. Hours. Where do we start? Is there a map?

"Relax, Kiara," Milo chuckles at my overwhelmed

expression. He leads us down the geometric tiled floor. "Today I will be your guide."

"Really?" I toss him a skeptical look. "What makes you qualified to give me the tour? I think the audio guide might be more educational."

"I am full of surprises." Milo gestures at a sculpture. "Prepare to be impressed."

And for the next two hours, he does just that. Impresses me. No matter what sculpture or painting I point to, Milo has a story, an explanation, a factoid. Knowledge. I eat up every word that rolls off his smooth tongue, truly stunned that he's so well versed in the history of this iconic cathedral that took six centuries to build. *Six.* The patience, the dedication, the craftsmanship, it's mind-blowing.

"What about this one?" I ask, pointing to a statue of an extremely chiseled bald man holding a book. "Do you think St. Bartholomew was *really* that muscular? Or is it like an old-fashioned version of Photoshop?"

I inwardly wince. I hope that question wasn't sacrilegious. I'm genuinely curious as to the accuracy of these depictions. Sorry, Nana.

"I suppose we will never know, tesoro." Milo expels an amused chuckle, checking his watch. "I am afraid we need to leave now; the sun is setting."

I pout. "But we only covered like a third of the church. There's so much more to see."

"We can always return." Milo reaches for my hand. "But right now, we need to go up to the *terrazza.*"

"Oh, I completely forgot there's rooftop access." He starts us toward the staircase that leads to the terrace on top of the cathedral.

"It has one of the best views of *Milano,*" Milo notes as we begin climbing the stairs. "My father used to bring me and Julia here every Spring. It was one of his favorite places."

And now it's one of mine.

"Is that how you know so much about the Duomo? From your father?"

"Everything I know is because of my father. He made sure that my sister and I received the best education. Oftentimes he would conduct the lessons himself if he found our tutors to be inept." He lets out a soft laugh. "Which was quite frequently, if I think of it."

"It sounds like you had a really caring father," I muse as we step out onto the terrace. "Not many children are blessed to have such involved parents."

"That is true." Milo smiles down at me. "I was very lucky."

"I was too," I sigh as we stroll by rows upon rows of statues resting on top of ornamental pinnacles. "My parents were wonderful."

"They must have been," Milo whispers as we reach the vantage point. "Come here." He wraps his arms around my waist. A sorbet sunset and an unobstructed view of the city greets us. "What do you think?"

"It's amazing." I relax into his hold and let out a melancholy breath. "I love sunsets. They remind us that even endings can be beautiful."

Milo rests his chin on top of my head, his arms tightening around me as we watch the vibrant colors melt into each other. "My father used to tell us that if we looked hard enough, we could find beauty even in the most peculiar places."

"Your father sounds like an Italian Dumbledore." I crane my neck up and cast Milo a small grin. "Just a little?"

He closes his eyes, a slight rumble in his chest. "I will take that as a compliment."

"As you should," I smile, biting my lip. "My dad wasn't as um...*articulate* as yours. I think the most poetic piece of advice he ever gave was: roll with the punches unless you got a mean right hook."

"Was your father a fan of boxing?"

"No," I snort. "He was a fan of pretending he was a philosopher. He actually *taught* philosophy at the local high school. I think it was the closest he could get to being Socrates."

"An admirable aspiration," Milo notes, the sky darkening around us. "What did your mother do for a living?"

A forlorn pang grips my chest. "She was a hospice nurse."

"Hmm... It all makes sense now."

I turn around in his arms, tilting my head to the side. "What makes sense?"

He peers down at me, his eyes softened as he caresses my cheek. "You."

"Oh." I manage a small smile as I lean into his palm, a flurry of comforting warmth spreading through my body. "If only *you* were that easy to figure out."

"Trust me, tesoro, I am not as complicated as you think."

He arches down, his lips brushing against mine like a tacit promise that he'll let me in. That there's hope. That I should have faith. And I want to believe him. I really do, but a zebra can't change its stripes no matter how strongly it believes it's a horse.

"You are the definition of complicated," I breathe, pulling away, my lips tingling. "That's a fact."

"No, Kiara." He expels a weakened sigh. "That is a hypothesis."

My gaze flickers across his face, searching for hints of falsity. "So, prove me wrong then."

Even though we're standing inches away, I still feel like we're miles apart. But that can change. He can close the distance. We're *so* close. Just not close enough.

Milo shuts his eyes, ripples flowing down his neck as he swallows. "We should head back to the hotel now," he says, checking his watch. "A ball awaits."

"Right." I walk past him, not wanting him to see the disappointment plastered all over my face. "We wouldn't want to be late."

The walk back to Hotel Di Vaio Milan is silent, charged with a duality of frustration and satisfaction. Of calmness and fear. Of hesitation and resolution.

Complicated.

Marchello and the rest of our entourage are dressed and drinking by the time we step foot into the suite. Well, they're starting early. What else is new?

"I will get ready out here," Milo says, laying his tuxedo out on the white sofa. "The bedroom is yours."

"I won't be long," I say, tossing him a small smile. "Thirty minutes."

He raises a dubious brow as the other men laugh at my timeline. "I will start the clock."

"Go ahead."

Who am I kidding? Thirty minutes is not enough time but I, for one, stick to my promises.

When I shut the bedroom door, I start a timer and transform myself into a jaded Cinderella. Once my hair and make-up are done, I slip on the red chiffon dress Milo bought for the gala and string on some jewelry.

With two minutes left on the timer, I triumphantly waltz out of the bedroom, the seven men in the living room all giving me a cheeky round of applause. Even Marchello is smiling at me. Must be the alcohol.

"Grazie, grazie," I grin, tossing them an elegant curtsy as Milo walks toward me, his covetous gaze flicking around my ensemble. "You like it?"

"Bellissima," he says, stopping in front of me. "Red is definitely your co—" He pauses, his face blanching as his eyes dart to the ruby stone hanging around my neck. "Where did you get that?"

"This?" I look down at the glimmering gem. "Julia and I were going through some of your mom's jewelry this morn—"

"Take it off."

*Prove me wrong.*

# CHAPTER 25

## LIFTING THE FOG

IT'S A SIMPLE QUESTION.

Three letters. Two consonants. One syllable.

Zero chances of getting a simple answer.

The room falls silent as I ask, "Why?"

His skin pales as he stares at me like he's seen a phantom. Blue flames glow in his hooded eyes, the icy heat burning and freezing my skin at the same goddamn time.

"Take it off, Kiara," he says through his teeth. "*Now.*"

"Why?" I whisper again, rolling the ruby heart stone between my thumb and index finger. "Because it's your mom's? It's just a necklace, Milo."

It's more than that. I know. It must be.

A gift from his father? An heirloom? A family jewel? If it were important to Antonia, she would have taken it with her, right? An uneasy knot forms in my stomach. Yes. She would've taken it.

"I do not know how you came to possess that necklace, but it is not my mother's."

Milo sucks in a stabilizing breath, his jaw tensing. Control. He's trying so hard not to explode. He's trying to remain calm in the midst of inner chaos. He's trying to not yell at me. He's trying *so* fucking hard.

For me.

"Take it off," he repeats himself, desperation trembling his hoarse voice. *"Please."*

A glass shatters in the distance.

I don't look. I don't care. All I want is for Milo to stop staring at me like I'm causing him physical pain. Agony. It's hurting me to see him like this. It's pricking my fucking heart.

And I hate that.

"Okay." Worry ripples down my throat as I wind my arms behind my neck and unclip the gold chain. *Not his mother's.* Dangling the necklace above Milo's palm, I ask, holding my breath, "Whose is it?"

Let me in. Please. Prove me wrong. I *want* to be wrong. Destroy my preconceived notions. Pummel my expectations. Wash away my prejudice, my fears, my worries.

Please.

Let me the fuck in.

Milo winces, snapping his fingers shut as I drop the chain in his hand. His fist vibrates like it hurts to hold, to touch, to remember.

He hesitates for a second, his gaze flitting across my pleading face before revealing, in a raw, coarse tone, "It belonged to someone who is no longer in my life."

"Oh," I hum, blinking at the dreary man in front of me as my stomach churns. He had a *someone.* A woman. A woman who has clearly left her mark. A dark, lingering stain on his guarded heart. "Okay."

But it's not okay. Not one bit.

Milo flicks his fingers in the air as he calls out, "Gio." His soldier appears by his side in an instant. Milo hands him the necklace. "Get rid of it. I don't want to see this ever again."

A giant stain.

Gio nods, fisting the chain. "Right away."

When my guard steps away, I tilt my head. "Are you alright?" I rest my hand on his rising chest, his heart beating into my open palm, fast, unsteady, frantic. "I'm sorry—"

Marchello clears his throat, drawing our attention. "We should head downstairs now," he states, stepping over broken glass. "People are expecting us."

"Yes." Milo casts me a weary glance and slowly reaches for my hand as we head out of the suite. "We should go."

He adjusts his grip, tightening his fingers around mine like he's afraid I'll fly away, disappear, turn into a ghost.

"I'm not going anywhere," I whisper under my breath, keeping my gaze on the tiled floor as we step into the elevator. "I promise."

Milo doesn't respond as he watches the numbers descend on the digital monitor. Maybe he didn't hear me. Maybe he doesn't care. Maybe the owner of the necklace has tarnished something I didn't know I wanted. Maybe this is it. This is all he can give me. A fragment. A sliver. A tainted shard of his broken heart.

Maybe it's enough.

It has to be.

When the elevator doors ping open, we make our way into the Royal Ballroom situated on the fifth floor. Muted laughter, soulful jazz, and the scent of roses overpower my dull senses as we enter the extravagant ballroom. Red florals decorate every table, thematic silk drapes converge at the center of the ceiling, dim atmospheric burgundy beams of light reflect off the faces of every guest.

"What now?" I ask Milo as he leads us through the hordes of people.

"Now we mingle," Milo murmurs lifelessly, expelling a labored sigh as he lets go of my hand. "We make our presence known."

When I was a little girl, I always dreamed of going to a ball. I dreamed of wearing a beautiful gown. I dreamed of dancing with a prince. But dreams are simply that, dreams. This isn't that sort of ball. Milo isn't that kind of prince. And this isn't a fairytale.

This is business.

Hours pass by as Milo drags me from table to table, introducing me to politicians, legislators, diplomats, the elite. I'm his friend. Just a friend. A friend that he refuses to touch or look at for more than two seconds. It's like I'm his accessory for the night. Like a luxury watch. A couture cuff-link. Merely there for show, for status, for decoration.

"If you'll excuse us," Milo says, smiling politely at the uppity couple we've been chatting with for the last ten minutes. "Enjoy the rest of your evening." For the first time in three hours, Milo dares to put his hand on the small of my back as he leads us out onto the terrace. "Is everything alright, Kiara?"

"Everything is great," I mutter, a gust of wind nipping my skin as we step out on the stone balcony. "Just great."

"You are cold." Milo frowns, pulling out a sleek black cigarette case from his pocket. "Here." He pops a Marlboro between his lips as he shrugs off his tuxedo jacket and drapes it over my shoulders. We side-step the entrance, settling in the corner of the patio near the ashtray. "Is that better?"

"Mhmm..." I lean against the glass windows as he lights his cigarette, the combination of his sweet cologne and the ashy cloud of chemicals filling my lungs. It shouldn't be comforting, but it is. "All better."

"I take it you are not having a good time," Milo astutely observes, blowing the smoke away from me.

I cross my arms. "Seeing as this is the longest conversation we've had all night, no, I am not having a good time." I tilt my head. "Are *you?*"

Milo closes his eyes, the crackling of the cherry burning filling the silence. "No, I am not."

"Well, at least we're on the same page." I let out a deep sigh. "Listen, you've been acting weird all night. Is it because of the necklace? I'm sorry for putting it on but I didn't know—"

"I know," he whispers, clenching his teeth. "You did nothing wrong, tesoro. I just—" He freezes as a gorgeous server with caramel-colored hair and a scowl on her face approaches us, a tray of champagne flutes in hand. "Cazzo."

"Mr. *Di Vaio,*" she slews in Italian, her judgmental gaze darting between the two of us. Her eyes linger on the jacket wrapped around my shoulders for a second too long before she continues. "*It's been a while. How are you?*"

"*Catarina,*" Milo says, the muscles in his neck tensing. "*I was not aware you would be working tonight.*"

"*This evening is full of surprises,*" she says, glancing at me, disgust written all over her face. "*Who is your friend?*"

"*This is Kiara,*" Milo replies in Italian. "*She's from America.*"

I smile, swallowing away the bitter taste in my mouth. The show must go on.

Catarina lets out a curt scoff. "*So soon? Have you already forgotten the last one?*"

Who the fuck is this woman?

"*Be very careful with your words, Catarina.*" Milo takes a

purposeful step forward, towering over the petite brunette. *"Remember who you are talking to."*

Her jaw clenches. *"I know exactly who you are, Milo. You are the angel of death. I am reminded of that fact every time I pass my sister's empty room."*

*"You should leave,"* Milo states, his expression darkening. *"Before you say something you might regret."*

Catarina takes a step back, turning her head toward me. "If you value your life," she says in English, "you will run. Fast. And never look back."

"Catarina!" Milo fumes. "Do not—"

"Have a good night," she cuts him off, turning on her heel and disappearing through the balcony doors.

I blink, taking in her ominous warning. "Who was that?"

Is that the owner of the necklace? An ex-girlfriend? She mentioned a sister? What sister? What happened? I'm so lost.

"Milo?"

Sixty excruciating seconds of silence hang in the air as Milo stays muted, staring out into the glowing cityscape. I chew on my bottom lip, trepidation bubbling inside my esophagus, making me ill, nauseous, scared.

"She is right," Milo finally whispers, running a hand through his hair as he turns away from me. "You should run. I will make sure you are protected wherever you go."

"Is that what you want?" My heart drops into a deep pit of panic. "You want me to leave?"

"Yes."

"Liar." I bite the inside of my cheek, my eyes glossing over. "You don't mean that."

With his back turned to me, he states, "I no longer require your services. Leave, Kiara. It is the smart thing to do."

"Who was she?" I don't budge, planting my heels firm on the ground. "Talk to me."

"A reminder that nothing good ever lasts," Milo whispers, still refusing to look at me. "Go. You are free now."

"No."

"Kiara, pleas—"

*Pop!*

Milo spins around, slamming my back against the window, shielding my body as a loud snap sounds from afar.

"Woah..." I press my palms against his heaving chest. His ragged, uneven breath fans against my forehead. "It's okay. Relax. It was just champagne."

"I thought it was—" he falters, wrapping his arms around my shoulders. He pulls me flush against his trembling body and presses his warm lips against my forehead. "Kiara..."

He thought it was a gunshot. He—

"You want me to leave yet you're willing to throw yourself in front of a bullet for me?" I grip his shirt with all my strength. *Don't fly away.* "What do you want from me, Milo? You need to decide."

I just did.

I don't want to leave. I want to be here. Not because I'm scared. Not because I'm in danger. Not because I have no choice. I want to be here because of him. Because of Milo. Because for the first time in weeks, I'm lucid. I'm *here.* And I don't want to be anywhere else.

"What do you want?" I ask again. "What do you want, Milo?"

"I—I cannot lose you," he whispers across my forehead. "I can't."

"You won't." I tilt my head back, caressing his stubbled cheek with my hand as I state in a breathy tone, "I'm right here."

He swallows, leaning into my palm, his eyes fluttering shut. "If you stay with me, people will try to hurt you. They will kill you—"

"I trust you to keep me safe." I meet his solemn gaze. "You'll protect me."

Milo shakes his head, the sharp edge of his jaw clenching. "I might not always be able to protect you, tesoro."

"I know that." I push myself up on my tippy toes and snake my arms around his neck, my fingers raking through his hair. "But it's a risk I'm willing to take."

"You are not a gambler," he breathes against my parted lips. "And I am a big risk."

"I like the odds." A low, building current courses through my body, not too overpowering, not too dull, just right. "I like them a lot."

"What happened to my pessimist?"

I manage a small smile. "She found something to believe in."

Conflict flashes across Milo's face for a millisecond as he cups my cheek, his thumb grazing my jawline. "What is it *you* want, Kiara? From me?"

"I want you," I reply honestly. And I mean every single word. "All of you."

"I am not a good person, tesoro, you said so yourself," Milo whispers, his soft touch making me dizzy. "I will hurt you one way or another."

"Maybe I like the pain." I press my body closer to him, my brain no longer filtering the words spilling out of my mouth. "It's better to feel something than nothing at all."

He drags his thumb along my lips, his gaze darkening as he scans my face like he's trying to read ancient Sanskrit, like he's struggling to understand me. "And what is it that you feel, tesoro?"

My chest rises with aching need as I writhe under his touch, heat collecting in my stomach. "I feel like we should go upstairs."

He hesitates for a moment before whispering, with absolute resolution, "Whatever you want, Kiara. It is yours."

*You need to decide what you want from him. And once you do, take it.*

And so, I do.

## Chapter 26

## Tapestry of Trust

THE PAST SEVERAL WEEKS HAVE BEEN TEMPESTUOUS, chaotic, unyielding with trauma and temptation.

The days were wild, tensions were high, and we were wrapped in emotional armor.

We were unwilling to shed our masks, unable to free ourselves from the shackles of fear.

We were trapped in the second circle of hell.

Until now.

As we slowly undress each other, the world seems to still, all the noise fading away until we're the only two people on earth.

Just us.

Moonlight reflects off Milo's face as he feasts upon my lips, his fingers gripping the roots of my hair, his hand tracing the soft edges of my curves.

Our tongues mesh and melt and meld together in heavenly perfection; every flick, every lick, every kiss more powerful, more intimate, more tender than anything I've ever experienced or will ever experience in my whole life.

*Whatever you want, Kiara, it is yours.*

And it *is* mine. I can feel it. It's in the way he's touching me, it's in his shallow breathing, it's in the melodic beating of his heart. It's in his lingering kiss.

I can *taste* his promise. It tingles my lips. It fills my heart with faith.

Milo pulls back, brushing his nose against mine as he rasps, "*Resta con me per sempre.*"

My breath hitches as I meet his dusky eyes, my heart thudding in my chest. "If you want me to stay with you forever," I whisper, gliding my palms over the taut, muscular ridges of his shoulders. "Don't give me a reason to leave."

Milo closes his eyes, his jaw clenching as he cups my cheek, his thumb grazing my lips. "I cannot promise that, tesoro. There will be days where you will loathe me and wish me dead."

At least he's being honest.

"Okay, in that case—" I guide him to the edge of the bed, my calves bumping against the king-sized mattress. "Instead of giving me a reason to leave, give me a reason to stay."

"That—" Milo lowers me down on the sateen sheets, hovering over me as his erection feathers my midsection. "I can do."

Anticipation and arousal collect in my belly as Milo settles himself between my legs, parting my thighs. I expel an airy moan, fisting the bedding as his tongue sails across my succulent folds, whirling, teasing, nipping at my sex.

"Oh my God," I whimper, lacing my fingers through Milo's hair, keeping him in place as he quickens his pace, sucking savagely on my swollen clit. "Fuck, yes. More. Please. *Oh my God.*"

"More?" A guttural groan escapes the back of his throat as he curls two fingers inside of me, pushing in and out in steady, controlled motions. "Is this what you want, Kiara?"

"Yes! Fuck!" He reaches my G-spot, expertly pushing me closer to the edge until a divine flash of release blinds me. My legs tremble as I come all over his lapping lips. "Holy shit..."

With a wolfish grin on his face, Milo peers up at me from between my legs, his mouth glistening with my juices. He licks his bottom lip, smirking. "I am not finished with you."

"I know," I breathe in a languorous state, grabbing onto Milo's neck and pulling him flush against my sated body. "Not even close."

I rain wet kisses down the slope of his neck as his arms wind around my waist. Rotating our bodies, Milo nibbles on my earlobe, his hands kneading my breasts, pinching my nipples. The sharp sensation of his touch spears heat into my aching core as I slide my hand down the length of his torso, curling my fingers around his pulsing erection.

A low moan tumbles from his lips, his cock twitching in my hand as I dip down and drag my tongue along his hard shaft, leaving streaks of saliva on every bit of his pink veiny flesh.

I don't tease him. No. I give him *everything* he wants but I take my time. We have *so* much fucking time. Milo sweeps my hair off to the side so he can look at me as I taste him, savor him, consume every last inch of his cock.

"Come here, tesoro," he rasps, caressing my hairline as my head bobs up and down, my hand stroking the wetted girth of his dick. "I want to feel you."

Milo sits up, running his hands over every crevice of my sensitive body as I straddle him, my wet sex rubbing against his throbbing cock. He grips the base of his shaft and lines it up at my entrance as he devours my lips in deep, passionate, celestial fucking kisses.

There's something different about the way he's holding me. There's no aggression, no dominance, no power.

It's balanced. Even. Harmonic.

"Oh, fuck." Milo lets out a wanton growl as I sink down on his length, my walls stretching to accommodate his size. "Kiara—"

"Mmm..." I swallow his hoarse groans as I move my hips, an orchestra of slapping flesh and mutual moans of pleasure permeating the air around us.

With our naked bodies woven together in a tapestry of trust, we move in blissful unison, heady, sweet sweat filling our lungs. Euphoric pants and gasps blow between our swollen lips as I drag my nails against his back, his shoulders, his neck.

I whimper as Milo switches the angle, thrusting his cock deep inside me as he tugs on my hair, tilting my head, and forcing my eyelids to spring open. My chest heaves as we stare into each other's eyes, picking up speed, my insides on the verge of ethereal spasm.

"Yes," Milo roars, latching onto my nipple, his thumb circling my clit as my walls clench around his cock. *Oh, God.* My head snaps back from elevated jubilation. "Come, baby. Come for me."

And with those words, I come undone, screaming out his name as I shake in his arms. Milo pumps faster, my body trembling with tranquility as he seeks his own erupting release.

With one final thrust, Milo spills inside of me, capturing my lips, groaning into my mouth, his body sticking to mine as his dick twitches within me.

With tangled limbs and rising chests, we topple over, basking in the glow of satisfaction and comfort.

We remain silent, speechless, because there's nothing more to say.

We've said it all.

After a few minutes of quiet recuperation, we clean ourselves off and climb back into bed. Milo draws me closer to his chest, my head resting on his shoulder as he secures me in his arms.

"You are tired, tesoro." Milo kisses my temple as I float my fingers up and down the bumpy texture of the healed scars on his arm. "We should sleep."

Having barely survived such an emotionally draining and tumultuous day, I *should* be tired. Yet, I'm not. I don't want to be. I don't want to sleep. Not yet. I want to hold on to this moment for a little while longer.

I trace a long closed-up wound on one of his triceps. "What happened here? It looks old."

"It is," Milo confirms in a distant tone, his mind wandering. "I fell out of a tree trying to keep up with my brother."

"You climbed trees with your brother?" I tilt my head up and kiss the underside of his jaw. "How precious."

Almost normal.

"I was seven at the time and Sergio was ten." A small, cynical chuckle slips from his lips. "He was very ambitious, even as a child."

I swallow, nuzzling my head deeper into his soft chest, no shields in sight. "What do you mean?"

"He always wanted more," Milo whispers, lazily playing with my fingers. "He wanted to climb the highest, run the furthest, lift the heaviest." A pause. "Ambition, it is a dangerous trait in this life."

"How so?"

Milo closes his eyes, inhaling a deep sobering breath. "When my father passed away, Sergio was more than happy to be named the new head of the family. He always wanted more power, more money, more control. He had a vision for us. That we would dominate the world, not just Italy."

I continue to caress Milo's lithe body as he lets me in, as he demonstrates his trust. "Did he succeed?"

"For the most part, yes." Milo expels a sardonic scoff. "Our hotel and casino business was growing steadily in Italy, but Sergio did not care about borders, he wanted to expand operations into neighboring countries. Over the years we had forged alliances across Europe, and he believed that they would be more than willing to cooperate."

"Like Manuel and Henri?" I ask, a shiver seizing my spine. Milo pulls the duvet over my chest as he cocoons me tighter in his arms.

"Exactly," Milo replies, the heat of his body warming mine. "He managed to secure agreements with gangs in France, Spain, Germany, and Poland. They would use our hotels and casinos to launder profits while we took a small percentage. It was a well-thought-out plan. Everything was fine until—" Milo swallows. "Until he decided he wanted to run Moscow."

The Russians.

"What went wrong?"

"Everything." His muscles tense. "We had no allies in Russia but Sergio didn't care, he thought he was invincible. Without consulting the family, he set up operations in Moscow. It took many months before the Pravda faction of the brotherhood found out about it but once they did—" He shakes his head. "It all went south."

I listen intently, rejoicing in the fact I'm finally getting the full story. "What happened? What went wrong?"

"*Pravda*. They requested a meeting with my brother. One-on-one. Igor, their leader, was adamant that it was only the two of them. I knew it was a bad idea. Marchello and I tried so hard to get Sergio to listen to us, but he was stubborn, high on power, on greed."

"So, he went alone?" I swallow. "And they killed him?"

"Yes," Milo croaks. "Sergio was gone for a whole week, no communication. We thought perhaps they were negotiating terms but then we received a package."

My eyes widen. "Oh, God..."

"It was a blue rose," Milo says lifelessly. "With his name carved into the stem. Their signature. They kept his body. They always keep the body. We—We couldn't give him a proper burial."

"I'm so sorry, Milo." I clench my teeth together, my eyes glossing over. "That's horrible. Everyone deserves a chance to say goodbye."

"I agree," Milo continues, his chest rising. "That is why I wanted to meet with Igor. In exchange for my brother's body, I would pull our operations out of Moscow. Sergio was naive and arrogant to think he could fight the brotherhood. I knew better. I did not want a war. I did not want to make the same mistakes my brother made." He pauses. "But then, right before I was going to make the call—" He looks down at me and tucks my hair behind my ear, his pained eyes flickering across my face. "They did something very foolish."

I blink, my throat closing up as I ask, "What?"

With anguish glowing his irises, Milo's jaw clenches. "At the time of Sergio's passing, I was with a woman, Vittoria." He chokes out the words like they're poison. "We had not been together very long, but she was there for me when he died. I—I cared for her."

And the pieces fall into place. A messy, dark place. One that leaves me uneasy, sick, worried.

Am I a rebound? A consolation prize? A distraction?

"The um—" I clear my throat. "The necklace was hers? V—" I stammer, her name like a dagger on my tongue. "Vittoria's?"

"Yes." Regret flashes across his falling face. "And the woman from the gala, Catarina, she is her sister." He lets out a shaky breath. "Catarina has many reasons to despise me, if her sister never met me, she would be alive."

"It's not your fault, Milo." I graze his stubble with the back of my hand, my heart aching for him. "You weren't the one who killed her."

Milo winces. "She disappeared, Kiara, from my own territory. I didn't even notice her absence until I received the rose. It *is* my fault. I couldn't protect her. I couldn't keep her safe."

Thick, tense air surrounds us as we lay together, intertwined in sadness and memories. My mind races, matching the speed of my beating heart.

"Did you love her?" I whisper, dreading to hear the answer.

He must have, right?

"I thought I did," Milo hums, his hot breath blowing against my temple. "But now, I am not sure."

I tilt my head up, my eyebrows drawn together. "But you started a war because of her. If you didn't love her, then why—"

"Reputation." Milo shifts uncomfortably under the covers. "There was no option but to retaliate."

Is he trying to convince me? Or himself?

"How did you retaliate?" I ask hesitantly. "What did you do? I remember um, Andre, he uh—mentioned guns or something."

Milo nods, avoiding my gaze. "We intercepted some of their arms shipments."

I cast him a wary frown. "I thought you don't traffic guns."

"We don't."

"Then where are the guns? What did you do with the shipments?"

"They're stored in a secure location." Milo shrugs, stifling a yawn. "Perhaps in the future, I will sell them to government agencies at cost. I have not yet decided."

"Government agencies aren't going to buy guns from the mafia," I say, wildly confused by his business plan. "That's illegal."

"You are adorable, tesoro," he says, a weak smile on his face. "We are not the only corrupt organization in the world. This should not be surprising for you to hear." A beat. "Money controls morals, Kiara. It always has and it always will."

Deep down, I know this to be true. It's the unfortunate reality we live in. Money over everything.

Wealth wins.

Always.

"How does this war end?" I ask, holding Milo a little tighter. "*When* will it end?"

"Soon, tesoro." Milo's soft gaze pierces mine as his lips curl into a fragile smile. "Very soon."

"You seem confident."

"I am," Milo hums into my ear. "Everything will go back to normal soon. I promise you."

"Okay," I murmur, unable to keep my eyes open. "If you say so."

What is normal?

"Go to sleep, tesoro," Milo whispers. "We can talk more in the morning."

"I want to go back to the Duomo tomorrow," I say, cuddling up to his body. "I want to watch the sunset again."

"We are here for two more days. We can watch all the sunsets you want."

"I love sunsets," I mutter, fatigue flowing through my veins.

"Me too..." He presses his warm lips against my forehead. "Sleep, tesoro."

*My father used to tell us that if we looked hard enough, we could find beauty even in the most peculiar places.*

Like in a broken man with a broken heart.

Or in a lonely girl who doesn't want to be alone.

Or in the chance encounter that brought them together.

Or in the storm that might blow them apart.

# CHAPTER 27

## GIFT OF THE PRESENT

EVEN THOUGH ENGLISH IS REFERRED TO AS THE universal language, it has many limitations. There are hundreds of beautiful words in foreign languages that describe emotions, senses, and experiences that are simply ineffable in my native tongue.

In Arabic, the word *ya'arburnee* is the hopeful declaration that you will die before someone you love deeply, because you can't stand to live without them. In German, the word, *waldeinsamkeit* describes the feeling of solitude and connectedness to nature when being alone in the woods. And in Norwegian, the word *forelsket* is the euphoria experienced as you begin to fall in love.

*Forelsket*. Could it be? Or is it merely infatuation? Fascination? Admiration?

Stockholm Syndrome? *Hah*. Possible but highly unlikely.

Leaning against the door frame, a stupid grin on my face, I soak in the sight of the gorgeously complex man in front of me. There are no words to describe how I feel as I watch him read the daily paper.

Grateful, perhaps, that he opened up about his brother? Hesitant, that he just recently lost a woman he cared for? Happy, that he finally trusts me enough to share? Hopeful, that this is the start of something new?

Something exciting, different, potentially world-defying?

All I know is that I've never felt like this before. It's as if my body went through an emotional cleanse overnight. I've flushed out the toxins, the bacteria, the filth of days past. And despite the fact his heart might not be solely mine, at least not right now, I feel renewed, refurbished, ready.

Ready for a new chapter in a story that's been told a thousand times. From Tolstoy to Shakespeare to Austen. Girl meets boy. It's how it always starts.

And the ending? I just pray that it's not Shakespearean.

A calming sense of comfort flows through my veins as I traipse toward the dining room table. Milo snaps his head up from the newspaper in his hand, his glistening eyes giving a slow once-over.

"Good morning, bella," he smiles, lifting a brow as I adjust the white button-up draped over my body. "Is that my shirt?"

"Yeah." I blush, inhaling the familiar oaky scent of his cologne that's seeped into the fabric. My favorite smell. "It was the first thing I could find. I hope that's okay."

"More than okay," he hums, licking his lips. How I envy that tongue. "It looks much nicer on you than on me."

"Obviously," I grin, rolling my eyes as I take a seat next to Milo and pour myself a cup of coffee from the French press. I look around the empty suite. "Where is everyone?"

"They are on an assignment." Milo passes me a plate of pastries. "They'll be back soon."

"Assignment?" I ask, taking a sip of espresso. "Do I want to know?"

"No, you do not." Milo checks his phone, a tiny frown marring his eyebrows. "But if everything goes according to plan, we will not have to worry about the Russians for much longer."

This doesn't make sense. After what happened in Monaco, I expected havoc to ensue. How is the war already ending? It barely even started. Or maybe it did, and I simply wasn't privy to that information. Either way, I'm grateful that it's almost over.

Grateful and a tad scared. It shouldn't be this easy. Something is amiss.

"Oh," I hum suspiciously, dipping a chocolate glazed biscotti into the espresso. "Whatever you're up to, it sounds dangerous."

"Do not worry, tesoro." His velvety voice suffocates my anxiety. "You are not in any danger."

"Is Marchello?" He's usually always with us. His absence, though appreciated, is unnerving. "Will he be okay?"

Milo lets out an amused laugh. "Marchello is a skilled man, Kiara. He will be perfectly fine." Folding the newspaper in half and placing it on the table, Milo leans closer to me. "That being said, we have two whole days to ourselves."

"No business? Just us?"

"I might have to answer a couple of calls, but other than that, no business." He reaches for my hand, his thumb caressing the underside on my wrist. "I am all yours."

"You are?" I meet his gentle gaze as my heart flutters in my chest like it's full of Monarch butterflies. "Mine?"

"Yes." The confirmation of his affection makes my head buzz with contentment. "Only yours."

"Good," I say, suppressing a satisfied smile. "I don't like to share."

"Neither do I," Milo says with a covetous grin. "So, Kiara, what would you like to do for the next few days?"

"Other than you?" I cock my head to the side. A glimmer of darkened lust flashes across his face. "I want to do everything. I know that might be impossible in two days, but we can try, right?"

"If you keep licking your lips, tesoro—" A mischievous smirk spreads on his face. "We might not have time to do anything other than fuck."

I clear my throat, casting him a playful scowl. "I can fuck you whenever I want, Milo, but the Christmas market only runs for two weeks."

He lets out a deep laugh. "You would rather walk around in the cold and look at handmade ornaments than spend the day in bed with me?"

"Mhmm. There's also music and drinks and food. I've always wanted to try *firunatt*."

Milo stands up and circles the table. "You are making me quite hungry, Kiara."

"Here." I hold a piece of biscotti over my shoulder as he runs his fingers through my tangled hair. "Have a snack."

He dips down, snapping the chocolate tip off the almond pastry with his teeth. *Double shit.* "Delicious," he coos into my ear, his hot breath blowing against my neck. *Bastard.* "Now for the main course."

"Milo—" Before I can feign protest, he swoops me up into his arms, knocking my chair down in his impulsive wake. I wrap my arms around his neck, glowering at him. "I wasn't done eating yet."

"I can think of a few things to put into your mouth," he rasps across my lips as he carries me into the bedroom.

"I—"

Milo drags his wet tongue along the slope of my neck. *Who am I kidding? The Christmas market will be there in an hour.* His warm palm circles my tender breasts as he kicks open the bedroom door. *Four hours.* He rolls my stiff nipples between his skilled fingers. *Tomorrow.* He drops me on the bed and removes his shirt, peering down at me with his goddamn sexy eyes.

Fucking hell, we can always come back next year.

"Cara!" Julia exclaims, dashing toward me and Milo as we enter the estate. "How I've missed you!"

"You need to find some new friends, Julia," Milo huffs, wrapping his arms around my waist as Gio brings our luggage inside and disappears down the hall with the rest of the men. "Kiara will be very busy from now on. I intend to take up most of her time."

"Shut up little brother and let me give her a hug." Julia yanks my wrist, pulling me into her arms as she sways me back and forth. "How was *Milano*? What did you do? Did you go to *Castello Sforzesco*? *Teatro Alla Scala*? Oh, did he take you to *Galleria Vittorio Emanuele*? I love it there, so beautiful."

"Uh—" I stammer, clearing my throat. "He took me to a lot of *very* magical places."

None of them were outside our hotel room but they were magical.

Otherworldly.

"Hmm." Julia pulls back, frowning as her inspective gaze floats down my body. "You are standing weird, wobbly, what happened to you? Are you sick? Hurt?"

Oh, God. Is that obvious? This is what happens when you try to mimic a contortionist. Idiot. The body is only meant to bend at certain angles. Never again.

Milo expels a knowing chuckle. I shoot him a glare. Fucking deviant.

"No, no!" I let out a nervous laugh, my cheeks burning up. "It was just a long drive."

"Alright," Julia says dubiously. "Well, dinner will be ready at eight. You will join us, no?"

"Of course, she will," Milo interjects, draping his arm around my shoulder and kissing my temple. "Right, Kiara?"

"Right..." I lean into his embrace. Dinner. With the whole family. For the first time. Not a big deal. No big deal. "I'll be there."

"Ah!" Julia claps her hands. "Excellent! I will inform Teresa to set another spot at the table."

"Next to me." Milo meets his sister's surprised expression. "On the right."

Julia blinks. "*Are you sure?*" she asks in Italian. Did she forget I can understand? "Milo—"

Milo nods, glancing down at me with a warm smile. "Yes, I am positive."

I purse my lips, my brows knitted together in confusion. "What's going on? What are you talking about?"

"Nothing, cara." Julia presses her lips into a thin line, her bright eyes glinting with approval. "Forget about it. Go get dressed and I'll see you at dinner, yes?"

"Okay..." My gaze darts between the two siblings who seem to be in on the same joke. "See you later, I guess."

"Go go," Julia says, shooing us up the stairs. "I must go get the good wine!"

Am I missing something?

"Care to explain what just happened?" I ask Milo as we

make our way up the stairs. "Why is Julia getting the good wine?"

"You are so full of questions, tesoro," Milo chuckles, kissing my knuckles as we round the staircase. "Let your mind relax. Just for a moment."

I let out a grumbled sigh. "It's hard to relax when you speak in code half the time."

"Don't worry," Milo laughs. "Soon you will be fluent in mafia. Give it a few weeks, you will catch on."

"I could catch on much quicker if you just translated for me. What is the significance of me sitting on your right? Tell me."

We stop at the top of the stairs. "It means that I care for you, tesoro," Milo says, brushing my hair behind my ear. "It means you are my woman."

His woman. Officially.

"So, it's like the Mob equivalent of changing your relationship status on Facebook?" A wave of clouded elation washes over me. "Something like that?"

Milo snorts. "Yes, Kiara, something like that."

"Good to know." I nod, biting my lip. Oh, God. This is a monumental step in our relationship. Am I ready? I am, right? A sheen of sweat covers my palms as I let out a small breath. "Is this going to go over well with the others? Or should I expect lots of judgmental stares?"

"Let them stare," Milo says nonchalantly, leading us into my bedroom. I lean against the vanity table as he continues. "The decision is mine, not theirs." He pauses. "And yours, of course." He tilts his head, scanning my antsy face. "This is what you want, is it not?"

When I was attempting to learn Mandarin, I came across the word *yuánfèn*; it loosely means fated coincidence or the fate between two people. I believe that I was fated to meet Milo. I was meant to be at the bank when he came in. Our lives were meant to collide.

But there's also a proverb in Mandarin, *yǒu yuán wú fèn*, which means have fate without destiny. Two people can be fated to meet but are not destined to stay together.

What a depressing proverbial sentiment. Awful, really.

I stare deep into Milo's rich brown eyes and pray to the heavens that our meeting was not some twisted karmic joke. I've lost too many people. There's no one left. I can't lose him too. Like with everything else in my life, this cannot fall apart. It has to last. It needs to transcend chance and circumstance.

Please. Let it last.

"Yes," I whisper, pressing my hand against his chest, his heartbeat reverberating into my palm. "It's what I want."

"*Grazie a Dio,*" he whispers, grazing his rough thumb along my cheek.

And I do. I thank Him for letting me find beauty in such a peculiar place.

With a smile on his face, Milo arches down, his lips melting against mine as he sucks all the oxygen out of my lungs. His touch filters away the hesitation, the doubts, the what ifs. His kiss deepens and my lungs are full again. Full of air that is pure, tender, devoted. Air that defies all logic and reason. Air that tethers us together. Air that makes me feel safe. Wanted. Cherished. Air that makes me want to keep breathing. That makes me want to keep living. Because I don't feel alone. Not now.

Not when I'm with him.

"Mmm," I hum in bliss, my hand slipping off the vanity table as Milo pulls back. Staggering to the side, I knock over a tray of jewelry. "Shit." I squat down, collecting the rings and necklaces sprawled all over the floor. I frown, tossing the last piece of jewelry into the ceramic bowl, a burst of anxiety gripping my heart. "My grandmother's locket. It's not here."

"I was hoping you wouldn't notice," Milo sighs as I stand up. "I was going to wait but—" He folds up a finger. "Give me a moment. I'll be right back."

I cast him a puzzled look. "What? Why?"

"Just stay there, Kiara," Milo says, exiting my room. "Do not move."

Crossing my arms, I tap my foot impatiently as I wait for him to return. What is he up to now?

With his hands behind his back, Milo strides toward me, a sly grin on his face. "Turn around, tesoro."

"Why?"

Milo lets out an exasperated sigh. "Kiara, please, just do as I say."

"Fine." I turn around and face the oval vanity, meeting Milo's gaze in the mirror as he dangles my nana's locket from his fingers. "I can't wear it, Milo, remember?"

"Hold up your hair, tesoro."

"Milo, I'm serious, I'll break out in hives."

He pinches the bridge of his nose. "Trust me, Kiara. You will be fine."

"I doubt it," I murmur, reluctantly pulling my hair into a bun as Milo clips the locket around my neck. When the icy metal hits my chest, I flinch, peering down at the shiny necklace. "Did you get this cleaned? It looks different."

"I had it dipped in white gold," Milo explains as I twirl the locket in my fingers.

"What?!" I spin around.

"This necklace seemed very important to you, Kiara. I wanted you to be able to wear it."

"When did you—"

"Weeks ago."

My eyes gloss over as I clutch the locket in my fist, my grandmother's positive energy coursing through my veins. She's here. With me.

"I can't believe you did this. You—" I bite the inside of my cheek. "This is the last piece of jewelry I have from my grandmother, I had to sell everything else when she died. Milo—" Tears roll down my face. "Thank you."

He frowns, wiping away the influx of joyful tears. "You had to sell everything? I do not understand."

"When my nana died, I got a letter in the mail," I explain, swallowing back the memories. "Apparently, we were living off credit. I didn't know. She told me we were fine, that we had money, but I guess she lied or she forgot, I don't know." I expel a shaky breath. "Her mental health had been deteriorating for years, it got even worse after my grandpa passed away. I wish she told me, she said everything was fine."

Milo pulls me into his arms, resting his chin on top of my head as he consoles me. "Perhaps she did not want to trouble you, Kiara. She did not want to make you worry."

"Probably," I sniffle, nuzzling my head into his chest. "Sounds like Nana Anne."

"Do you have any more debt?" he whispers, stroking my hair. "I will pay it all."

"No." I shake my head, stifling back aching sobs. "I paid it off by selling off most of her belongings. She had a lot of vintage collections. They meant a lot to her, and I sold them. I—I sold everything."

"I'm so sorry, tesoro," Milo hums, his voice raw, gruff, full of empathy. "That must have been very difficult."

"It was." An unfathomable longing tugs at my heart. "God, I miss her."

He rocks me back and forth. "It will get easier. It takes time, but it will get easier, I promise you."

"Yeah?" I pull back, wiping my nose on my sleeve. "How much time?"

He tucks a damp hair behind my ear as his soft eyes dance across my face. "The pain will never go away, Kiara, but you will learn to live with it. And in time, that pain will be a blessing, not a burden. It will make you stronger." I hiccup as he continues, "When a bone is broken, the place in which it heals becomes the strongest part."

"Is that why you're so strong?" I whisper. "Because you've been broken?"

"We are all broken, tesoro. Every single person. But some people ignore the pain and never heal. You must acknowledge your wounds, for they are a part of you. Forever."

"I get that—" I nod my head, taking in his wise words. "But sometimes it's easier to ignore the pain than address it."

"I know. But we must try, otherwise, we die long before we are dead."

"Wow." I sniffle, giving him a small smile. "My dad would've really liked you."

"He would?" Milo perks a brow. "Why?"

I shake my head, letting out a soft chuckle. "He was also an optimist."

"Can you please relay that message to my sister?" Milo laughs, kissing my forehead. "She is convinced I am full of negative energy. She once bought sage to cleanse my aura."

I stifle a snort. "I think an exorcism would be more fruitful."

"Is that so?" Milo casts me a playful grin. "Do you believe I am possessed?"

"Only sometimes."

"Fair..." Milo purses his lips. "I suppose life is all about balance, no?"

I let out a deep breath. "Yeah. All about balance."

After a moment of comfortable silence, Milo asks, "Do you still want to join us for dinner?"

"Yes," I state with absolute certainty. "I do."

"Alright, I will let you change." He pauses, hesitating for a second as he stares at me.

"What?"

He clears his throat. "I personally believe you look beautiful all the time; however, you might want to touch up your make-up. It is a bit smudged."

I spin around, my eyes widening as I look at my reflection. "Oh, God. I need to buy waterproof mascara."

Milo hugs me from behind. "Nonsense. I will simply have to ensure that you do not cry anymore."

I lean back into his arms. "That might be a challenge. I tend to cry a lot."

"I will fix that. No more tears, tesoro. Be happy."

"I am. I really am."

"Good." Milo kisses the top of my head. "I'll meet you in the dining room. Don't be late."

I toss him a scowl as he walks away. "I am never late."

"I know," he grins, exiting my room. "But you are so cute when you frown."

I roll my eyes, waving him off as I face the mirror. Despite the dried mascara on my cheeks and my bloodshot eyes, the woman looking back at me looks...happy.

Today I choose happiness. I get to decide how I feel. I will not be ruled by my past. I will not let the future scare me. Today I will live in the present, for it is a gift.

With one final glance at my Nana's locket, I suck in a solidifying breath and get dressed, slipping on a black cocktail dress and a pair of chunky heels. If the family is going to stare at me, I might as well give them something stunning to look at.

Twenty minutes later, I emerge in the dining room, the large banquet table covered in wine, antipasto, and rustic floral centerpieces. Milo and Paolo sit at the head of the table, Marchello, Gio, Matteo, Julia, Luisa, and a few others filling in the holes.

I smile at everyone as I straighten my shoulders and walk toward the empty chair on Milo's right. The eyes of the family follow me, quiet murmurs slipping from their tongues. I don't let their whispers faze me.

Today, I choose happiness.

"You look lovely." Milo places his hand on my thigh as I sit down. "Would you like some wine?"

I keep my voice low as I glance around the table. "I'd like a lot of wine."

Gio and Matteo are immersed in a deep conversation about football. Luisa and Paolo are divvying up the appetizers. Julia is grinning at me like a kid hopped up on sugar.

Oh goodness. She's way too excited.

Marchello clears his throat, drawing my attention across the table. He eyes me with a tight-lipped smile as he lifts up his glass.

"To the future," he says, nodding his head. "To Santi Oscuri."

The entire table repeats his words, toasting to the future. To the mafia. To the uncertain times ahead.

I join in.

Toasting to *my* future.

As a part of their world.

# Chapter 28

# The Curse of Cures

DECISIONS. DECISIONS. DECISIONS.

Red? Black? White? Lace? Satin? Charmeuse? Chiffon? God, this is frustrating. I hate choices.

"Jules?" I call out, whipping my head around the luxury boutique. "Julia?"

"Yes, cara?!" She waltzes toward me, several shopping bags in hand. "What is it?"

I hold up two lingerie sets. The first features a sheer black Chantilly lace bra with satin bow accents, a double strapped thong, and a matching high-waisted garter belt. The second, a Bordeaux red stretch satin bra with a lace finish, a rouleaux strapped thong, and finely stitched gold clasped suspenders.

"Which is sexier?"

Julia blinks, smiling awkwardly at the sales associate behind the counter. "Kiara, I adore you, truly, I do. But I am Italian, not *Targaryen*. Milo is my brother; I do not wish to assist you in seducing him."

An oversight.

"Right." I wince, slowly placing the sets on the counter. "I'll take both. *Grazie.*"

"Good choice." Julia lets out a soft laugh, spraying her wrist with sample perfume. "Always buy both, cara. Why decide when you can have everything?"

I lean against the counter as the associate scans the items. "If I follow that mindset, I'll need a bigger closet."

Julia shrugs. "So?"

I roll my eyes, turning my attention back to Claudia who is over the moon with me right now.

"Visa, please," I say, hesitantly handing her my credit card.

I know money is not an issue but nine hundred euros? Ouch.

"These are beautiful pieces," Claudia coos with excitement as she charges me an obscene amount of money for tiny scraps of fabric. "You have a very lucky man at home. You will bring him to his knees."

"That's the plan," I whisper, hoping the said man's older *sister* doesn't hear me. I thank Claudia and grab the handles of the matte black shopping bag as I cast Julia a small smile. "Okay, let's go."

"Come back again anytime!" Claudia exclaims. "Anytime!"

"Oh, I just love shopping! It makes me feel like royalty," Julia laughs, looping her arm through mine as we exit the store. Gio and Matteo follow closely behind as we stroll back to the SUV. "Do you like what you bought?"

"Mhmm," I hum, cringing. "Sorry about asking for your opinion. I wasn't thinking—"

"Forget about it, cara." Julia immediately waves me off. "It's not a big deal, I was half-joking anyway. I'm sure my brother would love you in anything. I haven't seen him this happy since—" She freezes, faking a cough. "In a long time."

A tiny pang of jealousy gripping my gut. "Since Vittoria?"

He was happy with her. That shouldn't bother me. It's disgusting that it bothers me. She's dead. I'm jealous of a dead woman? That's horrible.

*I'm* horrible.

Julia lifts a brow. "He told you about her?"

I nod, incredibly disappointed in myself. "Yeah, when we were in Milan. He told me everything."

"Oh," she hums as we cross the street. "That's a good sign, Kiara, that he's finally talking about it. I was starting to worry about him." She sucks in a sharp breath. "Milo, he is a private man. The fact that he's sharing with you is incredible. I'm proud of him."

I'm unable to hide the smile forming on my face. "Yeah, I am too." I bite my lip, mustering up the courage to be nosy. "Did you uh—know her well? Vittoria?"

"Mmm... Not really, I only met her a handful of times. Milo had only been dating her for six months before she—" She swallows. "It wasn't very long."

"Six months?" A lot of feelings can emerge in six months. Or six weeks. Hell, six days is plenty for some people. Ask Jane Austen. "How did they meet?"

"I believe they met at a club." Julia clears her throat, averting her gaze. "She was a dancer."

I blink. "A dancer?"

Julia twists her lips as she tosses me a meek glance. "A stripper."

"A stripper?!" My eyes bug out of their sockets. "Oh, okay. That's cool. You know, I read once that stripping requires lots of training. It's like a sport, really, very athletic. There are even competitions and—"

"You're rambling, cara." Julia cocks her head to the side. "It is okay if you feel a bit uncomfortable."

"What? Me? I'm fine." I expel a nervous laugh. "Not a big deal. Really. It's just a job." Readjusting my sweaty grip on the shopping bags, I ask, "So, uh, what was she like?"

Julia tosses me a dubious side-eye. "Why do you care, Kiara? It doesn't matter, she is not your competition."

"I know that... I just—I'm curious is all."

I don't want to push Milo into talking about her. Frankly, I don't want Milo to *think* about her. I want him to think about me. Only me. I want to be the first thought that crosses his mind when he wakes up and the last when he falls asleep.

Is that bad? Am I terrible for wanting that? Milo said that the pain from losing a loved one never goes away but I want *his* pain to go away. I want it to disappear. I want to scrub away the stain she left on his heart. I want it gone. I don't want to be a second choice. I don't want to live in her shadow.

I don't want to be a consolation prize.

Julia inhales a deep breath as Gio opens the car door for us and we slide inside. She faces me, revealing, "Vittoria was very, uh...vivacious. From what I remember she enjoyed being the center of attention, cocktails, and umm...she talked a lot. As I said, I did not know her well."

"Oh—"

"Kiara..." Julia's tone is gentle as she places a hand on my forearm. "Do not compare yourself to her, that is the worst thing you can do. She is gone, cara. She is not a threat."

I fiddle with my fingers. "It hasn't been that long since she passed away, Julia. What if he's not over her yet? What if I'm just a distraction? A band-aid?"

"You are not a band-aid, cara." Her raw faith punctures my self-conscious heart. "You are a cure. You are healing him; I can see it."

"Most cures have side effects."

"That is true, but they are usually temporary. The cure, however, is permanent."

If I'm a cure, I think I need to start giving him larger, more powerful doses.

I need to pump his body full of *me*.

And get rid of all of *her*.

When Julia and I enter the estate, I catch the back of Luisa's head as she turns a corner down the hallway.

"Luisa!" I call out, grabbing her attention. She stops and circles back toward us, eyeing our shopping bags, a barely noticeable frown marring her groomed brows. "Do you know where Milo is?"

"He and my father were gone for most of the day," she says. "I think he is in his office now." She bites her lip, scanning one of my bags. "You went to *Mimibella*? Did you like it? It is one of my favorite boutiques. Claudia is fantastic, no?"

"She was great," I say, reading her vaguely disappointed expression. Hmm. "Did you uh—want to come with us next time?"

If I'm going to be living here for the next foreseeable future, I should try and expand my pool of confidants.

Julia's not going to stay in Italy forever. Once she leaves, I'll only have Milo. He's more than enough but he's busy. A lot.

"Yes! Excellent idea!" Julia chirps, looking up from her phone. "We go again on Saturday, yes?"

"Oh," Luisa hums, crossing her arms, uncomfortably shifting her weight between both legs. "Uh—yes, that would be nice."

"Great! I can't wait," I smile, nudging my elbow against Julia's side. She's like a teenager. Always on her damn phone. "I'll see you at dinner, okay?"

"Where are you going?" she whines with an over-exaggerated pout. "I thought we could have some drinks before dinner. I can't drink alone, that is so sad. Why are you leaving me?"

"Maybe Luisa can drink with you." I toss Julia a coy grin as I wave the Mimibella bag in the air. "I have *other* plans."

Julia groans. "Fine! Go! I do not need you!" A startled squeal slips past Luisa's lips as Julia latches onto her wrist. "Come with me. We drink!"

And she marches away, a squirming Luisa in tow.

I shake my head, stifling a snort as I walk to Milo's office, a burst of excitement thrumming in my veins.

We've only been apart for a few hours, yet I desperately crave to be in his presence. To be held by him. To kiss him. To simply breathe the same air.

I knock on his office door. "Hello? Milo?"

The low timbre, melodic inflections, and sultry tone of his native tongue fill my ears as I twist the handle and step inside his office.

*"We do it tomorrow then, we have all that we need from him."*

I bite my lip, undressing Milo with my eyes as he paces back and forth talking on the phone, his statuesque silhouette making me hot. So fucking hot. He stops, snapping his head toward me, a devilish smirk on his face.

"*I will call you back, Marchello,*" he mutters, a wicked gleam in his irises as I stride toward him and drop the shopping bags by my feet. "*It is final, Marc—*"

His jaw clenches as I stop in front of him, my eager hands running over the muscular ridges of his wide shoulders. I press my body against his, my lips floating down the length of his neck.

"Get off the phone," I whisper, my fingers raking through his hair as I nip at his skin. "You can call him back."

Milo grumbles into the speaker, his voice strained as he hangs up and tosses the phone on his desk. Grabbing my waist, his lustful gaze sweeps across my face.

"You are very bad, tesoro."

"What are you going to do about it?" I taunt, drawing figure eights on his chests with my freshly done nails. "Hmm?"

"I can think of many things..." He coils his fingers around my hand, his thumb gliding across the red acrylic tips of my manicure. He lifts a curious brow. "These are new."

"Ye—" I glance down at his hand, pursing my lips as I take in his raw bruised knuckles. "So are these." I frown, peering up at him. "What happened?"

Milo ignores my question, examining the ridiculously long nails Julia pressured me into getting. "These are quite long," he notes, the arousal in his voice kindling the flame that's already burning in my belly. "And sharp."

"Very sharp." I tilt my head, bringing my fingers up to his throat. I drag my nails across his soft, vulnerable flesh. "It's like I have ten tiny daggers at my disposal."

His expression hardens, his grip tightening around my

waist. He fists my sweater, pinching my skin. "Are you threatening me, Kiara?"

"Of course not. Just merely stating facts."

"Well, your *facts* are going to get you into trouble one day," he breathes, his palm circling around my ass as he thrusts his hips forward. "A lot of trouble."

"I like trouble," I coo, batting my lashes. "I—"

Milo surges forward, his lips crushing against mine, coaxing them open, his tongue merciless in its assault. I kiss him back, only for a second, before pulling away, my breathing shallow as I say, "Not yet. I want to show you something."

"Whatever it is, it can wait." He arches down and nips at my neck as he attempts to remove my sweater. "This can't."

Despite the building ache in my core, I push him away, taking a step backward. "It'll be worth it." My gaze darts to the shopping bags. "I'll meet you in your room in ten minutes."

He glares at me with suspicion and elevated curiosity. "An early Christmas gift?" He leans against his desk. "What it is?"

"Just a little something for you to unwrap." I pick up the bags and head to the door. I crane my neck over my shoulder before exiting. "I know how much you love red." I pause, licking my lips. "And lace."

"Cruel woman," he hisses, his jaw twitching as he pushes himself off the desk and marches toward me. He coils his hand around the base of my throat, dragging his thumb along my bottom lip as his balmy breath fills my lungs. "You are maddening."

"Hmm..." My hand travels down to his pants and I stroke the outline of his growing erection. "You seem to like it." Pulling away, I cast him a devious smirk. "Ten minutes. Make yourself comfortable."

"Ki—"

"*Bye,*" I sing, quickly darting out of his office, a triumphant grin on my face as I run to my bedroom.

One dose of Kiara, coming right up.

# CHAPTER 29

## DIRTY LITTLE SECRETS

I AM NOT A CLASSICALLY TRAINED STRIPPER.

I probably shouldn't be doing this. I shouldn't be knocking on Milo's bedroom door with only a silk robe and skimpy lingerie covering my body. I shouldn't already be flushed from the idea of giving him a lap dance. I shouldn't be thinking that this is the perfect Vittoria antidote.

But I am.

Maybe I've lost my mind. Possible. But there's no way in hell I'm losing him. Not with what I have planned. Not in this outfit. Or lack-there-of.

Some cures are slow, they take time to work.

Personally, I prefer a more aggressive approach.

Fast acting.

"Enter."

My heart thuds in my chest as I open the door. Confidence. My stilettos click against the hardwood floor, my hips swaying seductively as I slowly walk toward him. Milo's sitting on a black leather armchair like it's a fucking throne and he's the goddamn king.

My mouth dries. Shit. This might be more difficult than I thought.

"Hi," I breathe, my chest rising as he looks up at me with a darkened, deviant expression. I bite my lip, slipping the robe off my shoulders, revealing the spilling flesh of my breasts. "Worth the wait?"

"Oh, fucking hell," Milo grunts, running two fingers over his lips as I approach. Ideal reaction. Thank you, Claudia. "Kiara, you—"

"Shh," I command, dropping the robe to my feet as I start moving my body in circular motions, using my frantic heartbeat as a metronome. "Don't move. Don't talk. Just watch."

I glide my hands over every curve of my body, my breasts, my hips, my stomach. My skin pebbles as I imagine that it's his hands touching me, groping me, making me so fucking horny. Turning around, I bend over, dragging my hand up the length of my thigh-high stockings, my neck craned over my shoulder as I wiggle my ass. Just a little.

"Like what you see?" I coo, sifting my fingers through my hair as I stride toward him. He doesn't say anything which pleases me greatly. "Cat's got your tongue, baby? Or maybe it's a kitten? A little gattina? Hmm?"

His lecherous eyes are narrowed, focused, locked in on my half-naked body, his mouth slightly agape as he orders, "Come here. Right now."

"As you wish, sir." Slithering up between Milo's parted, inviting legs, I lean forward, my back arched, my hips swaying as I grip either side of the armchair. "Let's play a little game, Mr. Di Vaio," I whisper, teasingly inching my breasts closer and closer to his tensed face. His shallow, hot breath blows against my chest. "What do you say?"

"I thought we were done playing games, tesoro," he

rasps, lifting his hand up to imprint me with his scalding touch.

"Ah, ah, ah..." I pull away and wave my index finger in the air as I click my tongue, a sense of control and power burning inside me. "That's part of the game. No touching."

Milo's pupils expand with carnivorous hunger. "That is impossible. Like asking a man not to breathe."

"If you succeed..." I arch down and wisp my lips against the soft shell of his ear. "I will let you fuck me—" I pause, circling my breasts in front of his face. "Anywhere."

A feral groan vibrates his throat, the thunderous sound reverberating against my red lips. "How long does this fucking game last?"

"Five minutes," I reply, my tone airy and full of anticipation. "Can you control your impulses for five little minutes, sir?"

"Are you certain you want me to succeed?" he asks through his teeth. "Are you certain you wish to grant me access to *every single* part of your body?"

"Absolutely certain." Milo's jaw locks, every muscle in his body clenching as I turn around and hover my ass just above his lap. "Five minutes starts... now."

Grabbing onto his knees, I expel a gasp as I lower my ass down to his pelvis and grind against his growing erection. "That was quick." I lean back and fondle my breasts in sensual movements. His balmy erratic breath fans against my neck as I continue to torture the man who's tortured me for weeks. "You're doing so good, baby."

"I can smell how wet you are, Kiara," Milo growls, his hard cock twitching against my gyrating hips. His evident discomfort only makes me grind harder. "Fuck..."

"Mmm...if only you could *feel* how wet I am." I glide two fingers over the smooth damp fabric of my panties, arching my spine as the back of my head rests on his shoulder. "I'm soaked. *So fucking wet.*"

"Dio aiutami." Milo grips the cushions of the armchair, his knuckles whiter than the purest cocaine. "How much longer?" His thick, strained voice is like a prayer to the heavens. Except in this moment, God is a woman. And Milo is just a man. A lowly mortal. Putty in my evil hands.

"There is power in restraint, Mr. Di Vaio." I rock my hips in stronger, deeper motions. His zipper creates delicious friction against my sex. "Control yourself."

"Enough!" Milo roars. I moan as he yanks my hair, tugging my head back, his tongue licking the slope of my neck. "True power lies in taking what you want." Oh, shit. His hands snap up to my chest, squeezing my breasts, my nipples helpless between his fingers as he twists and turns and torments. "I lose."

He jerks up, spinning me in his arms, violent yearning blazing in his irises.

"And what do you want?" I pant as he dips his thumb between my quivering lips, his right hand kneading my ass cheeks. I suck on his fingers, twirling my tongue. "Hmm?"

"I want to choke you with my cock," he growls, pushing me down to my knees, cupping my jaw. Tight. "And then I want to fuck you so hard that the dead will hear your cries."

And she will.

"As you wish." I release his pulsing erection and stroke his silky shaft, precum glistens on the tip like fucking diamonds. A girl's best friend. Gathering my hair in one hand, Milo surges forward, knocking the air out of my lungs as he fucking annihilates every inch of my willing mouth.

"Such a good girl," he growls.

I gag and groan and gasp for breath as he takes what he wants and gives me everything I need. He claims me and I mark him— the smudged red lipstick on the base of his cock a warning to all the bitches in the world that this man is mine.

With tears in my eyes and saliva dripping down my chin, Milo pulls me to my feet. Lurching forward, his lips devour mine, carnal and chaotic. We stumble toward his four-pillar bed, my pussy dripping, aching, needing to be filled.

Whipping me around, he throws me on the bed, my forearms and knees dipping the firm mattress as my chest heaves with vicious arousal.

"Don't you dare rip the fucking panties," I say, between pleasurable groans as he slaps my ass repeatedly, giving each cheek plenty of wanted attention. "They were expensive."

A dark, amused chuckle spills past his lips as his fingers curl under the luxurious fabric, pushing it to the side. "As you wish, baby," he mocks me as he buries his face inside my slick folds, his tongue probing, pillaging, penetrating all my fucking holes.

"Oh my God!" I cry, fisting the bedsheets so hard that they might disintegrate. "Holy shit!"

A husky groan escapes the back of this throat as he slips two fingers inside of me, swirling my juices like a goddamn cyclone. My abs contract as I near release, my eyes rolling back, my toes curling, my whole-body fucking humming with elation.

"Not yet" he commands as he replaces his fingers with his cock, teasing my sex for just a second before slamming inside me. My entire body jerks forward as he breeches my walls. My defense. My shield. It's down. Gone. Nothing there. He has me. All of me. And it feels so fucking good.

Snaking his arms around my torso, he yanks me

against his bare chest, destroying my pussy with every deep thrust. "You are fucking perfect," he mutters, his voice raw, hoarse as he scoops my breasts out of the bra and rolls my nipples between his fingers. "You are a goddess, a fucking savior."

"Oh my God, harder!" I beg, soaring through celestial skies, relishing in his worship, his wickedness, his bewitching power. "Milo!"

"Fuck, yes, yes, yes!" he grunts, slobbering wet kisses all over my sweaty body as my walls clench around his throbbing cock and we both come undone, our bodies shaking in a rapturous stupor.

Best nine hundred Euros I've ever spent.

Ever.

After catching our breath, Milo helps me off the bed, holding my body with a gentle touch as we go to the bathroom to clean up. What a disaster. I lean into the mirror, adjusting the tangled mess of lingerie that's still somehow intact.

"You didn't rip anything," I muse, tossing him a coy glance as he splashes cold water on his face. "I'm impressed."

"See? Self-control," he smirks, leaning against the counter. "Are you proud of me, tesoro? I am a changed man."

I snort. "You lost the game. Very early."

He cocks his head to the side, raking his fingers through my hair. "No, I definitely won."

"I'm not a prize," I retort, unable to stop myself from grinning.

"Correct, you are not a prize," he says, pulling me against his chest into a strong, tender embrace. "You are a treasure that I've been searching for my whole life."

"Your whole life?" I ask cautiously, kissing his neck as

my heart hammers in my chest. "As in you've never found it before?"

We both know what I'm asking.

I think.

"Never," he whispers, kissing my forehead. "Until now."

"Me neither," I admit, averting my gaze, suddenly feeling shy, exposed, bare. But it's the truth. A terrifying fact. "We uh—" I clear my throat. "We should get ready for dinner. Julia said Teresa is making Pansotti."

"Let's shower," he suggests, wiggling his eyebrows. "I will clean you. You are a very dirty girl."

"Tempting." I narrow my eyes, casting him an unimpressed scowl. "But we don't have time. It's almost eight."

"Fine," he says, with an unbothered shrug. "I don't mind if you smell like sex." He pauses, tilting his head. "Do you?"

"I'll use some perfume," I say, exiting the bathroom. "Chanel overpowers anything."

"You will need to use the whole bottle, tesoro." He slaps my ass on the way out. "Maybe two."

"Good thing you can afford it," I sing, picking up my robe and tossing it on. "See you in a few minutes."

His distant laugh spears into my skin like sunshine as I head to my bedroom. It's rare to admire someone who has two distinctly different sides. Milo is like an old book, his edges are rough, harsh, somewhat withered, but inside, there's a masterpiece, adventure, romance.

In a dazzling daze, I get ready for dinner, my cheeks hurting from the smile that refuses to leave my face. It's like I've been thrust into Aldous Huxley's *A Brave New World*, and I have Soma coursing through my body. I'm calm, pacified, in a total state of bliss.

Milo meets me at the top of the staircase as we walk

hand-in-hand to the dining room, taking our places around the table.

"You are glowing," Julia whispers in my ears as idle conversation surrounds us. "I take it he enjoyed your purchase."

"That's one way to put it," I grin, shoving a piece of ravioli in my mouth as I glance over to Milo who's chatting with Marchello. I let out a content sigh. "It's really good."

"Please be talking about the food, cara," Julia says, leaning away from me. "Please."

"Hmm?" I hum, choking on the walnut and mushroom stuffed pasta. "Oh, yeah. It's delicious."

Julia scowls. "Mhmm, okay."

"We're adults, Jules. Get over it."

"Still gross," she huffs, taking a sip of wine. Her phone vibrates on the table and she picks it up, grinning. "Ah! Look! Tutte! Tutte!" Julia holds out the phone, showing us a picture of Natalia dressed in a professional tutu. "Isn't she the most adorable sugar plum fairy?! Her class is putting on a production of The Nutcracker. Ah! So cute! Paolo look!"

"The Nutcracker is a little advanced for a three-year-old." I turn to Milo as Julia continues to gush over her precious daughter. "Right?"

"I do not believe it will be as choreographed as the original," Milo chuckles. "They mostly hop around...or cry."

"We attend every recital," Marchello says, checking his watch. "We support the children of this family."

"And we are so grateful for that!" Julia exclaims, joining our conversation. "Children are such a blessing, cara, believe me! When you have one of your own, you'll see. I remember when I was pregnant, God, I couldn't wait for it to be over so I could drink some fucking wine..." She trails off as I play with the food on my plate, a tiny pang of sadness grasping my heart.

A blessing I might never get to experience.

"Julia, enough." Milo's hand finds my thigh and he gives it a gentle, almost reassuring squeeze. He knows. He's seen my medical history. I look up from my plate to find him glaring at his sister. "Please."

Julia frowns, casting me an inquisitive side-eye. "What—"

"Later," I whisper with a weak smile. "It's fine."

"Oh," she hums warily. "I'm sorry, did I say—"

"It's fine," I assure her, taking a sip of wine. "So, when is the recital?"

"It's on—"

Marchello clears his throat. "Kiara," he says, nodding toward the bottle of Bordeaux on the table. "Pass me the wine."

"Oh, sure." I pick up the bottle and reach across the table to hand it to him. "Here."

"Thank—Merda!" Marchello fumes as I let go of the bottle and it falls on the table, toppling over, spilling on the dark linens, and dripping down the side onto his pants. "Fuck!"

"Oh my God!" I cover my mouth, my cheek burning up. "I'm so sorry! I thought you had it!"

"Clearly not," Marchello grumbles, yanking a napkin off the table and dabbing his lap. "This was the last bottle! Fuck sakes."

"It's just wine, Marchello," Milo says, letting out a sigh. "Relax."

"I'll go get another bottle!" I offer, hopping out of my seat. "If you clean your pants now, they won't stain. I'll be right back."

"Fine." Marchello's lips twist up into a scowl. "There should be one more bottle left in the kitchen."

"I'm on it!" I dip down to give Milo a kiss on the cheek. "Be right back."

Wincing, I clench my fists and scurry off to the kitchen. The man already doesn't like me very much and I do that?! Oh, God. Stupid.

It takes a minute to search the built-in wine cellar, but I find the bottle. Gripping it tightly, I head out of the kitchen. Don't drop this one. As I round the corner, I bump into the plump sturdy frame of Teresa.

"Oh! Teresa, hi. Sorry, I didn't see you there."

She spins around, a silver tray in hand. "Signorina," she swallows, her gaze darting down to the pile of brown mush on the tray. "Good evening. How is dinner? Good?"

"Yeah, it's super delicious," I say, narrowing my eyes. Is that risotto? Oatmeal? I can't tell. Either way, it does not look very appetizing. "Did you uh—want to come eat with us?"

"Oh, no no." She shakes her head, letting out a nervous laugh. "I go eat in my room. Not feeling well tonight." Teresa blinks. "This is old family recipe. Good for stomach."

I purse my lips, put off by her flustered demeanor. I scan the tray again. Plastic utensils? What? "Are you okay?" I ask, tilting my head, trying to get a read on her. A slight frown. Widened eyes. Tense posture. Guilt?

"I am fine, Signorina! Simply tired is all." She clears her throat. "I go now, yes?"

"Oh, umm...yeah sure," I say, forcing a smile, unease tugging at my gut. "Feel better."

"Grazie mille." Teresa turns on her heel and heads down the hallway.

What the hell was that? Whatever. I need to focus on the task at hand. Wine.

Exiting the kitchen, I freeze at the sound of descending footsteps. She's going *downstairs*? Why would she go to the basement? All the estate workers reside on the first floor.

Without thinking, I remove my heels and I follow the pitter-patter of her tiny steps down the staircase. I've officially lost my mind. Why am I stalking our cook? Because she was acting hella suspicious, a voice in my head replies. I roll my eyes. I live in a house full of criminals, everyone acts suspicious. I really need to get over these trust issues.

Keeping my distance, like a lunatic, I crane my neck over the railing as Teresa fumbles to open a lock to a door I've never seen before. I frown. Where is she going?

As soon as her body disappears through the weathered wooden door, I run toward it before it slams shut. Sticking my foot out, I hold it open and squeeze through, propping the bottle of wine under my arm as I tiptoe down the foreign stairs. I run my fingers along the untreated stone walls, the dim recessed lighting making it hard to see.

Where the hell are we?

The clamping sound of metal catches my attention as I turn the corner. My heartbeat quickens as I watch Teresa slide the tray of food – if we can call it that – through a steel slot carved in the prison-like door. She dusts her hands off as she stands upright and turns around.

"Signorina!" she gasps, covering her mouth as I slowly walk down the stairs. "What are you doing here?!"

"I could ask you the same question, Teresa," I say, my fingertips tingling from the sudden onset of anxiety and dread. "What's behind there?"

Teresa shakes her head, planting her body in front of the steel door, her head bobbing in front of the large sliding peephole in the center. "Nothing. Please, Signorina, you must leave."

I suck in a deep breath, gripping the straps of my shoes as a wave of trepidation nearly drowns me. "Teresa, move."

"No, per favore," she pleads. "You cannot be here. You need to leave."

"Move," I state, peering down at her with a stern expression. "Or I will make you move."

She whimpers, hobbling off to the side as I take a step toward the door. My throat clogs up as I slowly slide the hatch open. I narrow my focus on the back corner of the empty, dark room. There's someone sitting on a dirty mattress. Their shaved head is turned away from me, but I can see bruises and cuts on the side of their face.

A familiar face. So fucking familiar.

"Who is tha—"

The wine slips from my hands, shattering on the ground as they whip their head toward me, his beady blue eyes piercing mine.

I stumble backward, blinded by shock, rage, fucking betrayal.

"Signorina, the glass! Be careful!"

Andre.

# CHAPTER 30

## A FIGHT AGAINST FATE

TRUST.

It can take weeks, months, years to build trust. Trust is fragile. Like a flower. A beautiful rose bed. If you take good care of it, it flourishes, grows, survives. But if you don't, if you fuck up, if you grow that fucking flower in soil that's infested with lies and deception and betrayal then it dies. It's destroyed. And it's damn near impossible to grow anything healthy in that fucking soil ever again.

"You lying piece of shit!" I storm into the dining room, my vibrating gaze narrowed in on Milo. "I can't believe I fucking trusted you!"

"Kiara?" Milo twists his neck toward me as he abruptly stands up, his face plastered with confusion. "What is wrong? What happened?" He pauses, looking down at my feet. "You're bleeding."

"He's alive?!" I cry, incredulity searing through my goddamn veins. "He's fucking *alive*?!"

"Wha—"

"Signor Di Vaio! I am so sorry!" Teresa calls out, running

up behind me, panting to catch her elderly breath. "She saw him. She uh—she followed me. I tried to stop her but I—"

All the color drains from Milo's face. He knew. He fucking knew. Of course, he knew. This makes so much sense. The bruises on his knuckles. Why he was gone for hours on end but never left the estate. Oh my God. The sparrow. Andre was the fucking sparrow?!

"Kiara, please—"

"You fucking asshole!" I yell, every single one of my nerve endings buzzing with betrayal. "This whole time?! He was alive this whole time?! What the fuck is wrong with you?!"

"Do not talk to him like that!" Marchello slams his hand on the dining room table. "Know your place!"

"Shut up!" Milo snaps his head toward his underboss. Julia and Paolo's gaze darts between the two of us. "Everyone leave," he commands. "*Now.*" He peers over my shoulder at Teresa, his jaw clenching. "Please bring some antiseptic and bandages for Kiara's feet."

"No," I fume, shaking my head, angry tears on the verge of spilling. "You can all stay. *I'll* leave." I turn around, the pain from the shards of glass lodged in my feet incomparable to the pain in my stupid, naive heart. "I should've left long ago!"

I need to get out of here. I need to leave. I'm such an idiot. I can't believe I fell for him. I can't believe I *let* myself fall for him. This is what happens when you fall. You crash and burn and get your fucking heart broken. Smashed. Shattered. Stepped on and trampled.

"Kiara—" Milo jolts toward me, grabbing my hand. "Please, I can explain."

"Don't you dare touch me!" I yank my arm away,

heading down the hallway to the staircase. "Leave me alone."

"No," Milo says, his tone raw, trembling as he follows behind me. "I will not."

"Go away." I march up the stairs and into my bedroom. "I don't want to be near you. I don't want to talk to you. I don't want to fucking *look* at you." I throw my high heels on my bed and walk to the closet, pulling out a suitcase.

"What are you doing, Kiara?" Milo runs a frantic hand through his hair as I scoop piles of clothes from my dresser and throw them into the luggage set. "Kiara, stop!"

"Fuck off." I scramble around the room looking for more shit to pack. "I'm leaving." A maniacal laugh spills from my lips as I shove shirts into the carry-on. "Seeing as I didn't actually *kill* Igor's cousin, I'll take my chances with the Russians. Maybe they'll spare me!"

"Kiara, please! Stop and listen to me for fuck's sake!" Milo takes two strides toward me and coils his fingers around my arm. "Look at me." I don't move. "Kiara!"

"No!" I clench my teeth. "I can't look at you." My hands ball up into fists. "It hurts too much to fucking look at you! You lied to me! He—he was dead. I swear he was dead. I shot him! I thought—" Tears roll down my face. "I thought I killed him. You lied to me! Why would you do that? Why wouldn't you tell me? Why—"

"Kiara," Milo whispers, cupping my face as he tilts my head up. His thumb brushes away the tears, his touch so fucking soft, so delicate, so frustratingly tender. "I did not lie to you—"

"What?" I seethe, smacking his arm away, my eyes expanding with dis-fucking-belief. "You didn't *lie* to me? How can you say that? I saw him, Milo! He's alive!"

"I never said that you killed him." Regret flashes across his face. "I never—"

I blink. "Seriously? You never said I *killed* him? What—" I shake my head, losing my fucking mind. "You also didn't tell me that he's alive or that you have him locked up, downstairs, in a fucking dungeon! He was here the whole time! That is so fucked up! You made me think I killed someone, Milo! That I took a life, that—" I pause. "Oh, my God. That police report you showed me, is it even real? Or was that just some sick way of making me feel better? Huh?"

"Of course, it is real," Milo says, almost like he's offended. That's rich. "Everything I told you about him is the truth."

"Except for the fact that he's alive," I snap, turning my attention back to packing the suitcase. "You're unbelievable." I drop the blouse from my hand, whipping my head toward him. "Why? Why didn't you tell me? No, not even why, but how? How the fuck is he alive? I shot him. I saw the bullet enter his chest! I saw him bleeding out in the fucking parking lot. How? And why is he downstairs? What the fuck, Milo?!"

"When you shot him, you did not kill him. He had a pulse, it was very faint," Milo explains in a hushed tone as my entire body buzzes with livid rage. "But he was going to die. He was minutes from death but—"

"But what?"

"I was going to let him die." He winces. "But I—I changed my mind. I decided that it would be better to save him, to use his knowledge in order to end this fucking war. And it worked, we are so close to winning, Kiara. It's almost over."

"So, you healed him just to torture him?" I ask, a bitter taste coating my tongue. "Milo, you made me think that I was a murderer. You—" I let out a shaky breath. "You saw how his death affected me and you still didn't tell me? Why? You said you trusted me, you said—"

"I *wanted* to tell you, tesoro. I did but I was advised against it. You are not the only one who does not know. Only five people are aware that Andre is not dead. I couldn't risk it. I couldn't—"

"Risk what? Who the fuck was I going to tell? I have no one to tell! You fucked up, Milo. You—you broke my trust. You broke *us*. I can't stay here. I can't be around you anymore. I need to leave."

The sharp edge of Milo's jaw twitches. "You are not leaving, Kiara!"

"Watch me!"

"No!" Milo grabs my shoulder, spinning me around. "You are not going anywhere, Kiara. You cannot leave me. You—"

"Don't touch me!" I push on his chest. "You said you trusted me! That you cared about me! But you lied to me! You don't get to touch me anymore."

A blaze flickers in his dark irises. "I *do* care about you! I fucking love you!"

For a millisecond, the world stops, the gravity of his proclamation making my heart flutter with glee. But then the millisecond passes, and the glee morphs back into anger. A hurt, agonizing rage.

My jaw clenches as I slap Milo across the face.

"Love me? You love me?! Are you fucking kidding me? How can you say that? After all of this shit? If this is the way you show love, then I don't fucking want it! It doesn't change the fact that you lied to me!"

"For fuck's sake! Not everything is about *you*, Kiara!" Milo shouts, his booming voice sending a shudder down my spine. "It is not about you or me or us, it is about everyone else! This feud with the Russians transcends our relationship. I am responsible for so many fucking lives! They are *my* responsibility. Mine! So yes, I listened to Marchello when he told me not to tell you, because my brother, who is dead now, did not listen to advice. Ever. You can say that I lied to you or that I broke your trust, but I did what I had to do to ensure that my family would be safe, that we would remain in power, that no one else would fucking die!" He takes a ragged breath, closing his eyes as he adds in a softened tone, "Put yourself in my shoes, tesoro, try to understand. Please."

"I understand." I nod my head, biting the inside of my cheek. "Your loyalties lie with your family, with Santi Oscuri. Not with me. I get it."

"No—"

"Milo!" Marchello calls out, barging into my bedroom. "I need you downstairs. They are asking questions." He glares at me. "Deal with her later."

"*Her?*" I expel a low, defeated chuckle. "See? This would never work, Milo. I will never have respect in this house. I will never be one of you. I'll always be an outsider, always." My eyes well up with tears. "Sometimes love isn't enough."

Love isn't a cure. It's a disease. It's a sickness. It hurts. It kills. It's painful.

So fucking painful.

"You want respect? Is that what you want, tesoro?" Milo stalks toward me, his intense gaze packed with determination and resolve. He nods his head, scanning my face. "Alright, I will give it to you."

I blink. "What—"

"Marry me." He combs his fingers through my hair, my

knees weakening, my brain on the verge of complete shutdown. "Be my wife."

"Emilio!" Marchello barks, his lip twitching, his face red. "What are you doing?! Have you lost your fucking mind? She is a nobody! She is—"

"Enough!" Milo turns around, reaching for the Beretta that's tucked into the back of his pants. He points it directly at Marchello. I cover my mouth, letting out a frightened gasp. "Leave, right now or I will put a bullet between your fucking eyes."

"Oh my God, Milo, stop." I tug on his arm. Is he insane?! "Stop!"

"Emotions are dangerous, my boy," Marchello states, his gaze darting toward me. "Remember that."

"Get the fuck out of Kiara's bedroom." Milo readjusts his grip on the pistol. "I will not ask you again."

"Fine." Marchello swallows, a tight-lipped smile on his aged face. "I am leaving. We will talk later when you have calmed down."

Milo's features harden. "Do not provoke me, Marchello. Remember who is in charge. Leave."

Without another word, Marchello turns around and storms out of the room. When he's out of sight, Milo lowers his gun, staggering to the edge of my bed. He sits down, burying his face in his palms, his fingers rigid, tense.

"Marry me," he whispers, his tone hoarse, husky, heartbreakingly pleading. "Marry me, Kiara. I promise to never lie to you again. I will give you everything. I will give you the world. I will give you the fucking universe and all of its stars. Please, do not leave me."

"You're crazy..." I take a seat next to him, my pulse racing, my heart so goddamn conflicted. "You're fucking crazy."

"I love you," he whispers. "I am crazy because I love you." Taking a deep breath, he lifts his head up, his eyes red, glossy, full of emotion. "I am sorry, tesoro. I have failed you. I said I would stop your tears and yet you cry because of me."

"You hurt me. You broke my trust."

"I know," he breathes, dwarfing my fiddling hands. His touch is like a drug, a sedative, forcing my mind to slow down. To relax. To hear his words. Really hear them. For the first time. "I will never do it again." His thumb caresses the underside of my wrist. "I will dedicate my whole life to rebuilding that trust. I will make it whole, Kiara. I promise you that."

I stay silent, unable to respond.

Our relationship has grown on tainted soil. Everything that's sprouted, blossomed, flowered is covered in lies and deceit. And yet, when I look at his fucking face, it's still beautiful. It's the same face that fills my dreams. The same face that's stamped on my heart, my mind, my soul. But stamps fade. They're not permanent.

They don't last forever.

"Say yes," Milo whispers, interrupting my reverie as he leans his forehead against mine, his sweet breath fanning against my lips. "Be my wife, tesoro. Let me love you under God."

I close my eyes, my breath hitching. "Do you believe in God?"

"Yes." He cups the side of my face, his thumb grazing the damp apples of my cheeks. "He brought you to me. He brought me an angel."

"Sometimes God is cruel. He gives us things just to take them away."

"I will not let you go, Kiara. I will fight fate to keep you with me."

"People can't fight fate, Milo. That's why it's called fate."

"People can't. I can."

"You're not God."

"No, but I am a man in love." He kisses my knuckles. "And a man in love is just as powerful as any God."

This is all too much. Too fast. Too soon. Too overwhelming. I'm so tired. So fucking confused.

"I think you should leave." I bite my lip to stop myself from crying. "I need some time to think. I need—"

"You do not need to give me an answer right now." He stands up and runs a hand through his hair. "But soon, tesoro. I need it soon."

"What if I say no?" I peer up at him through damp lashes. "Will you let me leave?"

"You will say yes. I know you will say yes."

"Kiara!" Julia's voice cuts through the charged air. "Can I come in?"

"Yes," I call out, needing this conversation to end. I look at Milo, at his eyes, lips, nose. God, he's perfect. A perfect lie. "I'll talk to you tomorrow."

"Good night, tesoro." Milo sighs, giving his sister a weak smile on his way out.

Julia holds up a bottle of rubbing alcohol and some gauze. She looks down at my feet. "Are you still bleeding?"

"What?" I scan the dried blood on my heels and toes. "Oh, God. I didn't even feel it."

Julia sits on my bed, hiking my foot up on her lap as she administers first aid. "How are you feeling, cara? Are you okay? I—I did not know about Andre, I promise, I would have told you if I did."

"I know," I hum, wincing as she pads the cuts. "Jules?"

"Yes?"

"Milo, he uh—" I bite my lip. "He just asked me to marry him."

Julia freezes. "He what?"

"Yeah."

"Just now? Oh fuck, he is an idiot, truly," Julia grunts. "What was he thinking?"

"He's not very good at timing things, is he? I don't know what to do, Julia. What do I do?"

"That depends, cara. Do you love him?"

Is love enough?

## CHAPTER 31

## A GREY AREA

I've spent the last twenty-four hours thinking, reasoning, being mindful of what my heart wants, what my brain deems acceptable, and what my gut says is right. The polarizing conclusions from each internal department have left me with barely any functioning cells.

My heart is hurting, it's in pain but it misses Milo. My brain is furious with me, completely disappointed in my inability to leave, to make a damn decision. And my gut instincts are jammed, unable to send a clear signal.

What do I do? What the hell do I do?!

There is only one thing I didn't try. It's juvenile and not necessarily the best course of action, but I'm out of ideas. According to recent psychologists, Julia being one of them, pros and cons lists are often detrimental to the decision-making process as it leads to over-analyzing. Seeing as that ship sailed hours ago, I don't fucking care.

Nibbling on my bottom lip, my gaze bounces between the two columns jotted down in my notebook.

I inwardly scoff.

This is insane. If I'm basing my decision off this list,

then I should leave. I should pack my bags and get out of this fucking house. I should forget about Milo. I should try to start a new life. I should leave.

That's what I *should* do.

But I can't.

I fucking can't.

I groan, raking my hands through my hair as a knock on the bedroom door draws my attention.

Really? Again?

"Go away, Milo!" I call out, grateful that he hasn't stormed my quarters yet. "I don't want to talk to you."

Not yet. Not when I don't know what to tell him. *Marry me. Be my wife.* That's his brilliant solution? How? How is that supposed to fix anything? It's like trying to mend a broken dam with a band aid. He's clearly lost his fucking mind.

I refuse to lose mine.

"It's Luisa. Can I please come in?"

What? Luisa? He sent a spy? Typical.

"Uh, sure," I say, heavy hesitation in my voice. "Come in." My brows knit together as she enters my room, her red lips twisted up with mirrored emotions. "Is something wrong?"

"No..." She slowly walks toward my bed. "Everything is fine. I just—" She clears her throat, sitting down on the edge of the mattress. "I wanted to see how you're doing."

"Did Milo send you?" I narrow my eyes at her as I prop myself up against the headboard. "Because I already told him that I'll talk to him when I'm ready, and I'm not."

"No, he didn't send me," Luisa says, picking at her nails. "I came on my own."

"Oh," I hum, shifting uncomfortably. There's no trace of

deception in her features, at least none that I can read. "Sorry."

"It's fine." She waves me off, looking around my room. "So, how are you doing? Last night was—" She pauses, finding the right word. "Interesting."

I expel a low scoff. "Yeah, that's one way to put it." I scan her face, attempting to gauge her intentions. "Why are you here, Luisa?"

"I—I did not know either, about Andre," Luisa reveals in a hushed tone. "I was not told that he was still alive. My father—" She shakes her head, her jaw slightly clenching. "He didn't tell me."

"If you didn't know then who knew?" I ask, setting my notebook to the side. I cross my arms. "Milo said only five people knew the truth, who were they?"

"No idea." Luisa shrugs, mild irritation flashing across her face. "You know more than I do, Kiara. Even now, they don't tell me anything."

My blood thrums.

"Why? Why does *everything* have to be a secret? Marchello is your dad, how does he not trust you? I get why he doesn't trust me, he doesn't really know me, but you're his daughter. That makes no sense."

"I asked him what they are planning, if I could be of help but he told me that he did not need a woman's opinion," Luisa says with a defeated chuckle. "It is always like this. They don't tell us anything." She pauses, letting out a sigh. "This is why Julia doesn't ask anymore, why she pretends she doesn't care because she knows Paolo cannot tell her anything. That he *won't* tell her anything."

"I wouldn't be able to live like that," I admit. "I don't know how she does it."

"Me neither. Even though I know my father will not

reveal to me their plans, I still ask. And I will continue asking until one day, he tells me. And he will...I hope."

"So, you don't know *anything* about the feud with the Russians?" A frown mars my brows. "At all?"

"All I know is that they killed Sergio and Vittoria," she swallows. "I don't know anything after that." *She doesn't know about the guns? Really?* She sidles closer to me, her eyes flickering around my face. "You must understand Kiara, everything Milo and my father do is to make sure our family doesn't perish, that we remain strong. After Sergio's death, we became vulnerable, targets for the other clans. As much as I want to be involved, I understand the need for secrecy, for discretion. When he died, we became weak." She sucks in a small breath. "My father told me that weakness breeds disloyalty and distrust. I love my family, Kiara, more than I love my pride. I do not wish to see us fall."

A pang of guilt snatches my stomach. She is more in the dark than I am. Milo's told me snippets. He's told me secrets. He let me in. He trusted me more than Marchello trusted his own child.

He just didn't trust me enough.

"What's your point? Why are you telling me all of this?"

"Because," she says, running her fingers along my bedsheets. "It is something you need to bear in mind if you're going to become a part of the family. If you marry into Santi Oscuri, this is what you should expect."

I blink. "Marry? He told you?"

"Everyone knows that he asked for your hand." A sheepish smile spreads on her face. "You were very loud last night. Sound travels."

"Lovely. That's just great."

"Kiara—" She puts her hand on my knee. "It is important for you to understand the gravity of his proposal. If you say yes, your life will change, the way people treat you will change. The way my father spoke to you last night, that would never happen again if you became Milo's wife. If he ever showed you disrespect, he would die."

I purse my lips. Is that why he asked me? So that the men in this house would respect me?

"So, the only way I can earn respect is by marrying the boss? Really? That's so backwards."

"I am not saying it is right, but it is something you should consider if you see a future with Milo. Without a ring, Kiara, in their eyes, you are meaningless."

A future.

Do I see a future? Do I see us growing old? Exploring the world? Going on adventures? Making love on every continent? Living life, together, as husband and wife?

I throw my head back, slapping my hand over my forehead, an ache pulsing in my temples. "What do you think I should do?" I can't believe I'm asking Luisa for advice. I barely even know her. Maybe I *am* losing my mind. "Should I say yes?"

"It is not my place to say, Kiara. But I've known Milo my whole life, he is like a brother to me. I can see how happy you make him, and happiness is so difficult to find in this life. So, if you love him, then you should say yes."

"He lied to me." I close my eyes, a storm of uncertainty whirling around my mind. "How can I marry someone who lied to me?"

"It might not be easy, but you can try to forgive him." The mattress bounces as she stands up. "If you wish to be with Milo, that is the only thing you can do."

"If I said yes to him, you'd be okay with that?" I tilt my head as I sit up. "Your father said I was a nobody. That doesn't bother you?"

"I know we have not been the best of friends, but I like you. I think you and I are very similar. And I believe our family would benefit from having a woman like you at the head of the table."

"A woman like me? What do you mean?"

"Kiara—" She cocks her head to the side, a small grin on her face. "You called Milo a piece of shit and a fucking asshole in front of ten armed men. Do I need to say more?"

I snort, stifling a laugh. "I was really mad."

"More women need to get mad. That is how change happens."

"You think Milo can change?"

"He already has." Luisa checks her watch. "Shit, I must go and prepare Antonia's room. She arrives in a couple of days. The woman is very particular about her thread count."

"Milo's mom is coming?" I ask, swinging my legs over the side of the bed. "Why?"

"She always comes back for Christmas. It is tradition."

"Oh..." I tap my fingers against the duvet before standing up. "Do you know where Milo is right now? Is he in his office?"

"I think he is training in the gym." A beat. "Are you ready to talk to him?" she asks in a hopeful tone. "Are you going to say yes?"

"No." I expel a deep, stabilizing breath as I grab a cardigan off a chair and slip it on. "I'm not going to answer his question until he answers mine."

Luisa quirks up an eyebrow. "What question?"

"I have many."

Musky odor permeates the air as I enter the gym. Scanning the room, my gaze lands on Milo who's in the far corner, throwing calculated jabs at a red and black punching bag, all the muscles in his torso, shoulders, forearms contracting with every swing.

I swallow. Nope. Dismiss.

As if sensing my presence, his eyes land on mine as I walk toward him. "Kiara," Milo pants, grabbing a white towel off the floor. He drags it across his sweaty forehead. "What are you—"

"I'm ready to talk." I cross my arms, keeping my posture straight, confident. "Are you free?"

"Of course." He tosses on a light grey t-shirt, much to my disappointment. "Would you like to go to my office?"

"Nope, here is fine." I turn around, raising my voice so that all the men at various workout stations can hear me. "Hey! Can we please have the room?" Nothing. No acknowledgment. I clap my hands. "Hello?" A few heads turn to face me. "Leave, please." Four sets of eyes glance over my shoulder toward Milo. "Oh, my God!" I whip my head around. "Tell your sheep to fuck off."

"Sheep?" Milo attempts to suppress a grin as he joins my side. "*Ascolta!*" His baritone voice echoing off the walls. "*Tutti se ne vanno. Adesso.*"

"Unbelievable," I mutter as the room empties in seconds. "It's like you have them programmed."

"They will listen to you, tesoro, give it time. Once we are wed, you will have control."

The audacity.

"Don't get ahead of yourself." I glare at him, taking a seat on a bench press. "I didn't say yes." I point to an adjacent bench. "Sit."

"Oh." His face falls as he slowly sits down. In a low,

gruff tone he says, "You are here to tell me you are leaving then."

"No."

"No?" A gleam of puzzled hope flashes across his features. "You will stay?"

"I haven't decided yet. First, I need you to answer a few questions."

"Questions?"

"Yes."

"Okay." He rubs his hands together. "What do you want to know?"

Milo stays quiet as I organize my thoughts. I can't live like Julia. I don't want to be bitter like Luisa. I need answers. If I'm going to forgive Milo, if I'm going to look past his transgressions, then I need to know the who, what, why, where, and how.

And if he can't give that to me... I will leave.

"You said only five people knew Andre is still alive, who are they?"

"Me, Marchello, Paolo, Henri, and Antoine," he replies without missing a beat. "And Teresa, technically." I blink, taken aback. "I told you, Kiara. I will no longer lie to you."

I ignore the latter of his reply, I ignore the soft thumping of my heart. I ignore it all.

"Henri and Antoine know? Why?"

Again, no hesitation.

"If Igor believed that we killed his cousin, there would be a bloodbath and if he knew that Andre was alive and being held captive, none of the information he'd give us would be valuable, they would alter their operations. In order to avoid both of those circumstances, Henri and Antoine helped us fake his death. Drinking and driving.

They used a cadaver, the car exploded. No evidence, no body."

"Smart." That's why it's been so eerily quiet these past few weeks. "That was a good plan."

"Yes." A small proud smile clips his lips. "It worked. They do not know we have him."

*Him.*

I shudder, pressing on. "You've been torturing Andre." It's not a question. "For what?"

"Many things."

"Such as?"

Milo expels a sigh. "For the location of their safehouse, the whereabouts of Igor, names of suppliers, contacts, affiliates."

"What's your endgame?"

"To take Moscow away from *Pravda*."

"Too vague. I need details."

Milo closes his eyes. "It is dangerous, Kiara. I do not—"

"Tell me or I'm leaving." Harsh? Perhaps. "Either you trust me, or you don't. Decide."

"Fuck," he grunts, running a hand through his dark hair. "You are being very unreasonable, tesoro. I am telling you more than I should already. Is it not enough?"

"No, it's not enough. I don't want half-truths. I don't want half-ass explanations. I want to know everything. I want the details."

"You are impossible." His jaw clenches as he rests his forearms on his knees. "Kiara, please—"

"Tell me."

His dreary gaze meets mine as he reveals, "We will kill Igor and bomb their arms reserves."

Holy shit. I swallow. Knowledge is power. "When?"

"In a week from now," he grumbles, burrowing his face

into his hands. "Before the New Year." He peers up at me through his rigid fingers. "Satisfied?"

"Almost." Unease stirs in my belly. "Is—" I clear my throat. "Is Andre still alive?"

"Not for long."

Oh.

"Don't kill him," I whisper, my gaze flitting to the ground. "Turn him over to the Russian authorities. The families of his victims, they deserve justice."

"Tesoro," Milo hums, pushing himself off the bench and kneeling down in front of me. He grabs my hands, craning his head to meet my glossy eyes. "I cannot do that."

"Why not? You have all the information that you need, don't you? He deserves to rot in jail, Milo. Death seems almost like a gift. It's not fair. These families will live the rest of their lives thinking the man who murdered their daughters is still alive, breathing. That's not fair! That's not justice."

"Kiara, if we were to give Andre to the police, he would never see a day in prison," Milo cups my cheek, grazing his thumb along my hairline as he softens his tone. "He knows too much about the brotherhood. He would trade information for freedom and protection."

"That's fucked up," I croak. "That's not fair."

"I told you, tesoro," Milo hums regretfully. "We are not the only corrupt organization in the world. Your heart is in the right place but unfortunately, that is the truth."

I clench my teeth. "Did he suffer?"

"What?"

"Andre." I swallow, a sinister sense of disgust rising in my throat. "When you were torturing him, did he suffer?"

"Kiara—"

"Tell me." I grip the bench press, my fingers cramping. "I need to know."

"Yes," Milo admits in a strained tone, an almost shameful wince seizing his features. "Please do not—"

"Good."

"What?" Milo's puzzled eyes spring open. "Good? I thought you would be upset with me, I thought you would think me a monster."

There are many defining firsts in a person's life.

First step. First word. First missing tooth. First time riding a bike. First broken bone. First crush. First love. First heartbreak.

First time you see the world for what it is.

I was mistaken. There isn't only good and evil. Right or wrong. Black and white.

It's a nice thought but it's unrealistic.

It's a lie.

"You were right. There *is* a grey area. I see that now."

"Tesoro..." Milo frowns, curling two fingers under my chin. "I am sorry."

"For what?" I fight against every instinct not to lean into his touch. "For lying to me?"

"For lying to you," he breathes, arching down, his nose brushing against mine as our foreheads touch. "And for telling you the truth." I sniffle, tears on the cusp of spilling. "Perhaps now, Kiara, you understand why I tried to spare you, why I did not wish to burden you." His hot breath fans against my lips as he whispers, "You wanted the truth, tesoro, this is it."

"How do you sleep at night, Milo? Knowing what you know?"

"I didn't sleep." He pulls me against his chest, his safe, warm arms encircling my waist. "Not until I met you." He laces his fingers through my hair, his earthy brown eyes glowing with pure, untainted admiration. "I love you, Kiara, and I am sorry that I hurt you. Forgive me. I beg of you, please forgive me."

"I believe that you're sorry." I lift my hand up to his face, caressing the stubble on his cheek, outlining the edge of his strong jaw. And I do. I believe him. He's being real and raw and vulnerable. If only it were enough. "But I can't forgive you. Not yet. I need time, Milo. I need time."

"How much time?" he asks in a hoarse, rough tone as his grip around me tightens ever so slightly.

"I don't know," I whisper, pushing myself to my feet as I wipe away tears. "A day, a week, a month. I don't know."

"I understand," he says in a lowly tone. "Take as much time as you need, tesoro. And when you are ready, say yes."

Too much. Too soon. Too fast.

"I'm going to go help Julia decorate the Christmas tree now," I say, needing some space. Again. "I'll see you at dinner."

And with that, I head back to my room, my heart humming with happiness, my brain slowly coming around the idea of staying, and my gut telling me I made the right choice.

Crawling back into bed, I open my notebook and stare at the list.

### Cons:
He's the head of a mafia
He's killed people
He's a criminal
He tried to kill me
He kidnapped me
He lied to me

## **Pros:**
I love him.

Perhaps, I should have told him how I feel. I should have said it back. I should have given him some hope.

But he broke my trust.

I think I'll wait a bit before I give him full access to break my heart.

# CHAPTER 32

## UNDER A SPELL

GOLDEN HUES OF THE RISING SUN PEEK THROUGH THE arched windowpanes as I enter the library, a cup of coffee and a book in hand. Tightening a wool throw over my shoulders, I stare into the hypnotizing crackles of the fireplace, the sparking red embers flickering violently.

There is no rest for the wicked.

Or the hurt.

Sleep is the enemy and literature is the savior. Trading nightmares for literary escape is something that I'm used to. It's familiar, it's comforting. A book has an ending, a conclusion, it's there, on the last page. Will she, or won't she? Books are simple. Beginning, middle, end.

Am I at the end of a story?

Or at the beginning?

My gaze floats above the mantle to the oil paintings of generational criminals. Milo, his father, his mother, his brother. They're all there. Smiling. The soft brush strokes and muted colors of the paintings make them look harmless, normal, human. Just a family.

A family.

Sighing, I shake my head.

My future family.

Maybe?

"He was a handsome man, no?"

I gasp, my entire body jerking. Hot coffee spills over my hand as I spin around to find Antonia standing behind me. "Oh my God, you scared me. I thought you weren't coming until Christmas."

She takes a sip of espresso, her plum lipstick leaving a semi-circle stain on the tiny cup. "Natalia missed her mother." She strides toward me, her fingers twisting an emerald gem around her neck. "We arrived late last night."

"Oh," I hum, feeling mildly embarrassed as I wipe my coffee-drenched hand on my silk pajamas. "Well, welcome home. It's nice to see you again."

"It is nice to be back." Her eyes soften as she admires the paintings. "My husband was not a very photogenic man, but on a canvas?" She clicks her tongue, a ghost of a smile on her face. "He was beautiful."

"Milo looks just like him," I sigh, comparing the renderings of the two deadly men. "It's almost eerie."

"Yes, they are very similar, both in appearance and in heart," Antonia agrees as she faces me. "Emilio was Santino's favorite child." She expels a soft laugh. "Do not repeat this to Julia, she will argue otherwise."

"I would think most parents have a soft spot for their youngest," I muse as Antonia gestures for us to sit down on the couch. "I don't have any siblings but that's what I've heard."

"Very true." Antonia sets her coffee on the table. "Even when his hair turns grey, Milo will always be my baby." I shift uncomfortably as she slowly scans my face. "He told me what happened, Kiara."

I swallow, anxiety thudding in my chest. "He did?"

"Yes." She lets out a heavy sigh. "His exact words were: Mamma, I fucked up."

"Oh..." I blink, taken aback by the curse words slipping from her elegant mouth.

"He also told me that he proposed to you," she continues, her body language difficult for me to read. "But you have yet to give him an answer." She tilts her head. "Do you love my son, Kiara?"

"Uh—" I stammer, gripping the novel that's resting on my lap. I want to be offended that she'd ask such an intrusive and invasive question but the lack of malice or judgment in her tone makes me think that she comes in peace. "He has many qualities that I love and many that I don't."

"You cannot love pieces, Kiara," she states, glancing at the painting of her late husband. "You must love the whole man or love none of him."

*I'm trying.*

"You loved your husband?" I ask, following her sightline. "All of him?"

She swallows, her gaze distant. "Our marriage was determined long before I was even born," she reveals. "What I did not love at first, I learned to love." She looks at me, her dark eyes piercing mine. "Can you learn to love all of Milo, Kiara? If you can, then there is hope. But if you cannot, then please leave, do not hurt my child. Do not hurt my baby."

"I don't want to leave," I admit in a low hum, nibbling on my bottom lip. "But I also don't know how to forgive him. It's only been a few days; I can't just forget what happened. I want to, Antonia, but I can't."

"Kiara..." She takes my hand in hers and strokes my fingers. "If you do not want to leave, this shows to me that you already *have* forgiven him." Her tender grip tightens.

"Perhaps, it is no longer my son that you need to forgive but yourself."

I frown, not following her logic. "For what?"

"For letting yourself get hurt," she explains, her gentle touch reminding me of my nana's. "When we open our hearts, we allow pain to enter, and when it does, we tell ourselves never again. I have been where you are, Kiara. I have felt the same pain as you are feeling now but pain is a part of life, a part of love. Forgive yourself for loving him and the pain will go away."

Is she right? Am I angrier with myself than with Milo? I knew the kind of man he was, I knew his profession, his morals. I knew that he would hurt me. He told me that he'd hurt me. But I didn't listen. I didn't care. I still don't care. I want him. I want him so bad. I want all of him. I do. The good, the bad, the ugly, and the fucking beautiful. And there's so much beauty.

It's blinding.

"I don't think my heart can handle any more pain. It's at its capacity."

Antonia places her palm on my cheek. "Then let your heart be full of love. It will drive away all the pain. As a mother there is nothing I want more than for my children to love and to be loved."

That's what everyone wants.

"I don't know *how* to love him." Impending tears tickle my nose as I sniffle. "He's not a normal man. This isn't a normal family."

"And you are *clearly* not a normal woman," she says, tilting her head. "You are special, I can see fire in your eyes. I had the same fire, Kiara. That fire is what will keep you warm even on the coldest nights." She lets go of my hand and removes the emerald necklace around her neck, placing it in my palm. "I believe your fire will be of great benefit to my family."

I squeeze my hand shut, glancing down at my nana's necklace. I'm not ready to take it off. To trade one life for another. "Why are you giving this to me?"

"My husband's mother gave me that necklace before I got married. It was her blessing, as it is mine."

"I haven't said yes. I don't—"

"Perhaps you have not verbally agreed, but in your heart, you know the truth."

"Antonia, I—"

"Mamma!" Natalia screams, tiny thumping footsteps in the distance. "Mamma! I want to go play outside! Come! Play! Play!"

"Natalia!" Julia's groggy voice thunders through the walls. "It is so early! Why do you hate me?! My only child hates me!"

"Mamma, please!" Natalia begs. "Outside! Outside!"

Julia and her daughter round the corner, stopping outside the library. "Help me," Julia whimpers, rubbing her eyes and tightening her robe. "I gave birth to a demon. She does not sleep."

"Julia!" Antonia hisses, standing up. She tosses me one last knowing glance before she berates her child. "Go play with Natalia! *Dio, sei pigro!* You have not seen her in weeks!"

"But Mamma," Julia whines. "I need coffee first and I need to shower and I—"

"I'll take her outside," I offer, hoping Julia doesn't have a full-on meltdown. "I just need to change first."

"You are my hero, cara!" Julia pouts, running up to me and wrapping me in a hug. "Grazie! Grazie! Grazie!"

"Outside!" Natalia stumbles toward me and pulls on my sleeve. "Now! We go now!"

"Talia!" Antonia snaps, peering down at her grand-daughter. "You are being *very* rude right now. Perhaps you should not go outside after all."

Natalia's bottom lip quivers. "But Nonna!"

"Apologize to Kiara and thank her for volunteering to play with you," Antonia demands, crossing her arms. "Well?"

Talia's bright blue glossy eyes meet mine as she blubbers, "I'm sorry, Kiki. Please take me outside. Please!"

"Can you wait two minutes while I go get dressed?" I ask, running my fingers through her fine hair. "Hmm?"

She nods, wiping her snotty nose. "S*i*."

"Good," I chuckle, glancing up at Julia. "I'll be back in two minutes, okay?"

Julia mouths *thank you* to me as I exit the library, Antonia's necklace held firmly in my palm. She's giving me her blessing. Literally. God, what am I supposed to do? Seriously. God, tell me what to do. Help me. Give me a sign. A signal.

Anything.

Knowing there's a temperamental toddler waiting for me, I quickly change out of my pajamas and into a sweater and jeans, slipping on a pair of black leather booties before heading back downstairs.

"Alright." I zip up my jacket and hold out my hand to the jumping toddler. "Let's go!"

Natalia screams as we step into the courtyard. She darts to the woven box of toys, pulling out chalk, a jump rope, and bouncy balls. She hands me a piece of pink chalk. "Draw!"

"Yes ma'am," I chuckle, kneeling down beside her as we start doodling on the cobblestoned yard.

After playing with Natalia for over an hour, I've

concluded that children have the attention span of goldfish. I am no longer of interest to Natalia as she has found a bug in the crevices of the stones that is far more entertaining than I am. Perching down on a stone table built into the courtyard, I watch Talia crawl on all fours as she tries to trap the bug with a plastic cup.

"She will be busy for hours." I whip my head to the side, Milo's decadent, deep voice filling my cold ears. "Good morning, Kiara," he says, striding toward me, two cups of coffee in his hand. "You must be cold."

"A little." I take the large mug from his hands, warmth radiating off his body as he sits down beside me. "Thank you."

"Julia told me you volunteered to play with Talia." He smiles at his niece, his expression glowing with affection. "That was very kind of you."

I blow on the coffee before taking a sip. "I like kids. I actually wanted to be a teacher when I was younger. Mold young minds, make macaroni necklaces, finger paint. That was a long time ago. Before—" I sigh. "Everything changed."

"Your parents?"

"My parents, my grandpa," I murmur, an ache in my heart. "I wanted to get an early childhood education degree, but I couldn't do it. I needed to stay with Nana. It didn't seem like a big deal at the time, I figured one day I'd have kids of my own but—" I pause, shaking my head. "Well, you know."

I still remember how devastated I felt when my doctor informed me that my chances of getting pregnant are under five percent. At twenty years old, it's not something I was even thinking about, but to know it could never happen was soul-crushing. That day, my doctor took away a part of my future.

Milo places his mug on the bench and removes mine from my hands. "Do not look so sad, tesoro," he says, tucking a loose hair behind my ear. "There are many ways to have children."

"I know, but it's not the same." I lean into his touch, his rough hand keeping me stable, upright, present. "Don't you want kids of your own?"

"I do." His thumb grazes my temple, his rich dark eyes flickering across my face. "But I want you more."

"You shouldn't have to choose. Maybe this is a sign that we don't work. Maybe this wasn't meant to be."

"Nonsense." He twines his fingers through mine. "Life is a constant series of choices, and I choose you. Kiara—" He caresses the underside of my wrist. "I love the reality of you more than the possibility of children. And in the future, if we wish to become parents, we will figure it out, together."

"Why do you want to marry me?" I bite my lip, searching for more reasons to leave, to get out, to spare myself more pain. "We haven't known each other that long. Is it because you're afraid I'll leave? Is that why you asked?"

"It might seem as though I asked you out of desperation, and perhaps, at that moment, I did, but—" A sly smirk clips his lips as he cocks his head to the side. "But you have bewitched me, tesoro."

I expel a small laugh. "Are you trying to woo me with a line from *Pride and Prejudice?*" I tilt my head. "That line isn't from the book, it's from the movie. How do you even know that?"

Milo shrugs, a grin on his face. "It is Julia's favorite, I have seen it many times. But it captures exactly how I feel about you. I am under your spell, tesoro. You *have* bewitched me."

Impossible. He is making it fucking impossible not to

smile. I have zero control. I'm helpless. I am under his spell just as much as he is under mine. It's magic. I'm enchanted by his words, the sincere vulnerability in his voice, by the future in his eyes, by the promise in his touch.

But not all magic is good. Some magic is dark and sinister and all-consuming.

"Spells can break," I whisper, my skin hardening into a protective barrier. "They don't last forever."

"You are still unsure." Milo releases a labored, lifeless breath as he runs his hand through his hair. "It is understandable."

"I'm trying. I am."

"I know." A faint, heartbreaking smile captures his lips as his gaze flickers across my face. "I believe you." He lifts his hand to my cheek, leaning closer to me. "I want to kiss you, tesoro."

I wind my hands around his neck, my fingers digging into his skin. "Then kiss me."

My chest rises as his soft lips feather against mine, his sweet breath filling my lungs. It's a dream, a breathtaking illusion of happiness, of hope, of home. My grip tightens around his neck as I deepen our kiss, praying that some dreams come true.

"Gross!"

We pull away, our breathing shallow as we peer down at a cringing Natalia. "Are you spying on us, principessa?" Milo asks, lifting a brow.

"No!" she protests, stomping her foot. "I want to play with Kiki now! Go away Zio."

I stifle a laugh. "Tired of chasing bugs?"

She frowns, crossing her arms. "He too fast for me."

"Milo!" Marchello calls out from the doorway. He

glances at me, a small smile on his face as he nods. "We must leave now."

I frown. "Where are you going?"

"To *Milano* for a day, I need to meet with Nico about—" He glances down at Natalia who is watching us with a curious expression. "The sparrow." He looks at me. "I will be back tomorrow afternoon." He pauses, rubbing his chin. "Would you like to come with me?"

"No!" Natalia answers on my behalf. "She mine! You go!" She shoves his shins. "She mine!"

"Talia," Milo scolds, "do not push."

She scowls at her uncle. "Go, Zio! I want Kiki! Please!"

"Kiara—"

"It's fine." I hop off the stone table and dust off my jacket. "I'll see you when you come back." Natalia grabs my hand, twirling herself around my finger. I laugh. "I think she'll keep me busy until you return." I pause. "Don't do anything stupid, okay?"

"Never. I will see you tomorrow, tesoro."

"Tomorrow! Santa comes tomorrow!" Natalia sings, prancing around. "Presents! Presents! Presents!"

Santa already gave me my gift.

I'm just too scared to open it.

# CHAPTER 33

## STATE OF SURVIVAL

"KIARA!" JULIA HOLLERS FROM THE FOYER. "HURRY UP! The stores will be closing soon!"

"Who goes shopping on Christmas eve?" I call out from the powder room as I apply one more layer of taupe lipstick. "And didn't you already buy all your gifts?"

"Yes, but I want to buy more!" she shouts. "Come on, Kiara! Luisa's waiting for us in the car!"

I jog toward the front entrance, scowling at her. "Jules, I'm so tired, I don't want to go," I complain as she loops her arm through mine and drags me out of the house. "Can't the two of you go by yourselves?"

"And leave you alone so you can stare at the clock until my brother returns tomorrow? I don't think so!" She opens the backdoor to the SUV. "Get in!"

"Fine!" I grumble, sliding in beside Luisa. "Hi."

"Hi," she says hesitantly, scanning my face. "Are you okay? You don't look well."

"I—"

"She is fine!" Julia huffs as our driver starts the car and pulls out of the driveway. "And if she's not fine now she will be in ten minutes. Shopping fixes all problems. I'm a psychologist, trust me."

I roll my eyes. "I don't think that's factual."

Julia purses her lips as she scowls at me. "Studies have shown that shopping releases Serotonin which is a hormone that contributes to a person's happiness. So yes, it *is* factual, *Kiara*."

"I'm not *sad*," I protest, crossing my arms defensively. "I'm just tired."

"If you are not sad then why do you have that look in your eyes? Hmm? It is alright to be sad, Kiara, it does not make you weak, it makes you human," Julia says, cocking her head, her expression softening as she catches my slight frown. "What is wrong, cara? You can talk to us. We can help."

"I'm not sad," I double down, biting my bottom lip as my gaze bounces between Luisa and Julia. "I'm just—" I let out a defeated sigh, fiddling with my nana's necklace, Antonia's words muddling my mind. *Do not hurt my baby.* "I'm just confused and frustrated and tired."

"About Milo's proposal?" Luisa asks, shifting her body toward me. "Have you still not decided?"

"No. Not yet..."

"Talk to us, maybe we can help," Julia offers again. "Please?"

"Fine." I press a button on the console and raise the divider. Luisa and Julia give me their undivided attention as I lean back into my seat. "I feel like these past few days I've been stuck in this endless loop, and I can't seem to get out of it. It's like there's something holding me back from giving him an answer." I pause, my face falling. "And I don't know what it is."

"It's your brain, cara," Julia states with a weak smile. "That is the problem."

"My brain?" I knit my brows together. "What are you talking about?"

"Here we go," Luisa chuckles, tossing me a knowing side-eye. "The doctor has arrived."

"Oh, shut up." Julia casts Luisa a scowl before turning her attention back to me. "Listen, Kiara, in psychology, there is a concept of the Triune brain. Basically, a person's brain is broken up into three sections: the brain stem or survival state, the limbic system, the emotional state, and the prefrontal cortex, the executive state."

I blink. "Okay? And?"

"Well, the executive part of our brains helps us with problem-solving and making intentional decisions, only humans have this ability. The survival and emotional states exist in all mammals, they are instinctive, evolutionary. When a person is in a state of stress, their brains automatically default to the lower levels, emotional and survival. You are stuck in survival, Kiara. Milo hurt you and you are scared of being hurt again. Your brain is perceiving him as a threat, it is unable to differentiate between being chased by a lion and accepting a proposal."

"It is true," Luisa adds, drawing my attention. "Last year when I went through a break-up, I did not understand why it was taking so long to get over it. Julia said it was because my emotional state was preventing my executive state from letting me move on. Inside my brain, that break up was almost like being abandoned by my herd. It was why I was so upset over such a short relationship."

"Well, what the fuck am I supposed to do then?" I ask, flapping my arms. "How am I supposed to control my brain? You're not being very helpful right now, Jules."

"It is important to be aware of how your thoughts impact these states, Kiara. In order to move away from the survival state, you need to feel safe. You need to reassure your brain that you are *not* in danger, that Milo is *not* a threat."

"How do I do that?"

"You must believe it, cara," Julia says. "You cannot trick your body or your brain. You must be assertive, not passive in accepting change. And a proposal, a marriage, would be a big change. Your brain is trying to protect you. It is trying to keep you safe. But if you want clarity, you must take control of your feelings, your emotions. Do not let your primal instincts dictate your choices."

Mind over matter.

I close my eyes, taking in a deep breath. "He's not a threat," I whisper. Milo's soft touch, smooth voice, and comforting smell fills my mind. "He is not a threat."

"No, he is not, he loves you, cara," Julia hums, caressing my hand. "You must understand that he too has been stuck in the survival state for so long, practically his whole life."

My eyelids flutter open. "He has?"

"Of course," Julia says. "The men in this family, they do not trust because they are in a constant state of survival. It is their number one priority, always. It is difficult to rewire your brain, but Milo, he is trying. You were also once a threat to him. Remember that."

"I hadn't thought about it like that before," I say, flicking my nails. "But it makes sense."

I'm not the only one who's taking a chance. It's not just me. Relationships are not one-sided. There are two of us. Two people. Two hearts. Both equally vulnerable. Both equally scared.

The fear of loss is crippling. The fear of heartbreak is

debilitating. But the fear of being unable to love someone? That's unacceptable.

Milo is not a threat. He's not. I know this. I do. He's not a fucking threat. Do you hear that, brain? He's a blessing. A fucking gift. He was brought into my life not to destroy me but to heal me.

I don't want to just survive. I want to live. I want to thrive. I want control.

I want love.

The car comes to a halt, snapping me out of my head.

"I know you're tired, cara," Julia says, getting out of the car as Luisa and I follow suit. "But let's try to enjoy ourselves, yes?"

"Two hours," I say, suppressing a yawn. "Then we're leaving, okay?"

"Two, four, something like that," Julia mutters as we stop outside the door to Mimibella. "Maybe you can find a gift for Milo inside."

My eyes widen. "Oh my God, I didn't get him anything. Is he going to expect a Christmas present? Julia!"

"Dio, relax! You are so wound up all the time!" Julia huffs. "We will find something; we have all day."

"You guys go in," I mumble, fishing my phone from my purse. "I need to make a call."

"Fine! Don't be too long, I need opinions," Julia says.

"Julia," Luisa whispers, nodding at our silent guards. "Can you?"

"We do not need you," Julia says, addressing Gio and Mateo. "Go for a walk."

"We are not supposed to leave you," Gio says.

Julia's expression hardens. "I said go." Gio and Mateo exchange a conflicted look before striding away. "Okay,

Kiara, you have one minute then I am dragging you inside, yes?"

"Okay, okay."

Unlocking my phone, I dial Milo's number, staring into the store as I pace back and forth in front of the semi frosted windows of the lingerie store. Claudia, the sales associate, rounds the checkout counter, throwing her arms around Luisa. She tucks back a piece of Luisa's hair as she gives her a lingering kiss. My mouth drops as the line continues to ring in my ear. Oh...

"Tesoro, do you miss me already?" Milo asks in a cheeky tone. "I have only been gone a few hours."

"Uh—" I stammer, clearing my throat as I notice a rosy hue spread on Luisa's face. Claudia giggles, biting her lip as they talk.

"Kiara? Are you there?"

"Yeah, sorry," I mutter, expelling a nervous laugh as I turn around, giving the two women some privacy. "Um, how are you?"

"Is something the matter? You sound strange."

"No, no, everything is fine, I'm just shopping with your sister and Luisa." I narrow my eyes at Gio and Mateo who are smoking half a block down. Is that why Julia sent them away? They don't know?

"Kiara?"

"Yes?"

"Why did you call me?"

I blink. "Right, um...is there anything you want for Christmas?"

Milo chuckles. "I want you to say yes."

I suppress a grin. "Something perhaps that I can buy in a store?"

"No," he says in a gentle tone. "I do not need anything

else." He pauses, muffled voices in the distance. "I must go now, tesoro."

"Okay," I say, my body humming with elation. "Oh, and I do."

"You do what?"

"I miss you."

"I miss you too, Kiara," Milo whispers. "I would much rather be with you right now, believe me."

"Can you come back tonight instead?" *He is not a threat.* "I don't want to sleep alone again. It's Christmas Eve. We should be together."

"I will try, Kiara." Milo's deep breath fills my ears. "But it might be late."

"Then wake me up."

"I will. See you soon, tesoro."

"Bye." Hanging up, I enter the store and immediately dart to Julia. "Hey, Jules!" I tug on her sleeve. "Are Luisa and Claudia—"

"We are." Luisa's voice startles me, and I spin around. "But please do not tell Milo. No one knows. Promise me, Kiara? I am trusting you."

"Would Milo care?" I ask, frowning.

"I don't know," Luisa sighs, her gaze darting to her girlfriend. "It is forbidden. I would rather not risk it. If my father ever found out—" She closes her eyes. "Please do not say anything."

"I won't," I say, squeezing her hand. "Thank you for trusting me though. That means a lot."

"And you can also trust me," she says. "I would like for us to be friends, Kiara."

"We are," I smile, nodding toward Claudia. "So how did you meet?"

"We were getting fitted for bras this past summer," Julia

pipes up, tossing Luisa a smirk. "She liked it more than I did."

Luisa rolls her eyes. "The way you tell the story makes it sound so romantic, Julia. Thank you."

"I have a way with words," Julia teases, handing me a white lingerie set. "Try this one. It will make you look like a slutty angel. Perfect for your wedding night."

"Oh my God, Jules, stop," I say, shoving it back into her hands. "I haven't said yes."

"But you will!" she sings in a taunting tone, striding away from me.

"Ignore her," Luisa says. "It is your decision to make, Kiara. Do not feel pressured." She nods to the counter. "Would you like to officially meet Claudia?"

"Of course, I'd love to." I hesitate, before stating, "I'm sorry you have to keep your relationship a secret. It's not fair."

"I do not have the power to change tradition," she says, smiling at me. "But you do...or you will."

"I thought you said no pressure," I say, casting her a playful scowl. "That seems like a lot of pressure."

"It is important to seize opportunities, my father taught me that." Luisa shrugs unapologetically, gazing adoringly at Claudia. "I was scared too, Kiara, but I decided to choose love over fear. I had to be honest with myself, that took a long time, but once I accepted my feelings, I felt whole." She glances at me. "So be honest with yourself, Kiara, and choose love."

"You're willing to risk everything for her?"

"I don't want to die with regrets."

Neither do I.

## CHAPTER 34

# TIDAL WAVES

I'M IN A DREAM RIGHT NOW.

White sand stretches as far as the eye can see. Frothy crests of aquamarine waves break on the beach and ebb away. Tranquil silence surrounds me as I dig my heels into the warmth of the fine-grained sand, the sun beating down on my face, my body, seeping into my pores.

I know this is a dream because I've had it hundreds of times. I sit in the same spot, on the same beach, staring out into the same ocean. But the sensation of peace that thrums through my veins as I watch the waves crash never lasts.

It's a mirage, an illusion, a *delusion*.

The wind will pick up and the waves will get larger, stronger, faster. They will charge at me like aquatic warriors, gaining confidence, bravado with every gust, every tremble of land.

In the distance, I'll see a wave that looks like a mountain, like moving earth. It'll taunt me, it'll get higher and closer, and then it'll wash me away.

It'll drown me. It'll leave me breathless. It'll kill me. It always does.

Except for today.

I've been here for hours, for days, maybe even years and there's no tidal wave. My body feels so warm, so safe, so fucking calm. The hot, humid air, it's hugging me, enveloping my entire being in an embrace. The gentle cool breeze is whispering in my ear that it loves me, that it treasures me, that it's never going to betray me.

It takes only a second of consciousness for me to realize that it's not the air that's keeping me warm, but his arms. It's not the wind that's breathing adoration into my lungs, but his words. And it's not the deserted island that's keeping me safe, comfortable, at peace – it's him.

I roll over in his arms, the bright glow of the moon illuminating the sharp edge of his jaw, his cheekbones, the slope of his neck. He's here. He's my island. My refuge. A shield from the storm.

"I can feel you staring at me," Milo whispers, his eyelids fluttering open, a ghost of a smile on his face.

"What time is it?" I ask, my vision adjusting to the dark. "When did you get here?"

"It's 4 a.m." Milo feathers his fingers across my arm. "Go back to sleep, Kiara. Close your eyes."

"You didn't wake me up..." I run my hand down the sculpted ridges of his bare chest. "You should've woken me up."

"Clearly I did," he murmurs, cupping my face in his hand, his thumb grazing my lips. His gaze flickers across my shadowed, flustered face. "Go back to sleep, Kiara."

"No." I shake my head, my chest rising with need as I mold my body against his, my breasts spilling out of my nightgown. "I don't want to sleep."

"What *do* you want?" His knowing dark eyes float down to my parted lips. "Use your words," he whispers as I find his hand and guide it to my sex. His fingers curl under my panties, feathering my wet folds. "Kiara—"

"I want to feel you," I breathe, closing my eyes as he rolls on top of me, his growing erection grazing my midsection. I release his cock, stroking the hard length of his smooth shaft. "Please."

"Fuck," he groans, grasping the hem of my nighty and slipping it off my body in one swift motion. He rips off my panties and tosses them aside. Looking down, he studies every inch of my naked body, his gaze predatory, protective, promising. A total contradiction. He wants to destroy me and save me. Protect me and harm me. Fuck me and make love to me. All at the same fucking time. And I want it too.

I want his chaos.

"Milo," I whine impatiently.

My desperate plea is all it takes for his lips to claim mine. Our tongues collide and we feast upon each other, starved, deprived, damn near feral. He coils his fingers around my wrists, pinning my hands over my head. His knee parts my thighs as he captures my nipples in his mouth, his teeth biting at the tender peaks. I moan, writhing under his touch.

"Do you forgive me, tesoro?" he rasps into my ear, teasing my clit, dipping only the tip of his fingers inside me. "Tell me that you forgive me."

"Yes," I whimper, lifting my hips to the heel of his hand, rocking my pelvis into his touch, my pussy aching to be full, touched, fucked. "I do."

"Good." A gust of relief slips past his lips. "On top." He pinches my nipples between his fingers as I straddle him, rubbing my sex against his cock. "I want to watch you."

He grabs the base of his shaft, keeping it steady as I ease myself down on him. It hurts so fucking good as he fills me to the hilt, stretching my walls, snapping the barrier that's kept us apart for too goddamn long. His eyes never leave mine as he thrusts, spearing his cock deeper inside my clenching pussy.

Crying out in pleasure, I lean back, grabbing his ankles as I ride him, feel him, savor him. God, how I've missed him. I missed being close to him, not just in proximity but in spirit, in fucking soul. He's inside of me. A part of me. We are one.

A chaotic, catastrophic, cathartic fucking being.

As his thumb circles my clit, as my moans fill the air, as his possessive grip on my hips tightens, I feel whole. I feel complete. The shards of broken self, of broken morals, of broken hearts, they slowly mend together, one powerful thrust at a time. One piece, two, three. All the lies, all the doubt, all the hesitation, they slip away, they vanish, replaced by trust, faith, and blissful hope.

"Look at me," he growls, his voice strained. "Look at me, Kiara." I stare down at him, and I see it. I see it so fucking clearly. He grabs my waist, locking me in place as he thrusts sharply inside me. "I fucking love you. You're fucking mine." I close my eyes, on the brink of ecstatic release. "Say it!"

"I'm yours," I choke out, my whole body violently shaking as I come undone. "I'm yours."

With a guttural groan, Milo finds his release, pulling me flush against his sticky chest. "I love you."

Unable to keep my eyes open or form coherent words, I simply nod. Unable or unwilling? It's right there. On the tip of my tongue. Just say it. For fuck sakes, say it!

"I know," I hum, hating myself for being so weak. "I know."

*I love you too.*

Crouching down by the side of the bed, I rest my head on the edge of the mattress. "Hey," I whisper, caressing Milo's cheek. "Wake up, we need to go downstairs."

He stirs, opening his eyes, a low, sleepy groan escaping his lips. "Or we can stay in bed," he says in a suggestive tone. "Come here."

I chuckle, standing up and crossing my arms. "Get up," I demand, tilting my head. "Julia won't let Natalia open any presents until we're all together. Your niece is about ten minutes away from a full-blown temper tantrum."

Milo pouts. "But it's Christmas, Kiara. A day of giving." He peers down at his half-erect penis. "What am I to do? I need help."

"Mind over matter, baby." I grab a pile of clothes off the foot of the bed and toss it to him. "Get dressed. You have two minutes."

Milo scowls, propping himself up and slipping on a black shirt. "You are very bossy this morning, tesoro." He climbs out of bed, his dick on full display. I blush, pressing my lips into a thin line as my throat dries. He smirks, cocking his head. "Mind over matter, *baby*."

"Shut up and put some fucking pants on."

Milo laughs as he slides on a pair of briefs and jeans. "Your loss, gattina."

I roll my eyes, chucking him his watch. He slips it over his wrist. "Okay, let's go." He yawns, wrapping his arm over my shoulder as we head downstairs. "Are you still tired?"

"Yes." He squeezes his eyelids open and shut. "I need an espresso."

"Yeah, you had a long day yesterday." I bite my lip as we

round the staircase. "How did everything go in Milan by the way? Any problems?"

"Surprisingly no. I thought Nico would fuck something up, but everything is going according to plan. My associates in Moscow are ready to go on our command."

"When are you doing it?" I whisper, swallowing back unease. "You said before the new year, right?"

"New Year's Eve," Milo reveals, unbothered by the fact he's going to murder someone. "Igor is hosting a party, we will do it then. Their arms warehouse will be unmanned. It is the perfect opportunity. How is it you Americans put it? Two birds, one stone?"

"That's a really big stone," I murmur in a low hum. "Are you sure this is a good idea? What if they try to retaliate? What if it gets worse? How do you know this will put an end to all of this?"

Milo stops us at the bottom of the staircase. He cups my cheek, meeting my worried eyes. "*Pravda* is not a very organized faction of the brotherhood. They are reckless and arrogant. Without Igor, they will not be able to remain in power." He strokes my hair, placing a soft kiss on my lips. "Do not worry, tesoro, they will not be a problem anymore."

I blow out a slow exhale, leaning into his touch. "You're confident? I don't want you to get hurt."

"Yes, Kiara, I am confident." He links his fingers through mine. "Let's not think about this today, yes?"

"Okay," I hum as we follow the whimpering cries of Natalia into the living room.

"Talia!" Milo exclaims, holding out his arms. "Buon Natale, mia principessa. Why are you crying?"

"Zio!" Natalia darts toward us, her baby pink dress bouncing with every step. "Mamma won't let me open my presents!"

My gaze darts to Julia who's already sipping on a glass of white wine. "Do not judge me, cara," she states in a sour tone. "You did not give birth to a demon child."

Paolo comes up behind his wife, wrapping his arms around her waist. "Julia, smile, baby, it's Christmas." He kisses her neck. "Relax, please?"

Antonia claps her hands, drawing our attention. "I think it is time to put Talia out of her misery." She looks at her granddaughter. "You may now open your gifts."

Natalia screeches, stumbling toward the fourteen-foot-tall Christmas tree by the fireplace. Teresa saunters into the room with a tray of espresso and a glass of wine. "Buon Natale," she says to me and Milo before walking to Julia.

"She will be wasted by ten," Milo notes with a soft laugh, taking a seat next to his mother on the couch. He gives her a kiss on the cheek. "How many glasses has she had?"

Antonia scowls. "Too many." She peers up at me. "Do you drink, Kiara?"

I blink, taking a sip of coffee. "I do."

"In the morning? Before breakfast?" Antonia adds, sighing, "Lord save my daughter."

"*Mamma*," Milo says in a drawn-out playful tone. "It could be worse; she could be snorting cocaine."

Antonia gasps as she slaps Milo's knee. "Stop that. Dio mio, Emilio. Natalia is right there." She lets out a shaky breath. "I raised animals. Both of you."

Milo cranes his neck toward me, tossing me a wink. "Yes, I *am* an animal, aren't I?"

My jaw drops. In front of his mother?! "I think I need some cream, if you'll excuse me."

"I will go with you," Milo offers and I cast him a hardened glare. "On second thought, I will stay here."

"Good idea." Christmas with the Di Vaio's. Definitely not normal. Turning the corner toward the kitchen, I bump into Marchello and Luisa. "Good morning, Luisa." I give her a hug. Glancing over her shoulder, I smile at her father. "Merry Christmas, Marchello."

"To you too, Kiara," he says with a warm smile that doesn't reach his eyes. "It is nice that we are all together."

"Yes, the whole family under one roof, it doesn't happen very often," Luisa notes with a sly smirk. "And maybe today we will celebrate more than just Christmas? Hmm, Kiara?"

I shrug, casting her a knowing smile. "Maybe."

She beams. "Really?!"

"Luisa," Marchello says, keeping his tone level as he tugs on his daughter's arm. "You can talk later; we should go see Milo. You can give him your gift."

Luisa subtly rolls her eyes. "Of course, papà."

"I'll see you in a minute," I say, choosing not to be affected by Marchello's lack of enthusiasm.

"How many presents did you guys get her?" I scan the once visible hardwood floor which is now covered with shredded wrapping paper, bows, and toys. "Don't you think you're spoiling her a bit?"

Milo chuckles, kissing my temple. "Are you jealous, tesoro? Do you wish to be spoiled?"

"Yeah, I'm jealous of a three-year-old," I jeer, giving him a slight shove. "But seriously, it's been like two hours and she's still opening gifts? Seems a bit over the top."

"Perhaps." Milo shrugs, gazing at Julia and Paolo who are on the floor trying to help Natalia put together a toy. "But look how happy she is."

I roll my eyes. "I'm just saying, our children would get like a maximum of ten presents. Anything more than that is just absurd."

Milo whips his head toward me, a grin on his face. "*Our* children?"

Shit. I clear my throat. "It's a figure of speech."

"A very *telling* figure of speech." Milo smirks as he stands up. "I think it is time for *your* present, tesoro. Come with me."

"What?" I flap my arms. "I thought we weren't doing gifts! Milo..." Great. Fuck sakes. I knew I should've gotten him something.

Ignoring my frazzled expression, he looks around the room, nodding at his underboss. "We will be back shortly."

Marchello smiles, pulling out his phone. "Lunch will be served soon, do not be long."

Without another word, Milo grabs my hand and drags me down the hallway. "Close your eyes, Kiara." I frown, pursing my lips. "Please?"

I grumble, begrudgingly following his instructions. "Fine."

"Are you not a fan of surprises?" he laughs, guiding me down the hall.

"Not really."

"I think you will like this one." He leads me through a creaking door and positions me in the center of the mystery room. "Do not peek."

"Where are we?" I open my right eye just a crack. "It's really dark in here."

Milo clicks his tongue. "You are peeking."

"No, I'm not," I lie. "I'm just very intuitive."

Milo snorts, letting go of my hand. "You can open your eyes in twenty seconds, yes?" I nod. "I will be right back."

"Wait! What? Where are you going?"

"Trust me." His voice is faint as he walks away from me. "Start counting."

I let out a sharp breath, crossing my arms as I count down from twenty out loud, a faint electrical buzz sounding from afar.

What the fuck is going on?

"Alright," Milo says, appearing by my side. "Open."

As soon as my eyelids flutter open, my heart stops, and I let out a loud gasp. *Nana.* "Oh my God." At the front of the dark room, dressed in her iconic baby blue pleated skirt and cloche hat, is my grandmother. She's pixelated, but she's there. Nana Anne. And she's smiling at me. She's looking at me. Holy shit. "Milo, what did you do?"

"Merry Christmas, sweetheart," Nana says, her comforting, angelic voice immediately forcing my eyes to well up with tears. I grip my chest, my knees weak as I'm flooded with emotions. She looks so real. *So fucking real.* Her voice. Her hair. Her mannerisms. It's her. It's Nana. *Oh my God.* "I miss you so much, Kiara, every day." She tilts her head, her soft green eyes piercing my soul as tears roll down my face. Milo laces his fingers through mine as I stare in awe at the hologram. "My wish this Christmas is for you to never stop dreaming. Do not limit yourself to the familiar, Kiara, instead embrace the unknown. All God's children were given wings. Use yours, sweetheart. Fly. Fly like a bluebird."

"She's said this to me before," I mumble under my breath, my heart beating in my chest, my grip tightening around Milo's hand. "This is from—"

"Whenever you are feeling sad, Kiara, simply remember that—" Nana pauses, taking a deep breath as familiar instrumental music flows from the hidden speakers. How did he do this? How did he—Nana opens her mouth and starts singing *Over the Rainbow*.

"Oh my God. How did you do this? Milo—" I gasp for breath. "Oh my God."

Milo stays silent as my grandmother sings me a song from my favorite movie. When I was little, I wanted so badly to be Dorothy. I wanted to escape my life, the pain of losing my parents, the darkness of reality.

I wanted magic, adventure, *color*.

Nana claps her hands, grinning at me. "You're a blue-bird, Kiara. Just spread your wings and don't be afraid to fly." She takes a small breath. "I love you sweetheart, Merry Christmas."

And she vanishes.

"Holy shit," I hum as soft lights turn on and I realize we're in the theater.

He glides his thumb across my wet cheek. "Please tell me those are happy tears, tesoro."

"How did you do that?" I ask, glancing back to the front of the room. "She looked so real, she sounded so real. What she said I— It was her."

"I had some of my men visit your home in Hawthorne, they collected old VHS footage of your grandmother and a few cards she's written to you over the years," he explains, cupping my face. "I wanted to give you something authentic."

That was authentic all right.

"You broke into my house?" I ask, hiccupping. "That's very illegal."

"Are you upset with me?" Milo asks, a small frown marring his brows.

"No," I fan myself as a wide smile spreads on my face.

"I'm not upset. This was—" I shake my head. "This was the best gift I've ever received. I can't believe you did this."

"Your grandmother meant a lot to you." He caresses my hand, his honest gaze flickering around my face. "And you mean a lot to me. Kiara—" He sinks down on one knee and produces a velvet box from his pocket. My heart hammers in my chest as he opens the baby blue box, a teardrop diamond ring glistening in the center. "From the moment I saw you, I knew I would fall in love with you. You are a remarkable woman, Kiara, and I want to spend the rest of my life by your side. Will you please do me the honor of becoming my wife?"

"I think I knew too." I kneel down in front of him, resolution coursing through my veins like liquid gold. "Milo—" Caressing his cheek, I scan his beautifully vulnerable face. I'm not scared anymore. I'm not frightened. This is right. This is fate. "Milo, I lo—"

"Emilio!" The door swings open and Gio barges inside, his eyes wide with shock. "You need to come with me right now!"

Milo's jaw clenches as he shoots daggers at Gio. "We are in the middle of something, can you not see? Fucking idiot!"

"Milo, *now*," Gio says unapologetically.

Milo's posture harden as we stand up. "What is happening? Tell me."

"Come," Gio says, his body language tense as Milo grabs my hand and we follow him down the hallway.

"This better be important," Milo grunts. "Fucking unbelievable."

"Yeah—" I pause, frowning as Gio opens the front door for us. "Where are we going?"

He doesn't reply.

A sick feeling creeps into the pit of my stomach as we

walk down to the front of the estate. What is going on?! The nausea intensifies as I scan all the family members huddled around the brass gates. Julia looks at me, her expression more distraught than Gio's.

"What is happening?" Milo asks as we approach the hordes of white faces.

"Milo," Julia whispers, casting me a sympathetic look as everyone clears the way for us. Once the path is empty, all the color washes out of Milo's face and he drops my hand, staggering backward. "Milo, breathe, please."

I whip my head around, following his sightline. On the dampened ground, wrapped in a tattered fur jacket is a red-headed woman. She snaps her head up, her hazel eyes locked on Milo.

"No," Milo breathes, covering his mouth. "This cannot be."

"Who is sh—"

The redheaded woman scrambles toward Milo, her painted lips teetering between a frown and a smile. She throws herself into his arms.

Oh God, is that—

"Amore mio!"

*My love?* Oh, no.

No. No. No. No. No.

This isn't happening. How is this happening?

Milo's hands hover above her back for ten agonizing seconds until he slowly, so *fucking* slowly lowers them. *No. Please no.* As he tightens his arms around her waist, it's like he's choking me, killing me, *drowning* me.

I was mistaken. I was so fucking wrong.

There's always a tidal wave.

Always.

# CHAPTER 35

# ON THE SURFACE

UNTIL THE WATER SUBSIDES, AND THE DEBRIS IS cleared, it is difficult to see the damage caused by a tidal wave. Nana taught me to never make assumptions, she taught me to be logical, rational, calm. It's easier said than done. But I'm trying, I really am.

Although their embrace lasted for only a second before Milo pulled away and ordered everyone inside, I still can't gauge the extent of the damage. He won't look at me. Or her. Or anyone. But I don't need to see his face to know that he's conflicted. It's in his body language, it's in his footsteps, it's in his clenched knuckles. He's struggling, and frankly, I don't blame him. I know exactly how he's feeling. He's relieved. He's angry. He's confused. That's how I felt when I found Andre. Milo blamed himself for her death. But she's here. In the flesh.

Vittoria is alive.

But how? And why? It doesn't make sense. Curiosity is outweighing dread. Faith is outweighing doubt. And my love for Milo is outweighing all the fear thrumming through my veins.

I made my decision and it'll take more than the return of a dead ex-girlfriend to make me leave. I won't let her drown me. Us. Not after everything we've been through. This is just another hurdle. It's taller, longer, wider than the rest but this time, *we're* stronger, faster, and more capable of making the jump. At least, I hope. I have to believe that. I have to believe that we will survive. There's no other option. None.

The living room is silent as Milo paces back and forth in front of Vittoria who is seated in the center of the couch, a hot cup of tea in her hands. I glance at Marchello, Julia, and Luisa who are scattered around the room. No one dares to make a sound. We're flies on the wall, observing, studying, holding our breaths.

"Milo," Vittoria whispers in a timid tone. "Say something."

Milo's jaw clenches as he stops in front of her. "I thought you were dead. We received a rose, Vittoria, it had your name on it. I thought *Pravda* took you. I thought—"

"They did." Vittoria looks down, tucking a piece of hair behind her ear. "I was at the beach when they took me."

"And yet you are alive," Milo says, the tiniest glimmer of hope in his voice. "Is Sergio alive as well? Is he—"

"No." Vittoria swallows, unable to look at him. "He is dead."

Milo swallows back reality. "And why are you not dead, Vittoria? Hmm? What did you do? What did you tell them?"

Vittoria snaps her head up, her lips curled into an offended frown. "You think I betrayed you? You think I sold you out?" She lets out a low scoff. "How? What would I tell them, Milo? Your favorite flavor of gelato? Where you buy your shoes?! I know nothing of value."

Milo runs a frustrated hand through his hair. "Then how is it that you are here? What happened, Vittoria? Explain it to me because I have never heard of anyone surviving *Pravda*."

"They were—" She clears her throat, lowering her head. "They were going to kill me but then—" She sniffles. "Igor changed his mind. He said that I was too beautiful to die, so he—" She glances up at Milo, tearing up. "He made me his mistress."

"He what?" Milo spits.

Vittoria dabs the corner of her eye with a napkin. "He brought me to his brothel. He made me do things, Milo."

Earth-shattering guilt flashes across Milo's face. "What kind of things?"

Vittoria lets out a small shaky breath as she goes into further detail. The story slipping out of her mouth is devastating, disgusting, demoralizing. And I feel ill. Nauseous. But the unease stirring in my stomach is not from her words, no, it's from the disconnect between her words and her face.

The frown between her eyebrows is over-exaggerated, the trembling of her lips is theatrical, and her eyes lack any emotion; they're empty, blank, disconnected.

The pain in Milo's voice breaks my heart as he asks, "Why did he let you go, Vittoria?"

"I don't know." She shrugs, taking a sip of tea. "Maybe his wife found out about me? Maybe she wanted to kill me?" She clears her throat. "Igor, he uh—he said he loved me. He fell in love with me. The last thing I remember is going to my room and the next moment, I woke up outside your house. I don't remember how I got here."

On the surface, she looks like she's been through hell; ripped black nylons, smeared mascara, wild unkempt hair, a few streaks of dirt smudged on her face and hands. Yet, examining her with a critical eye, I notice that her manicured nails are spotless, that the rings on her fingers are glistening under the yellow light of the chandelier, that her fur coat is mink. Nana loved mink.

I've spent my whole life studying emotions in order to be able to read people, in order to be one step ahead of liars and cheaters, in order to shield myself from pain and hurt. I've learned that the surface is easy to fake. I've done it. I still do it. But there are some things that cannot be hidden. That cannot be faked. And Vittoria, she's a shiny counterfeit bill.

She's lying. She's fucking lying. But unfortunately, based on Milo's aghast expression, he doesn't see it.

"He is a sick man, Vittoria." Milo's face contorts with disgust. "I am so sorry you had to go through that, I really am."

"But now it is all okay," she says, reaching out to grab Milo's hand. "Now I am home. I am with you."

"Vittoria," Milo whispers, taking a step back and pinching the bridge of his nose. "I—"

The French doors to the living room swing open as Paolo walks inside. "Milo, we checked the security footage," he says, glancing at Marchello. "It was an unmarked black van, no plates. Nothing. They pushed her out and drove off. We cannot track them."

"Try," Milo says through his teeth. "Tap into the city lines, I do not give a shit. If *Pravda* is in *Genova*, I need to know."

"Right away," Paolo says, giving Julia's hand a squeeze before exiting the room.

"Luisa," Milo says, his expression weary. "Please take Vittoria upstairs."

"No, don't leave me," Vittoria whines, pouting. Breathe.

Stay calm. I am staying calm. "Do not leave. I don't want to be alone. Milo, please."

"I cannot do that," Milo says, his tone low. "You are free to stay here for as long as you need but—"

"Milo," Marchello says, taking a step forward. "Take the poor woman upstairs. Look at her, she is scared."

I inwardly roll my eyes, immediately feeling like a piece of shit. I have no evidence that she's lying. I can't prove anything. For all I know, maybe she's telling the truth. And if she is, then I'm a horrible, awful person.

"You can take her," I say, speaking for the first time in what feels like hours. "It's fine, Milo."

Vittoria whips her head toward me, frowning. "Who are you? You are new."

"That is Kiara," Milo says, taking a breath. "She is my—"

"Friend," Marchello cuts him off, shooting me a hard-ened look. "She is a friend."

Respect.

"Actually," I say, meeting Milo's gaze. This is not the right time or the right place, but I don't care. I refuse to be a casualty in her destructive wake. "I'm his fiancée."

Marchello's lip twitches but he doesn't say anything.

"What?!" Vittoria grabs her chest, letting out a loud gasp as she looks at Milo. "Your *fiancée*? Milo, how could you? Did I mean nothing to you?"

Milo's body tenses. "I think it is time for you to go upstairs, Vittoria. Get some rest."

"Maybe call your sister?" I suggest in a gentle tone. "I know she misses you."

Vittoria's eyes light up with genuine excitement. "My sister? You have spoken to her? When? Where? Is she okay?"

I frown at her. Odd reaction. "In Milan, a few weeks ago. She will be very pleased to hear that you are alive."

Marchello clears his throat. "Perhaps Milo is correct, it is time to rest, Vittoria."

She blinks, averting his gaze. "Fine. I will go."

"I will be in my office," Milo says, pulling out his phone. "If you need me." He looks over his shoulder. "Kiara? Come with me."

I cast Julia a nervous side-eye as I follow Milo out of the living room. Instead of going to his office, Milo leads us into the kitchen. He darts to the liquor cabinet, pouring himself a glass of scotch and downing it. He hangs his head, gripping the edge of the granite counter, letting out a deep sigh.

"Hey..." I come up behind him and rest my cheek on his back, wrapping my arms around his torso. "Are you okay?"

"No," he admits, spinning around. "All this time, she was alive. She was suffering all this time." His jaw tightens. "He was hurting her, he was—"

"It's not your fault, Milo." I caress his cheek, my heart hurting for him. "It's not your fault."

"I should have looked for her, Kiara. I should've done something." He takes my left hand and grazes his thumb over my fingers. He looks up at me, his eyes hooded, drowning in pain. "Are you saying yes to my proposal because of Vittoria?"

"No," I breathe, tightening my grip around his hand. "I'm saying yes because I love you, Milo." I tilt my head. "I love you."

Milo swallows. "I do not deserve your love, Kiara. I don't deserve anything."

"Stop that. This wasn't your fault, Milo. What happened to Vittoria wasn't your fault. You thought she was dead. How could you have known?"

Milo slumps against the counter, dragging his hand across his face. "If anything were to ever happen to you, Kiara, I would not be able to live with myself. I love you more than the air I breathe, but you were right, I cannot keep you safe, that is a fact."

"Nothing's going to happen to me. And if it does, then so what?"

Milo's eyes spring open. "So what? What do you mean, so what?"

"People die every day, Milo," I say, lacing my fingers through his. "It's the circle of life. No one gets to live forever."

"And what if the same thing that happened to my grandmother and Vittoria, happens to you, Kiara?" Milo says, his tone rising. "There are far worse fates than death. You must see that by now." He shakes his head, turning away from me. "I do not wish to wield your fate, Kiara."

My heart hammers in my chest. "What are you saying? That you don't want to marry me? You don't want to be with me?" I yank on his arm. "Look at me!"

"I can't."

"Yes, you can!" Frustration blurs my vision. "You think that I don't know the hazards that come with being your wife? You think that I haven't thought about that? I have. I've thought about it a lot. And I'm *still* saying yes. I'm still here. I want to be here."

"I cannot protect you," he whispers. "I cannot keep you safe."

"Oh my God!" I rake my hands through my hair. I'm going to lose it. "What happened to Vittoria is not your fault. It's not—" I let out a manic chuckle. "She's not even telling the truth, Milo! She's fucking lying to you!"

Milo's head snaps toward me. "What?"

"She's lying," I say, flapping my arms. "Everything she's told you is a fucking lie."

"Why would she lie about something like that? For what reason?"

"Oh, I don't know? Sympathy? A shoulder to cry on?" I motion between our two bodies. "This! Us fighting. I can see it in her eyes, Milo, it's written all over her face. She's not telling you the truth, she's not."

"I understand that you are upset, Kiara, but you are out of line."

"And you're blind. How can you not see it? Don't you think it's convenient that she shows up *now*? After all this time?"

Milo sighs, pouring himself another drink. "Perhaps it is time for you to leave, Kiara. Save yourself."

"Oh, don't be a fucking martyr, Milo. It's not a good look on you," I sneer, digging my nails into my palm. "I am not leaving."

"Kiara," he breathes in a defeated tone. "Your life would be much easier without me in it."

I expel an incredulous scoff. "Yeah, no shit, Milo! But evidently, I don't want easy, I want complicated and messy and fucking deranged." I pull on his arm, swinging his body around. "I want *you*." I grab the collar of his shirt. "And you want me, so just fucking kiss me and give me the *goddamn ring*."

Milo blinks, suppressing a grin. "You are quite frightening when angry."

"Then don't provoke me," I state through my teeth. "Listen, I know you must be in shock right now and I'm probably not handling this the proper way, but I love you, Milo and I'm not going anywhere, so you might as well just get over this whole 'I can't keep you safe' shit so we can move on. Okay?!"

"Okay."

"And just because something bad happened to someone else, doesn't mean it's going to happen to—" I pause. "Wait, did you say okay?"

Milo's expression softens as he lets out a small laugh. "You are crazy, Kiara,'" he says, reaching into his pocket. "And for some reason, it makes me love you even more." He holds out the velvet box, opening it with one hand. "Your ring."

"*Thanks*." I yank the diamond and slide it on my finger. "Now, was that so hard?"

Milo shakes his head, rubbing his chin as he scans my flustered face. "You're very sexy right now. Perhaps I should anger you more often."

"If you wish to walk around with both of your balls intact, I would advise against that."

"You are ruthless."

"Well, I am marrying into the mafia. I need to start acting the part."

"Fuck." Milo runs a tired hand down his face. "I need to go review the footage Paolo collected."

"Can I help?" I twirl the engagement ring around my finger. "Please."

Milo grins, gesturing to the door. "After you, Mrs. Di Vaio."

I purse my lips, mentally exhausted but physically thriving. "Has a nice ring to it, don't you think?"

"Definitely," Milo agrees with a mischievous smirk as he places his palm on the small of my back.

We exit the kitchen and make our way upstairs. Entering Milo's office, we find Paolo and Marchello sitting on the couch, talking to Vittoria. I clench my fists, attempting to keep my expression neutral.

"I thought you were going to call your sister," I say, scratching my nose with my left hand. Petty, I know. "What happened?"

Paolo and Marchello exchange a look. "Vittoria just told us some very concerning news," Paolo says.

Milo frowns. "What is it?"

"Tell him what you told us," Marchello says.

Vittoria clears her throat. "Two days ago, I overheard Igor talking on the phone," she explains, her gaze darting between the two of us. "He mentioned a mole."

Milo's body stiffens. "A mole?"

"Yes." Vittoria subtly glances up at me, a barely noticeable smirk clipping her conniving lips. "Here. In *Santi Oscuri.*"

Oh, this fucking bitch.

# CHAPTER 36

## HIDDEN IN PLAIN SIGHT

THE ABILITY TO CONTROL YOUR EMOTIONS IS AN invaluable skill, one that comes in pretty fucking handy when a redheaded bitch is essentially accusing you of being a spy. But since she hasn't said it point-blank, I'll go ahead and pretend as if I'm not rattled by her not-so-subtle insinuation.

"A mole? Here?" I ask, my tone even, calm. "Really?"

"Yes," Vittoria says, fiddling with her fingers. "That's what I heard."

"What *exactly* did you hear?" Milo asks, running a hand through his hair as he paces in front of the couch. "Word for word, Vittoria."

"My memory is still a bit foggy from being drugged," she says in a broken tone as she looks up at my fiancé. "But he was thanking whoever was on the phone. He said that they were much more competent than—" She clears her throat, looking between Milo, Paolo, and Marchello. "Than Enzo."

Milo's jaw locks.

I blink, unfamiliar with the name. "Who's Enzo?"

"The rat from Manchester," Marchello spits, disdain in

his voice. "Fucking rat. He deserved more than a bullet in the brain."

I frown at Vittoria. She's lying yet she knows about Enzo? It doesn't make sense. How would she know? Unless she's telling half-truths. Or reading a script.

"That is all you heard?" Milo asks. "No name?"

"No." Vittoria shakes her head, keeping her gaze on the floor. "No name."

"If this mole is Enzo's replacement," Paolo muses, his brows pinching together, "That means they have only recently joined our organization."

"That is what it sounded like." Vittoria tilts her head up, batting her lashes at Milo. "Is there anyone new that you do not trust?" She glances at me. "Or that fits that description?"

I bite my tongue to keep myself from lashing out at her. That's what she expects. I know it. But I won't fall into her trap. Calm, cool, collected. That's me. Oh, and smart. Smarter than her.

"Do you speak Russian, Vittoria?" I ask, eliciting confused glances from the three men.

She frowns. "No, I do not. Why?"

I shrug. "Well, I'm just wondering how you understood what Igor was saying on the phone if you don't speak Russian."

"He was speaking in English."

"Really?" I say in a drawn-out breath. "Interesting." I bite my lip, glaring at Vittoria. "When was this again? When did you overhear this conversation?"

"Two days ago."

"What time?"

She blinks. "It was late."

"Where were you?"

"At the brothel," she says without missing a beat. "In the other room."

"What were you wearing?"

"Uh—"

"What did you eat that day?" I ask, crossing my arms. "What was the weather like? Hot? Cold? Sun? Rain? Snow?"

"It was—it was snowing, I think," Vittoria stammers, her breath quickening.

"What color were the walls at the brothel, Vit?" I ask, not believing her for a second. "What kind of bed did you sleep on? Did you have your own room? Or did you have to share? Was the room small, big? Did it have windows? Air conditioning? Where in Moscow was it?"

"I—I don't know. I—"

"Or maybe you just forgot your lines," I state sharply, unfazed by the tears welling up in her eyes. "Perhaps next time, use a teleprompter."

"Kiara," Milo scolds, frowning at me. "What are you doing?"

"Me?"

"I'm sorry!" Vittoria cries, burying her head into her hands, her shoulders vibrating as she begins to sob. "I don't want to think about it! I don't want to remember. Please don't make me! Please!"

"It's alright, Vittoria," Paolo whispers, rubbing her back as he casts me an unimpressed scowl. Great, *I'm* the bad guy? "It's alright. Shh."

I scoff. "So dramatic."

"Kiara, may I speak with you outside?" Milo grabs my arm and drags me to the hallway. He closes the door to his office, his eyes widened with confusion as he scans my irritated face. "What is going on with you? Why are you being so hostile with Vittoria? Why ask her all those questions? She is clearly traumatized."

"She's not traumatized, Milo, she's fucking acting! And quite poorly might I add. You don't seriously believe her, do you?"

"She knew about Enzo," Milo says, letting out a sigh. "How would she know about him if she weren't truly being held by Igor?"

"I don't know, but what I *do* know is that she's lying. Don't you see what she's trying to do? She's implying that I'm the mole."

"What? You?"

"Yes!" I shake my head. God, he's dim. "That's where all of this is leading. You don't see it? Really? Other than me, who else is technically new? Hmm? She's trying to put a wedge between us, Milo. How can you not see that?"

"Tesoro," Milo hums, taking my hand. "In the last few months, we have had three new members join our organization, it is not only you." He runs his thumb across my knuckles. "I trust you, Kiara. I know you are not the mole."

I close my eyes, his touch relaxing my stiff muscles. "I'm glad that you trust me, Milo, I really am but what about the others? They don't know me like you do. They have no reason to trust me."

"Baby—" Milo cups my cheeks, placing a soft kiss on my lips. "They will trust whoever I tell them to trust."

"Why are you so quick to believe her?" I rest my forehead against his. "For all we know, *she's* the fucking mole."

"Do not worry, Kiara. We will not tell her anything. I might believe her, but I do not trust her." He kisses my nose. "Not like I trust you."

"Fine," I grumble, sucking in a deep breath. He's not

budging. "Well, what's your plan then? What are you going to do?"

"I will have to re-run background checks on the new recruits, track their movements and calls for the last few months." Milo sighs apologetically. "I am sorry today has turned into such a disaster."

"Yeah..." I fiddle with my Nana's locket as I admire my engagement ring. "So much for a celebration."

"We *will* celebrate, tesoro." Milo pulls me against his chest, his chin resting on my head. "Once this is all over." He kisses my forehead. "Go downstairs, Kiara, try to enjoy the rest of the day. Please? Your Christmas does not need to be ruined. It is salvageable."

"Yeah, whatever." I pull away from Milo, my head throbbing, my body weak from stress. "I'll be downstairs if you need me."

"I love you, Kiara," Milo says, squeezing my hand. "Remember that."

I force a smile. "I love you too, Milo."

He turns around reaching for the door handle. "I'll come find you soon, yes?"

"Mhmm."

If he wants proof, then I'll just have to find it.

How? No fucking idea.

<hr />

"Cara!" Julia leaps off the couch and runs up to me. She grabs my hand and lets out an excited shriek. "Look at this rock! Holy fucking shit! It's bigger than mine!"

I stifle a yawn. "It's a bit extra."

"Come sit, Kiara, you look exhausted." Luisa pats the seat beside her, a sympathetic smile on her face. I sit down between my two friends. "How are you feeling? It is crazy, no? I cannot believe she is alive."

"It is horrible," Julia says, passing me a glass of wine. "But at least she is safe now."

"I'm good." I shake my head, pouring myself a glass of sparkling grape juice. Alcohol and headaches don't mix. I purse my lips. "So, you believe her? That she was held captive all those months?"

Luisa frowns, taking a bite of a cream-filled pastry. "Of course, who would lie about something like that?"

I scoff. "Vittoria."

Julia blinks. "You don't believe her? Why?"

"Because her story doesn't make sense, because I can see it in her eyes, her lips, her body language. She's lying, Jules. I know she is."

"Kiara—" Julia places her hand on my thigh. "Everyone reacts to trauma in different ways, just because she is not presenting the typical signs of abuse does not mean she is lying. We must believe her." A little grin appears on her face as if she's trying to lighten the mood. "I thought you were a feminist, cara."

"I am!" I exclaim, irritation spiking in my tone. "But just because I'm a feminist doesn't mean I have to blindly trust all women, especially not Vittoria who is acting her little ass off upstairs saying that there's a fucking mole here."

"What?" Luisa gasps, her mouth hanging open. "She said there is a mole?"

"Yup," I say, chugging the shitty grape water. "And she basically insinuated that it was me."

"She said that?" Julia asks, setting down her glass. "She said it was you?"

"No, but she hinted at it. It was very subtle, but I caught it right away." I slump into the couch. "If Milo doesn't nip this in the bud, I don't see how anyone is ever going to trust me."

Luisa bites her lip. "This is not good, Kiara. To be accused of being a mole, it never works out well."

"Yeah, I know! Plus, I'm new and I'm with Milo and he's told me things, but like how conniving and diabolical does she think I am? Would people honestly believe that I was at the bank on purpose? That I somehow lured Milo to my till? He could've chosen fucking Evie! That was his decision. And why would I shoot Andre if I was working for the Russians? Huh? That makes no sense at all!" My eyes spring open. "Oh my God!"

"What?" Julia asks, blinking. "What is it?"

"Andre!" I say, jumping off the couch, my head spinning. "I can go ask Andre if Vittoria is lying or not. As far as I know, he's still in the basement."

"Kiara—"

I clap my hands at my brilliant idea. "Yes, this is perfect. I'll go down there and get him to confirm my theory, that Vittoria is a lying bitch." I purse my lips in thought. "Where's Teresa?"

"I don't think that is a good idea, Kiara," Luisa says. "He is dangerous. Do not go alone."

"Then come with me," I say, cocking my head to the side and yanking on her arm. "Girl power, let's go!"

"I think you need to calm down, cara," Julia hums, giving me a worried stare. "Maybe you need to sleep."

"I agree with Julia," Luisa says, her eyebrows knitting together. "You have had an emotional day. You are not thinking clearly. Go rest, Kiara."

"You know what? You're right." It would seem as though I'm on my own. "I think I'll go take a nap. Sleep it off."

"That is a good idea," Julia says. "I will wake you when dinner is ready, yes?"

"Thanks," I say in a warm tone, heading out of the living room. Glancing over my shoulder to make sure they're not watching me, I duck into the adjacent room and dart to the kitchen, following the smell of Italian cuisine. Teresa hovers over a pot of aromatic pasta sauce as I enter the kitchen. "Hi, Teresa."

She jumps, grabbing her chest. "Signorina, you scare me."

"Sorry." I lean against the counter, scanning her plump face. "Teresa, I need the keys to the basement."

She frowns. "The basement?"

"Yes, to the room you bring food." I'm not sure how much she knows. "I need the keys to the room. Please."

Conflict flashes across her face. "I am not supposed to—"

I put my left hand on her forearm, making sure she sees the ring. "It's fine, Teresa. I grant you permission."

She blinks at the glistening diamond. "Oh, congratulations, Signorina!" she exclaims, smiling up at me. "One moment, I will be back."

"Grazie," I say, tapping my nails on the counter as she scurries to the back room.

Scanning the cutting station, my gaze lands on a small fillet knife. Hmm. Perhaps some form of protection would be wise. After all, he is a rapist and a murderer. I shouldn't just go in unarmed. Opening one of the wooden drawers, I take out a sharp knife and slide up my sleeve, blade down.

Teresa returns a moment later, keys in hand. "Be careful, yes?"

With the icy metal of the Chef's knife pressed against my forearm, I know I'll be just fine.

# CHAPTER 37

# NO MORE TEARS

DOING A QUICK GOOGLE SEARCH ON MY WAY DOWN TO the basement, I learn that there are three rules to talking to a psychopath. Number one: Establish boundaries and don't get manipulated. Basically, stand your ground. Number two: Remain calm and don't give them the satisfaction of a reaction. Number three: Stay focused on the goal at hand, don't get distracted by diversion tactics.

Easy enough.

Sucking in a deep breath, I slide the steel divider and peek into the rundown dimly lit room. "Andre." A chill zaps down my spine as he cranes his neck toward me, his face thin, dirty, bruised, and broken. "I have a couple of questions for you."

"Who are you?" Andre shifts on the mattress, the rattling of metal sounding from where he sits. He squints, a small smile forming on his face. "Oh, Kiara," he says with a hoarse laugh. "I remember your pretty little eyes. Please, come inside."

"I think this is fine," I wince, bile rising in my throat. "I need to ask you a couple of questions about your cousin."

"And I will answer all your questions. But not through a door." He cocks his head. "Don't be scared, *kukulka*—" He shimmies his wrist. "Your boyfriend chained me, like a dog."

Fuck.

"Fine," I sneer, unlocking the door. The hinges creak as I open it and step inside, all my senses on high alert. "Okay, now for my questions."

He smirks, giving me a slow, disgusting once-over. "You are the best Christmas gift I've ever received. And I've gotten many treasures over the years."

I wince at the word treasure. "Do you know a woman by the name of Vittoria?" I ask, hiding my discomfort. "Red hair? Italian?"

"Maybe..." He props himself against the weathered stone wall. "Maybe not. " He smirks at me. "Why?"

"I'm not here to play games, Andre," I state, keeping my distance. "Answer the question or I'm leaving."

"Fine." Andre's eyes harden. "The name sounds familiar." He pauses. "I thought your questions were going to be about my cousin, not some woman I don't know."

"Igor never mentioned that name before?" I ask, taking a step forward. "Maybe ten/ eleven months ago? Around the same time you killed Sergio?"

"That was a good day," Andre chuckles. "Idiots, all of these Italians."

I clench my jaw. "So, you did kill him? Sergio?"

"I believe *Milo* can confirm that," he says in a knowing tone. "He has a pretty blue rose to remember him by. Perfect for a funeral." He shrugs. "No, body though, so sad."

"How many roses did you send here?" I slowly stride toward the bed. "Only one?"

Andre purses his lips. "One, maybe two. I don't remember."

"Try. Did you or did you not kidnap and hold hostage a woman named Vittoria?"

He grins, peering up at me. "Red hair, right?"

"Andre." I stop at the foot of the bed. "Answer the fucking question."

He scans the room, a pensive look in his eyes. "I am curious, Kiara," he muses. "Why is it that you are here alone?" He licks his lips. "Does anyone know you are down here?"

"Yes, they do," I answer immediately.

"Too fast, *kukulka*," he notes, clicking his tongue as he shifts on the mattress. "I think you are lying." He tilts his head, a devious grin on his face. "Truly a great Christmas."

Before I can react, the handcuffs slip off his right wrist as he surges forward, wrapping his hand around my throat. My head whips back, slamming against the wall as he presses his body against mine.

"Get off me," I croak, gasping for air as he licks the side of my face, his hand inching along the hem of my sweater.

"I've wanted to do this since I first saw you at the casino," he whispers into my ear, sliding his hand up my shirt, his filthy fingers grazing my midsection.

"Milo will kill you," I say between ragged breaths. "If you touch me, he will kill you. Let me go."

Andre laughs, pushing his hips forward, his half-erect dick pressing against me. "He will kill me in six days anyway," he says, thrusting harder. "At least this way, I'll die with your sweet pussy on my cock." My heart hammers in my chest as I writhe under his strong hold, trying to get my right arm loose. The blade of the knife digs into my wrist.

Fuck, just a little bit further.

He lowers his arm and reaches for his zipper. "I love it when they squirm."

It's instinctual. Primal. Innate. The desire to live. To be

spared from harm. To survive. There's no time to think or reason or hesitate. And I don't. I don't hesitate. I don't hesitate when I release my grip on the blade and slide it down my arm into my hand. I don't hesitate when I look at Andre in the eyes, the sharp tip of the knife slicing through fabric, skin, muscle, fat. I don't hesitate when he lets go of me and I twist the blade, eviscerating his organs, his agony-infested cries like music to my fucking ears.

Andre drops to his knees, gripping his stomach, blood spurting from his abdomen as he looks up at me. "Help me," he croaks. "Please."

"Why?" I stare at him as I grip the slimy handle of the knife. "Why should I help you?"

"Please." His voice is barely audible as he topples over. "Help me."

I tilt my head to the side, smiling down at him as I press the tip of my boot on his open wound. He cries out in pain. "Does that hurt, *kukulka?*" Blood pools around him as his body twitches. I stand over him for what feels like hours until he stops moving, until he stops breathing, until I know he's gone for good. With a sigh of relief, I mumble, "Goodbye, Andre."

It's funny. I feel nothing. No regret. No remorse. Nothing. Huh. Interesting. Maybe I'll see him in hell, but something tells me that only one of us will burn for all of eternity. I know I'm not the judge, but I think I'm an excellent candidate for clemency.

I look up heavenward. Right?

"Kiara!"

Shit.

I spin around to find Milo and Marchello standing at the door, both their gazes locked on Andre's dead body.

Milo's head snaps up. "Kiara!" He dashes toward me,

scanning the knife in my hand. "What the fuck happened? Why are you down here? Are you hurt?"

"I'm fine." I give him the knife, my movements and tone oddly calm. "I came here to ask him questions about Vittoria."

"Is that so?" Marchello asks, narrowing his eyes at me. "If you came only to ask questions, why is he dead?"

"He attacked me," I explain, speaking only to Milo. "I thought he was handcuffed to the radiator. But he must have loosened the cuffs or something."

"He attacked you?!" Milo fumes. "Did he touch you, Kiara? Tell me."

"He tried." I wince, running a hand across my midsection. "But he didn't get too far."

"Fucking scum," Milo seethes, peering down at Andre. "If only it were possible to kill a man twice."

Marchello clears his throat. "So, what did Andre say, Kiara? When you asked about Vittoria?"

"Not a lot," I reply, wiping my blood-stained hand on my jeans. "But I don't think he knows who she is."

"You don't *think*?" Marchello hums. "Well, you are the expert in lying, aren't you?"

"Do you have something to say, Marchello?" I take a step toward him. "Say it. What's on your mind?"

"Oh, nothing," he muses in a flippant tone. "I just find it strange that we came down here to ask Andre the same questions only to find him dead." He glances at Milo. "It would seem like Kiara just murdered the only person who might know the identity of the rat."

"Enough!" Milo glares at his underboss, grabbing my hand. "I do not appreciate what you are implying, Marchello. Not another word, understand?"

Marchello holds up his hands. "It was just an observation."

"Right. You can check the cameras if you'd like. I'm sure they'd corroborate what happened."

"No audio though." Marchello sucks on his teeth. "Convenient."

"I said enough!" Milo spits. "I am taking Kiara upstairs." He looks over his shoulder. "Feed him to the dogs."

"But—"

"Now," Milo orders, leading me out of the room. "I will meet you in my office in an hour." He grumbles under his breath, pulling me up the stairs. "Fucking hell, Kiara. Why would you go down there by yourself? Do you know what could have happened? He could've—"

"Well, good thing I brought a knife, right?" I say, frustrated by the entire turn of events. Marchello is right. I look so fucking suspicious now. I did the exact opposite of what I was trying to do. "How bad is this, Milo? Tell me the truth."

"It is not good, tesoro," Milo sighs, opening my bedroom door. He follows me into the bathroom, slumping against the counter. He watches as I remove my shirt and wash Andre's blood from my hands. "Are you hurt?"

"It's not mine." Light pink water circles the drain as I scrub my hands. "I'm sorry for killing him. I know I created more problems for you."

"You're sorry?" Milo crosses his arms, his gaze fluttering around my face. "Are you sure?"

"What?" I dry my hands, slipping on a clean t-shirt. "What do you mean am I sure?"

He hesitates for a second before stating, "It takes around five minutes for a man to bleed out, Kiara. If you wanted to save him, you could've gotten help."

I swallow, averting his gaze. "I know that."

"You wanted him to die," Milo muses, his expression tight, almost uncomfortable. "You wanted him to suffer."

"Is that wrong?" I look at myself in the mirror. This time, I don't hate the woman looking back at me. I admire her. "Does that make me a bad person?"

"Not in my eyes, no. But how do *you* feel, Kiara?" Milo asks in a low voice, trying to read my mood. "Do you want to talk to Julia? Maybe she can help."

I walk to the bed and take a seat on the edge. "Do I *look* like I need help?"

"No," Milo observes, hovering above me, studying me carefully. "But last time—"

"I'm fine, Milo," I interrupt him, crawling under the sheets. He frowns. "Really, I'm fine. I don't—" I rest against the headboard, expelling a sigh. "I feel fine."

"You just murdered a man, Kiara..." Milo sits down beside me and takes my hand. "Are you positive you are alright?"

"He was a rapist and a murderer, and he attacked me," I say flatly. "Am I supposed to feel bad? Plus, technically, it was self-defense." I pull my hand away, suddenly feeling quite annoyed. "Why are you so concerned? You kill people all the time."

Milo's lip twitches. "I do not wish for you to become me, Kiara."

"And I do not wish to continue this conversation," I state, turning away from him. "I want to sleep. You can leave now."

"Tesoro," Milo whispers, caressing my hair. "Do not be mad at me. I am worried about you."

"Worried about me? Why?" I aggressively roll over, narrowing my eyes. "Should I have not killed him? I should've just let him rape me? I don't understand what you're trying to say."

Milo swallows. "I know how much you value your humanity, Kiara. I do not wish to see you fall apart and resent me in the future."

I expel a deep sigh, feeling guilty for being so snippy. "Baby," I squeeze his hand, "I'm fine, I promise. I don't feel any less human, I really don't. Andre deserved what he got, he did. Maybe I wasn't thinking about the consequences in the grand scheme of things because I know this is going to be a headache to clean up, but I don't regret doing it. I don't."

Milo's expression softens. "Clean up?"

I roll my eyes, suppressing a smile. "See? I'm becoming fluent."

"Yes." He arches down, pressing his soft lips against mine. "Yes, you are."

"I love you," I whisper, leaning into his touch. "I really do."

Milo smiles, kissing my cheek. "Rest now, Kiara. I will wake you up in a few hours."

"No, it's fine. Just let me sleep. I'm ready for this day to be over." Milo climbs into bed with me. "What are you doing?"

"Close your eyes, tesoro," he whispers, pulling me against his chest. "I will stay until you fall asleep."

"Are you worried I'll start crying once you leave?"

"No." Milo tightens his arms around me, kissing my temple. "I am not."

And neither am I.

# Chapter 38

## Missing Piece

I wake up in an empty bed, my gaze darting to the digital clock on the nightstand. 11 p.m. I groan, rubbing my eyes. Great. I should've gotten Milo to wake me up. Why did I think I could sleep through the night?

I take a sweater off the armchair and slip it on, grabbing my phone on the way out of the bedroom. He's probably still working. Of course, he's still working.

God, when will this end? Where's the light at the end of the tunnel? I don't see it. I don't. I fucked up. I *really* fucked up and now he has to fix it. He has to undo all the damage I caused.

But can he?

No matter how much sway and power Milo has, some messes are impossible to clean up. He can scrub and bleach and disinfect, but my dirty actions aren't going to wash away that easily. Not when there's a mole on the loose. Not when I'm a suspect in the eyes of the family. Not when lies are spreading like a disease. Not when everyone is catching the infection.

I walk down the hallway toward Milo's office, pausing outside the guest bedroom.

*"I don't know,"* Vittoria says in Arabic. What? *"Maybe a month? Two?"* I press my ear against the door. *"I know. I know."* She pauses. What is going on? *"Yes, okay. I love you too. Bye."*

Who is she talking to? And in Arabic? Oh my God, nothing makes sense. Nothing. I knock on her door. Let's see her lie her way out of this one. "Vittoria?"

"Yes?" Distant fumbling sounds from inside. "Come in." I open the door, staying out in the hallway. "Oh, Kiara. Hi."

"Hi. Were you just on the phone?"

She blinks. "Oh, yes with my sister. It's been a long time since we talked."

"Your sister?" Strike one. "Really? How's she doing?"

"Good." She clears her throat. "She is very happy to hear from me."

"I can imagine. It's not every day your sibling rises from the dead."

"She said it was a miracle." Vittoria sits down on her bed and flicks her nails. "A gift from God."

"A gift from *someone*, that's for sure," I agree, studying her movements. "Vittoria, can I give you a tip?"

Her brows pinch together as she looks up at me. "What?"

"If you want to get away with lying, you should learn how to hold eye contact for more than a second." I lean against the door frame. "And your hands? Too much fiddling. Dead giveaway." I click my tongue. "Well actually, that could also be a sign of anxiety or nervousness but in your case? I think it's all of the above. What do *you* think?"

She places her palms on her knees, staring at me. "I am not lying to anyone."

I pout, shaking my head. "Remember to blink, Vittoria. *Too* much eye contact is also bad."

She swallows. "I'm not lying."

I sigh, tilting my head. "See? You keep saying that but it's not the truth, is it? It's almost like you're trying to convince yourself. But why? What actually happened, Vittoria? Hmm? You might as well tell me because I will find out."

She clenches her fists. "You seem to be the only one who does not believe me, *Kiara*."

"Because I'm objective, Vittoria. And observant, and quite frankly, more intelligent than everyone else here. I know, I know, I shouldn't brag, but it's the truth." I take a step forward. "You see, Milo, I think he only believes you because he's been eaten alive by guilt. He's unable to look past that. But me? I can see right through you. You're like the cheapest brand of cellophane. So fucking transparent."

She opens her mouth to say something, but I hold up a finger.

"I know you're hiding something, Vittoria, and it's only a matter of time before I find out what it is, and when I do—" I stop in front of her, my gaze cold. "You will regret ever lying to me and to the man I'm going to marry. You will regret causing us such a headache and you will *definitely* regret ever stepping foot in this house. Now—" I smile. "Is there anything you'd like to tell me while you still have the chance?"

She silently stares at me, her expression for the first time, unreadable. "No. I don't have anything to say."

"Are you sure? I can see that there's something on your mind. What is it?"

Her face tenses. "Sometimes in life, Kiara, you must do what is necessary to survive."

I frown. "What does that mean?"

"You're the genius, right?" Her lips curl into a scowl. "Figure it out." She points to the door. "And get the fuck out of my room."

I scoff, heading to the door. "If I were you, I'd be careful, Vittoria. I just killed a man, perhaps I'm a little unhinged right now. Don't provoke me, okay?"

Her face pales. "Leave."

She's tougher than I gave her credit for. A shame. She was so close to cracking.

"Sweet dreams, Vittoria."

I make my way to Milo's office, my brain pulsing as I try to wrack my head around what the fuck is going on. What is she planning? Who does she work for? Does Igor speak Arabic? Was she actually in Russia? Survival? What was she talking about? So many questions and none of them link together. There's no common ground. I can't solve a puzzle with half the fucking pieces missing. It's impossible.

I bust into Milo's office without knocking. "Did you know Vittoria speaks Arabic?"

Marchello and Milo look up from the computer. "What?" Milo asks as I sit down on the chair in front of him.

"Arabic," I repeat myself. "I just overheard her on the phone speaking to someone. Thought you'd want to know."

Milo pinches the bridge of his nose, reclining in his chair. "Kiara, she studied abroad for a year when she was in university. I think it was in Dubai."

"Oh." I cross my arms. "Does her sister also speak Arabic?"

"I don't know, Kiara," Milo says in a tired tone. "Why?"

"When I asked her who she was talking to, she said it was her sister. Doesn't that seem weird to you? Why would she speak Arabic to her sister?"

"Why were you eavesdropping on her?" Marchello asks, taking a sip of coffee. "That is also weird, don't you think?"

I shoot him a glare. "I just happen to be passing by."

"Mmm, of course," he hums, checking the time. "Perhaps you should go back to sleep, Kiara. We have a lot of work to do."

I roll my eyes, ignoring him. "Milo, come on, you don't think that's suspicious behavior?"

"Kiara," he sighs. "I have just spent seven hours going through footage and recordings of our new recruits, trying to find the mole. I do not have the energy to deal with this right now."

"Why are you looking through footage? She's lying. There's no mole! You're wasting your time."

"Kiara, please," Milo pleads, his tone low. "We have more footage to comb through and we need to adjust our plans for the Russians. Can you please just let this go? Please?"

"No. God, why don't you believe me? Seriously, Milo? Why? You said you don't trust her, yet you're changing your *plans*? What plans? For new year's?"

Milo nods. "Yes, we cannot follow through. It could be a trap."

"Oh my God," I whimper, losing my mind. "There's no trap, baby, there isn't. Trust me, please." This is insane. What is he doing?! "Don't change your plans. You said everything is ready to go! It's almost over, Milo. You're so close. Don't stop now just because she *claims* there's an insider."

Marchello frowns. "She *knows* about new year's?" he growls. "Milo! Are you an idiot? Why would you tell her?!"

Milo slams his hand on the table. "You do not speak to me like that!"

Marchello grinds his teeth, glaring at me. "Why is it that you do not want us to believe there is a mole? Huh, Kiara? Why are you so adamant that we follow through with our plans? Hmm? Maybe perhaps it is because you have something to *gain*."

Oh my fucking God!

A frantic gust of air slips past my lips. "Shut the *fuck* up, Marchello!" I look at Milo. "You don't believe me, do you? Why? Why is Vittoria's word more valid and believable than mine?" I narrow my eyes, realization dawning on me. "Oh my God, you *did* love her, didn't you? You said you weren't sure, but you did. That's the only explanation. It's—"

"That is incorrect, Kiara," Milo states, his jaw clenching. "I am doing *all* of this because even if there is a *small chance* that she is telling the truth, I need to be prepared. There is no room for error. Our family cannot and will not survive another mistake. I need stability, Kiara. I need to reclaim power, and I cannot do that unless I am one hundred percent certain that I am not sending my men to fucking die!"

"I think it is time for you to leave," Marchello says, nodding at the door. "Let the men work."

"Men? Plural?" I scoff. "Funny, I only see *one*."

"Watch your mouth, woman!" Marchello growls.

"Or what?" I ask. "What are you going to do? Hmm?"

Milo bangs his fist on the table. "Both of you, stop fucking talking!"

"Fine!" I abruptly stand up, my blood thrumming with irritation. "I'll leave you *boys* to it then." I grab a jacket from Milo's coat rack. "Bye."

"Kiara, where the fuck are you going?" Milo asks, his tone defeated.

"For a walk! I need some fresh air."

"Do not leave the estate," he says as I slip on his trench coat. "Understand?"

"Don't tell me what to do," I snap back. "I'll go wherever I damn well please. I can't stay in this house any longer. I'm losing my fucking mind."

"If you must leave then take Gio or Mateo with you," Milo says.

"Why? Clearly, I'm not in any danger seeing as *I'm* the mole, right Marchello? Why do I need a guard? I'm the bad guy, right?"

"For fuck's sake, Kiara!" Milo stands up. "At least take your gun."

"Oh, you trust me with a gun? Really? Even though I work for the Russians?"

"I never said that Kiara," Milo sighs. "Why are you being so difficult?"

"Difficult? Me?" I flap my arms. "God, I need to leave before I strangle you."

"Marchello, give her your gun," Milo says. "Now!"

"What?" Marchello frowns. "I'm not—"

"I said now!"

"Fine!" He reaches into his holster and reluctantly hands me his pistol. "Don't fucking lose it."

"Wouldn't dream of it," I scowl, pocketing the gun. I glare at Milo. "Don't wait up."

"Do not leave the neighborhood, Kiara," Milo warns. "I will know."

I roll my eyes. "Don't you have footage to comb through? Better get to it."

"Kia—"

I don't give him time to finish before I march out of his office, slamming the door. God, I need a drink. This is absurd. Am I the only sane person here? This is how inno-cent inmates on death row must feel. It's infuriating, blood-curdling, fucking maddening.

I shove my feet into a pair of boots by the front door. Exiting the house, the clear star-infested sky greets me as I make my way out of the gates.

What do I do? Think, Kiara, think! I turn right, walking aimlessly up the block, my fingers curled around the heavy pistol in my pocket. What are the facts? What do I know for certain? Oh my God. Nothing. I don't know anything. It's all a jumbled mess of maybes. How do I solve a riddle with no clues?

God, am I in the wrong here? Am I being paranoid? Is Vittoria telling the truth? I don't know anymore. I don't. I grip the locket around my neck. Nana, help me! Please! Give me a sign, a signal, a crumb!

A wave of nausea washes over me. *Oh, God.* Feeling lightheaded, I sit down on a random bench, nestling my head between my knees. Breathe. *In and out. In and out. In and out.* My phone rings. Milo. I ignore the call. It rings again. I ignore it. And again.

"What do you want?"

"You've been gone an hour, Kiara," he says in a gentle voice. "Come back, tesoro. I'm sorry for yelling at you. Please."

"I'll be back in a bit, okay? I just—" I close my eyes. I can't go back until I have a plan. Until I have something to go on. I need to figure out what's happening, otherwise, there might be nothing to go back to. "I need to think."

"About what?"

"Just everything," I whisper, hanging up.

Slipping my phone into my pocket, I stand up, continuing my journey. According to researchers, walking increases creativity by sixty percent. That's a lot. And I need to be creative. This problem isn't a linear equation. It's complicated, complex, with so many variables. Vittoria. Igor. Enzo. The Russians. Arabic. The rose. The Mole. Andre. God, that's too many variables. Too many variations of the truth. Too many possible answers. I can't do it. I can't solve it. I can't.

I circle a corner, entering a dimly lit street, the humming of an engine behind me. I twist my neck toward the slowly moving vehicle. Too slow. I can barely see it, no headlights. I pick up my pace as my brain stem activates survival mode. The car follows me at a distance.

Trepidation seizes my insides as the car speeds up and a man jumps out of the passenger's side door.

Fuck! I start running, my heart racing as I fumble around for my cell phone. The man follows me, only a few feet behind. My vision blurs, panic setting in as I try to dial Milo's number, my legs heavy as I sprint. As I'm about to press call, I trip on the uneven pavement, my body lurching forward, the phone flying out my hands and smashing on the ground.

No!

I scramble to get up as the man approaches me. I study his face, reaching for the gun. I don't know him. He's not familiar. I raise my shaking arms, the pistol heavy in my hands. Too heavy.

"Who are you?" I ask, pointing the silver revolver at the six-foot-tall man. "Who sent you?" He raises his hands in the air, the SUV stopping behind him. They probably have guns as well. Shit. "Who are you?! Let me go or I'll fucking kill you!"

He doesn't say a word, but I know something's wrong.

He smiles as he looks over my shoulder into the distance. And that's when I hear it. Footsteps behind me.

I spin around but it's too late.

A blunt object hits the back of my head.

Game over.

# CHAPTER 39

## THE BIG PICTURE

Bolts of thundering pain pulsate through my brain, every one of my nerve endings activated as jarring cold water collides with my face. I gasp, receded grey edges hindering my vision as I struggle to open my eyes.

Fuck. My head.

I wince, another flood of freezing water crashing against my face, jolting me awake into a state of confused consciousness. I blink, my hazy vision coming in and out of focus.

"Who are you?" I croak, my throat dry as I try to make out the man in front of me. "Where am I?"

He doesn't reply.

"Let me go." Abrasive material burns my wrists and ankles as I writhe in the cushioned chair, attempting to stand up. Shit. Come on. Focus. Focus! Slowly, like a dial-up connection, the fog stifling my ability to think, to see, to process, begins to lift.

The man watches me as I look around the room, frowning as I take in the upscale and sophisticated design of my surroundings. The walls are slightly curved, blinds rolled down on all the windows. The white furniture and sleek marble accents cause a sharp pain in my eyes.

Where the hell am I?

The floor beneath my feet is unstable, swaying, subtly rocking my body like I'm floating.

A boat? I glance around the room again. No. A yacht. A marina. We must be at a marina. That means there might be people. There might be help.

As if sensing that I'm about to scream, the man moves his coat to the side, revealing a gun. No words. I don't need words to heed his warning.

Scream and you'll die. Got it.

"Do you speak English?" I look up at the bald middle-aged man. He doesn't move a muscle, standing still, stoic and impassive. Let's try again. "Russian?" Nothing. "Arabic?" No. "Ita—"

"Italian, yes. He does."

I whip my head around toward the familiar voice, my eyes widening with disbelief as Marchello strides toward me, waving his revolver in the air.

"Marchello? What—what are you..." Realization dawns on me. "Oh my God, you? *You're* the mole?"

"Me? A mole?" He throws his head back and laughs, his nefarious cackles rattling my bones. "I like you, Kiara, I really do," he stops in front of me, "but you are not nearly as intelligent as you think you are. There is no mole, *idiota*. Well—" He clicks his tongue. "I suppose there is now." He cocks his head to the side. "You."

"I don't—"

"You don't understand?" he cuts in, a sly grin on his face. "I know you don't. See, that is the problem, you are *incapable* of understanding. Do you know why? Because you do not belong here, Kiara. You will *never* belong here."

"Go fuck yourself," I seethe, struggling to free myself from the ropes binding my limbs.

"I will not be disrespected!" His features harden as he whips me across the face with his pistol. Pain spreads through my body, metallic odor filling my nostrils and coating my tongue. "You will keep your mouth shut, understand?"

I clench my jaw, my left eye welling up with tears. Don't fucking cry. I look up at him, spitting blood-infused saliva into his face.

"Fuck you."

He blinks, glaring at me as he wipes two fingers across his cheek. "I would hit you again, but I am afraid I might kill you."

"Isn't that your plan? To kill me?"

"Maybe, it depends on your answer," he says, pacing in front of me as he sucks on his teeth. "The truth is, Kiara, it was never supposed to come to this but unfortunately you have proved to be a very *malignant* form of cancer." He stops, peering down at me. "You are more difficult to remove than I had originally thought."

I swallow, my brows knitting together in confusion as I keep my mouth shut. Based on the curl of his lips, the gleam of pride in his eyes, and his boastful tone, I don't need to ask any questions. He thinks he's won whatever game we were playing.

This is a victory lap, his moment to shine.

He twists the revolver around his index finger. "I created many opportunities for you to leave on your own accord. I planted the necklace, I led you straight to Andre, I even brought that cheating whore Vittoria back from the dead, and yet you stayed."

He lets out a maniacal laugh that sends chills down my

spine. So, Vittoria wasn't kidnapped. I was right. Or she was. Just not by the Russians.

Marchello continues, not giving me time to ask what happened. "Not only did you *stay* but you accepted his proposal. I was certain bringing back Vittoria would be the end, but I was wrong. When you referred to yourself as Milo's fiancée, I thought it was over. I thought I lost, but then, I had a moment of pure genius."

"A mole."

"Yes," he grins. "A mole. It was perfect, I thought in time I would be able to convince Milo that you were a traitor, a spy, but then you go and kill Andre, all on your own. It was beautiful but it changed my plans. I had to act quickly. I had to strike while the iron was hot. So tonight, Milo will think that you fled, that you ran away. That in fact, you *were* the mole."

I blink, attempting to make sense of everything he's saying. "So, you orchestrated all of this because you don't want me to marry Milo?" I pause, narrowing my eyes. "Why? I don't understand."

He takes a deep breath. "Because, Kiara, there is no room for love in *Santi Oscuri*. There is only power, loyalty, and money." He scans my bleeding face. "Not only do you make Milo weak—" He points the gun at my uterus. "But you are also a broken woman, and you have no place by his side. When the time comes for Emilio to produce an heir, my daughter will gladly offer up her womb because she understands the importance of legacy."

My face falls. "I don't think your daughter will be as *willing* as you think."

"It is not about will, Kiara, it is about duty. I have served this family since I was fifteen years old, almost *fifty* years. I have been at the forefront of battles, of wars, standing beside the Di Vaio's, ensuring that our legacy lives on, even after I am dead. And I will not let you, Vittoria, or any other woman, jeopardize our position as leaders."

"Vittoria?" I ask in a low hum. "What did you do? Why—"

"Milo, he was not groomed to be *capo*. That was always Sergio's birthright but then he died, and Emilio was going to undo *everything* his brother was trying to accomplish." Marchello's lip twitches. "He was going to relinquish control of Moscow, and for what? His brother's body? So sentimental, so foolish. A body is nothing, Kiara. It is flesh and bones and blood, nothing of value, nothing important."

"So, you kidnapped Vittoria and framed the Russians," I say, the pieces finally falling into place. "Why? To make Milo angry? To make him want revenge?"

Marchello casts me an impressed grin. "Exactly, he needed motivation, he needed *fuel*, so I gave it to him. Not too long after Sergio's death, I caught Vittoria in a *very* compromising position with one of our men, so I gave her a choice, the same choice I am now going to give you."

"Yeah?" Fucking bastard. "And what's that?"

Marchello squats down in front of me, his gaze flickering around my face. "Either I kill you, right now." He drags the pistol across my battered cheek as the silent man brings over a briefcase. "Or you take this money and disappear. You go far, *far* away. And never return."

I blink. "Why not just kill me? Get rid of me for good? If I'm such a cancer, why risk keeping me alive?"

"Because, Kiara, I look at the big picture. I plan ahead. That is my job. If you are willing to take this money—" He taps the metal case. "That tells me that you have a price. And if I keep you alive, I can buy you again, in the future, if I ever need to. You will be my pawn; I will own you."

"Vittoria took the money," I whisper under my breath. "You paid her to come back. You paid her to say—"

"Of course, she took the money!" Marchello scoffs. "That was the only reason she latched her nails into Milo in the first place. She never loved him, she loved this—" He motions around. "She loved luxury, diamonds, champagne. So yes, she took the money and she moved to Dubai. She was smart, Kiara. And I hope you will be smart too."

That explains the Arabic. That explains everything.

"There's one thing I don't understand." I purse my lips, a thought popping into my head. "You said your job is to ensure the legacy of this family, right? Don't you think this whole thing is counterproductive then? Milo is changing the plans against the Russians. You would've reclaimed power in six days, but now? You fucked everything up by bringing in a fake mole. Did you think of that?"

"Once again, Kiara, big picture," Marchello hums with an unbothered shrug. "We will have another opportunity to take down Igor, but I will not have a better opportunity to get rid of you. So now—" He stands up. "I need your answer. Do you wish to die tonight? Or live a long, healthy life?"

The last time my life flashed before my eyes, I saw nothing. It was empty, deprived of meaning, emotion, substance. But this time, I don't see my past. I see my future. I see Milo. I see his face. I hear his laugh. I feel his touch.

I feel his love.

It's inside me. It's coursing through my veins, keeping me alive. It's given me life. He resurrected me. Brought me back from the brinks of existential death. Without him, I have no one. Not one single person on God's green earth loves me as much as he does.

And I know he does. I do.

He gave me his heart.

And I'll give him my life.

"I won't take your money," I whisper, my breathing shallow. "I would rather die than be blackmailed by you. I will not be your pawn, Marchello. So, kill me."

Marchello frowns. "Kiara, be logical, take the money."

"No." I stare at his gun. "I don't want your money."

"This is what I mean." He takes four steps backward as the bald man puts a gun with a silencer in his palm. Marchello holds out the pistol, pointing it at my head. "Love makes you stupid. It is truly the most destructive emotion." He sighs. "Any last words, Kiara? A prayer, perhaps?"

I close my eyes, a small twinge of peace gripping my heart. "I'll see you soon, Nana," I murmur under my breath. "I'll see you soon."

A loud bang echoes around the room.

"You son of a bitch!"

My eyes spring open, Milo, Gio, and Mateo storming into the room, guns drawn.

Relief washes over me.

"Untie her," Milo spits, glancing at Gio who rushes toward me. He re-grips his gun, pointing it at Marchello as Gio unties the ropes from my wrists and ankles. "You fucking little shit. I trusted you and you have been manipulating me this whole time!"

"What—How...How do—" Marchello stammers, backing away until his back hits the wall. He raises his arms in surrender. Milo nods at the cameras in the corners of the room. "But I—I disabled them. I—"

"Even you, Marchello, do not know everything," he growls, burning rage twisting his face. "I heard every single word that came out of your traitorous mouth!"

"Traitor?!" Marchello's voice rises as I stand up. I keep my distance, rubbing my sore wrists. "I am not a traitor! I am loyal! More loyal than you will ever be, Emilio! Everything I have done is for the sake of our family. For you! For our future!" He takes a step forward, pressing his chest against the tip of the Beretta. "You needed to become a leader, Milo, and I made that happen. I made you into the man we needed, into a man who will rule the fucking world!"

"You betrayed me, Marchello," Milo says, his jaw clenching. "You were like a father to me, and you betrayed me."

"I did what I had to do, Emilio," Marchello spits. "I did my duty. I stayed loyal to Santi Oscuri."

"No." Milo cocks his head to the side, his tone deep, menacing as he states, "I *am* Santi Oscuri, and you, Marchello, have broken the code. And for that, you must die."

My gaze darts between the two men.

Loyalty. Power. Wealth.

*Stability.*

No.

No.

"Stop," I shout as Milo racks the slide, chambering a round. "Milo, stop! Stop!"

His head snaps toward me, his eyes chocked full of agonizing pain as his gaze flickers around my face. "Look at you, tesoro," he breathes, his voice trembling. "Look at what he did. He needs to die."

"No," I whisper, placing my hand on Milo's stiff arm. "You can't kill him." Marchello shoots me a dubious look as I glance at him. "You can't kill him."

"Yes, I can. He broke the code."

"It doesn't matter," I whisper, removing the Beretta from his hands. *Big picture.* "If you kill Marchello, we'll look weak. We'll lose power, Milo. The other families, they'll know. It'll get around. It'll—" I swallow. "It'll start another war. A *civil* war."

"Kiara—"

"You need stability, baby," I say, clenching my teeth as my fingers coil around the gun. "*We* need stability. At least for a little while."

"I have underestimated you, Kiara." Marchello expels a low laugh, drawing our attention. "Perhaps you *do* belong here after all."

"You will keep your mouth shut, understand?" I repeat his words as I stride toward him. "You said that there is no room for love in *Santi Oscuri*, right? But you're wrong."

"Wh—"

"Did I say you could talk?" I meet his defiant gaze as he snaps his lips shut. "Better. You're wrong because if I didn't love Milo, I *would* let him kill you. I would let him unload this entire magazine into your *fucking* body." I take a deep, calming breath. "But you see, I *do* love him, and I've grown to love his family. Julia, Natalia, *Luisa* even. And I don't want to see this family, *my* family, be catapulted into another *unnecessary* war on the basis of internal conflict. So, thank whatever God you worship that love *does* exist in Santi Oscuri, because without it, you would be dead."

Marchello swallows.

"I cannot trust him anymore." Milo glares at his under-boss. "What do you suggest we do with him?"

"You can trust me, Emilio!" Marchello pipes up. "You can."

"We'll think of something." I cast Marchello an ominous smile. "The floors in my bathroom looked a little dirty. He can start there." I turn to Milo, my head throbbing. "Let's go, I need to have a word with Vittoria."

"The floors?!" Marchello shouts, his chest puffing up.

"You expect me to clean your fucking bathroom?! After all the years I gave to this family? After all the sacrifices I made?!"

Dull pain pulses in my temples as I whip my arm out and fire a bullet into his shoulder.

He staggers backward, sliding down the wall as he presses his palm against the bullet hole.

"Shut up, Marchello, you're giving me a headache."

"Jesus, Kiara," Milo murmurs as Gio lurches forward.

I hold out my hand. "No, don't help him." I nod toward the galley kitchen. "Go get some paper towels and spray." I smile, peering down at the whimpering old man. "You're getting blood all over the carpet. *Clean it up.*" I expel a deep sigh, looking up at Milo. "As I was saying, I need to have a word with Vittoria."

Milo blinks. "Whatever you want, tesoro, just don't shoot me."

"Here. Take it." I hand him back the gun. "For your own safety."

I am not a pawn.

Not anymore.

I'm a fucking queen.

And queens don't cry.

They don't.

I walk past Milo, needing to get off this damn boat.

# CHAPTER 40

## THE LIGHT INSIDE

"Kiara, slow down," Milo calls out after me as I rush up the unlit walkway toward the black SUV idling on the street. "Kiara, be careful!" I stop at the top of the bridge, waiting for him to catch up. Milo grabs my shaking hands, scanning my face. "You're hurt, you need to slow down."

"I'm fine," I say in a trembling tone, my eyes welling up. "I just want to get home, slap Vittoria, and go to sleep." A flood of tears roll down my face. Holy shit, what is happening to me? I wipe away the tears, wincing as I accidentally touch the wound on my cheek. "I'm sorry, I don't know why I'm crying, I'm okay, really. I don't know—"

"Shh, it's okay," he whispers, pulling me against his chest, his fingers gripping the back of my head. "I am so sorry, tesoro. This is all my fault. I should have never doubted you; I should have believed you."

"I had no proof," I sniffle, fisting the sides of his jacket, my body unable to pick a fucking mood. "I get it, Milo. You were just trying to be cautious; you were trying to—"

"No," he hums into my hair, his arms tightening around me. "There is no excuse. I was wrong and I was almost too late. If I came just a minute later—" His jaw clenches. "I cannot say it."

I'd be dead.

"How—how did you know where I was?" I take a deep breath and pray that my body powers down. I peer up at him through damp lashes. "Are there sensors on the boat or something? You pointed to the cameras."

"No, Marchello disabled the sensors and the cameras. I only turned them back on when I saw your location." Milo brushes a piece of hair away from my face, the strand sticking to the drying blood on my cheek. "Fucking hell, Kiara, you might need stitches. We must see Aldo first before anything else."

I frown. "What do you mean you *saw* my location? I don't have a phone with me."

He swallows, his weary gaze fluttering down to my Nana's necklace.

"What?" I look down and open the locket, a tiny red flashing light shining through my nana's photo. Oh, God. "Seriously? You put a tracking device in here? Milo!"

"I did it to protect you, Kiara," he says, his voice faint, timid. "To keep you safe." He pauses, taking a breath. "I tried calling you again earlier, but your phone went to voicemail, and I knew something was wrong." He runs the tip on his index finger across the locket. "For this, I am not sorry. I'm not."

"Although I don't appreciate being *tagged* like some animal, I suppose I can't really be mad, it's served its purpose." I expel a deep sigh, twisting the necklace between my fingers. "Good thing I didn't take it off and wear your mom's necklace. I'd probably be fish food by now."

"Kiara—"

"Can we please go?" I open the car door and hop inside, pain thudding in the back of my skull. "My head hurts."

"Of course." Milo slides in beside me, reaching for my hand. He hesitates for a moment before whispering, "Kiara, I appreciate your loyalty to me, but you should have taken the money."

"What?"

"The money Marchello was offering." His hand dwarfs mine as I rest against his shoulder, crisp air blowing through the cracked windows. "You should have taken it. I am not worth dying over."

"Yeah? Would *you* have taken the money?" My heart rate slows down as I glance up at Milo. "If the roles were reversed, what would you have done?" He doesn't respond, avoiding eye contact. "That's what I thought."

"It is different..." He looks out of the window at the bright full moon. "Your life is more precious than mine, Kiara. You are more worthy of life. I would die a thousand deaths if it meant you'd be able to live just one."

I can see it. An intricate woven chain. One end is wrapped around his heart, the other around mine. We're tethered. Bound together by fate, by destiny, by the blessings of angels. We're connected in a way that defies death, defies circumstance, defies logic.

"It doesn't work like that anymore," I whisper, shaking my head as I take in his solemn features. "I love you, Milo. Your life *is* my life, so I forbid you to die, do you understand? You have to promise me that you will never leave me. That you will stay with me until it's our time to go, no sooner."

"I would never dream of leaving you." He hesitates for a second before arching down and giving me a soft, heavenly kiss. "*Sei la cosa più bella che mi sia mai capitata. Ti amo,*

Kiara." He brushes his thumb across my lips. "You are my light, tesoro, without you, I would be lost."

"I've felt lost my whole life, Milo, and when I'm with you, it finally feels like I'm home," I say, caressing his stubbled cheek. "You have more light inside of you than you think." I smile, losing myself in his earthy eyes. *"The devil is not as black as he is painted."*

"Do you truly believe that Kiara?" He leans into my palm. "The things I have done—" He sighs. "I am not sure how much light remains."

"The dichotomy between light and darkness, it's—it's dynamic, Milo, it changes, it's not stagnant. Every day one might outshine the other, but you'll always have both, *always.*"

He smiles, lacing his hands through my hair as he kisses my forehead. "Your father would be very proud of you, Kiara. You are a philosopher in the making."

"I stabbed one man to death and shot another all in the course of thirty-six hours," I murmur, resting my head on his shoulder. "I'm not so sure he'd be proud of me right now."

"He would understand, tesoro. He would."

"Maybe." I close my eyes, letting out a grunt. "Shit, I probably shouldn't have shot Marchello. That was an impulsive and rash decision. He knows too much, what if he—"

Milo's body tenses as he begrudgingly states, "He won't. Marchello has proven to be a great disappointment and I'd like nothing more than to kill him, but he has always held *Santi Oscuri* above all else. I do not believe he will betray the family. You were right to stop me, Kiara. There would have been severe consequences if I had killed him."

"I'm sorry," I whisper. "I know how much you trusted him."

"It wasn't personal," Milo says in a strained tone. "This was business. It's always business."

"Still—" I crane my neck up. "He hurt you, you're allowed to feel that."

"According to Marchello, I am not allowed to feel anything. Or else I risk destroying our legacy."

"I think that depends on what kind of legacy you want to leave behind. Marchello's version of the future doesn't have to be yours. He wants world domination, which is unrealistic and dangerous. The future lies in *your* hands, Milo. What do you want to be remembered by?"

Milo stays quiet, gazing out the window for several comfortable moments of much-needed silence.

"I want to conquer Europe," he finally says. "That will be my legacy."

I manage a small laugh. "Europe's still really big, baby."

He faces me, a smirk creeping up on his face. "But it's smaller than the world."

I roll my eyes, my temples instantly pulsing. "Taking control of fifty countries in your lifetime will be impossible. How do you plan on doing that?"

"What you meant to say is, how do *we* plan on doing that," Milo counters with a grin. "And easy—" He cocks his head. "One country at a time." The car stops in front of the estate. "We can discuss this later, right now, you need to see a doctor."

"No," I say, climbing out of the car. "I need to see Vittoria."

"Kiara, please, she is not going anywhere. First a doctor, you could have a concussion," Milo pleads, placing his hand on the small of my back as we enter the house. It's quiet. Everyone must be sleeping. I ignore him, heading to her room. "Kiara—"

"I'll be quick," I say, pausing at the top of the staircase. I need a plan. Strategy. Stability. Damage control. "Who knows about this? About Marchello? Obviously Gio and Mateo, anyone else? Paolo? Luisa?"

"No, I didn't have time to tell them," Milo says. "Why? What are you thinking?"

"I think we need to keep this quiet for a while," I whisper, biting my lip. "The fewer people that know the better."

"They will ask questions, Kiara. They will wonder why Marchello is not by my side. It will lead to speculation. We need to be honest."

I purse my lips. "He's injured right now. Unfit for duty. We can go with that."

"It's just a gunshot, Kiara. A scratch. He can still function."

"Then break his fucking legs," I say dryly, eyeing Vittoria's door. "We can't risk the other families finding out about this, Milo. We can't. We'll have to tell everyone that Vittoria was the mole and that we killed her after catching her talking to Igor or something. We can put Marchello on desk duty. It's not ideal but it'll have to do."

"*Break his legs?*" A low chuckle tumbles from Milo's lips. "Who are you?"

"Your future wife," I say, crossing my arms. "So, what do you think? Will it work?"

Milo sucks in a long breath. "Only one way to find out." He nods at the door. "She's all yours."

"Excellent." I turn on my heel and enter Vittoria's bedroom, flicking on the lights. "Wake up!"

"What the fuck?" Vittoria grumbles, jerking upright. Her face pales as her gaze darts between me and Milo. "What—what do you want?" She pauses, cringing. "Dio, what happened to your face?"

"What do you think?" I walk toward her, my head spinning. "I gave you the chance to tell me the truth, Vittoria, yet you continued to lie. That was a mistake. Do you remember what I said would happen when I found out the truth? Hmm?"

She swallows looking at Milo. "You—you know?"

"Yes." I glare down at her. "We know about the cheating, the money, Dubai. We know you came back because Marchello paid you." I shake my head. "It takes a very special type of person to lie about being raped, Vittoria. It's disgusting and you should be ashamed of yourself."

"He would have killed me if I didn't take the money. I didn't want to die—" Her bottom lip quivers. "And I didn't want to come back! I didn't! I was happy in Dubai, I met a nice man, I—" She wails into the comforter. "But Marchello, he said he would kill my sister if I didn't return and say all those horrible things. I didn't want to, believe me." She peers up at Milo. "I'm sorry, I really am. I didn't—"

"Actions have consequences, Vittoria," I say, catching a glimpse of Milo, his expression neutral, unaffected. Whatever fraction of his heart she was holding hostage is now free. Good.

"I know," she whimpers, shame flashing across her face. "I know that! I think about it all the time, okay? I made a mistake. Please don't kill me! Please."

"This is what's going to happen. You are going to leave tonight. You are going to go back to Dubai, and you will never come back to Italy." I pause, pursing my lips. "Have you called your sister yet? I know you were not talking to her last night."

"No," she whispers, sniffling. "I didn't think it would be safe."

"Good. You will never contact her again. She will continue to think you are dead."

"But—"

I shoot her a glare and she stops talking. "You will forget about this life, about Milo, about *Santi Oscuri*. Do you understand?"

She blinks. "You're not going to kill me?"

"No, I'm not going to kill you. Not today at least," I say, shaking off the sudden onset of fatigue. "But if we ever find out that you have opened your mouth about this to anyone, we *will* kill you *and* your new boyfriend *and* his entire family *and* your sister." I tilt my head as her eyes widen with terror. I glance at the clock. "You have ten minutes to get ready and then Gio will drive you to the airport. You will take the jet back to Dubai and never come back. Is that clear?"

She nods. "Yes."

"Good." I glance over at Milo. "Anything you'd like to add?" He shakes his head. "Okay." I turn to Vittoria. "Get dressed."

"Thank you," she mumbles.

Without another word, I exit her room, feeling light-headed. Milo closes the door behind us. "I am surprised you are letting her live," he whispers as we walk down the hall. "Are you sure that is wise?"

"I feel bad for her," I say, dancing black spots infiltrating my vision as we reach the staircase. "She was just a—just a pawn. Plus, umm...I think that living in a state of constant fear is worse than uh—worse than death." I grab the railing, steadying myself as my head spins. "It's the—" I blink, my knees giving out. "The uh—"

"Kiara!"

# CHAPTER 41

## BEATING HEARTS

THE STERILE SCENT OF DISINFECTANT FILLS MY LUNGS as my eyelids flutter open. Attempting to prop myself up, I wince, glancing at the IV needle inserted into my right forearm. Oh, God. I hate needles. I look around the private room, the humming of various medical machinery ringing in my ears. I frown, unease stirring in my stomach. I hate hospitals even more.

"Oh, thank God." I crane my neck toward the far end of the room, smiling as Milo walks out of the ensuite bathroom, relief gracing his worried face. "You're awake."

"Where—" I clear my throat, my mouth dry as he sits down on a stool beside me. "Where am I? What happened?" I blink, looking out the large windows, the sun beaming through the blinds. "What time is it?"

"You have been unconscious for eight hours, Kiara," Milo whispers, his grip gentle as he takes my hand in his. He passes me a glass of water off the side table and I take a slow sip. "I was worried you sustained head trauma." He sucks in a deep breath, caressing my cheek. "Fuck, baby, I am so happy to see your eyes."

"Eight hours?" I hum, squeezing his hand as I shift my weight in the surprisingly comfortable bed. "Am I—am I okay? That seems like a long time."

"Yes," he smiles, kissing my knuckles. "Aldo came with us and I made him run every test imaginable. It is a miracle that you do not even have a concussion."

"I don't?" I peer up at the IV drip. "What is this for?"

"Hydration." I whip my head to the door as Dr. Giardini enters the room with a clipboard in hand. "Hello, Kiara, welcome back. How do you feel?"

"Good? I think? My head doesn't hurt as much anymore." I sit up, Milo refusing to let go of my hand. "I don't have a concussion? Really?"

"Yes," Aldo confirms, flipping through the documents. "All your injuries were superficial and minor."

I frown. Didn't feel minor last night. "Then why did I faint?"

"There is only so much stress and fatigue a person can take, Kiara," Aldo explains. "This was your body's way of letting you know that you need to slow down and relax." He looks down at Milo. "However, since Milo refused to believe my initial diagnosis, I have the last of your lab results here."

"Lab results?" I ask, glancing at Milo. "For what?"

"I thought perhaps Marchello had drugged you," Milo says in a bitter tone. "I did not want to take any chances." He nods at the clipboard. "So, everything is normal?"

"We found no trace of sedatives in your blood. However —" Aldo purses his lips, his gaze darting between me and Milo. "We did discover high levels of hCG."

Milo blinks, glancing at me as I take another sip of water. "hCG? What is that?"

"Human chorionic gonadotropin hormone." Aldo clears

his throat as he elaborates gingerly, "It's a hormone only produced during pregnancy."

"What?!" Water spurts out of my nose. "Pregnancy?!" My gaze darts to Milo who's grinning, a glow of pride in his dark eyes. "But I can't...get pregnant. I have—"

"Are you sure?" Milo asks, his tone hopeful. "She is pregnant?"

Aldo nods. "Yes, roughly five weeks."

My jaw drops. "Five weeks?! How is that even—" I pause, attempting to calculate my last period. Fuck, it's always irregular. Sometimes it doesn't even come. The last time was— Shit. We should've used a condom. It completely slipped my mind. "Oh God." I gasp, jerking upright as I peer down at my stomach. "Five weeks? That means, the first time we—"

"Amazing," Milo muses, rubbing his chin as he lets out a low, cocky chuckle. "Evidently, the potency of the Di Vaio seed transcends modern medicine!"

"Milo!" I shoot him an incredulous look as I smack his shoulder. "Shut up!" I peer up sheepishly at Dr. Giardini. "I was told that my chances to conceive were under five percent, I don't understand how this happened."

"Five percent is not zero percent." Aldo shrugs, suppressing a grin. "But perhaps Milo is correct. Powerful sperm."

I blink. "You have very poor bedside manners, *Doctor*."

"Kiara, please," Milo smirks. "It is his *professional* opinion. We must listen to him."

"You seem *very* pleased with yourself."

"I am *overjoyed*, tesoro," Milo whispers in a sweet tone. "I love you and I know you will be an amazing mother." He places his palm on my stomach, his eyes soft and dreamy as he adds, "This baby does not know how lucky it is."

Holy shit.

"Baby," I mutter under my breath, my heart racing with confused elation. "We're going to have a baby?"

"A baby?! Oh my God! A baby?!" Julia exclaims, busting through the door, balloons and flowers in her hands. Antonia, Natalia, Luisa, and God, everyone else, piles into the cramped room. "Ah! Are you serious, cara?" She vibrates with excitement, looking at Milo. "I will be a *zia*?! Me?"

"Julia, please do not scream, we are in a hospital." Milo's unable to rein in a wide, proud grin. "But yes, it would seem that Kiara is pregnant."

"Baby?" Natalia coos, running up to the bed and poking my stomach. "In there? A baby?" She turns around and looks at her mother. "*How?*"

"Uh—" Julia stammers, casting her husband a flustered look. She cringes, forcing a smile. "A miracle?"

"It is a *gift*," Antonia states, striding toward me. She cups my cheek. "It is a blessing, Kiara." She pauses, frowning as she scans my face. "I cannot believe that *bitch* did this to you."

Before I can open my mouth, Julia says with a sour expression, "Milo told us what happened with Vittoria. Truly unbelievable. I say the world is a better place without her in it."

"I agree," Luisa scowls. "She was an idiot to think we would not find out."

"It is over now." Milo squeezes my hand, casting me a knowing look. He did it. He told them that she was the mole. "Let us move on, yes?"

"Yes!" Julia claps her hands, a cunning smile on her face. "Now we can start planning the wedding." She gasps, covering her mouth. "Oh my God! We must do it now! Before she gets fat!"

"Julia!" Antonia clicks her tongue. "Pregnant is not fat."

"Tell that to Chanel!" Julia bites her lip in thought. "Oh! We can do it on New Year's Eve! We are having a party anyway; we will make it a wedding! It is perfect!"

Milo clears his throat, drawing everyone's attention. "New Year's Eve will not work," he says, glancing at Paolo. "It is too soon."

I purse my lips. "Is there somewhere you need to be on New Year's?" If he thinks he's going to Russia to blow up the warehouses himself, he's lost his damn mind. "Well?"

"Paolo and I will be out of town," Milo states. "We will return on New Year's Day."

"Paolo!" Julia crosses her arms. "When were you going to tell me about this? You are leaving? Why? For what?"

Irritation and fear flush my cheeks. He is *not* going to fucking Russia.

"I think New Year's Eve is a great idea, Julia," I state, casting Milo a subtle glare. "I'm sure whatever is happening that night does not require their *personal* attendance. Right? Perhaps, you can participate from *afar*?"

"No, I cannot—"

"Milo, please!" Julia snaps. "What is more important than Kiara? Hmm? She is carrying your fucking child! Do you not want to marry her?"

I suppress a grin as Milo's jaw clenches. Julia, my greatest weapon. "Of course, I want to marry her, Julia."

"Then what is the problem?" Julia asks through her teeth. "If it is a matter of time constraint, do not worry, little brother, I will take care of *everything*."

"Yes, baby," I say, feigning a pout. "What's the problem?"

Milo sighs, glancing at Paolo who nods in approval. "I suppose there is no problem."

"Then it's set!" Julia exclaims, giddiness exuding from her body. "Luisa and I will get started on preparations right away! We only have five days! There is so much to do!" She perches on the edge of the hospital bed. "What kind of flowers do you like? Colors? Silver or gold? And your dress? Mermaid? Ball-gown? A-line? Trumpet? White? Cream? Champagne?"

"Uh—" I stammer, suddenly feeling overwhelmed and nauseous. "I—"

"Perhaps this can wait until Kiara has fully recovered," Dr. Giardini pipes up, catching my flustered demeanour. "I think it is best if you all leave. She will return home later today but for now, we should let her rest."

I mouth *thank you,* casting him a grateful smile before squeezing my future sister-in-law's hand. "Honestly, Julia, I trust your judgment. Do whatever you want." I look over at Luisa. "Can we keep this small? Under fifty people? Is that possible?"

Luisa scrunches her face. "It is doable, but we might offend some of our allies if they are not invited."

Our allies. *My* allies.

I take in the smiling faces of everyone around me. They're here for me. They're here because they care about me. Because they love me. Because I am one of them.

They're my family.

The last time I was in a hospital, I was alone. Thirteen and alone.

I don't feel alone anymore.

I place my hand on my belly. I will never be alone again.

"Okay," I say, letting out a content breath. "Invite everyone we know."

"Big is always better, cara!" Julia exclaims as Natalia

attempts to crawl up on the bed. "Talia, what are you doing?"

"I want to say hi to baby!" Natalia frowns, struggling to lift her tiny body.

"Here—" I give Natalia a boost up on the bed.

Natalia kneels beside me, lowering herself down to my stomach as she whispers, "Hi, little baby. You be my friend?" She looks at me with doe-like eyes. "It hear me?"

"Yes, it can hear you," I sniffle as Milo grabs my hand, caressing the underside of my wrist.

"I would like to be alone with my future wife," Milo says, kissing the back of my hand. "We will see you all at home."

"Thank you all for coming. It means a lot," I whisper, wiping the tears from under my eyes as I get swarmed with hugs and kisses.

When the room empties, I tug on Milo's arm. "Lay down with me." I roll to my side as he climbs into the bed. "Milo—" I run my fingers through his hair. "Were you going to go to Russia? Was that your plan?"

He sighs. "Marchello was supposed to go and lead the operation but now I cannot trust him."

"So, you were going to go yourself?" I ask, shaking my head. "It's too dangerous Milo. Your men can do it themselves. You said you had everything ready to go."

"There cannot be any errors, Kiara," Milo says, tracing the little circle on my arm. "That is why I wanted to go myself."

"You said you'd never leave me. I can't risk losing you." I glance down at my stomach. "*We* can't risk losing you."

"And that is why I will stay." He pulls me against his chest, his sweet breath fanning against my forehead. "I love you, Kiara. I know this is all happening so fast, but I have never been more happy in my whole life. To have a child with a woman I love, that is truly a gift."

"You're not scared?" I swallow. "I'm scared."

"The greatest challenges yield the greatest rewards, tesoro," Milo whispers, brushing his nose against mine. "And there is no doubt in my mind that we are capable of providing this child with a beautiful life."

"Are you going to be mad if it's a girl?" I ask in a low murmur. "I know you probably want a boy. An heir."

Milo's chest rumbles as he laughs. "Kiara, if our daughter is anything like you, she will one day rule the fucking world."

I blink. "You're putting a lot of pressure on our unborn child."

He grins. "Pressure makes diamonds, tesoro, and our child will shine brighter than the burning sun." He drags his thumb across my bottom lip before arching down and giving me a gentle kiss. "God, I love you. I cannot wait to call you my wife."

"I love you too, so much." I close my eyes, every wound I've suffered over my lifetime, closing up, healing, disappearing. Tolstoy was right. Life and love. It's the only remedy for pain. "I wish my nana was here. I think she'd like you."

"Where is she buried?" Milo asks, smiling against my lips. "We can move her to our family plot if you'd like."

I peer up at him. "You can?"

"Of course, Kiara. She is part of the family."

Family.

Maybe *that's* the true remedy for pain.

# CHAPTER 42

## DUST TO DUST

DEATH SURROUNDS US.

Rows upon rows of resting souls. It should make me sad; it should prick my heart with longing, with sorrow, with pain.

But it doesn't.

All I feel is love.

These people were loved.

And love doesn't die with a person. Love lives on through memories, through stories, through *us*.

The blood coursing through my veins is historic, ancient. I am a vessel that carries the life, the memories, the love of my family.

I *am* my nana. I *am* my grandpa. I *am* my mom. I *am* my dad.

We *are* the dead.

And they are us.

"My family has been buried here since the 19th century," Milo says, linking his fingers through mine as we walk down the dusty path toward the far end of the cemetery. "When I was a child, I would beg my parents to leave me at home when they came to pay their respects." He glances at me with softened eyes. "I was scared of ghosts. Silly, I know."

"That's not silly at all. The laws of thermodynamics state that energy cannot be created or destroyed, so when a person dies, where does all that energy go?" I grin. *"Ghosts."*

Milo blinks. "Thermodynamics?"

"There's a lot you don't know about me Mr. Di Vaio," I singsong, offering him a coy shrug.

"Clearly." He lifts an amused brow. "What other secrets are you hiding from me, *Mrs. Di Vaio?"*

"Plenty," I say as we cut through the grass toward a tall building in the distance.

"Such as?"

"Wouldn't you like to know," I tease, giving him a playful shrug. "I guess you'll just have to force it out of me."

"Is that so?" he grins. "Need I remind you that I am an expert in extracting information. My techniques can make mute men sing."

"Do you plan on torturing me?" I tilt my head to the side. "That seems a bit excessive."

Milo's eyes harden. "True torture is sleeping in bed next to a gorgeous woman who was advised by an idiotic doctor to refrain from any physical activity for two whole days."

I snort. "You poor little baby, how have you survived?"

"A man needs his woman, Kiara," Milo mutters. "It is a matter of sanity."

I scoff. "Maybe that's why all wars are started by men."

"I would gladly start a war if it meant I got to taste you," Milo smirks as we pass a mourning couple.

My cheeks burn up. "I hope they didn't speak English."

Milo shrugs shamelessly. "I hope they *did."*

"Maybe now's not the time, baby. Let's try to be respectful."

"You started it," Milo murmurs under his breath as we stop in front of the grand white stone mausoleum.

"Wow. It's really big."

"Big family."

"Lucky." I examine the intricate detailing of the mausoleum. Chiseled into a slate of marble hung above the distressed archway reads *Gloria Non Morietur*. "Glory never dies?"

"Very good." Milo casts an impressed smile. "Yes, it is our family motto."

"A little pretentious, don't you think? They just assumed you'd be glorious?"

"Humility has never been a Di Vaio strong suit." Milo expels a small laugh as we enter into the dark room, natural light beaming through the cracks in the foundation. "Over here."

"Evidently not." My gaze darts around the gold embellished crypts lining the walls, pulse quickening with sudden nervousness as we stop in front of several crypts.

"This is my father, Santino," Milo says. He nods at the subsequent crypt. "And one is for my brother." He takes a step to the side. "And this is your grandmother, Annabelle Payne."

I suck in a sharp breath, pressing my palm against the cold stone. "Hi Nana, it's been a while." I swallow, glancing at Milo. "Nana this is Emilio—" I squeeze his hand. "We're getting married in two days. Isn't that crazy?" I chuckle to myself. "But I guess you were always a fan of crazy." I peer up at Milo. "On my fourteenth birthday, she lined our basement with plastic wrap and filled the room with foam. She thought it would cheer me up."

Milo laughs. "That is quite odd."

"Yeah," I snort, shaking my head. "She was a very odd woman."

"Did it?" he asks.

I frown. "What?"

"Cheer you up? I am making a mental list of ways to keep you happy. Julia told me I should expect many mood swings in the foreseeable future."

"Worried you won't be able to handle me? I think I've been pretty stable so far."

Milo presses his lips into a thin line. "The past few days would suggest otherwise."

"That wasn't hormones, that was stress."

"Whatever you say, Kiara."

I blink. "Do not patronize me, it's very unbecoming."

"I am joking, tesoro." He arches down and kisses my forehead. "You are perfect in every way."

"You're just saying that so I won't shoot you."

"No," he whispers, lifting my hand up to his lips. "I am saying it because it is true." He nods at the crypts, a warm smile on his face. "Did you want to show them the photo?"

"Oh, good idea." I reach inside my jacket pocket and pull out a sonogram. I clear my throat, holding out the black and white print for the whole family to see. "We're having a baby." I flip the photo around and narrow my eyes. "It's this tiny little dot right here, can you see?" I keep my index finger on the tiny little angel as I flip the photo back around. "It's about the size of an orange seed so no worries if you can't. To be honest, I couldn't see it at first either."

"*I* saw right away," Milo says with a sly grin. "But us Di Vaios, we have excellent vision."

"Anyway—" I roll my eyes, suppressing a smile. "We're um... we're really excited. And uh—we just wanted to share this news with all of you." I pause, reading my nana's name. "If it's a girl, I want to name her Annabelle, after you, Nana."

"And Sergio if it is a boy," Milo says, taking a deep breath.

"Yeah," I hum, resting my head on his shoulder. "Sergio if it's a boy." Comfort washes over my body as I trace the outline of my nana's name. "I hope you're happy here, Nana, I know how much you and grandpa wanted to visit Italy. I'm sorry it had to be like this but at least you're here, right?"

"Speaking of your grandfather, he is over here with your parents," Milo whispers, pointing to an enclosed glass section with three ornate urns resting on the shelf. "I had my men take the liberty of retrieving them from your home in Hawthorne, I hope you don't mind."

"Oh my God, thank you." I cover my mouth, tears welling up in my eyes as I walk toward the urns. "Hi Mom, hi Dad, hi Grandpa." I shake my head, chuckling under my breath. "They're all here. Everyone."

Milo comes up behind me and wraps his arms around my waist. "What is so funny, tesoro?"

"Nothing," I laugh. "This is just the most morbid *meet the parents* ever. Seriously, this is so not normal."

"Perhaps not for the average person," Milo muses, resting his chin on the top of my head. "But we are not average, tesoro. You and I, we were not born to be normal. We were born to be extraordinary."

"Ah, there's the humility I know and love," I tease, craning my neck up. "Pride is a sin, baby. Didn't they teach you that at church?"

"So is gluttony," Milo smirks. "And yet I said nothing when you ate three hamburgers on the drive here."

My jaw drops. "I am eating for two now!"

He blinks. "Yes, I am sure the tiny orange seed needed a

Big Mac. It is amazing how they are able to pack in so many nutrients between two buns."

"I would sleep with one eye open if I were you," I warn him. "It would be a shame for my child to be fatherless so early in life."

"Again, I am joking." He lets out a laugh, wrapping me in a hug. "You are just so cute when you are angry, I cannot help myself."

"If you wish to see your name on one of these crypts, please go ahead and continue *joking*. I'll show you just how *cute* I can be."

"God, I love it when you threaten me." He tucks a piece of hair behind my ear. "It is such a turn on." He drags his finger down the slope of my neck. "I could fuck you right now."

I blink. "If you could refrain from saying shit like that in front of my parents, that would be great. They're right there!"

"Come on, baby," Milo coos, brushing his nose against mine. "I am just showing my love."

"Well keep your *love* in your pants until we get home," I say, pushing past him as I walk out of the mausoleum. "So disrespectful."

"Kiara, wait!" Milo catches up to me, his laughter filling the air. "I was obviously kidding. Slow down. Please!"

"Fine." I cross my arms, stopping in the middle of the cemetery. "God, you're in a good mood today, aren't you?"

"Of course, I am in a good mood," he says, lacing his fingers through my hair. "I have a beautiful woman to sleep beside every night, a child on the way, a growing empire. What else does a man need to be happy?" He cocks his head. "Forgive me, baby. I will be gentler with you."

"It's fine." I lean into his touch, unable to stay mad at him. "Just tone it down like twenty percent."

"For you, my love, *twenty-five*," he smirks. "I like to exceed expectations."

"How very studious of you." I raise myself on my tippy toes and give him a kiss. "Okay, it's getting cold, we should leave." I check my phone, letting out a sigh. "Your sister just asked me about my thoughts on ice sculptures." I look up. "Any strong opinions?"

"On *ice*?" Milo asks. "No, I cannot say I do."

"Me neither," I hum typing out a quick text. "God, this wedding is going to be insane. Ice sculptures? Is that even necessary?"

"You can always tell Julia you would prefer something simpler," Milo suggests, taking my hand as we stroll back to the parking lot.

"Hah, yeah sure," I snort, pocketing my cell phone. "Have you met your sister? She bought Champagne infused with 24-Carat gold flakes, Milo. People will *literally* be drinking gold. I don't think simple is her style."

"It is our wedding, tesoro, not hers," Milo notes with a shrug. "If you don't like something, tell her."

"No, it's fine. I don't have the energy to argue with her anyway. Plus, if she gets mad at me and quits then I'd have to decide on all of these things myself."

"You will still have Luisa," Milo says as we exit through the gates of the cemetery. He pauses. "Did she tell you if she is bringing Claudia?"

I blink. "What?"

Milo cocks his head. "Claudia? The woman she is dating."

"You know? She told you?"

"No, she didn't tell me. I heard her," Milo explains.

"Luisa has many skills but speaking quietly on the phone is not one of them. I've known for several months now."

"Oh," I hum, biting my lip. "Should I tell her to bring Claudia then? I don't think she was going to because well— you know."

"I personally do not care." Milo shrugs nonchalantly. "It is up to Luisa; it is her life."

"Okay, I'll let her know—"

"Milo!" We whip our heads toward the hoarse voice. Marchello strides toward us, looking around. "May I have a word with both of you?" He nods at me, keeping my gaze. "Signora, I hear congratulations are in order."

"Thank you," I say warily. "How's your shoulder doing?"

Marchello swallows. "It is healing."

"Oh, good. I'm glad."

"What are you doing here, Marchello?" Milo asks, his jaw clenching. "I thought we told you to take a *vacation*."

"I will go but I—I have a request."

"I do not think you are in any position to request *anything*," Milo says through his teeth. "Leave now, Marchello, before I take Kiara's advice and break your fucking legs."

"Please listen to me," Marchello pleads. "Please."

I narrow my eyes. "What do you want?"

Marchello clears his throat. "You have every reason to say no, but—" His gaze bounces between us. "Let me go to Russia. Let me finish this. Let me prove my loyalty."

"You want to go to Russia?" Milo asks, shaking his head. "How do I know you will not betray us? My trust in you, Marchello, is non-existent right now."

"I understand that but—" Marchello lowers himself on his knees as he takes a blade from his pocket, cutting a deep gash into his palm. "I vow to you, Emilio, that I will not betray you. I will bring honor to our family. Let me go. Please." He hands Milo the knife. "Please."

"*Mors Votum?*" Milo asks, taking the knife. "Are you sure?" I tug on Milo's hand. He faces me to explain. "If he breaks the vow, it is instant death."

"Oh."

"Let me do this, Milo," Marchello states. "Please."

Milo's quiet for a minute as he studies Marchello's desperate face. "I have no reason to trust you."

"I will not let you down," he insists, blood streaming from his hand. "I will not let *Santi Oscuri* down. You can trust me."

"Let him go," I whisper, meeting Marchello's solemn features. No hint of falsity in his tone, eyes, lips. He's being sincere. "He has to earn our trust somehow."

"Fine." Milo sucks in a deep breath, dragging the blade across his palm. He holds out his hand. "*Mors Votum.*"

Marchello grabs Milo's hand, a gleam of hope in his eyes. "*Mors Votum.*"

Death surrounds us.

It's in our blood.

## CHAPTER 43

## A NEW REIGN

Noise.

Sometimes it's loud. Sometimes it's impossible to ignore. Like the howling of the wind during a storm or the pulsing growls of erupting volcanoes.

But sometimes the noise is a whisper. A faint voice in the back of your head. Like static on a TV or a heart beating a little too fast.

Noise. It never truly goes away. It sneaks up on you when you least expect it.

Can I do this? Is this right? Will I be successful? Will I be able to uphold the values of this family? Am I capable? Am I worthy? Am I enough? Am I *strong* enough?

Are *we* strong enough?

Noise is destructive. I know that. I do. But some noise is valid, it has merit, yet oftentimes, it's just a manifestation of all your worst fears. Either you can listen to the static, grant it permission to hum in your ears and infiltrate your mind or, with enough faith, you can mute it. You can silence the noise, the doubt, the fear.

Faith is louder than fear.

And I have faith. Faith in Milo, faith in family, and most importantly, faith in myself.

And so, I'm pressing mute. I'm turning down the volume. I *am* in control.

Me.

Only me.

I take a deep breath, closing my eyes as Julia's piercing voice stings my temples.

Now if only I could mute the gaggle of Italian women bickering in front of me.

"She cannot wear the tiara, *mamma*!" Julia yells, slamming her hand on the table. "She is already wearing your necklace and earrings! She will look cheap! Coco Chanel said when leaving the house, look in the mirror and take something off! Do you want her to look like she robbed a fucking jewelry store?"

"Please Julia do not make me laugh!" Antonia scoffs, giving her daughter a once-over. "You are the last person who should advocate for *less is more*." She tugs on a piece of Julia's hair. "How many extensions are you wearing, ah?"

"Ow!" Julia whines, swatting her mother's hand away. "You will rip my hair out!"

"I will rip your *head* off if you continue to argue with me!" Antonia picks up the sparkling tiara with five pear-shaped diamonds interspersed with pearl accents. "It is tradition for all brides to wear the crown, Kiara is no exception!"

Julia crosses her arm, looking down at me. "Why don't we ask Kiara what she wants, hmm?" She casts me a warm smile. "Well? Cara?"

I blink, tightening the white satin robe over my shoulders. "Um, I mean if it's tradition I suppose I should—" I look up to my future mother-in-law. "Wear it?"

"Excellent!" Antonia beams. "You will look marvelous walking down the aisle. All eyes will be on you!"

The noise is back.

"No!" Julia snaps, her eyes widening as she kneels down beside me. "Kiara, you are wearing emeralds already. You cannot mix in diamonds and pearls and rubies. You are not a mutt!"

"A mutt?!" Antonia roars, looking around the room. Her gaze lands on Luisa. "Did she just say mutt? Would a mutt wear a crown? Would they?!"

"Uh—" Luisa clears her throat, unease flashing across her face as she glances at Claudia. "I—uh..."

Oh my God. No. I've had enough. I fake check the time.

"Listen," I say, forcing a smile as I look around the makeshift bridal suite in the east wing of the estate. "I appreciate all your help, I really do, but I think I can finish getting ready myself. Maybe *all* of you should head downstairs. The guests have probably started to arrive. We wouldn't want to be rude now, would we?"

Julia frowns, scanning my face. "Are you okay, cara? You look a little pale."

"I'm fine," I lie, checking my reflection in the vanity mirror. "I'd just like to be alone right now. I will see you all downstairs in half an hour." I nod at the door. "You can go, I'll be fine, I promise."

"Are you sure?" Julia asks, glaring at her mother. "Perhaps *I* should stay. You will need help getting into your dress."

"Julia," Luisa says in a gentle tone. "Let's go downstairs, yes? Let Kiara have a moment of peace and quiet before her life changes forever."

More noise.

"Fine," Julia says with a forced smile. "We will meet you

in the gardens in thirty minutes." She glances at the tiara. "I suppose if anyone could pull off a *clusterfuck* of gems, it would be you. Wear it if you want."

Antonia leans down and kisses my cheek. "You will look beautiful, Kiara," she whispers. "You were born to wear this crown. It is yours now."

"Thank you," I murmur, my throat drying as Luisa and Claudia both give me a quick hug. "I'll see you all very soon."

When the room clears, I close my eyes, taking several deep breaths, the weight of the crown pressing down on my chest.

The Di Vaio name is not merely a name, it's a title, it carries significance, it holds meaning, it's powerful. The most powerful name in Italy.

And it'll be mine.

My burden. My blessing. My responsibility.

I can do this.

Releasing a long, steadying exhale, I stand up and walk toward the wardrobe. As I unzip the garment bag protecting the beaded Alencon lace strapless ball gown, my tense shoulders relax. I run my hand across the white tiered ruffles on the back of the dress, my gaze following the chapel length train.

I *am* doing this.

White has always represented innocence, purity. But as I step into the fragile gown, I don't feel impure, I don't feel corrupted. I have seen acts of evil. I have committed acts of evil, and yet, I don't *feel* evil.

Perhaps innocence is not preserved through actions or words but through heart. When I look at Milo, I can *see* his innocence. It's in the way he laughs, the way he plays with his niece. It's his love for his mother, his sister, his family. It's in the way he touches me, holds me, loves me. I rest my palm against my belly. Loves *us*.

Yes. I can do this. I *will* do this.

The noise is gone.

"Shit," I gasp as a knock on the door startles me. Oh, good, she came back. "Come in, Jules," I call out, attempting to zip up the dress. Apparently, I need her help after all. .

"Wow." The lock clicks shut.

"Milo—" My breath hitches as I snap my head toward the door. He strides toward me, a slim-fitted black tuxedo wrapping his lithe body, a knowing smirk on his face. "What —what are you doing here?"

"I was talking to Julia downstairs," he says in a raspy tone, his dark hungry eyes dancing around my body. "She said you sounded...*nervous*."

My chest rises as he stops a foot away from me.

"I was worried you might be having...second thoughts." He pauses, licking his lips. "You look—" He shakes his head. "Radiant."

"Thank you." A shiver courses down my spine as I face the mirror. "Zip me up?"

"Are you nervous, tesoro?" Milo feathers his fingers across my shoulder blades as he leans into my ear, my submissive pulse quickening as he asks, "Should I make you...less nervous?"

"No," I breathe as his hand floats down my bare back. "I'm not nervous about marrying you, I'm just—" I close my eyes, his soft touch stirring heat inside my core. "I'm nervous about walking down the aisle in front of three hundred people I don't know...what if they judge me? What if—"

"If they judge you, tesoro—" Milo's hot breath fans against my ears as he pinches the zipper, slowly tugging it down. "It is only because they are jealous." He nips at the soft flesh of my lobe. "Every single woman sitting outside under the stars will be wishing they were you."

"Wrong way." I bite my lip as he rains wet kisses down the slope of my neck. "Milo, we...we can't." He tugs the zipper lower, past my ass. The ball gown slips off my body, dropping on the floor around my ankles. "It's already bad luck to see the bride before the—"

"But you like bad," he rasps, snaking his arm around my waist. I let out an aching moan as he cups my breast in his palm, his fingers rolling my nipples. "Isn't that right, tesoro?" He drags his hand down my stomach as I lean back, resting my head on his shoulder. He groans, curling his fingers under the hem of my panties. "You seem to like it...*a lot.*"

"Milo," I whimper, opening my legs for him as he dips one finger inside my folds. "Oh, God."

"You are so wet, baby." Milo wraps his left hand around the base of my throat as he teases me with just the tip of his index finger. "So fucking wet." His grip tightens around my neck. "Open your eyes, Kiara, and watch. I want you to see what I see." His thumb grazes my bottom lip. "I said open your eyes. Or I will stop."

"Don't stop," I plead, forcing my eyelids to flutter open. My face flushes with desire, need sizzling the atoms bouncing through my body as I look at myself in the mirror. He adds a second finger, a devilish gleam in his irises as I expel a yelping moan.

"Shh, shh, shh," Milo taunts, grazing his teeth down the side of my neck as he continues his ministrations. "You need to be quiet, tesoro. The walls, they are so very thin."

"More," I whine, pressing my ass against his hardened shaft. "I need more."

"Such a greedy girl," he whispers, his chest rumbling against my spine. I reach back, rubbing my hand down the length of his erection. He grunts. "Mmm, you want my cock, baby?" He plunges a third finger inside my pussy. "Is that what you want?"

"Yes!" I pant, fumbling to unfasten his trousers. "Please. Fuck me."

"Hands on the mirror." Milo pushes me forward, slapping my ass as he drops his pants. He arches over me, fisting my hair as he tugs my head back, pushing my panties to the side. With a husky moan, his cock coaxes open my dripping wet folds. "Watch, baby. Keep your eyes open." I gasp, pleasure searing through my body as he surges forward. "Eyes open!"

"Holy fuck," I moan as he pulls me flush against his chest, his unyielding cock thrusting inside me, deeper and deeper and deeper, filling every fucking inch of my pussy as his thumb flicks my sensitive clit. "Oh my God."

"Yes, baby," he growls, his heady sweet breath filling my lungs as he fucks me, worships me, fucking obliterates me. "Are you going to come for me?"

"Yes," I whimper as someone knocks on the door. "Oh my God, harder!"

"Kiara?" Julia shouts. "Hello?"

He slaps his hand over my mouth. "Shh, baby, we wouldn't want to get caught now, would we?" My walls clench around him. "Oh fuck, come on baby. Come for me." He lowers his voice, applying just the right amount of pressure on my clit to send me over the goddamn edge. With one final thrust, he explodes inside me. "Fuck!"

"Oh God," I pant, catching my breath, my vision blurry. "Holy shit."

Another knock. "Kiara? Is everything alright?"

"Yes!" I croak, attempting to float back down to earth. I clear my throat. "One minute!" I cringe, looking at my reflection in the mirror. "Shit, Milo, help me put the fucking dress on."

"Here—" Milo smirks, handing me a tissue to clean myself off with. "You look so sexy right now, Kiara. Perhaps one more time?"

"Shut up!" I smack his shoulder, scrambling to get the gown on as he tucks in his shirt and readjusts his bow tie. "Help me!"

"Kiara?!" Julia calls out. "Are you sure you're alright?"

"Milo," I whine, attempting to fix the smudged mascara under my eyes as Milo zips up my dress. I spin around, taking a deep breath. "How do I look? Normal? Good?"

"You look amazing, tesoro," Milo chuckles, reaching for the tiara on the vanity and placing it on top of my head. "Like a queen." He arches down, giving me a lingering kiss. "I love you, baby. I will see you at the altar."

Oh, God.

"I love you too," I whimper, fixing my hair as Milo heads to the door. He tosses me a wink before twisting the handle.

"Julia," he states in a cool tone, nodding at his sister. "She is all yours." He pauses, a grin on his face. "For now."

"What are you—" Julia's eyes widen as her gaze darts between the two of us. "Are you fucking kidding me? Three hours! You could not have waited three fucking hours? *Dio mio*—" She slaps Milo's shoulder. "Go downstairs! You are late!" She rushes inside the room, shaking her head in disapproval. "Oh, for fuck's sakes, cara! You look like you were swept up in a fucking tornado!"

"It's not that bad!" I insist as Julia grabs a brush off the vanity table. She scolds me under her breath while touching up my make-up. "Better?"

"Lucky for you, I am *extremely* talented," Julia huffs, examining her handy work. She tucks back a strand of my curled hair. "Alright, Kiara. Now you are ready." She tilts her head. "You are ready, no?"

"Yes," I say, taking a comforting breath as I glance at myself in the mirror. "I'm ready."

"Fantastic!" Julia exclaims, grabbing my hand as she leads me out of the suite, toward the gardens. "*Andiamo!*"

When we get downstairs, Luisa hands me my bouquet, a small frown on her face. "You look beautiful, Kiara."

"What's wrong?" I ask, tilting my head as classical music starts playing. "Are you alright?"

"I'm fine," she sighs. "My father hasn't called yet, that is all." She shakes her head. "Don't worry about it, Kiara. Enjoy this moment, yes? You will only get one."

"It is time," Julia says, nodding at the French doors. "Remember to breathe, Kiara. Ignore everyone else, just focus on Milo."

"I'm ready," I whisper as two attendants open the doors.

Luisa and Julia walk slowly ahead of me down the navy-blue carpet. I close my eyes, feeling the presence of my family. They're here. With me. Watching. Smiling. Loving. I nod, stepping through the threshold.

I'm ready.

The garden is decorated with dozens of chandeliers hung from exposed golden beams, extravagant arrangements of pastel florals, and strands of crystals strung over the hundreds of seated guests.

*Canon in D Major* fills the air as I stride through the white rose petals, distant whispers and murmurs from the attendees barely registering in my head as I see Milo standing at the altar, his eyes on me, only me.

It's just us.

No one else.

With every step I take, I am walking away from my past

and toward my future. Toward an ocean of endless opportunities, infinite love, and boundless faith.

There will be noise. There will be storms. There will be waves. But I'm not scared. Not one bit.

He is my life raft.

And I am his.

Together, we will weather all storms.

Together, we will *cause* the storms.

We will blow the world away.

We will be remembered.

Forever.

Milo holds out his hand as I step up on the platform, handing Julia my bouquet. He smiles at me, mouthing *relax, tesoro* as we face the priest.

I nod, my body humming with excitement.

"We are gathered here today to celebrate the joining of two hearts. In this ceremony we will witness the union of Emilio Di Vaio and Kiara Payne," the priest begins. "If there is anyone present who has just cause why this couple should not be united, let them speak now or forever hold their peace."

Milo looks over his shoulder, his eyes hardened. I suppress a chuckle. Not a peep from the guests. I suppose no one wishes to die tonight.

"Good," the priest continues. "You have come together today so that the Lord may seal and strengthen your love in the presence of God—" Milo squeezes my hand as the sermon continues. "The bride and groom have written their own vows. Emilio."

Milo takes a small breath, the moonlight glowing in his eyes. "Kiara, my vow to you is simple. I vow to bring you joy every day of your life. I vow to never make you cry. And I

vow to love you, even after death, for death cannot stop me."
My eyes well up. "No tears, tesoro.''

"Okay." I sniffle, nodding my head. *Breathe.* "Milo, I've
spent the majority of my life running away. From regrets, from
pain, from mistakes. But starting today, I vow to you that the
only place I will run is into your arms, nowhere else. *I promise.*"

The priest smiles. "Emilio, do you take Kiara to be your
Wife?"

It's instant. No hesitation. No doubt. "I do."

"Do you promise to love, honor, cherish and protect her,
forsaking all others and holding only unto her forevermore?"

"I do."

"Kiara, do you take Emilio to be your Hus—"

"I do," I say, grinning at Milo.

"Okay," the priest chuckles under his breath. "Do you
promise to love, honor, cherish and protect him, forsaking
all others and holding only unto him forevermore?"

"Yes. I do."

"Rings please." Julia hands the priest two rings. "The
ring is a symbol of the unbroken circle of love. May these
rings always remind you of the vows you have taken. Repeat
after me—"

And we do.

As golden rings slide on our fingers and bind us together
for life, we promise to love each other in joy and in sorrow,
for richer and for poorer, in sickness and in health.

In light and in darkness.

With our fingers linked, we stare up at the priest with
hopeful, dreamy eyes, waiting for him to say the words that
will launch a new reign.

For Milo, I will be strong. I will be tough.

For my child, I will be gentle. I will be warm.

For myself, I will be kind. I will be smart.

And for my new family, I will be ruthless.

I will be a queen.

"By the power vested in me, I now pronounce you husband and wife." The priest looks at Milo. "You may kiss your bride."

I gasp as fireworks crackle in the air, lighting the dark sky on fire.

"Come here, *Wife*," Milo grins, raking his fingers through my hair, his soft lips slamming against mine. "You are mine forever, tesoro."

"Forever?" I whisper, melting into his touch as applause and cheers surround us. "That doesn't seem nearly long enough."

Thousands of miles away, at this very moment, a warehouse full of weapons is being bombed and a man's life is ending.

This whole chapter is ending.

It's finished. It's finally over.

As red and white sparks twinkle in the sky and cascade down, I stare at my husband, taking in his rich brown eyes and the future they hold.

A life might be ending.

But mine is just beginning.

A life with him.

My husband. My king. My love.

Milo.

# Epilogue

---

## Legacy

*Five Years Later*
## MILO

I KNOW SHE IS HERE.

I can *see* her crouched down on the grass, her arms around Anna as they play. I can *smell* her perfume, the femininity and allure of her scent forever ingrained into my memory. If I were to stand up and take five strides forward, I could *touch* her. I could *feel* the soft curves of her body, run my fingers through her thick hair, rub that sweet pussy that is always so fucking wet for me.

She is here, right in front of me, and yet, as I bring a cup of espresso up to my lips, she does not seem real.

How can something so perfect exist in such an imperfect world?

It is a miracle that she has not vanished, that she has not yet disappeared without a trace, that her entire existence has not been a cruel joke. Every night when I fall asleep with her in my arms, I am afraid I will wake up and it will all have been a dream.

But she *is* here.

And only God knows why.

But I do not dare ask God the reasons for him bringing me an angel.

He might realize his mistake and take her away.

A mortal man does not stand a chance against a deity, but for my angel, my treasure, I would raise the servants of hell to keep her beside me. I would sell every ounce of my soul to the devil himself if it meant that she would stay.

But thankfully, for my soul, my sanity, and my heart, she *is* here, in front of me, playing with *our* child.

"You need to use both hands, Anna," Kiara instructs in a patient tone, her hair glistening in the sun like topaz. "Make sure you have a firm grip, okay?"

"Like this?" our daughter asks, flashing a hopeful smile.

"Yes, exactly like that," Kiara says, kissing Anna's head as she whispers something into our child's ear. Anna giggles as she nods. "Okay, now, aim at the target, and when you're ready, fire."

"Okay, mamma!"

Anna pinches her eyebrows together as she squints in concentration, pointing toward the pink bullseye. Suddenly, she whips her body toward me, her eyes gleaming with humor as she pulls the trigger and streams of water spurt out of the toy gun and onto my dress shirt.

"Annabella!" I scold, standing up. "What are you doing?!" I slam the newspaper on the patio table. "You are in big trouble, principessa." I hold my arms out, wiggling my fingers as I stalk toward my wife and daughter. "Big *big* trouble."

"Ah! No!" Anna shrieks, giggling as she hides behind Kiara. "Mamma made me do it! I'm sorry, papa, don't tickle me. Please!"

"I did no such thing!" Kiara's jaw drops as she dramatically crosses her arms. "It was *all* Anna."

Anna peeks around Kiara's thigh, flashing me a bright smile. God, they are identical. There are two of them. Two angels. My angels.

"Mamma's lying," she whispers. "She's lying."

"Oh, is she?" I hum, grinning at my daughter. "Why don't you go inside and find Claudia. I think she is with your brother." I briefly glance at my wife, casting her a knowing glare. "I have a traitor to interrogate."

"Uh oh, mamma," she squeals. "He gonna tickle you now."

"Yes." I lick my lips as I meet Kiara's sheepish gaze. "I am going to tickle her so *so* hard." I look down at Anna. "Go get Claudia, yes?"

"Okay," she says, dashing into the house. "Claudia! Where are you?!"

When our daughter is out of sight, my expression hardens. "You got me wet, tesoro." I take a step toward her. "You must pay for your crimes."

"Scared of a little water, baby?" Kiara smirks, backing away from me. "You just looked so hot, I wanted to cool you down."

"Hot? Interesting. What about me is so—" I cock my head to the side. "*Hot?*"

"Hmm," Kiara hums, biting her lip. "It's so hard to pick just one thing."

I reach out and grab her waist, yanking her toward me. "We have time, tesoro," I rasp, brushing my lips against hers. "I would like a *comprehensive* list."

"Well, let's see—" Kiara expels an airy laugh, wrapping her arms around my neck. "Your mouth, your chest, your hands—" She tugs on my hair. "Your co—"

"Milo, Kiara!" Gio calls out as he enters the gardens. "Are you ready? We have the jet on standby."

My jaw tenses. "He always has the worst *fucking* timing."

"We have the whole flight to Germany to finish the *list*," Kiara coos, tossing me a wink before spinning around in my arms. "Hey, Gio, we just need to say bye to the kids then we can leave." She pauses, a slight frown marring her brows. "Is Luisa back yet?"

"She will meet us at the airport," Gio replies, his tone low. "I will bring her bags with us."

"Okay, give us fifteen minutes," she says. Gio nods, heading back inside. Kiara clicks her tongue as she looks up at me. "Luisa's been there all day, maybe we should've gone with her."

"We offered," I note, lacing my fingers through my wife's hair, a twinge of pain gripping my gut. "She said she wanted to be alone with him."

"I know," Kiara sighs, leaning into my palm. "But it's his birthday. We should have gone to pay our respects. If it weren't for him—" She sighs. "He deserves our respect."

"Marchello was a loyal man, Kiara," I whisper, taking a deep breath as I pull her against my chest. "But he was not sentimental. I do not believe he would be offended if we missed his birthday. Plus, he is not alone, Luisa is there."

"Sometimes I think she hates us," Kiara admits. "Do you ever get that feeling?"

"No." I press my lips against her forehead. "Her father died a hero, Kiara. He died saving the lives of seven of our men. He did his duty. He stayed loyal until the end."

"But we let him go," Kiara whispers, shaking her head. "We sent him there. We both know how it feels to lose a parent, I just—" She swallows. "I just feel bad for Luisa. He was her only family."

"You are wrong, tesoro." I sweep away a few stray strands of hair off her shoulder as Claudia appears in the doorway, Sergio in her arms and Annabella by her side. "*We are her family. She knows that Kiara. She does not blame us.*"

"Mamma! I found Claudia!" Anna yells, running up to us. She frowns, scanning Kiara's face. "Why you sad?"

Kiara blinks, forcing a smile as she strokes our daughter's cheek. "I'm not sad, baby, I'm just going to miss you and your brother *so* much."

"He just woke up," Claudia says, smiling fondly at Sergio, a child that she grew for us, that she kept safe and warm for nine months. We owe Claudia a debt of gratitude. She helped make our family whole. Complete.

"Can I come with you?" Anna asks, tugging on Kiara's dress as Claudia hands off Sergio. "Please?"

Kiara pouts, shooting me a defeated side-eye as she bounces Sergio on her hip. "Sorry, baby but this is a business trip. Mamma and papa have to go alone. But when we come back, we can all go somewhere together, how does that sound?"

"But Luisa and Gio are going," Anna whines, crossing her arms. "I wanna go too!"

"Milo," Kiara whispers, nodding at Anna. "Help."

"Anna—" I kneel down in front of my daughter, taking her hands in mine. "We will only be away for three days, principessa," I say. "You will not even notice we are gone. Plus, you love playing with Claudia, right?"

Anna nods, her bottom lip quivering. "Yes."

"Then you should be happy!" I scoop Anna up in my

arms, tickling her belly. "Claudia might even give you gelato for dinner!"

"Really?" Anna bursts with excitement as she looks at her mother. "Gelato?"

"Mhmm, sure," Kiara hums, tossing me an icy glare as we head inside. "Whatever you want, baby."

"Yay!" Anna claps her hands as I set her on the floor. "I go color now!"

"We love y—" Kiara begins to say but Anna is already halfway down the hallway. "Wow, I think she just played us."

"Welcome to my life," Claudia laughs, handing Kiara her purse. "Your daughter is cute but very manipulative."

I smile proudly. "That means she will have the brightest of futures."

Kiara rolls her eyes, flicking Sergio's chubby cheeks. "Maybe this one will love us unconditionally." She plants kisses all over his face. Sergio giggles, squirming in her arms. "You love me more than gelato, right? Right?"

"Do not worry, tesoro, at least *I* love you unconditionally," I smirk as we walk to the front door. "You can find solace in that."

"Very funny," Kiara says, handing me Sergio as she changes into a pair of heels. "Remember, I can teach these children eleven languages, nine of which you will never understand. Don't fuck with me."

I snort, kissing Sergio's soft head. "Are you implying that you will turn my children against me?"

"Words are more dangerous than guns, baby, bear that in mind." Kiara straps a Beretta into her holster. "Alright, I'm ready. Let's go."

"Should I be worried about this trip?" Claudia asks as she takes Sergio. "Luisa did not tell me much."

Kiara smiles. "There's nothing to worry about, Claudia. It's just a friendly trip. That's all."

"Okay," Claudia sighs, opening the front doors for us. "I will see you in a few days."

"Take care of our children," I say, placing my hand on the small of Kiara's back as we head to the idling SUV. "A *friendly* trip?"

Kiara shrugs, hopping in the backseat. "The less she knows the better. She'll just worry about Luisa the whole time. It's useless to stress about things you have no control over."

"True," I agree, closing the car door. "Plus, I do not anticipate this trip going awry."

"No?" Kiara asks, tilting her head. "And why's that?"

"Because I will not let anyone destroy my legacy."

"We don't control Germany yet," Kiara notes. "It's not really ours."

"That is not my legacy," I whisper, dragging my thumb along her cheek, her jawline, her lips. "*You* are my legacy, tesoro. Our *children* are my legacy."

I could rule the entire world but without my family, I would be the poorest man alive.

But I am rich. So fucking wealthy.

Because of her.

Because she *is* here.

With me.

Forever.


The end.

# About the Author

E.L. Lewis is a multi-genre romance author who writes swoon-worthy stories full of sugar and spice. With books ranging from dark romance to rom coms, new adult to young adult fiction, she has a happily ever after for every mood. When she's not dreaming up characters and plots, she enjoys reading Dramione fanfics, listening to T-Swift on repeat, cheering on the Kansas City Chiefs, and arriving far too early at airports. She lives in Orange County with her husband and their lil pup.

*For more books and updates:*
www.ellewiswrites.com

## Contact
Instagram: @ellewiswrites
TikTok: @ellewiswrites
Facebook: Author E.L. Lewis
Inquiries: ellewiswrites@outlook.com

Printed in Great Britain
by Amazon

53064436R00249